Praise for *One of Our Thursdays Is Missing*

PENGUIN BOOKS

ONE OF OUR THURSDAYS IS MISSING

Jasper Fforde is the author of five previous Thursday Next novels: *The Eyre Affair, Lost in a Good Book, The Well of Lost Plots, Something Rotten,* and *First Among Sequels.* He is also the author of the novel *Shades of Grey,* as well as the Nursery Crime series, featuring Detective Jack Spratt, which includes *The Big Over Easy* and *The Fourth Bear.* All of Jasper Fforde's books are available from Penguin. He lives in Wales.

THURSDAY NEXT

IN

One of Our Thursdays Is Missing

A NOVEL

Jasper Fforde

PENGUIN BOOKS

PENGUIN BOOKS

Published by the Penguin Group

Penguin Group (USA) Inc., 375 Hudson Street, New York, New York 10014,
U.S.A. • Penguin Group (Canada), 90 Eglinton Avenue East, Suite 700, Toronto, Ontario,
Canada M4P 2Y3 (a division of Pearson Penguin Canada Inc.) • Penguin Books Ltd,
80 Strand, London WC2R 0RL, England • Penguin Ireland, 25 St. Stephen's Green,
Dublin 2, Ireland (a division of Penguin Books Ltd) • Penguin Books Australia Ltd,
250 Camberwell Road, Camberwell, Victoria 3124, Australia (a division of Pearson
Australia Group Pty Ltd) • Penguin Books India Pvt Ltd, 11 Community Centre,
Panchsheel Park, New Delhi–110 017, India • Penguin Group (NZ), 67 Apollo Drive,
Rosedale, Auckland 0632, New Zealand (a division of Pearson New Zealand Ltd) • •
Penguin Books (South Africa) (Pty) Ltd, 24 Sturdee Avenue, Rosebank,
Johannesburg 2196, South Africa

Penguin Books Ltd, Registered Offices: 80 Strand, London WC2R 0RL, England

First published in the United States of America by Viking Penguin,
a member of Penguin Group (USA) Inc. 2011
Published in Penguin Books 2012

1 3 5 7 9 10 8 6 4 2

Illustrations by Bill Mudron and Dylan Meconis

Publisher's Note: This is a work of fiction. Names, characters, places, and incidents either
are the product of the author's imagination or are used fictitiously, and any resemblance
to actual persons, living or dead, business establishments, events, or locales is entirely
coincidental.

THE LIBRARY OF CONGRESS HAS CATALOGED THE HARDCOVER EDITION AS FOLLOWS:
Fforde, Jasper.
One of our Thursdays is missing / Jasper Fforde.
p. cm.
ISBN 978-0-670-02252-6 (hc.)
ISBN 978-0-14-312051-3 (pbk.)
1. Next, Thursday (Fictitious character)—Fiction. 2. Literary historians—
England—Fiction. I. Title.
PR6106.F67O64 2011
823'.92—dc22   2010043581

Printed in the United States of America
Set in Berling LT Std

For Tif Loehnis

*To whom I owe my career
and by consequence
much else besides*

Contents

One of Our
Thursdays
Is
Missing

1.

The BookWorld Remade

The remaking was one of those moments when one felt a part of literature and not just carried along within it. In less than ten minutes, the entire fabric of the BookWorld was radically altered. The old system was swept away, and everything was changed forever. But the group of people to whom it was ultimately beneficial remained gloriously unaware: the readers. To most of them, books were merely books. If only it were that simple. . . .

Bradshaw's BookWorld Companion (2nd edition)

*E*veryone can remember where they were when the Book-World was remade. I was at home "resting between readings," which is a polite euphemism for "almost remaindered."

But I wasn't doing nothing. No, I was using the time to acquaint myself with EZ-Read's latest Laborsaving Narrative Devices, all designed to assist a first-person protagonist like me cope with the strains of a sixty-eight-setting five-book series at the speculative end of Fantasy.

I couldn't afford any of these devices—not even Verb-Ease™ for troublesome irregularity—but that wasn't the point. It was the company of EZ-Read's regional salesman that I was interested in, a cheery Designated Love Interest named Whitby Jett.

"We have a new line in foreshadowing," he said, passing me a small blue vial.

"Does the bottle have to be in the shape of Lola Vavoom?" I asked.

"It's a marketing thing."

I opened the stopper and sniffed at it gingerly.

"What do you think?" he asked.

Whitby was a good-looking man described as a youthful forty. I didn't know it then, but he had a dark past, and despite our mutual attraction his earlier misdeeds could only end in one way: madness, recrimination and despair.

"I prefer my foreshadowing a little less pungent," I said, carefully replacing the stopper. "I was getting all sorts of vibes about you and a dark past."

"I wish," replied Whitby sadly. His book had been deleted long ago, so he was one of the many thousands of characters who eked out a living in the BookWorld while they waited for a decent part to come along. But because of his minor DLI character status, he had never been given a backstory. Those without any sort of history often tried to promote it as something mysterious when it wasn't, but not Whitby, who was refreshingly pragmatic. "Even having no backstory as my backstory would be something," he had once told me in a private moment, "but the truth is this: My author couldn't be bothered to give me one."

I always appreciated honesty, even as personal as this. There weren't many characters in the BookWorld who had been left unscathed by the often selfish demands of their creators. A clumsily written and unrealistic set of conflicting motivations can have a character in therapy for decades—perhaps forever.

"Any work offers recently?" I asked.

"I was up for a minor walk-on in an Amis."

"How did you do?"

"I read half a page and they asked me what I thought. I said I understood every word and so was rejected as being overqualified."

"I'm sorry to hear that."

"It's okay," he said. "I was also offered a four-hundred-and-six-word part in a horror last week, but I'm not so sure. First-time author and a small publisher, so I might not make it past the second impression. If I get remaindered, I'd be worse off than I am now."

"I'm remaindered," I reminded him.

"But you were *once* popular," he said, "so you might be again. Do you know how many characters have high hopes of a permanent place in the readers' hearts, only to suffer the painful rejection of eternal unreadfulness at the dreary end of Human Drama?"

He was right. A book's life could be very long indeed, and although the increased leisure time in an unread novel is not to be sniffed at, a need to be vigilant in case someone *does* read you can keep one effectively tied to a book for life. I usually had an understudy to let me get away, but few were so lucky.

"So," said Whitby, "how would you like to come out to the smellies tonight? I hear *Garden Peas with Mint* is showing at the Rex."

In the BookWorld, smells were in short supply. *Garden Peas with Mint* had been the best release this year. It only narrowly beat *Vanilla Coffee* and *Grilled Smoked Bacon* for the prestigious Noscar™ Best Adapted Smell award.

"I heard that *Mint* was overrated," I replied, although I hadn't. Whitby had been asking me out for a date almost as long as I'd been turning him down. I didn't tell him why, but he suspected that there was someone else. There was and there wasn't. It was complex, even by BookWorld standards. He asked me out a lot, and I declined a lot. It was kind of like a game.

"How about going to the Running of the Bumbles next week? Dangerous, but exciting."

This was an annual fixture on the BookWorld calendar, where two dozen gruel-crazed and indignant Mr. Bumbles yelling, "More? MORE?!?" were released to charge through an unused chapter of *Oliver Twist*. Those of a sporting or daring disposition were invited to run before them and take their chances; at least one hapless youth was crushed to death every year.

"I've no need to prove myself," I replied, "and neither do you."

"How about dinner?" he asked, unabashed. "I can get a table at the Inn Uendo. The maître d' is missing a space, and I promised to give her one."

"Not really my thing."

"Then what about the Bar Humbug? The atmosphere is wonderfully dreary."

It was over in Classics, but we could take a cab.

"I'll need an understudy to take over my book."

"What happened to Stacy?"

"The same as happened to Doris and Enid."

"Trouble with Pickwick again?"

"As if you need to ask."

And that was when the doorbell rang. This was unusual, as random things rarely occur in the mostly predetermined Book-World. I opened the door to find three Dostoyevskivites staring at me from within a dense cloud of moral relativism.

"May we come in?" said the first, who had the look of some-one weighed heavily down with the burden of conscience. "We were on our way home from a redemption-through-suffering training course. Something big's going down at Text Grand Central, and everyone's been grounded until further notice."

A grounding was rare, but not unheard of. In an emergency all citizens of the BookWorld were expected to offer hospitality to those stranded outside their books.

I might have minded, but these guys were from *Crime and Punishment* and, better still, celebrities. We hadn't seen anyone famous this end of Fantasy since Pamela from *Pamela* stopped outside with a flat tire. She could have been gone in an hour but insisted on using an epistolary breakdown service, and we had to put her up in the spare room while a complex series of letters went backwards and forwards.

"Welcome to my home, Rodion Romanovich Raskolnikov."

"Oh!" said Raskolnikov, impressed that I knew who he was. "How did you know it was me? Could it have been the subtle way in which I project the dubious moral notion that murder might somehow be rationalized, or was it the way in which I move from denying my guilt to eventually coming to terms with an absolute sense of justice and submitting myself to the rule of law?"

"Neither," I said. "It's because you're holding an ax covered in blood and human hair."

"Yes, it is a bit of a giveaway," he admitted, staring at the ax, "but how rude am I? Allow me to introduce Arkady Ivanovich Svidrigailov."

"Actually," said the second man, leaning over to shake my hand, "I'm Dmitri Prokofich Razumikhin, Raskolnikov's loyal friend."

"You are?" said Raskolnikov in surprise. "Then what happened to Svidrigailov?"

"He's busy chatting up your sister."

He narrowed his eyes.

"My sister? That's Pulcheria Alexandrovna Raskolnikova, right?"

"No," said Razumikhin in the tone of a long-suffering best friend, "that's your mother. Avdotya Romanovna Raskolnikova is your sister."

"I always get those two mixed up. So who's Marfa Petrovna Svidrigailova?"

Razumikhin frowned and thought for a moment.

"You've got me there."

He turned to the third Russian.

"Tell me, Pyotr Petrovich Luzhin: Who, precisely, is Marfa Petrovna Svidrigailova?"

"I'm sorry," said the third Russian, who had been staring at her shoes absently, "but I think there has been some kind of mistake. I'm not Pyotr Petrovich Luzhin. I'm Alyona Ivanovna."

Razumikhin turned to Raskolnikov and lowered his voice.

"Is that your landlady's servant, the one who decides to marry down to secure her future, or the one who turns to prostitution in order to stop her family from descending into penury?"

Raskolnikov shrugged. "Listen," he said, "I've been in this book for over a hundred and forty years, and even I can't figure it out."

"It's very simple," said the third Russian, indicating who did what on her fingers. "Nastasya Petrovna is Raskolnikov's landlady's servant, Avdotya Romanovna Raskolnikova is your sister who threatens to marry down, Sofia Semyonovna Marmeladova is the one who becomes a prostitute, and Marfa Petrovna Svidrigailova—the one you were *first* asking about—is Arkady Svidrigailov's murdered first wife."

"I knew that," said Raskolnikov in the manner of someone who didn't. "So . . . who are you again?"

"I'm Alyona Ivanovna," said the third Russian with a trace of annoyance, "the rapacious old pawnbroker whose apparent greed and wealth led you to murder."

"Are you *sure* you're Ivanovna?" asked Raskolnikov with a worried tone.

"Absolutely."

"And you're still alive?"

"So it seems."

He stared at the bloody ax. "Then who did I just kill?"

And they all looked at one another in confusion.

"Listen," I said, "I'm sure everything will come out fine in the epilogue. But for the moment your home is my home."

Anyone from Classics had a celebrity status that outshone anything else, and I'd never had anyone even remotely famous pass through before. I suddenly felt a bit hot and bothered and tried to tidy up the house in a clumsy sort of way. I whipped my socks from the radiator and brushed off the pistachio shells that Pickwick had left on the sideboard.

"This is Whitby Jett of EZ-Read," I said, introducing the Russians one by one but getting their names hopelessly mixed up, which might have been embarrassing had they noticed. Whitby shook all their hands and then asked for autographs, which I found faintly embarrassing.

"So why has Text Grand Central ordered a grounding?" I asked as soon as everyone was seated and I had rung for Mrs. Malaprop to bring in the tea.

"I think the rebuilding of the BookWorld is about to take place," said Razumikhin with a dramatic flourish.

"So soon?"

The remaking had been a hot topic for a number of years. After Imagination™ was deregulated in the early fifties, the outburst of creative alternatives generated huge difficulties for the Council of Genres, who needed a clearer overview of how the individual novels sat within the BookWorld as a whole. Taking the RealWorld as inspiration, the CofG decided that a Geographic model was the way to go. How the physical world actually appeared, no one really knew. Not many people traveled to the RealWorld, and those who did generally noted two things: one, that it was hysterically funny and hideously tragic in almost equal measure, and two, that there were far more domestic cats than baobabs, when it should probably be the other way round.

Whitby got up and looked out the window. There was nothing to see, quite naturally, as the area *between* books had no precise definition or meaning. My front door opened to, well, not very much at all. Stray too far from the boundaries of a book and you'd be lost forever in the interbook Nothing. It was confusing, but then so were *Tristram Shandy*, *The Magus* and Russian novels, and people had been enjoying them for decades.

"So what's going to happen?" asked Whitby.

"I have a good friend over at Text Grand Central," said Alyona Ivanovna, who had wisely decided to sit as far from Raskolnikov and the bloody ax as she could, "and he said that to accomplish a smooth transition from Great Library BookWorld to Geographic BookWorld, the best option was to close down all the imaginotransference engines while they rebooted the throughput conduits."

This was an astonishing suggestion. The imaginotransference engines were the machines that transmitted the books in all their subtle glory from the BookWorld to the reader's imagination. To shut them down meant that reading—*all* reading—had to stop. I exchanged a nervous glance with Whitby.

"You mean the Council of Genres is going to shut down the entire BookWorld?"

Alyona Ivanovna nodded. "It was either that or do it piecemeal, which wasn't favored, since then half the BookWorld would be operating one system and half the other. It's simple: All reading needs to stop for the nine minutes it requires to have the BookWorld remade."

"But that's insane!" exclaimed Whitby. "People will notice. There's always someone reading *somewhere*."

From my own failed experience of joining the BookWorld's policing agency, I knew that he spoke the truth. There was a device hung high on the wall in the Council of Genres debating chamber that logged the Outland ReadRate—the total number of readers at any one time. It bobbed up and down but rarely dropped below the 20-million mark. But while spikes in reading were easier to predict, such as when a new blockbuster is published or when an author dies—always a happy time for their creations, if not their relatives—predicting slumps was much harder. And we needed a serious slump in reading to get down to the under-fifty-thousand threshold considered safe for a remaking.

I had an idea. I fetched that morning's copy of *The Word* and turned to the week's forecast. This wasn't to do with weather, naturally, but trends in reading. Urban Vampires were once more heavily forecast for the week ahead, with scattered Wizards moving in from Wednesday and a high chance of Daphne Farquitt Novels near the end of the week. There was also an alert for everyone at Sports Trivia to "brace themselves," and it stated the reason.

"There you go," I said, tapping the newspaper and showing it to the assembled company. "Right about now the Swindon Mallets are about to defend their title against the Gloucester Meteors, and with live televised coverage to the entire planet there is a huge potential fall in the ReadRate."

"You think that many people are interested in Premier League croquet?" asked Razumikhin.

"It *is* Swindon versus Gloucester," I replied, "and after the Malletts' forward hoop, Penelope Hrah, exploded on the forty-yard line last year, I would expect ninety-two percent of the world will be watching the game—as good a time as any to take the BookWorld offline."

"Did they ever find out *why* Hrah exploded?" asked Whitby.

"It was never fully explained," put in Ivanovna, "but traces of Semtex were discovered in her shin guards, so foul play could never be ruled out entirely. A grudge match is always a lot of fu—"

Her voice was abruptly cut dead, but not in the way one's is when one has suddenly stopped speaking. Her voice was clipped, like a gap in a recording.

"Hello?" I said.

The three Russians made no answer and were simply staring into space, like mannequins. After a moment they started to lose facial definition as they became a series of complex irregular polyhedra. After a while the number of facets of the polyhedra started to lessen, and the Russians became less like people and more like jagged, flesh-colored lumps. Pretty soon they were nothing at all. The Classics were being shut down, and if Text Grand Central was doing it alphabetically, Fantasy would not be far behind. And so it proved. I looked at Whitby, who gave me a wan smile and held my hand. The room grew cold, then dark, and before long the only world that I knew started to disassemble in front of my eyes. Everything grew flatter and lost its form, and pretty soon I began to feel my memory fade. And just when I was starting to worry, everything was cleansed to an all-consuming darkness.

#shutting down imaginotransference engines, 46,802 readers
#active reader states have been cached
#dismounting READ OS 8.3.6
#start programs
#check and mount specified dictionaries
#check and mount specified thesauri
#check and mount specified idiomatic database
#check and mount specified grammatical database
#check and mount specified character database
#check and mount specified settings database
Mount temporary ISBN/BISAC/duodecimal book category system
Mount imaginotransference throughput module
Accessing "book index" on global bus
Creating cache for primary plot-development module
Creating /ramdisk in "story interpretation," default size=300
Creating directories: irony
Creating directories: humor
Creating directories: plot
Creating directories: character
Creating directories: atmosphere
Creating directories: prose
Creating directories: pace
Creating directories: pathos
Starting init process
#display imaginotransference-engine error messages
#recovering active readers from cache
System message=Welcome to Geographic Operating System 1.2
Setting control terminal to automatic
System active with 46,802 active readers

"Thursday?"

I opened my eyes and blinked. I was lying on the sofa staring up at Whitby, who had a concerned expression on his face.

"Are you okay?"

I sat up and rubbed my head. "How long was I out?"

"Eleven minutes,"

I looked around. "And the Russians?"

"Outside."

"There is no outside."

He smiled. "There is now. Come and have a look."

I stood up and noticed for the first time that my living room seemed that little bit more realistic. The colors were subtler, and the walls had an increased level of texture. More interestingly, the room seemed to be brighter, and there was light coming in through the windows. It was *real* light, too, the sort that casts shadows and not the pretend stuff we were used to. I grasped the handle, opened the front door and stepped outside.

The empty interbook Nothing that had separated the novels and genres had been replaced by fields, hills, rivers, trees and forests, and all around me the countryside opened out into a series of expansive vistas with the welcome novelty of *distance*. We were now in the southeast corner of an island perhaps a hundred miles by fifty and bounded on all sides by the Text Sea, which had been elevated to "Grade IV Picturesque" status by the addition of an azure hue and a soft, billowing motion that made the text shimmer in the breeze.

As I looked around, I realized that whoever had remade the BookWorld had considered practicalities as much as aesthetics. Unlike the RealWorld, which is inconveniently located on the *outside* of a sphere, the new BookWorld was anchored on the *inside* of a sphere, thus ensuring that horizons worked in the opposite way to those in RealWorld. Farther objects were higher in the visual plane than nearer ones. From anywhere in the BookWorld, it was possible to view anywhere else. I noticed, too, that we were not alone. Stuck on the inside of the sphere were hundreds of other islands very similar to our own, and each a haven for a category of literature therein.

About ten degrees upslope of Fiction, I could see our nearest neighbor: Artistic Criticism. It was an exceptionally beautiful island, yet deeply troubled, confused and suffused with a blanketing layer of almost impenetrable bullshit. Beyond that were Psychology, Philately, and Software Manuals. But the brightest and biggest archipelago I could see upon the closed sea was the scattered group of genres that made up Nonfiction. They were positioned right on the other side of the inner globe and so were almost directly overhead. On one side of the island the Cliffs of Irrationality were slowly being eroded away, while on the opposite shore the Sands of Science were slowly reclaiming salt marsh from the sea.

While I stared upwards, openmouthed, a steady stream of books moved in an endless multilayered crisscross high in the sky. But these weren't books of the small paper-and-leather variety that one might find in the Outland. These were the collected *settings* of the book all bolted together and connected by a series of walkways and supporting beams, cables and struts. They didn't look so much like books, in fact, but more like a series of spiky lumps. While some one-room dramas were no bigger than a double-decker bus and zipped across the sky,

"O brave new world, that has such stories in't!"

others moved slowly enough for us to wave at the occupants, who waved back. As we stood watching our new world, the master copy of *Doctor Zhivago* passed overhead, blotting out the light and covering us in a light dusting of snow.

"What do you think?" asked Whitby.

"O brave new world," I whispered as I gave him a hug, "that has such stories in't!"

2.

A Woman Named Thursday Next

A major benefit of the Internal Sphere model of the remade BookWorld is that gravitational force diminishes with height, so it is easier to move objects the higher you go. You have to be careful, though, for if you go too high, you will be attracted to the gravitational dead spot right in the center of the sphere, from where there could be no return.

Bradshaw's BookWorld Companion (6th edition)

*M*y father had a face that could stop a clock. I don't mean that he was ugly or anything; it was a phrase that the Chrono-Guard used to describe someone who had the power to arrest time to an ultraslow trickle—and that's exactly what happened one morning as I was having a late breakfast in a small café quite near where I worked. The world flickered, shuddered and stopped. The barman of the café froze to a halt in midsentence, and the picture on the television stopped dead. Outside, birds hung motionless in the sky. The sound halted, too, replaced by a dull snapshot of a hum, the world's noise at that moment in time paused indefinitely at the same pitch and volume.

"Hello, Sweetpea."

I turned. My father was sitting at a table behind me and rose to hug me affectionately.

"Hi, Dad."

"You're looking good," he told me.

"You, too," I replied. "You're looking younger every time I see you."

"I am. How's your history?"

"Not bad."

"Do you know how the Duke of Wellington died?"

"Sure," I answered. "He was shot by a French sniper early on during the Battle of Waterloo—why?"

"Oh, no reason," muttered my father with feigned innocence, scribbling in a small notebook. Once done, he paused for a moment.

"So Napoléon *won* at Waterloo, did he?" he asked slowly and with great intensity.

"Of course not," I replied. "Field Marshal Blücher's timely intervention saved the day. This is all high school history, Dad. What are you up to?"

"Well, it's a bit of—hang on," said Dad, or rather the character *playing* my book-father. "I think they've gone."

I tasted the air. He was right. Our lone reader had stopped and left us dangling in a narrative dead zone. It's an odd sensation: a combination of treading on a step that isn't there, someone hanging up the telephone midspeech without explanation and the feeling you get when you've gone upstairs for some reason but can't think why. Scientists have proved that spaniels spend their entire lives like this.

"I was *marvelous*," intoned my book-father haughtily, the implication being that it was somehow my fault the reader didn't last until even the end of the first page. "You need to *engage* the readers more, darling. Project yourself. Make the character come *alive*."

I didn't agree that I was at fault but wasn't going to argue. He had played my father longer in the series than I had played Thursday, so he had a kind of seniority, even if I was the protagonist, and first-person player to boot.

"Sometimes I yearn for the old days," he said to Hector, his dresser, but obviously intending for me to hear.

"What do you mean by that?"

He stared at me for a moment. "This: It was a lot better when we had the previous Thursday play Thursday."

"She was violent and immoral, Dad. How could that *possibly* be better?"

"She might have been a shit of the highest order, darling, but she brought in the readers. I'll be in my dressing room. Come, Hector."

And so saying, he swept from the café setting with his ever-present dresser, who pouted rudely at me as they left. My book-father had a point, of course, but I was committed to promoting the type of Thursday the *real* Thursday wanted to see in the series. The series had originally been written to feature a violent and disorderly Thursday Next, who slept her way around the BookWorld and caused no end of murder, misery and despair. I was trying to change all that but had met with stiff resistance from the rest of the cast. They saw my attempt to depict reality as damaging to the overall readability—and for a character, the only thing worse than being read badly is to be badly unread.

I sighed. Keeping everyone within my series happy and fulfilled and focused was about as hard a job as acting in the book itself. Some books had a page manager to do all that boring stuff, but for financial reasons I had to do it myself with only a defective Mrs. Malaprop for assistance. Making us all readable was the least of my worries.

I walked slowly home through my book-version of Swindon, which was forty times more compact than the real one. Due to the limited number of locations mentioned in my series, I could go easily from the café to my mother's house to the GSD church and then on to the SpecOps Building in the space of a few minutes, something that would take the best part of an hour in the real Swindon. There were a few handy shortcuts, too. By opening a door at the back of Our Blessed Lady of the Lobster, I could find myself in the mockup of Thornfield Hall, and by taking the first door on the right past Jane's bedroom, I could be in the Penderyn Hotel in Wales. All told, the series covered about five acres on six levels and would have been larger if we hadn't doubled up the East facade of Thornfield with the front of Haworth Parsonage in Yorkshire, and the Gad's Hill Museum with the redressed lobby of the SpecOps Building. Economies like this were commonplace in remaindered books and helped us keep the cast at almost full strength. Doubling up characters *was* possible, but it caused problems when they were in scenes with themselves. Some characters could handle it, others could not. On one memorable occasion, Vronsky played *all* the parts in an abridged version of *Anna Karenina* whilst the rest of the cast were on strike for more blinis. When asked what it was like, he described it as "like, totally awesome, dude."

"Good morning, Pickwick," I said as I walked into the kitchen, which not only served as the command center of my series but also as the place where tea and toast could be made and eaten. "Good morning, Mrs. Malaprop."

"Cod Moaning, Miss Next," said the defective Mrs. Malaprop, bobbing politely.

"May I have a word?" asked Pickwick, in a not very subtle aside.

"Is it important?"

"It is vitally *crucial*," said Pickwick, rolling her eyes oddly.

We moved out to the hallway.

"Okay, what's the problem?" I asked, since Pickwick *always* had a grievance of some sort—whether it was the cold or the heat or the color of the walls or a hundred and one other things that weren't quite right. Whitby and I referred to her as "Goldilocks without the manners"—but never to her beak.

"It's Mrs. Malaprop," said the dodo in an affronted tone.

"She's becoming increasingly unintelligible. It would be okay if it were faintly amusing, but it isn't, and . . . well, quite frankly, there is the risk of infection, and it frightens me."

To a text-based life-form, unpredictable syntax and poor grammar is a source of huge discomfort. Ill-fitting grammar are like ill-fitting shoes. You can get used to it for a bit, but then one day your toes fall off and you can't walk to the bathroom. Poor syntax is even worse. Change word order and a sentence useless for anyone Yoda except you have.

"Now, then," I said, using an oxymoron for scolding effect, "it is totally unproven that malapropism is inflectious, and what did we say about tolerating those less fortunate than ourselves?"

"Even so," said Pickwick, "I want you to tell her to stop it. And her shoes squeak. And while we're on the subject, Bowden referred to me as 'that bird' again, the baobab in the back garden is cutting out the light from my bedroom, and I'm taking next Wednesday off to have my beak oiled, so you'll need to get a replacement—and not the penguin like last time. She didn't do justice to my dynamic personalty and poetic sensibilities. Played it all a bit . . . *fishcentric*, if you know what I mean."

"I'll do my best," I said, making a mental note to *definitely* rebook the penguin.

"Good," said Pickwick. "Have you the paper?"

We returned to the kitchen, and I found *The Word* for her.

"Hmm," she said thoughtfully, staring at the City pages. "Metaphor has risen by seventeen pounds a barrel. I should dump some metonym and buy into synecdoche futures."

"How are things going with Racy Novel?" I asked, since the political problems up in the North had been much in the news recently. A long-running dispute between Racy Novel, Women's Fiction and Dogma had been getting worse and was threatening to erupt into a genre war at the drop of a hat.

"Peace talks still on schedule for Friday," replied Pickwick, "as if that will do any good. Sometimes I think that Muffler nutjob wants nothing but a good scrap. By the way," she added, "did you hear about *Raphael's Walrus?*"

"No."

"Got their eviction papers this morning."

This wasn't surprising. *Raphael's Walrus* was a book six doors down that hadn't been read for a while. I didn't know them well, but since we were located at the Speculative end of Fantasy, the real estate was valuable. We'd have a new neighbor almost the moment they left.

"I hope it's not Sword and Sorcery," said Pickwick with a shudder. "Goblins really drag down the neighborhood."

"Goblins might say the same about dodos."

"Impossible!" she retorted. "Dodos are cute and cuddly and lovable and . . . don't steal stuff and spread disease."

People often wondered why my written dodo was such a pain in the ass when the real Pickwick was so cute. The reason was simple: lack of choice. There are only three dodos in fiction. One was dangerously psychotic, the second was something big over in Natural History, which left only one: The dodo from *Alice* is the same bespectacled know-it-all in my series. Her name wasn't actually Pickwick—it was Lorina Peabody III, but we called her Pickwick, and she didn't much mind either way. She put down the paper, announced to the room that she would be taking her siesta and waddled off.

"Mrs. Malaprop," I said once Pickwick had left, "are you still attending your therapy sessions?"

Mrs. Malaprop arched a highbrow. She knew well enough who had complained about her.

"Eggs tincture is too good for that burred," she said in a crabby tone, "but isle do as Uri quest."

The average working life of a Mrs. Malaprop in *The Rivals* was barely fifty readings. The unrelenting comedic misuse of words eventually caused them to suffer postsyntax stress disorder, and once their speech became irreversibly abstruse, they were simply replaced. Most "retired" Mrs. Malaprops were released into the BookWorld, where they turned ferrule, but just recently rehoming charities were taking note of their plight. After they'd undergone intensive Holorime Bombardment Therapy to enable them to at least *sound* right even if they didn't *read* right, people like me offered them a home and a job. Our Malaprop was an early model—Number 862, to be precise—and she was generally quite helpful if a little tricky to understand. There was talk of using Dogberry stem cells to cure her, but we didn't hold our broth.

I stared at the diagnostics board that covered one wall of the kitchen. The number of readers on the Read-O-Meter was stuck firmly at zero, with thirty-two copies of my novels listed "bookmarked and pending." Of these, eighteen were active/resting between reads. The rest were probably lying under a stack of other unfinished books. I checked the RealWorld clock. It was 0842. Years ago I was read on the train, but that hadn't happened for a while. Unreadfulness was a double-edged sword. More leisure time, but a distinct loss of purpose. I turned to Mrs. Malaprop.

"How are things looking in the series?"

She stared at her clipboard.

"Toll rubble. Twenty-six care actors Aaron leaf or training courses; all can be covered by eggs Hastings characters. Of the settings, only Hayworth House is clothes bee coarse of an invest station of grammasites."

"Has Jurisfiction been informed?"

"We're low prior Tory, so they said a towers."

"How close is our nearest reader?"

"Nine teas heaven minutes read time away."

It wasn't going to be a problem. He or she wouldn't pick up the book again until this evening, by which time the problem would have resolved itself.

"If the reading starts early for any reason," I said, "we'll use the front room of Thornfield Hall as a stand-in. Oh, and my father has a flea in his ear about something, so keep an eye on him in case he tries to do his own lines. I got a letter last week from Text Grand Central about illegal dialogue flexations."

Mrs. Malaprop nodded and made a note. "Come harder hearing cold," she said.

"Sorry?"

"Comma DeHare ring cooled."

"I'm . . . still not getting this."

Mrs. Malaprop thought hard, trying to place the correct words in the correct place to enable me to understand. It was painfully difficult for her, and if Sheridan had known the misery that using acyrologia in a comedic situation would bring, he would possibly have thought butter of it.

"Come hander hair-in culled!" she said again in an exasperated tone, sweating profusely and starting to shake with the effort.

"Commander Herring called?" I said, suddenly getting it. "What about?"

"A naval antecedent," she said urgently, "in evasion."

She meant that a novel had met with an accident in Aviation.

"Why would he be calling me after I blew it so badly last time?"

"It sea reprised me, too. Here."

She handed me a scrap of paper. Commander James "Red" Herring was overall leader of the BookWorld Policing Agency. He was in command not only of the Fiction Police known as Jurisfiction but also of Text Grand Central's Metaphor Squad and at least eighteen other agencies. One of these was Book Traffic Control—and part of that was the Jurisfiction Accident Investigation Department, or JAID, a department I occasionally worked for. The overhead book traffic, despite its usefulness, was not without problems. Fiction alone could see up to two thousand book-movements a day, and the constant transportation of the novels across the fictional skies was not without mishap.

I spent at least a day a week identifying sections that had fallen off books passing overhead, trying to get them returned—and, if possible, find out why they'd come unglued. Despite safety assurances, improved adhesives and updated safety procedures, books would keep on shedding bits. The loss of a pig out of *Animal Farm* was the most celebrated incident. It fell several thousand feet and landed inside a book of short stories by Graham Greene. Disaster was averted by a quick-thinking Jurisfiction agent who expertly sewed the pig into the narrative. It was Jurisfiction at its very best.

"Did Commander Herring say which book or why he was calling me?"

"A very spurious accident, Walsall he said. You're to to me, Tim, at this address."

I took the address and stared at it. Commander Herring's calling me *personally* was something of a big deal. "Anything else?"

"Your new-ender study is waiting to be interviewed in the front room."

This was good news. My book was first-person narrative, and if I wanted to have any sort of life outside my occasional readings—such as a date with Whitby or to have a secondary career—I needed someone to stand in for me.

I walked through to the front room. My potential understudy looked pleasant enough and had troubled to integrate herself into my body type and vague looks. She had a Thursday Next outfit on, too. She wanted this job badly.

"The written Thursday Next," I said, shaking her hand.

"Carmine O'Kipper," she replied with a nervous smile. "ID A4-5619-23. Pleased to be here."

"You're an A-4, Miss O'Kipper?"

"Call me Carmine. Is that a problem?"

"Not at all."

An A-4 character was theoretically only three steps down from the Jane Eyres and Scout Finches. To be able to handle first person, you had to be an A-grade, but none of the other understudies had been higher than an A-9.

"You must be at least an A-2, yes?" she asked.

"Something like that," I replied as we sat. "Do you know of the series?"

"I used to keep a scrapbook of the *real* Thursday Next."

"If you're here to catch a glimpse of her, it's unlikely. She dropped in once soon after the remaking, but not since then."

"I'm really just after the work, Miss Next."

She handed me her CV. It wasn't long, nor particularly impressive. She was from an original manuscript sitting abandoned in a drawer somewhere in the Outland. She would have handled loss, love, uncertainty and a corkingly good betrayal. It looked like it might have been a good gig. But after fifteen years and not a single reader, it was time to move on.

"So . . . why do you want to work in my series?"

"I'm eager to enter a new and stimulating phase of my career," she said brightly, "and I need a challenging and engaging book in which I can learn from a true professional."

It was the usual bullshit, and it didn't wash.

"You could get a read anywhere," I said, handing back the CV, "so why come to the speculative end of Fantasy?"

She bit her lip and stared at me.

"I've only ever been read by one person at a time," she confessed. "I took a short third-person locum inside a *Reader's Digest* version of *Don Quixote* as Dulcinea two weeks ago. I had a panic attack when the read levels went over twenty-six and went for the Snooze."

I heard Mrs. Malaprop drop a teacup in the kitchen. I was shocked, too. The Snooze Button was reserved only for dire emergencies. Once it was utilized, a reverse throughput capacitor on the imaginotransference engines would cause the reader instantaneous yawning, drowsiness and then sleep. Quick, simple—and the readers suspected nothing.

"You hit Snooze?"

"I was stopped before I did."

"I'm very relieved."

"Me, too. Rocinante had to take over my part—played her rather well, actually."

"Did the Don notice? Rocinante playing you, I mean?"

"No."

Carmine was just what I was looking for. Overqualified understudies rarely stayed long, but what with her being severely readerphobic, the low ReadRates would suit her down to the ground. I was mildly concerned over her eagerness to hit Snooze. To discourage misuse, every time the button was pressed, one or more kittens were put to death somewhere in the BookWorld. It was rarely used.

"Okay," I said, "you're hired. One caveat: You don't get the Snooze Button access codes. Agreed?"

"Agreed."

"Excellent. How much reading time do you have?"

"Aside from my own book, I've got eighty-seven pages."

It was a lamentably small amount. A single quizzical reader hunting for obscure hidden meanings would have her in a stammering flat spin in a second.

"Get your coat and a notebook," I said. "We're going to go greet our new neighbors—and have a chat."

3.

Carmine O'Kipper

Outland tourism was banned long ago, and even full members of Jurisfiction—the BookWorld's policing elite—were no longer permitted to cross over to the RealWorld. The reasons were many and hotly debated, but this much was agreed: Reality was a pit of vipers for the unwary. Forget to breathe, miscalculate gravity or support the wrong god or football team and they'd be sending you home in a zinc coffin.

Bradshaw's BookWorld Companion (17th edition)

After taking a pager off the counter so Mrs. Malaprop could reach me in case a reader turned up unexpectedly, we stepped out of the main gate and walked down the street. The remade Geographic BookWorld was as its name suggested—geographic—and the neighborhoods were laid out like those in an Outland housing estate. A single road ran down between the books, with sidewalks, grass verges, syntax hydrants and trees. To the left and right were compounds that contained entire novels with all their settings. In one was a half-scale Kilimanjaro, and in another a bamboo plantation. In a third an electrical storm at full tilt.

"We're right on the edge of Fantasy," I explained. "Straight ahead is Human Drama, and to your right is Comedy. I'll give you Wednesdays off, but I expect you to be on standby most of the time."

"The more first-person time I can put in," replied Carmine,

"the better. Is there anything to do around here when I'm off-duty, by the way?"

"If Fantasy is your thing," I said, "plenty. Moving cross-genre is not recommended, as the border guards can get jumpy, and it will never do to be caught in another genre just when you're needed. Oh, and don't do anything that my dodo might disapprove of."

"Such as what?"

"The list is long. Here we are."

We had arrived on the top of a low rise where there was a convenient park bench. From this vantage point, we could see most of Fiction Island.

"That's an impressive sight," said Carmine.

There was no aerial haze in the BookWorld, and because the island was mildly dished where it snuggled against the interior of the sphere, we could see all the way to the disputed border between Racy Novel and Women's Fiction in the far north of the island, and beyond that the unexplored Dismal Woods.

"That's the Metaphoric River," I explained, pointing out the sinuous bends of the waterway whose many backwaters, bayous, streams and rivulets brought narrative ambiguity and unnecessarily lengthy words to the millions of books that had made their home in the river's massive delta. "To the east of Racy Novel is Outdated Religious Dogma."

"Shouldn't that be in Nonfiction?" asked Carmine.

"It's a contentious issue. It was removed from Theology on the grounds that the theories had become 'untenable in a modern context' and 'were making us look medieval.'"

"And that island off the coast of Dogma?" she asked, pointing to a craggy island partially obscured by cloud.

"The smaller of the two is Sick Notes, and the larger is Lies, Self-Delusion and Excuses You Can Use to Justify Poor Behavior. South of Dogma is Horror, then Fantasy, with Adventure and Science Fiction dominating the south coast."

"I'll never remember all that."

I handed her my much-thumbed copy of *Bradshaw's Book-World Companion*. "Use this," I said, showing her the foldout map section and train timetables. "I've got the new edition on order."

Whilst we had been sitting there, the recently evicted book had been unbolted by a team of Worker Danvers.

"*Raphael's Walrus* has been unread for over two years," I explained, "so it's off to the narrative doldrums of the suburbs. Not necessarily permanent, of course—a resurgence of interest could bring it back into the more desirable neighborhoods in an instant."

"How come your series is still here?" she asked, then put her hand over her mouth. "Sorry, was that indelicate of me?"

"No, most people ask that. The Text Grand Central Mapping Committee keeps us here out of respect."

"For you?"

"No—for the *real* Thursday Next."

A smattering of soil and pebbles descended to earth as *Raphael's Walrus* rose into the air, the self-sealing throughput and feedback conduits giving off faint puffs of word vapor as they snapped shut. This was how the new Geographic Book-World worked. Books arrived, books left, and the boundaries of the various genres snaked forwards and backwards about the land, reflecting the month-to-month popularity of the various genres. The Crime genre was always relatively large, as were Comedy, Fantasy and Science Fiction. Horror had gotten a boost recently with the burgeoning Urban Vampires sector, while some of the lesser-known genres had shrunk to almost nothing. Squid Action/Adventure was deleted quite recently, and Sci-Fi Horse Detective looked surely set to follow.

But the vacated area was not empty for long. As we watched, the first of many prefabricated sections of the new book arrived, fresh from the construction hangars in the Well of Lost Plots. The contractors quickly surveyed the site, pegged out strings and then signaled to large transporter slipcases that were hovering just out of sight. Within a few minutes, handling ropes were dropped as the sections moved into a hover thirty feet or so above, and the same small army of Worker Danvers, cheering and grunting, maneuvered the sections into position, and then riveted them in place with pneumatic hammers. The first setting to be completed was a semiruined castle, then a mountain range, then a forest—with each tree, rabbit, unicorn and elf carefully unpacked from crates. Other sections soon followed, and within forty minutes the entire novel had been hauled in piecemeal from the overhead, riveted down and attached to the telemetry lines and throughput conduits.

"It's a good idea to be neighborly," I said. "You never know when you might need to borrow a cupful of irony. Besides, you might find this interesting."

We walked up the drive and across the drawbridge into the courtyard. Notices were posted everywhere that contained useful directions such as THIS WAY TO THE DENOUEMENT or NO BOOTS TO BE WORN IN THE BACKSTORY and even DO NOT FEED THE AMBIGUITY. The contractors were making last-minute adjustments. Six were arranging the clouds, two were wiring the punctuation to the main distribution board, three were trying to round up a glottal stop that wasn't meant to be there, and two others had just slit a barrage balloon full of atmosphere. The ambience escaped like a swarm of tiny midges and settled upon the fabric of the book, adding texture and style.

"Hello!" I said to the cast, who were standing around looking bewildered, their heads stuffed unrealistically full of Best Newcomer prizes and a permanent place in every reader's heart. They were about to be published and read for the first time. They would be confused, apprehensive and in need of guidance. I was so glad I wasn't them.

"My name's Thursday Next, and I just dropped in to welcome you to the neighborhood."

"This is indeed an honor, Miss Next," said the king, "and welcome to *Castle of Skeddan Jiarg*. We've heard of your exploits in the BookWorld, and I would like to say on behalf of all of us—"

"I'm not that one," I replied, before it all got embarrassing. I had denied I was the *real* Thursday Next more times than I would care to remember. Sometimes I went through an entire week doing little else.

"I'm the *written* Thursday Next," I explained.

"Ah," said one of several wizards who seemed to be milling around. "So you're not Jurisfiction, then?"

"I got as far as a training day," I replied, which was still a proud boast, even if I had been rejected for active service. It was annoying but understandable. Few make the grade to be a member of Fiction's policing elite. I wasn't tough enough, but it wasn't my fault. I was written to be softer and kinder—the Thursday who Thursday herself thought she wanted to be. In any event, it made me too empathetic to get things done in the dangerously dynamic landscape of the BookWorld.

They all returned my greeting, but I could see they had lost interest. I asked them if I could show Carmine around, and they had no objections, so we wandered into the grand hall, which was all lime-washed walls, flaming torches, hammerhead beams and flagstones. Some of the smaller props were only cardboard cutouts, and I noted that a bowl of fruit was no more than a Post-it note with "bowl of fruit" written on it.

"Why only a Post-it?" asked Carmine. "Why not a real bowl of fruit?"

"For economic reasons," I replied. "Every novel has only as

much description as is necessary. In years past, each book was carefully crafted to an infinitely fine degree, but that was in the days of limited reader sophistication. Today, with the plethora of experience through increased media exposure, most books are finished by the readers themselves."

"The Feedback Loop?"

"Precisely. As soon as the readers get going, the Feedback Loop will start backwashing some of their interpretations into the book itself. Not that long ago, books could be stripped bare by overreading, but since the invention of the loop, not only do books suffer little internal wear but readers often *add* detail by their own interpretations. Was that a goblin?"

I had just seen a small creature with pixie ears and sharp teeth staring at us from behind a chair.

"Looks like it."

I sighed. Pickwick *would* have something new to complain about.

"What is Thursday like?" asked Carmine.

I got asked this a lot. "You've heard the stories?"

She nodded. Most people had. For over fifteen years, Thursday Next had worked at Jurisfiction, tirelessly patrolling the BookWorld like a narrative knight-errant, bringing peace and justice to the very edge of acceptable prose. She was head and shoulders above the other agents—giants like Commander Bradshaw, Emperor Zhark, Mrs. Tiggy-winkle or even the Drunk Vicar.

"Did she really take Hamlet into the RealWorld?" asked Carmine, excited by my mentor's audaciousness.

"Among others."

"And defeat Yorrick Kaine?"

"That, too."

"What about the Great Samuel Pepys Fiasco? Did they *really* have to delete two weeks of his diary to make everything okay?"

"That was the least of her worries. Even Thursday had occasional failures—it's inevitable if you're at the top of your game. Mind you," I added, unconsciously defending my famous namesake, "if Samuel Pepys hadn't set Deb up in a pied-à-terre in the backstory of *Sons and Lovers* with Iago coming in for half-costs on alternate weekdays, it would never have escalated into the disaster it became. They could have lost the entire diaries and, as a consequence, anything in Nonfiction that used the journal as a primary source. It was only by changing the historical record to include a 'Great Fire of London' that never actually happened that Thursday managed to pull anything from the debacle. History wouldn't speak to the council for months, but Sir Christopher Wren was delighted."

We walked back out into the courtyard. The king and queen invited us around for a "pre-reading party" that evening, and I responded by inviting them around for tea and cakes the following day. Thus suitably introduced, we made our way out to the street again.

"So how do you want me to play you?" asked Carmine.

"You're not playing *me*, you're playing *her*. There's a big difference. Although I've been Thursday for so long that sometimes I think I am her, I'm not. I'm just the written her. But in answer to your question, I try to play her dignified. I took over from the *other* written Thursday—long story, don't ask—soon after the Great Samuel Pepys Fiasco was deleted—even longer story, still don't ask—and the previous Thursday played her a little disrespectfully, so I'm trying to redress that."

"I heard that the violent and gratuitous-sex Thursday had a lot more readers."

I glared at Carmine, but she simply stared back at me with big innocent eyes. She was making a statement of fact, not criticism.

"We'll get the readers back somehow," I replied, although I wasn't wholly convinced.

"Can I meet the real Thursday?" asked Carmine in a hopeful tone of voice. "For research purposes, naturally."

"She's very busy, and I don't like to bother her."

I was exaggerating my influence. Despite overseeing my creation, the real Thursday didn't like me much, possibly for the very same reasons she thought she might be improved. I think it was a RealWorld thing: the gulf between the person you want to be and the person you are.

"Look," I said, "just play her dignified—the individual interpretation is up to you. Until you get into the swing of it, play her subtly different on alternate readings. Hamlet's been doing it for years. Of course, he has twenty-six different ways of playing himself, but then he's had a lot of practice. In fact, I don't think even he knows his motivation anymore—unless you count confusing readers and giving useful employment to Shakespearean scholars."

"You've met Hamlet?"

"No, but I saw the back of his head at last year's BookWorld Conference."

"What was it like?" asked Carmine, who seemed to enjoy celebrity tittle-tattle.

"The back of his head? Hairy," I replied cautiously, "and it might not have been him. In any event, keep your interpretation loose, and don't telegraph. Let the readers do the work. If you're going to explain *everything*, then we might as well give up and tell everyone to stick to television and movies."

"Were there any goblins?" asked Pickwick as soon as we walked back in.

"I didn't see any. Did you, Miss O'Kipper?"

"No, no, not a single one."

"Mrs. Malaprop," I said, "we'll be having royalty for tea tomorrow. Better bake some silver and have the buns cleaned."

"Very good, Mizzen Exe."

"Here," I said to Carmine, handing her the complete script for my part. "I have to go out for an hour. I'll test you on it when I get back."

She suddenly looked nervous. "What if someone starts to read us while you're away?"

"They won't," I replied, "and if they do, Mrs. Malaprop will point you in the right dictation. Just take it smooth and easy. The rest of the cast will help you along."

"What do I do with Skimmers?" she asked with a faint tinge of panic in her voice. All rookies feared Dippers, Skimmers and Last-Chapter-Firsters.

"There's no hard-and-fast rule. Skimmers move in a generally forward direction, and with experience you'll figure out where they're going to land next. But the main thing is not to waste time with the nuisance reader—in a word, *prioritize*. Find the stable, methodical, bread-and-butter readers and give them your best. Leave the Skimmers and Dippers high and dry if there's a crisis. When things die down later, you can pick them up then."

"And students?"

"A breeze. They'll pause at the end of each sentence to think quasi-intellectual deep thoughts, so as soon as a full stop looms, you can be off dealing with someone else. When you get back, they'll still be pondering about intertextuality, inferred narratives and the scandalously high price of the subsidized beer in the student union."

She was quiet and attentive, so I carried on.

"You should show no discrimination with readers. Treat the lip movers as you would the *New York Times* critic. You might not be able to distinguish between the two at first, but you soon will. Yossarian said that you can get to know individual readers by the *way* they read you. Mind you, he's been doing it a long time, and *Catch-22* gets reread a lot."

"You've met Yossarian?"

"He was just leaving the room after giving a talk. I saw his foot."

"Left or right?"

"Left."

"I met someone who was beaten about the head boy Sir John Falstaff," remarked Mrs. Malaprop in an attempt to show that she, too, hobnobbed with celebrities.

"I talked to someone who held Pollyanna's hat for three whole pages," added Carmine.

"Small fry," remarked Pickwick, eager to outdo us all. "Sam Spade *himself* actually spoke to me."

There was silence. This was impressive.

"What did he say?"

"He said, 'Get that stupid bird out of my way.'"

"Well, pretend to be a soldier and elope with my ward," remarked Mrs. Malaprop, her word choice rendered clean and clear by the sarcasm. "You can dine out on *that* one for years."

"It's better than your dumb Falstaff story."

"The thing to remember," I remarked, to stop the argument before it got to the next few stages, which were insults, crockery throwing and punches, "is that the more readers there are, the easier it becomes. If you relax, it actually becomes a great deal of fun. The words spring naturally to your lips, and you can concentrate on not just giving the best possible performance but also dealing with any readers who are having problems—or indeed any readers who are trying to *cause* trouble for you and change the book. You'll be surprised by how strong the power of reader suggestion can get, and if you let readers get the upper hand, it'll be *Smilla's Sense of Snow* all over again."

Carmine looked thoughtful. The Sea Worms incident was a sobering lesson for everyone, and something that no one wanted to repeat.

"I'll be back as soon as I can," I said, preparing to leave. "I have to meet with Commander Herring. Mrs. Malaprop, will you show Carmine around the series and do the introductions? Start with the Gravitube and the Diatryma. After that it's all fairly benign."

4.

The Red-Haired Gentleman

Despite the remaking of the BookWorld, some books remained tantalizingly out of reach. The entire Sherlock Holmes canon was the most obvious example. It was entirely possible that they didn't know there was a BookWorld and still thought they were real. A fantastic notion, until you consider that up until 11:06 A.M. of April 12, 1948, everyone else had thought the same. Old-timers still speak of "the Great Realization" in hushed tones and refer to the glory days when the possibility of being imaginary was only for the philosophers.

Bradshaw's BookWorld Companion (4th edition)

I stepped out of the front door and walked the eight blocks to the corner of Adams and Colfer. A bus arrived in a couple of minutes—they always do—and after showing my pass to the driver, who looked suspiciously like a Dr. Seuss character on furlough, I took a seat between a Viking and a nun.

"I'm on my way to a pillage," said the Viking as he attempted to find some common ground on which to converse, "and we're a bit lean in the 'beating people to death with large hammers' department. Would you like to join us?"

"That's most kind, but it's really not my thing."

"Oh, go on, you might rather like it."

"No thank you."

"I see," said the Viking in a huffy tone. "Please yourself, then." And he lapsed into silence.

It was the nun's turn to speak.

"I'm collecting," she said with a warm smile, "for the St. Nancy's Home for Fallen Women."

"Fallen in what respect?"

"Fallen *readership*. Those poor unfortunate wretches who, through no fault of their own, now find themselves in the ignominious status of the less well read. Are you interested?"

"Not really."

"Well," said the nun, "how *completely* selfish of you. How would you like to be hardly read at all?"

"I *am* hardly read at all," I told her, mustering as much dignity as I could. There was an unfair stigma attached to those characters who weren't read, and making us into victims in need of saving didn't really help, to be honest.

The Viking looked at me scornfully, then got up and went to the front of the bus to pretend to talk to someone. The nun joined him without another word, and I saw them glance in my direction and shake their heads sadly.

I took the bus across the Fantasy/Human Drama border, then changed to a tram at Hemingway Central. In the six months since the BookWorld had been remade, its citizens had learned much about their new surroundings. It was easier to understand; we had usable maps, a chain of outrageously expensive coffee shops in which to be seen, known as Stubbs, and most important, a network of road, rail and river to get from one place to another. We now had buses, trams, taxis, cars and even paddlewheel steamers. Bicycles might have been useful, but for some reason they didn't work inside the BookWorld—no matter what anyone did, they just wouldn't stay up. Jumping directly from book to book had rapidly become unfashionable and was looked upon as hopelessly Pulp. If you really wanted to be taken seriously and display a sense of cool unhurried insouciance, you walked.

"So what do you think?" asked a red-haired, jowly gentleman

who had sat next to me. He was dressed in a double-breasted blue suit with a dark tie secured by a pearl tiepin. His hair was long but combed straight, and there seemed rather a lot of it. So much, in fact, that he had gathered the bright red locks that grew from his cheeks into fine plaits, each bound with a blue ribbon. Aside from that, his deep-set eyes had a kindly look, and I felt immediately at ease in his company.

"What do I think about what?"

"This," he said, waving a hairy hand in the direction of the new BookWorld.

"Not enough pianos," I said after a moment's reflection, "and we could do with some more ducks—and fewer baobabs."

"I'd prefer it to be more like the RealWorld," said the red-haired gentleman with a sigh. "Our existence in here is very much life at second hand. I'd love to know what a mistral felt like, how the swing and drift of fabric might look and what *precisely* it is about a sunset or the Humming Chorus that makes them so astonishing."

This was a sentiment I could agree with.

"For me it would be to hear the rattle of rain on a tin roof or see the vapor rise from a warm lake in the chill morning air."

We fell silent for a moment as the tram rumbled on. I didn't tell him what I yearned for above all, the most underappreciated luxury of the human race: free will. My life was by definition preordained. I had to do what I was written to do, say what I was written to say, without variance, all day every day, whenever someone read me. Despite conversations like this, where I could think philosophically rather than narratively, I could never shrug off the peculiar feeling that someone was controlling my movements and eavesdropping on my every thought.

"I'm sure it's not all hot buttered crumpets out there in the breathing world of asphalt and heartbeats," I said by way of balance.

"Oh, I agree," replied the red-haired gentleman, who had, ·

I noticed, nut-brown hands with fingers that were folded tight along the knuckle. "For all its boundless color, depth, boldness, passion and humor, the RealWorld doesn't appear to have any clearly discernible function."

"Not that better minds than ours haven't tried to find one."

The jury had been out on this matter for some time. Some felt that the RealWorld was there only to give life to us, while others insisted that it *did* have a function, to which no one was yet party. There was a small group who suggested that the RealWorld was not real at all and was just another book in an even bigger library. Not to be outdone, the nihilists over in Philosophy insisted that reality was as utterly meaningless as it appeared.

"What is without dispute," said my friend once we had discussed these points, "is that the readers need us just as much as we need them—to bring order to their apparent chaos, if nothing else."

"*Who are you?*" I asked, unused to hearing such matters discussed on a Number 23 tram.

"Someone who cannot be saved, Miss Next. I have done terrible things."

I started at the mention of my name and was suddenly suspicious. Our chance meeting was no chance meeting. In fiction they rarely are. But then again, he might have thought I was the *other* Thursday Next.

"Sir, I'm not her."

He looked at me and smiled. "You're more alike than you suppose."

"Physically, perhaps," I replied, "but I flunked my Jurisfiction training."

"On occasion, people of talent are kept in reserve at times of crisis."

I stared at him for a moment. "Why are you telling me this?"

"I don't have much time. I think they saw us talking. Heed this and heed it well: *One of our Thursdays is missing!*"

"What do you mean?"

"This: Trust no one but yourself."

"Which 'yourself'? I have several. Me, the real me and Carmine who is being me when I'm not me."

He didn't get to answer. The tram lurched, and with a sharp squeal of the emergency brakes we ground to a halt. The reason we had stopped was that two highly distinctive 1949 Buick Roadmaster automobiles were blocking the road, and four men were waiting for us. The cars and their occupants were among the more iniquitous features of the remaking. The Council of Genres, worried about increased security issues with the freedom of movement, had added another tier of law enforcement to the BookWorld. Shadowy men and women who were accountable only to the council and seemed to know no fear or restraint: the Men in Plaid.

The doors of the tram hissed open, and one of the agents climbed inside. He wore a well-tailored suit of light green plaid with a handkerchief neatly folded in his top pocket.

I turned to the red-haired gentleman to say something, but he had moved across the aisle to the seat opposite. The Man in Plaid's eye fell upon my new friend, and he quickly strode up and placed a pistol to his head.

"Don't make any sudden movements, Kiki," ordered the Man in Plaid. "What are you doing so far outside Crime?"

"I came to Fantasy to look at the view."

"The view is the same as anywhere else."

"I was misinformed."

The red-haired gentleman was soon handcuffed. With a dramatic flourish, the Man in Plaid pulled out a bloodstained straight razor from the red-haired gentleman's pocket. A gasp went up from the occupants of the tram.

"This lunatic has been AWOL from his short story for twenty-four hours," announced the agent. "You are fortunate to have survived."

The red-haired gentleman was pulled from the tram and bundled into the back of one of the Buick Roadmasters, which then sped from the scene.

The Man in Plaid came back on the tram and stared at us all in turn.

"A consummate liar, whose manipulative ways have seen two dead already. Did he say anything to anyone?"

The red-haired gentleman had admitted to me that he'd done terrible things, but that wasn't unusual. Out of their books, crazed killers could be as pleasant as pie.

"He murdered two women," continued the first Man in Plaid, presumably in order to loosen our tongues. "He cut the throat of one and strangled the other. Now, did he say anything to anybody?"

I remained silent, and so did everyone else. In the short time the Men in Plaid had been operational, people had learned they were simply trouble and best not assisted in any way.

"Are you a Man in Plaid?" asked one of the passengers.

The man stared at the passenger in a way you wouldn't like to be stared at. "It's not plaid. It's tartan."

The agent, apparently satisfied that the red-haired gentleman had not spoken to anyone, stepped off the tram, and the doors hissed shut. I shivered as a sudden sense of foreboding shuffled through the four hundred or so verbs, nouns and similes that made up my being. The red-haired gentleman had told me he thought that "one of our Thursdays is missing," and by that I took him to mean Thursday Next, the *real* Thursday Next. My flesh-and-blood alter-better ego. But I didn't get to muse on it any further, for a few minutes later we arrived at the border between Human Drama and Thriller.

5.

Sprockett

The logic of cog-based intelligences is unimpeachable. Unlike the inferior electronics-based intelligences, they cannot show error, for the constantly enmeshed cogs, wheels and drives never slip or jump. I think one can safely attest that there is no puzzle that Men of the Cog cannot solve, given sufficient oil, facts and winds.

Bradshaw's BookWorld Companion (6th edition)

*T*here was a queue to cross into Thriller, bookpeople either being permanently transferred or on a Character Exchange Program designed to stop characters from getting bored, restless and troublesome. There were a few traveling artisans, salesmen and a dozen or so tourists, apparently on a Get Beaten Senseless by Bourne package holiday, which had just overtaken the Being Shot in the Leg by Bond break for popularity, much to the Fleming camp's disgust.

As little as two months ago, I would have been waved across with nary a glance, but the heightened security risk due to the potentially inflammable political situation up at Racy Novel had made everyone jumpy.

I took a TransGenre Taxi as far as the Legal part of Thriller, then continued on foot. I took a left turn by *The Firm* and picked my way along a weed-covered path and across a plank that spanned a ditch of brackish water, the best method to get into Conspiracy without being waylaid by deluded theorists, who always wanted to explain in earnest terms that President

Formby was murdered by President Redmond van de Poste, that bestselling author Colwyn Baye was far too handsome and clever and charming to be anything other than an android or a reptile or an alien or all three.

I took a left turn at the Lone Gunman pub, and walked past a hangar full of advanced flying machines that all displayed a swastika, then entered a shantytown that was home to theories that lived right on the edge of Conspiracy due to a sense of overtired outrageousness. This was where the *Protocols* lived, along with alien abductions, 9/11 deniers and the notion that FDR somehow knew about the attack on Pearl Harbor. I had hoped I might tread unnoticed within the genre, but I was mistaken. Despite avoiding eye contact, I was spotted by a wild-looking loon with hair that stuck out in every direction.

"There's no such thing as time," he confided, with an unwavering sense of belief in his own assertions. "It's simply a construct designed by a cabal of financiers eager to sell us pensions, life insurance and watches in their pursuit of a global, timepiece-marketing agenda."

"Really?" I asked, which is probably the only answer to anything in Conspiracy.

"Definitely. And the seal is not a mammal—it's an insect. The truth has been suppressed by the BBC and Richard Attenborough, who want to promote a global mammalcentric agenda."

"Don't you mean *David* Attenborough?"

"So you agree?" he said, eyes opening so wide I was suddenly worried I might see his brain. "Would you like to stone a robot?"

"What?"

"Stone a robot. Just one of the first generation of mechanical men, designed to be placed amongst us in order to take over the planet and promote a clockwork, global cogcentric agenda."

"I'm not really into stoning anyone."

"Oh, well," said the theorist as he picked a rock off the ground. "Suit yourself."

And he walked off. Intrigued and somewhat concerned, I followed him to New World Order Plaza, where a small crowd had gathered. They were an odd bunch that comprised everything from small gray aliens to reptilian shape-shifters, Men in Black, Elvises, lost cosmonauts and a smattering of Jimmy Hoffa/Lord Lucan secret genetic hybrids. They were arranged in a semicircle around a tall man dressed in a perfectly starched frock coat, striped trousers and white gloves. Of his clockwork robotic origins there seemed little doubt. His porcelain face was bland and featureless, the only moving part his right eyebrow, which was made of machined steel and could point to an array of emotions painted in small words upon the side of his head. From the look of him, his mainspring was at the very last vestige of tension—he had shut down all peripheral motor functions, and if his eyes had not scanned backwards and forwards as I watched, I might have thought he had run down completely.

"They banish us here to Fiction," said a rabble-rousing gray alien, pointing his finger in the air, "when we should be up there, in Nonfiction."

The crowd agreed wholeheartedly with this sentiment and clacked their stones together angrily.

"And then," continued the alien, "they have the temerity to send robots amongst us to spy on our every movement and report back to a centralized index that holds the records of everyone in the BookWorld, all as a precursor to thought-control experiments that will rob us of our minds and make us into mere drones, lackeys of the publishing world. What do we say to the council? Do we politely say, 'No thank you,' or do we send their messenger home in a sack?"

The crowd roared. I didn't know much about Conspiracy,

but I did know that its theorists were mostly paranoid and tended to value conviction above evidence.

I was just wondering what, if anything, could be done to stop the needless destruction of a finely crafted automaton when the mechanical man caught my eye, and with the last few ounces of spring pressure available to him, he moved his eyebrow pointer among an array of emotions in a manner that spoke of fear, loss, betrayal and hopelessness. The last plea from a condemned machine. Something shifted within me, and before I knew what I was doing, I had spoken up.

"There you are!" I said in a loud voice as I strode into the semicircle of stone-wielding conspirators. "I *knew* I should have given you an extra wind at lunchtime."

The aliens and Elvises and alien Elvises looked at one another suspiciously.

"Thursday Next," I said as I searched the automaton's pockets for his key. The crowd looked doubtful, and the alien ringleader blinked at me oddly, his large, teardrop-shaped eyes utterly devoid of compassion.

"Thursday Next is too important to trouble herself with the fortunes of a mechanical man," he said thinly, "and she told me personally she would rather kneel on broken glass than ever visit Conspiracy again."

This was doubtless true, and I could see why.

"You are an impostor," said the alien, "sent by the council as part of a plan to destabilize our genre and promote your own twisted evidence-centric agenda."

There was a nasty murmuring among the crowd as with fumbling hand I found the large brass key and inserted it into the socket located on the back of the automaton's neck. I gave him a quick wind to get him started, and I felt his body shift slightly as the gyros, motors, cogs and actuators started to reboot his mechanical cortex.

. . . and with the last few ounces of spring pressure available to him,
he moved his eyebrow pointer among an array of emotions in a
manner that spoke of fear, loss, betrayal and hopelessness.

"You're the *written* one," said someone at the back. "The dopey one who likes to hug a lot."

The situation had just taken a turn for the worse. But since this was Conspiracy and facts weren't necessarily the end of an argument, I thought I'd try a bluff. I reached into my pocket and held out my JAID shield. From a distance it might be confused with a Jurisfiction badge. I had to hope that no one would look too closely.

"Read it and weep," I said, swallowing down my nervousness. "Make a move on me and I'll have Jurisfiction dump forty tons of Intelligently Reasoned Argument right on your butt."

"So *you* say," said the small alien. "Elvis? Check her badge."

The two dozen Elvises looked at one another and began to squabble as they tried to figure out which Elvis the alien was talking to, and once this was established, I had half wound the mechanical man. If it came to a fight, I wouldn't be on my own.

"Steady on, lads," said the Elvis after looking at my badge. "She's not bluffing—it's her all right."

"I am?" I said, then quickly added, "Yes, I am. Now piss off."

The small group hurriedly made some excuse about having to view some reverse-engineered alien technology hidden in a hangar somewhere in a desert, and within a few moments the clockwork man and I were entirely alone.

"Permission to speak, madam?" said the automaton once I had wound him sufficiently to reboot his memory and thought processes. He spoke with the rich, plummy tones of the perfect gentleman's gentleman, but with a faint buzz—a bit like a bumblebee stuck inside a cello.

"Of course."

"I am one of the older Duplex-5 models, so if madam would only wind me as far as twenty-eight turns, I would be most grateful. My spring will take a full thirty-two, but the last four winds have an *unpredictable* effect upon my central reasoning gears that render me unable to offer my best."

"I'll remember that," I said.

"And if I might be so bold," added the clockwork man, "I would highly recommend that you do not let me fall *below* two winds, as I fear I might become somewhat languorous in my movements and may stray unforgivably into short-tempered impertinence."

"Between two and twenty-eight it is."

I finished winding him but, as requested, was careful not to go beyond the red mark on the mainspring tension indicator just under his chin. Once I was done, he turned to face me, and his single expressive eyebrow quivered momentarily and then pointed to "Uncomfortable." I knew exactly what he meant: that the winding of a manservant is a mildly embarrassing undertaking, and to preserve both employer and employee's mutual respect, should not be commented upon again.

"That's a very useful eyebrow."

"It's a standard feature of the Duplex-5s. Since we have few genuine emotions, it helps to telegraph how we think we should be feeling, given the circumstances."

"It works for me, Mr. . . . ?"

"Sprockett," said Sprockett. "Ready and willing to enter your employ."

"I'm not sure I need a butler."

"In that you would be in error, ma'am. It has been long proven that *everyone* needs a butler. Besides, you saved my life."

It was complex, but I knew what he meant. Because I had saved him, he was indebted to me—and to refuse him an opportunity to reciprocate my kindness would leave him burdened by a favor unpaid. And if you had a potential life of a thousand years or more, you could be a long time fretting, and fretting increases wear on cogs. Clockwork life-forms could be annoyingly steadfast, but it was their saving grace, too.

"All right," I agreed, "but for a trial period only."

"Very good, ma'am. Would you care for a cocktail? I do a very good Tahiti Tingle—without the umbrella if you think they are a bit passé."

"Not now. I'm working."

"In Conspiracy, ma'am?"

I pointed at the book traffic that was moving constantly overhead.

"One of those came down last night, and I'm here to find out why."

"I see," said Sprockett, his eyebrow pointer nodding toward "Worried" as he looked upwards. "I will assist in whatever capacity I can."

We made our way toward the regional offices. Sprockett talked and thought well for an automaton, and aside from a slight limp, his empty features and a muted buzz when he moved or thought, he was reasonably lifelike. I asked him where he was from, and he told me he was from Vanity—in a pilot book for a series titled *The League of Cogmen*, about the many adventures that befall a series of mechanical men designed by an Edwardian inventor. Sprockett had been initially built as a butler but soon transcended his calling to become a dynamic machine of action. A mixture of *The Admirable Crichton*, *Biggles* and *The 1903 Watchmaker's Review*. When unemployment beckoned, he reverted to domestic service—butlers are more sought after than are action heroes.

"What was your book like?"

"Uneven," replied Sprockett. "A fine concept, but lacking in legs to carry it off. Sadly, I have too few emotions to be engaging as a principal character."

"Because you were designed as a butler?"

"Not at all—because I'm only a Duplex-5. The empathy escapement was never quite perfected before we went into production. I can indicate a range of emotions through my eyebrow pointer, but that's about it. I can recognize your sorrow and act accordingly—but I cannot feel emotions nor truly understand what 'emotion' or 'feel' actually means."

"But surely you felt danger when you were about to be stoned and relief when rescued?"

"Yes, but only in the context that to be destroyed would deny me the opportunity to serve cocktails—and that would contravene the second law of domestic robotics."

Sprockett told me that his books were hastily printed, had not been read once in seventeen years and now, aside from a few copies in the circulation of friends and family, were sitting unread in a cardboard box in the writer's garage in Cirencester.

"And becoming damp, too," he added. "Sometimes rain is blown under the garage doors. There is mold and damp seeping up the print run—look."

He rolled up a trouser leg to reveal a green patch of patination on his otherwise shiny bronze leg. His would be a long, lingering journey to unreadfulness. He would gradually look more tarnished and increasingly lost over the years until the last copy would be destroyed and—unless picked up in another book—he'd suddenly wink out of existence.

"What's it like living in Vanity?"

"May I be candid?"

"I'd welcome it."

"We tend not to use the term Vanity anymore. It sounds derogatory. We refer to it as Self-Published or Collaborative, and you'd be surprised just how much good prose is interspersed with that of an uneven nature."

This was true. Beatrix Potter, Keats and George Eliot had all been self-published, as was the first issue of *Alice in Wonderland*. I looked across to where the island of Vanity lay just off the coast beyond the Cliff of Notes. Even from here the high-stacked apartment buildings could clearly be seen. The turbulent waterway between Vanity and the mainland was swept with dangerous currents, whirlpools and tidal rips. Despite this, many Vanitarians attempted to make the perilous journey to brighter prospects on the mainland. Of those who survived, most were turned back.

"I'd like to come out and see the conditions for myself," I said, the unease in my voice setting Sprockett's eyebrow to flicker twice before pointing at "Worried."

"No, really," I said, "I would. You can't believe anything you read in *The Word* these days."

Sprockett demurred politely, but his eyebrow said it all—speaking of an entire genre kept marginalized, right on the edges of Fiction. The "Vanity Question" was one of many issues that had dogged the political elite since the remaking. The problem was, no published books liked anything self-published in the neighborhood. They argued—and quite eloquently, as it turned out—that the point of having similar books clustered in neighborhoods and genres was for mutual cross-fertilization of ideas, themes and topics. Having something from Vanity close by would, they claimed, "lower the tone of the prose." Liberal factions within the Council of Genres had attempted a cross-genre experiment and placed *The Man Who Died a Lot* right into the middle of McEwan on the basis that the localized erudition could only have a bettering effect on the Vanity book. It was a disaster. None of the characters within McEwan would talk to them and even claimed that some descriptive passages had been stolen. It was then that McEwan and the nearby Rushdie and Amis threatened to go on strike and lower their Literary Highbrow Index to a shockingly low 7.2 unless *The Man Who Died a Lot* was removed. The offending book was gone before teatime, and no one had tried anything since. Vanity's contribution to Fiction in general was an abundance of cheap labor and the occasional blockbuster, which was accepted onto the island with an apologetic, "Gosh, don't know how that happened."

We continued our walk through Conspiracy, past something odd that had been dug up on the Quantock Hills, and Sprockett asked me if I conducted many accident investigations.

"My last investigation was in a book-club edition of *Three Men in a Boat*, which had sprung a leak," I told him, "and lost forty thousand gallons of the river Thames as it passed across Crime Noir, where it fell quite helpfully as rain. My theory had been that it was a sticky pressure-relief valve on the comedy induction loops, probably as a result of substandard metaphor building up on the injectors. I penned an exhaustive report to Commander Herring, who congratulated me on my thoroughness but tactfully pointed out that comedy induction loops were not introduced until April 1956—long *after* the book was built."

"Oh," said Sprockett, who perhaps had been expecting a story with a happier ending. "So what had *really* happened?"

I sighed. "Someone had simply left the plug out of the Thames and it had drained away."

We walked on in silence for a moment.

"Ma'am, if you would forgive the impertinence, might I place one small condition upon my employment?"

I nodded, so he continued.

"I have an overriding abhorrence for honey. No matter what happens, it always seems to end up in my insides, and it is the very devil to remove. In my last employ, my master insisted upon honey for breakfast, and a small quantity became lodged in my thought cogs. Until steam-cleaned, I became convinced I was the Raja of Sarawak."

"No honey," I said. "Promise."

And so, fully introduced, we talked about the much-heralded

and much-delayed introduction of the advanced Duplex-6 clockwork automaton. And, after that, the relative merits of phosphor-bronze over stainless steel for knee joints. So it was that I arrived, thoroughly versed in the Matters of the Cog, at the regional Conspiracy offices a few minutes later.

6.

The Bed-Sitting Room

The ISBN security numbering system achieved little. Thieves simply moved into stealing and trading sections of older books. The members of the Out-of-Print Brigade were furious; after looking forward to a long and happy retirement, they instead found their favorite armchairs pinched from under them as they dozed. Entire books were stripped of all nouns, and in the very worst cases large sections of dramatic irony were hacked from the books and boiled down to extract the raw metaphor, rendering once-fine novels mere husks suitable only for scrapping.

Bradshaw's BookWorld Companion (14th edition)

*T*he local genre representative was sitting on a wicker chair on the veranda of his office, a clapboard affair that looked much ravaged by overreading. The rep was described as what we termed "UK-6 Aristocracy Dapper-12," which meant that he had a fine pencil mustache and spoke as though he were from the Royal Academy of Dramatic Art. I told Sprockett to wait for me outside, which he unhesitatingly agreed to do.

The rep did not rise from his chair and instead looked me up and down and then said in a disparaging tone, "You're a long way from Mind, Body and Soul, old girl."

It's true that I may have looked a bit New Agey, but I didn't really need this. Bolstered by my earlier claim to be the real Thursday, I decided to try the same here.

"The name's Thursday Next," I said, waving my shield.

The reaction was electric. He choked on his afternoon tea and crumpet and, in his hurry to get to his feet, nearly woke a large and very hairy Sasquatch who dozed in a wicker chair a little way down the veranda.

"Good gracious!" exclaimed the genre rep. "Please excuse me. The name's Bilderberg. Roswell Bilderberg. My office is your office. Hey!" He kicked the foot of the Sasquatch, who opened one eye and stared at him indifferently. "Thursday Next," hissed Roswell, nodding in my direction.

The Sasquatch opened his eyes wide and jumped to his feet. "I was nowhere near the Orient Express that evening," he said hurriedly, "and even if I was, I had nothing against Mr. Cassetti—isn't that right, Roswell?"

"Don't drag me into your web of deceit," replied Roswell out of the side of his mouth, still smiling at me. "Now, how can we help you, Miss Next? Pleasure or business?"

"*Official* business," I said as the Sasquatch nonchalantly picked up a set of snowshoes and sneaked guiltily away.

"What sort of official business?" asked Roswell suspiciously. "We've heard that the Council of Genres was planning on moving us across to Juvenilia as part of a secret cross-BookWorld plan to marginalize those genres that don't toe the official line. And if we didn't comply, we would all be murdered in our sleep by government assassins who can drip poison into your ear down a thread—if such a thing is possible, or even likely."

As far as I knew, no such plans were afoot. But you didn't live in Conspiracy for long without imagining all sorts of nonsense. Not that Conspiracy always got it wrong. On the few occasions they *were* correct, a rapid transfer to Nonfiction was in order—which threw those who were left behind into something of a dilemma. Being in Fiction meant a wider readership, something that Nonfiction could never boast. Besides, a conspiracy theory that turned out to be real wasn't a theory anymore, and the loss of wild uncorroborated speculation could be something of a downer.

"I'm working with JAID—the Jurisfiction Accident Investigation Department."

"Ah!" he replied, suddenly realizing what I was here for. "The Lola incident. I believe that Commander Herring is already up there. Can I stress at this time that we will afford Jurisfiction's representatives all possible help and assistance?"

It was all he could say, really. No one wanted to fall afoul of Jurisfiction or the Council of Genres. This was Fiction. There were skeletons in everyone's closet.

"It came to earth nine hours ago," he said as we walked past two faked moon landings, three UFO abductions and a grassy knoll. "It bounced on a pamphlet regarding the notion that Diatrymas are being bred by the Goliath Corporation to keep people out of the New Forest, then landed on a book outlining the somewhat dubious circumstances surrounding the death of Lola Vavoom."

With Sprockett following at a discreet distance, we took a shortcut through a field of crop circles, passed a laboratory covertly designing infectious diseases for population control, moved aside as a white Fiat Uno drove after a black Mercedes, then entered the subgenre of Lola Vavoom Suspicious Death. Roswell pushed open the swinging doors of a concrete multistory car park that opened directly onto the tenth floor, and standing next to a large lump of tattered wreckage the size of a truck were two men. I didn't recognize the more disheveled of the two, but the older, wiser and clearly the boss was someone I did recognize: Regional Commander Herring of the BookWorld Policing Agency.

He was very much a hands-on type of administrator. He had no staff, carried all his notes in his head and was one of the few people who still jumped from book to book rather than taking a taxi or public transport. He was a BGH-87 character type.

Male, persnickety and highly efficient, but seemingly without humor. He was about fifty and was dressed in a short-sleeved white shirt with an infinite quantity of pens in his top pocket and a garish tie. He wore spectacles, but only for effect. He was high up in the chain of command at the Council of Genres and had access, it was said, to Senator Jobsworth himself. He was the most powerful man I knew.

"About time," he said when I appeared. "Places to be, people to visit—wheels within wheels."

"Wheels within wheels," echoed the man next to him.

"This is Martin Lockheed," explained Herring. "You'll answer to him, as I am a busy man. After this meeting I do not expect us to meet again."

"Yes, sir."

"Your *Three Men in a Boat* investigation didn't really impress," he began.

"Yes, I'm sorry about that."

"Apologies don't really cut it, Next, but I am a man loyal to friends, and the real Miss Next has always intimated in the past that you may show promise one day."

"I'm very grateful to her . . . and you," I managed to stammer.

"So I look upon you as an investment," replied Herring, "and a long-standing favor to a valued colleague. Which is why we are here now. Do you understand?"

"I think so."

"Good."

"That's good," said Lockheed, as if I might not have heard what Herring said. The regional commander waved a hand at the wreckage.

"Easy one for you to cut your teeth on. It has all the signs of being another unprecedented event that despite all expectations has become repeatedly unrepeatable. Don't let me down, will you? Wrap it up nice and neat and don't get all showy or anything. Fiction has a 99.97 percent book-safety record, and the last thing we want is the residents of this fair island worried that the fabric of their world is prone to shredding itself at the drop of a particle, hmm?"

"I'll do my very best to discover that it's an unrepeatable accident," I told him, "and with indecent haste."

"Very good. Twenty-four hours should suffice, yes?"

"I'll see what I can do, sir, and I'd like to thank you for the opportunity."

"No need. Lockheed?"

"Yes, sir?"

Herring snapped his fingers impatiently, and the rather harassed Lockheed passed him a clipboard.

"These are the reported items of debris," Herring said, handing the clipboard straight to me without looking at it. "Not good, having narrative falling from the skies, so let's keep it simple, eh? Wheels within wheels, Thursday."

"Wheels within wheels," added Lockheed earnestly.

"Wheels within wheels, sir. Would you thank Miss Next for me when you see her?"

"When next I see her. She's very busy."

He then looked at Sprockett, who was standing off from the group, being unobtrusive. "Who's that?"

"Sprockett," I replied, "my butler."

"I didn't know you had a butler."

"Everyone needs a butler, sir."

"I have no argument with that. Duplex-3, is he?"

"Duplex-5, sir."

"The Fives were prone to be troublesome without sufficient winding. I'll let you get on. You can call Lockheed anytime you want for guidance. Any questions?"

I thought of asking him if he had seen the real Thursday Next recently but decided against it. The red-haired gentleman had spoken of "being able to trust no one but myself," and besides, I didn't want to look a fool if the man on the tram really *was* a murderous nutjob.

"No questions, sir."

"Good luck, Miss Next."

He gave me a half smile, shook my hand and vanished.

"I'll be off, too," said Lockheed, handing me a business card and a folder full of health-and-safety literature. "Commander Herring is a great and good man, and you are lucky to have been given this opportunity to converse. He doesn't usually speak to people as low as you."

"I'm honored."

"And so you should be. I was his assistant for three years before he deigned to look me in the eye. One of my proudest moments. If you need me, the JAID offices are at Norland Park."

And he walked off. Eager not to waste the opportunity I had just been given, I turned my attention to the wreckage.

The chunk of book had splintered off the main novel as it broke up. But this wasn't pages or ink or anything; it was a small part of *setting.* Despite the ragged textual word strings that were draped across and the graphemes lying scattered on the floor nearby, the misshapen lump seemed to be a room from a house somewhere. It had landed on the asphalt covering of the car park and cracked the surface so badly that the textual matrix beneath the roadway was now visible. The battered section had landed upside down just behind Lola Vavoom's Delahaye Roadster, which had prevented her from reversing too quickly from her parking place, breaking through the barriers and falling eighty feet to her death. It had always been a suspicious accident, but nothing untoward was ever found to suppose it wasn't just that—an accident.

"Will this take long, dahling?" asked Lola, who was dressed in tight slacks and a cashmere sweater with a pink scarf tied around her hair. Her eyes were obscured by a pair of dark glasses, and she was casually sitting on the trunk of her car smoking a small Sobranie cigarette.

"As long as it must," I said, "and I'm sorry for the inconvenience."

"Do your best, dear," she intoned patronizingly, "but if I'm not dead in mysterious circumstances by teatime, someone is going to have some serious explaining to do."

I turned my attention to the wreckage. Spontaneous breakups were uncommon but not unheard of, and it was JAID's job to try to find the cause so that other books wouldn't suffer the same fate. Losing a cast of a thousand or more was not just a personal tragedy, but expensive. When a book-club edition of *War and Peace* had disintegrated without warning a few months ago as it passed over Human Drama, all those within the debris field were picking brass buttons and lengthy digressions out of their hair for a week. The JAID investigator assigned to the case painstakingly reconstructed the book, only to find that a batch of verbs had been packed incorrectly at the aft expansion joint and had overheated. Punctuation lock had no effect, and in a last desperate attempt to bring the book under control, the engineers initiated Emergency Volume Separation. A good idea, but undertaken too quickly. The smaller and lighter Epilogues could not alter course in time and collided with Volume Four, which in turn collided with Volume Three, and so forth. Of the twenty-six thousand characters involved in the disaster, only five survived. Verb quality control and emergency procedures were dramatically improved after this, and nothing like it had happened since.

"It seems to be a bed-sitting room of some variety," murmured Sprockett as he peered inside the large lump of scrap. "Probably ten pounds a week—furnished, naturally."

"Naturally."

"Are we looking for anything in particular?"

"An International Standard Book Number," I said, "an ISBN. We need to know what the book is and where it came from before we can start trying to figure out what went wrong. It's sometimes harder than it seems. The wreckage is often badly mangled, widely scattered—and there are a lot of books out there."

We stepped into the upside-down bed-sitting room, all its contents strewn around inside. It was well described, so it was either a popular book given depth and color by reader feedback, or pre-feedback altogether. The room hadn't been painted for a while, the carpets were threadbare, and the furniture had seen better days. It might seem trivial, but it was these sorts of clues that allowed us to pinpoint which book it was from.

"Potboiler?" I suggested.

"It's from HumDram if it is," replied Sprockett as he picked up a torn *Abbey Road* album. "Post-1969, at any rate."

We searched for half an hour amongst the debris but found no sign of an ISBN.

"This book could be any one of thousands," said Sprockett. "*Millions*."

With nothing more to see here, we stepped back outside the bed-sitting room, and I laid a map of the BookWorld on the hood of Lola's car and marked where the section had been found. This done, I called in Pickford Removals, and within twenty minutes the bed-sitting room had been loaded onto the back of a flatbed for onward delivery to the double garage at the back of my house. This was ostensibly to allow the books in which they had landed to carry on unhindered. Not that a ton of tattered paragraph would necessarily be a problem. The entire cast of *A Tale of Two Cities* has steadfastly ignored a runaway pink gorilla that has evaded capture for eighty-seven years but, as far as we know, has not been spotted by readers once.

"I'm sorry to have troubled you," I said to Lola, who stubbed out her cigarette and climbed into her car. She stomped on the accelerator, and the Delahaye shot across the car park, drove straight through the wooden barrier behind her and landed with a crunch on top of the Mairzy Doats sandwich bar ten stories below.

"Come on," I said to Sprockett. "Work to be done."

The debris field extended across four genres, and we spent the next three hours listening to residents who claimed that falling book junk had "completely ruined their entrance," and on one rare occasion it actually had. There was a reasonable quantity of wreckage, but nothing quite as large as the bed-sitting room. We found a yellow-painted back axle, the remains of at least nine tigers, a few playing cards, some lengths of silk, a hat stand, sections of a box-girder bridge, nine apples, parts of a raccoon and a quantity of slate. There was a lot of unrecognizable scrap, too, much of it desyntaxed sentences that made no sense at all. We found only one piece of human remains—a thumb—except it might not have been a thumb at all but simply reformed graphemes.

"Graphemes?" asked Sprockett when I mentioned it.

"Everything in the BookWorld is constructed of them," I explained. "Letters and punctuation—the building blocks of the textual world."

"So why might that thumb not actually be a thumb?"

"Because once broken down below the 'word' unit, a grapheme might come from anywhere. The same *s* can serve equally well in a sword, a sausage, a ship, a sailor or even the sun. It doesn't help that under extreme pressure and heat, graphemes often separate out and then fuse back together into something else entirely. At Jurisfiction basic training, we were shown how a 'sheet of card,' once heated up white-hot and then struck with a blacksmith's hammer, could be made into 'cod feathers' and then back again."

"Ah," said Sprockett, "I see."

"Because of this, anything under a few words long found at an accident site can be disregarded as evidence—it might once have been something else entirely." Oddly enough, the process of graphusion and graphission, while occurring naturally in the Text Sea, was hard to do synthetically in the BookWorld but simplicity itself in the Outland. The long and short of it was that victims of extreme trauma in the BookWorld were rarely found. A sprinkling of graphemes was soon absorbed into the fabric of the book it fell upon and left no trace.

Once Sprockett and I had logged everything we'd found and dispatched it via Pickford's to my double garage, I called Mrs. Malaprop to check that all was well. It was, generally speaking. Pickwick was suspicious that there really might be goblins around, and Carmine was spending her time rehearsing with the various members of the cast. Whitby Jett had called to say that now that Carmine was there, he would be taking me out to Bar Humbug for a drink and nibbles at nine—and no arguments.

I'd known him for nearly two years, and I think I'd just come to the end of a very long trail of excuses and reasons that I couldn't go out on a date. I sighed. There was still one. Perhaps the *only* one I'd ever had. I told Mrs. Malaprop I would be home in half an hour, thought for a moment and then turned to Sprockett.

"Can I shut you down for a while?"

"Madam, that is a *most* improper suggestion."

"I'm about to do something illegal, and since you are incapable of lying, I don't want you in a position where you have to divide your loyalties between your duties as a butler and your duties to the truth."

"Most thoughtful, ma'am. Conflicting loyalties do little but strip teeth off my cogs. Shall I shut down immediately?"

"Not yet."

We hailed a cab at the corner of Heller and Vonnegut. The cabbie had issues with clockwork people—"all that infernal ticking"—but since Sprockett was, legally speaking, nothing more nor less than a carriage clock, he was consigned to the trunk.

"I don't mind being treated as baggage," he said agreeably. "In fact, I prefer it. Promise you'll restart me?"

"I promise."

And after he had settled back against the spare tire, I pressed the emergency spring-release button located under his inspection cover. There was a loud whirring noise, and Sprockett went limp.

I shut the trunk, settled into the cab and closed the door.

"Where to?"

"Poetry."

7.

The Lady of Shalott

Here in the BookWorld, the protagonists and antagonists, gate-keepers, shape-shifters, heroes, villains, bit parts, knaves, comedians and goblins were united in that they possessed a clearly defined motive for what they were doing: entertainment and enlightenment. As far as any of us could see, no such luxury existed in the unpredictable world of the readers. The Outland was extraordinarily well named.

Bradshaw's BookWorld Companion (4th edition)

*T*he taxi was the usual yellow-and-check variety and could either run on wheels in the conventional manner or fly using advanced Technobabble™ vectored gravitational inversion thrusters. This had been demanded by the Sci-Fi fraternity, who had been whingeing on about hover cars and jet packs for decades and needed appeasing before they went and did something stupid, like allow someone to make a movie based on the title of the book known as *I, Robot*.

The driver was an elderly woman with white hair who grumbled about how she had just given a fare to three Triffids and how they hadn't bothered to tip and left soil in the foot wells and were horribly drunk on paraquat.

"Poetry?" she repeated. "No worries, pet. High Road or Low Road?"

She meant either up high, dodging amongst the planetoid-size books that were constantly moving across the sky, or down low on the ground, within the streets and byways. Taking the High Road was a skillful endeavor that meant either slipstreaming behind a particularly large book or latching onto a novel going in roughly the same direction and being carried to one's destination in a series of piggyback rides. It was faster if things went well, but more dangerous and prone to delays.

"Low Road," I said, since the traffic between Poetry and Fiction was limited and one could orbit for hours over the coast, waiting for a novel heading in the right direction.

"Jolly good," she said, clicking the FARE ON BOARD sign. "Cash, credit, goats, chickens, salt, pebbles, ants or barter?"

"Barter. I'll swap you two hours of my butler."

"Can he mix cocktails?"

"He can do a Tahiti Tingle—with or without umbrella."

"Deal."

We took the Dickens Freeway through HumDram, avoided the afternoon jam at the Brontë-Austen interchange and took a shortcut through Shreve Plaza to rejoin the expressway at Picoult Junction, and from there to the Carnegie Underpass, part of the network of tunnels that connected the various islands that made up the observable BookWorld.

"How are you enjoying the new BookWorld?" I asked by way of conversation.

"Too many baobabs and not enough smells," she said, "but otherwise enjoyable."

The baobabs *were* a problem, but it was hardly at the top of my list of complaints. After a few minutes with the cabbie telling me in a cheerful voice how she'd had Bagheera in the back of her cab once, we emerged blinking at the tunnel exit and the island of Poetry, where we were waved through by a border guard who was too busy checking the paperwork on a consignment of iambic pentameters to worry much about us.

We made our way slowly down Keats Avenue until we came to Tennyson Boulevard, and I ordered her to stop outside

"Locksley Hall" and wait for me around the corner. I got out, waited until she had gone, then walked past "The Lotos-Eaters" and "The Charge of the Light Brigade" to a small gate entwined with brambles and from there into a glorious English summer's day. I walked up the river, past long fields of barley and rye that seemed to clothe the wold and meet the sky, then through the field where a road ran by, which led to many-towered Camelot. I walked along the river, turned a corner and found the island in the river. I looked around as aspens quivered and a breeze and shiver ran up and down my spine. I really wasn't meant to be here and could get into serious trouble if I was discovered. I took a deep breath, crossed a small bridge and found myself facing a square gray building with towers at each corner. I didn't knock, as I knew the Lady of Shalott quite well, and entered unbidden to walk the two flights of stairs to the tower room.

"Hullo!" said the lady, pausing from the tapestry upon which she was engaged. "I didn't expect to see you again so soon."

The Lady of Shalott was of an indeterminate age and might once have been plain before the rigors of artistic interpretation got working on her. This was the annoying side of the Feedback Loop; irrespective of how she had once looked or even *wanted* to look, she was now a Pre-Raphaelite beauty with long flaxen tresses, flowing white gowns and a silver forehead band. She wasn't the only one to be physically morphed by reader expectation. Miss Havisham was now elderly whether she liked it or not, and Sherlock Holmes wore a deerstalker and smoked a ridiculously large pipe. The problem wasn't just confined to the classics. Harry Potter was seriously pissed off that he'd have to spend the rest of his life looking like Daniel Radcliffe.

"Good afternoon, my lady," I said, curtsying. "I would like to conduct more research."

"Such adherence to duty is much to be admired," replied the lady. "How are your readings going?"

"Over a thousand," I returned, lying spectacularly. If I didn't pretend to be popular, she'd never have granted me access.

"That's wonderful news. Make good use of the time. I could get into a lot of trouble for this."

Satisfied, she left her tapestry and summoned me to the window that faced Camelot. The Lady of Shalott took great care not to look out of the window but instead gently stroked a mirror that was held in a large bronze hanger and angled it towards the windows, as if to see the view outside. But this mirror wasn't like other mirrors; the surface grew misty, turned the color of slate, then displayed an image quite unlike the reflection one might expect.

"Usual place?" she asked.

"Usual place."

The image coalesced into a suburban street in the Old Town of Swindon, and the Lady of Shalott touched me on the shoulder.

"I'll leave you to it," she told me, and quietly returned to her tapestry, which seemed to depict David Hasselhoff in various episodes from *Baywatch*, Series 2.

I stared into the mirror. The image flickered occasionally and was mildly desaturated in color, but it was otherwise clear and sharp.

"Left forty-five degrees."

The mirror shifted to look up the suburban road to the house where Thursday and Landen lived. But this wasn't a book somewhere, or a memory. This was the RealWorld, the Outland. The Lady of Shalott uniquely possessed a window into reality and could see whatever she wanted, whenever she wanted to. Great lives, great events—even *Baywatch*. The images she saw were woven into a tapestry, and she couldn't look outside her own window on pain of death. It was all a bit weird, but that's Tennyson for you.

The view was live, and aside from the fact that it was mute, was almost as good as being there.

"Move forward six yards."

The viewpoint moved forward to a front door that was very familiar to me. I had a similar front door in my own book, but my version didn't have peeling paint or the random fine crackle that natural weathering brings. I sensed my heart beat faster.

"Go inside."

The viewpoint drifted through the door, where the hall was less familiar. Thursday and Landen's real house was only ever described briefly to the ghostwriter who wrote my series, so the interior was different. I jumped as someone moved past the mirror. It was a young girl aged no more than twelve, and she looked very serious for her years. This would have been Thursday and Landen's daughter, Tuesday, as brilliant as Uncle Mycroft but in the "confusing petulant" state of pubescence. Nothing was right and everything was wrong. If it wasn't problems over the revectoring of electrogravitational field theory, it was her brother, Friday, whom she regarded as a total loser and layabout.

"Advance two yards."

The viewpoint moved forward to the hall table. I could see that Thursday was not in, as her bag, keys, cell phone and battered leather jacket were absent. It didn't say she was missing; only that she wasn't at home right now.

"Advance six yards, rotate left twenty degrees."

The viewpoint moved into the kitchen, where a man was sitting at the table attempting to help Tuesday with her GSD uni-Scripture homework. He was graying at the temples and had a kindly face that was *very* familiar. This was Landen Parke-Laine, Thursday's husband. I blinked as my eyes moistened. They were talking, and he laughed. I couldn't hear him, but imagined as best I could how he might have sounded. Sort of like . . . *music.*

"One-twenty degrees to the right, pull out a yard."

The mirror did as I asked so I could see the family scene. I didn't have this. None of this. No husband, no children. Despite the real Thursday's wishes that Landen would be included in the series after I took over, he wasn't—and neither were any of the children. Thursday was overridden by a senator named Jobsworth over at the Council of Genres. So they reverted to the previous plan and had Landen continue to die in a house fire in the first chapter of *The Eyre Affair*, a clumsy attempt to give purpose to the written Thursday's fictitious crime fighting. The plot device might have been clunky, but the loss had been exceptionally well written; I felt it every minute of every day. Being fictional is a double-edged sword. You get to savor the really good times over and over, but the same is true of the bad. For every defeat of the Goliath Corporation, there is the loss of Miss Havisham, and for every moment in Mycroft's company there is a day in the Crimea. The delight at returning Jane Eyre to her book and thwarting Acheron is forever tempered by the inevitable loss of Landen, again and again forever.

So I stood there, staring at what should have been mine. I wanted to be with the children I should have been allowed to have and to spend my life expending time and energy in the glorious hope that I would one day become parentally redundant. In my bleaker moments, Pickwick and Mrs. Malaprop attempted to console me by explaining I had loss only to give relevance to what drove my character through the narrative, but it was meager consolation. I should have had a written Landen and written children to keep me company.

I watched Landen for several more minutes. Every movement, every nuance. I watched how he spoke to Tuesday with humor and infinite patience. I watched how he scratched his ear, how he laughed, how he smiled.

Friday joined them. My would-be son was a fine fellow—handsome like his father. Perhaps a bit rudderless at that age, but thought and function would eventually arrive in the fullness of time. I wanted to give him some guidance, but he had his mother for that. The real me. The real *her*. Besides, the mirror saw only in one direction. They had no idea that I was there, no idea that I felt as I did. I watched for a few more minutes, until Landen got up and walked to the sink, drew himself a glass of water and stared out the window.

"Pull out into the garden three yards, right ninety degrees."

My viewpoint drifted through the kitchen wall, and after a brief glimpse of central-heating pipes and a bored-looking mouse, I was now outside looking at Landen, who was just on the other side of the window. Although he couldn't see me, we were staring into each other's eyes.

"Whitby has asked me out to the Bar Humbug," I whispered. "I wanted you to know that I'm going."

Landen couldn't hear me, but I knew I had to tell him. It was by way of apology. I blinked away tears but then frowned. Landen was blinking away tears, too. *Something had happened.* Thursday wasn't here, but for how long? An argument? Had she *died* in the Outland? I looked at the children, who were busy with homework. They seemed unconcerned.

Whatever it was, it was a burden shouldered by Landen alone.

"When did you last see Thursday?" I whispered.

Landen took a deep breath, wiped his eyes and returned to the children. I put out my hand to touch the mirror, but it simply rippled, like water in a pool.

"Left thirty degrees, three yards forward."

The mirror complied, and I found myself close enough to the memo board above the telephone to read the notes. I peered amongst the receipts, pictures and old theater tickets before finding what I was looking for. A telephone message in Thursday's hand telling Landen that his sister wanted to talk to him. It was dated seven days ago. If Thursday *was* missing, it was for the maximum of a week.

"Did you see what you wanted?"

I jumped. The Lady of Shalott had returned and was standing just behind me.

"I think so," I replied hastily. "It was the . . . ah . . . state of her memo board I was looking at. You know what they say: 'A view into a woman's ephemera is a window to her soul.'"

"Do they say that?" asked the Lady of Shalott doubtfully.

"Frequently."

I made ready to leave. The visits to Shalott were as frequent as I could make them without arousing suspicion, the views they offered all too fleeting. I wanted to know where Thursday was, sure, but I had to see Landen and the kids, too. *Had* to.

I thanked her, and she walked me to the door. But this wasn't a favor, and she and I both knew it. I wasn't allowed to be in Poetry without just cause, and I certainly wasn't allowed to sneak-peek the Outland. She handed me a wooden box.

"You will look after them, won't you?"

"Of course," I replied, and placed the box in my shoulder bag. I walked outside the castle and returned to where the taxi was waiting to take me home. I was none the wiser as to where Thursday was, but I could reasonably surmise she was missing in the Outland, too. I took a deep breath. It had been, as always, *difficult*. I loved and hated seeing him, all at the same time. But it helped when it came to finally going on a date with Whitby. It lessened the sense of betrayal.

8.

The Shield

The evidence for the existence of Dark Reading Matter remains obscure at best. Supposedly the vast amount of unread material either forgotten or deleted, DRM is also said to be home to the Unread: zombielike husks of former characters, their humanity sucked from their heads by continued unreadfulness. It is generally agreed that these stories belong to metamyth—stories within stories—and are used by drill sergeants at character college to frighten recruits into compliance.

Bradshaw's BookWorld Companion (8th edition)

*T*he queue to get out of Poetry was long, as always. The smuggling of metaphor out of the genre was a serious problem, and one that made the border guards extremely vigilant. The increased scarcity of raw metaphor in Fiction had driven prices sky-high, and people would take unbelievably foolish risks to smuggle it across. I'd heard stories of metaphor being hidden in baggage, swallowed, even dressed up to look like ordinary objects whose *meanings* were then disguised to cloak the metaphor. The problem at that point was trying to explain why you had a "brooding thunderstorm" or "broad sunlit uplands" in your luggage.

"Can we take the High Road?" I asked.

She turned around to look at me. Taking the High Road out of Poetry meant only one thing—that I wanted to avoid any entanglements with the border guards.

"My friend Jake was carrying a mule without realizing it last week," said the cabbie in a meaningful tone. "The mule had two kilos of raw metonym on him—hidden in the saddlebags."

Metonym wasn't as dangerous as smuggling raw metaphor, but the underworld would try anything to turn a buck and had set up labs to enrich variable forms of metaphor into the real McCoy. Extracting the "like" from simile was the easiest method, but the resulting metaphor was as weak as wet paper. Synecdoche was used in much the same way; the best minds in Jurisfiction were constantly trying to outwit them, and raided met labs on an almost daily basis.

"Did he get to keep his cab?" I asked. "Your friend Jake, I mean."

"His entire car was reduced to text with the metonym still in it."

"Reduced to text?" I echoed. "Sounds like a hammer to break a nut."

"Poeticals are like that," said the cabbie with a disrespectful snort. "Prone to fits of violent passion. I think it's all that absinthe. The point is this: I can get you out of Poetry, but it will cost."

"I'll lend you my butler for an afternoon."

"One afternoon and a garden party."

"A garden party."

"Done."

The cabbie flipped the vectored thrust nozzles, and in an instant we were climbing almost vertically upwards. It took less than a minute to reach the low-lying book traffic, and within a few seconds we had latched onto an academic paper moving from Physics to Biology. We stayed there for a few minutes and then detached, hovered for a moment and then reattached to the keel of an oil tanker that was part of a Bermuda Triangle book on its way to Fiction. We were under the massive rudder at the back, with one of the vast propellers looming over us.

"We'll ride this baby all the way into Fiction," said the cabbie as she took out some knitting, "about twenty minutes. We could fly the whole way, but we'd probably be picked up by the book-traffic controllers and get busted."

"Don't look now, but I think we just have."

The flashing red lights of a Jurispoetry squad car close by had alerted me to the fact that the cabbie wasn't quite as good as I thought she was. We could have detached there and then and dropped the mile towards the Text Sea before leveling out and making a run for the coast, but it was a risky undertaking. Cutting and running meant only one thing: guilty.

"Oh, crap," said the cabbie, dropping a stitch in surprise. "I hope you've got some friends in high places."

"Hullo," I said to the officer who was now standing outside the car. He was dressed in a baggy white shirt and smelled strongly of rhyming couplets. He stared at me with the supercilious look of someone who knew he had the upper hand and was certainly going to milk it.

"Oh, to sneak across the border, when it's plain you should not oughta?"

I had to think quickly. Unlike the Poetry government officials who conversed in rhyme royal, this was a lowly traffic cop who spoke only the gutter doggerel of the streets. He was using a soft-rhyming AA and so was probably not that bright. I hit him with some AABCCB.

"*Au contraire*, my friend, we did not intend to break any poetical code. We were waved through by others of your crew and simply took the upper road."

But he didn't go for it.

"I can see your little plan, but your stanzas barely scan. You, madam, I must nab, so get your butt from out the cab."

I climbed out and succumbed to a search. He soon found the box the Lady of Shalott had given me.

"Well, lookee here, what have we got? Is this metaphor or is it not?"

"Not one but other, I must confess, the situation's now a mess."

He opened the box and stared. It wasn't metaphor, but contraband nonetheless.

"You're in big trouble smuggling this junk. What else you got? Let's pop the trunk."

We did, and there was Sprockett. The officer stared at him for a moment.

"I'm sure you can explain away why a dead butler's in your trunk today?"

"He's a *clockwork* butler, Duplex-5, and even paused he's still alive."

The officer had seen enough and brought out a report sheet to take down some details.

"Name?"

"Thursday Next."

The officer looked at me, then at my New Agey clothes, then at Sprockett.

"Now, which one could that be? The heroine or the one who likes to hug a tree?"

In for a penny, in for a pound. I had to hope that this guard could be fooled as easily as the Elvis back in Conspiracy.

"I am she, the Thursday proper. Those that cross me come a cropper."

"That seems likely, but before I yield, let me check your Jurisfiction shield."

I passed it across. The officer took one look at it, put away his report sheet and told his partner that they were leaving. He smiled and handed me back my badge.

"It's an honor, I'll be reckoned. Sorry to have kept you for even a second."

I signed my name in his autograph book and with growing confusion climbed back into the cab as the Jurispoetry car detached from the hull and fell away from the tanker, leaving us to continue our trip unmolested.

"You're Thursday Next?" said the cabbie, her attitude suddenly changed. "This ride is for free, kiddo. But listen, the next time you're in the RealWorld, can you find out why there have to be over a hundred different brands of soap? I'd really like to know."

"Okay," I muttered, "no problem."

The remainder of the journey was unremarkable, except for one thing: I spent the entire trip staring at the Jurisfiction shield that had allowed me not once but twice to squeak out of trouble. It wasn't my shield at all. It was Thursday's. The *real* Thursday's. *Someone had slipped it into my pocket that morning.* And the more I thought about the morning's events, the more I realized that I might have become involved—quite against my will—with a matter of some considerable consequence.

9.

Home

Rumor has it that undiscovered genres were hidden among the thick vegetation and impenetrable canopy in the far north of the island. Primitive, anarchic, strange and untouched by narrative convention, they were occasionally discovered and inducted into the known BookWorld, where they started off fresh and exciting before ultimately becoming mimicked, overused, tired and then passé. BookWorld naturalists argued strongly that some genres should remain hidden in order to keep the BookWorld from homogenizing, but their voices went unheeded.

Bradshaw's BookWorld Companion (3rd edition)

I had the most curious dream," mused Sprockett as soon as I had rewound him completely, "in which I was a full-hunter silent repeater. There was also this gramophone—you know, one of those windup varieties—and she was running overspeed and playing 'Temptation Rag.' And then there was this monkey hitting cymbals together, and I—"

He checked himself.

"I'm frightfully sorry, ma'am. My protocol gearing can become a bit gummy during deactivation. You are not offended by my drivel?"

"Not in the least. In fact, I didn't know machines *could* dream."

"I dream often," replied the butler thoughtfully. "Mostly about being a toaster."

"Dualit or KitchenAid?"

He seemed mildly insulted that I should have to ask.

"A Dualit four-slot, *naturally*. But perhaps," he added, his eyebrow pointer clicking from "Indignant" to "Puzzled," "I only *believe* I dream. Sometimes I think it is merely a construct to enable me to better understand humans."

"Listen, I should warn you about Pickwick," I said as we walked up the garden path.

"What is a Pickwick?"

"It's a dodo."

"I thought they were extinct."

"They may yet become so. She's trouble, so be careful."

"Thank you, ma'am. I shall."

I pushed open the front door and was met by the sound of laughter. Carmine was sitting at the table with Bowden Cable and Acheron Hades, two of the other costars from the series. They were all sharing a joke, or at least they were until I walked in, when everyone fell silent.

"Hello, Thursday," said Bowden, whom I'd never really gotten along with, despite the fact that his counterpart in the RealWorld was one of Thursday's closest friends. "We were just telling Carmine the best way to play Thursday."

"The best way is the way I play her," I said in a firm yet friendly manner. "Dignified."

"Of course," said Bowden. "Who's your friend?"

"Sprockett," I replied, "my butler."

"I didn't know you needed a butler," said Bowden.

"Everyone needs a butler. He was going to be stoned, so I took him with me."

"What do cog-based life-forms get stoned with?" asked Bowden in an impertinent manner. "Vegetable oil?"

"Actually, sir," intoned Sprockett, "it's sewing-machine lubricant for a mild tipple. Many feel that the exuberant effects of 3-in-One are worth pursuing, although I have never partaken myself. For those that have hit rock bottom, where life has become nothing more than a semiconscious slide from one partial winding to the next, it's WD-40."

"Oh," said Bowden, who had been put firmly in his place by Sprockett's forthrightness, "I see."

"Hmm," said Acheron, peering at Sprockett's data plate with great interest. "Are you the Duplex-6?"

"Five, sir. The Six's release has been delayed. A series of mainspring failures have put beta testing back several months, and now I hear the Six has pressure compensation issues on the primary ethical escapement module."

"What does that mean?"

"I have to admit I'm not entirely sure, sir. The main problem with clockwork sentience is that we can *never* understand the level of our own complexity—for to do so would require an even *greater* level of complexity. At present we can deal with day-to-day maintenance issues, but all we can ever know for sure is that we function. We tick, therefore we are."

Pickwick asked me how I thought we could afford such an extravagance, but the real disapproval came from Mrs. Malaprop.

"Good afternoon, Mr. Sprockett," she said coldly. "I hope you are fully aquatinted with the *specific* roles of mousecreeper and butler?"

"Indeed, Mrs. Malaprop," replied Sprockett, bowing low. "And I don't require much space—I can easily fit in the cupboard under the stairs."

"You will knot," replied Mrs. Malaprop with great indignation. "*I* am resizing there. You may have the earring cupboard."

"Then with your permission I shall go and repack," announced Sprockett.

"You mean you're leaving?" I asked.

"Repack my knee bearings," he explained. "With grease.

Knees, despite much design work, continue to be the Duplex-5's Achilles' heel."

And leaving us all to muse upon his odd choice of words, he departed.

"At least *try* to be nice to him," I said to Mrs. Malaprop when he had gone. "And I want you to order some oils of varying grades to make him feel welcome—and make sure all the clocks are kept wound. Cog-based life-forms take great offense at stopped clocks."

"As madam washes," replied Mrs. Malaprop, which was her way of telling me to get stuffed.

"If you don't need us, we're going to go and rehearse Acheron's death scene on the roof of Thornfield Hall," said Carmine.

"You'll need to unlock Bertha," I replied, handing her the key. "And don't forget to put the bite mask on her."

I watched them go with an odd feeling that I couldn't describe. Despite my being the protagonist, most of the characters were already here when I took over, and few of them were happy with my interpretation of Thursday, even though it was the one that Thursday herself had approved. They had all preferred the sex-and-violence Thursday who'd turned a blind eye to the many scams they had had cooking. Because of this, I hadn't really gotten on with any of them. In fact, the out-of-book relationship with the rest of the cast could best be described as barely cordial. Carmine seemed to get on with them a lot better. I shouldn't have minded, but I did.

"She's going to be trouble, that one," said Pickwick, who was doing the crossword while perched on the dresser.

"All she has to be is a good Thursday," I murmured. "Everything else is immaterial. Mrs. Malaprop?"

"Yes, madam?"

"Did you put anything in my pocket this morning? For a joke, perhaps?"

"*Joke*, madam?" she inquired in a shocked tone. "Malaprops always keep well clear of potentially hummus situations."

"I didn't think so. I'll be in my study. Will you have Sprockett bring in some tea?"

"Very good, madam."

"Pickwick? I need the paper."

"You'll have to wait," she said without looking up. "I'm doing the crossword."

I didn't have time for this, so I simply took the paper, ripped off the crossword section and handed it back to her. I ignored her expression of outrage and walked into my study and shut the door.

I moved quietly to the French windows and stepped out into the garden to release the Lost Positives that the Lady of Shalott had given me. She had a soft spot for the orphaned prefixless words and thought they had more chance to thrive in Fiction than in Poetry. I let the defatigable scamps out of their box. They were kempt and sheveled but their behavior was peccable if not mildly gruntled. They started acting petuously and ran around in circles in a very toward manner.

I then returned to my study and spent twenty minutes staring at Thursday's shield. The only way it could have gotten into my pocket was via the red-haired gentleman sitting next to me on the tram. And if that was the case, he had been in contact with Thursday quite recently—or at least sometime in the past week. It didn't prove she was missing in the BookWorld any more than it proved she was missing in the RealWorld. I had only a telephone note, a husband's tears and the word of a murderer.

"Your tea and shortbread, ma'am," said Sprockett, placing the tray upon my desk. "A very comfortable house you have. I must confess that in a weak moment, and quite against your advice, I lent that odd-looking bird twenty pounds for her kidney operation."

"I warned you about Pickwick," I said with a sigh. "She doesn't need a kidney operation, and her mother isn't in 'dire straits,' no matter what she says."

"Ah," replied Sprockett. "Do you think I might be able to get my money back?"

"Not without a lot of squawking. Is Mrs. Malaprop causing you any trouble, by the way?"

"No, ma'am. We agreed to arm-wrestle for seniority in the house, and even though she attempted to cheat, I believe that we are all square now."

"I was given this by someone on a tram," I said, passing the real Thursday's shield across to Sprockett.

His eyebrow pointed to "Puzzled," then "Thinking," then "Worried."

"That would explain the ease by which I escaped the stoning in Conspiracy."

"And later, getting out of Poetry."

"I don't recall that."

"You were dreaming about gramophones. Can you call the Jurisfiction front desk and ask for Thursday Next? Tell them it's me and I need to speak to her."

Sprockett stood in the corner to make the calls. A request like this would be better coming from my butler.

"They tell me that she is 'on assignment' at present," replied Sprockett after talking quietly to himself for a few seconds.

"Tell them it's the written Thursday and I'll call again."

I wondered quite how she could be on assignment without her shield and idly turned over the newspaper. I stopped. The banner headline read, FAMED JURISFICTION AGENT TO LEAD PEACE TALKS. Thursday was due to table the talks on Friday, less than a week away. All of a sudden, her "absent" status took on a more menacing angle. If she was missing now, things could get very bad indeed.

For the past three years, Racy Novel and its leader, Speedy

Muffler, had been causing trouble far in excess of his size, readership or importance. Sandwiched precariously between Women's Fiction and Outdated Religious Dogma, with Erotica to the far north and Comedy to the south, the large yet proudly anarchic genre had been troublesome ever since it was declared a member of the Axis of Unreadable along with Misery Memoirs and Celebrity Bio. Muffler, stung by the comparison to voyeuristic drivel or the meaningless nonadventures of celebrities, decided to expand his relevance within Fiction by attempting to push out his borders. The CofG responded to his aggression by transferring *Lady Chatterley's Lover* out of Racy Novel and into Human Drama, then moving *The History of Tom Jones* to Erotica. Sanctions soon followed that prevented anyone from supplying Racy Novel with good dialogue, plot or characterization. This did nothing to appease Speedy Muffler, and he claimed that the sanctions were preventing him from developing as a genre—quite against BookWorld law and the Character's Charter. The trouble was, Muffler and Racy Novel couldn't be ignored, since they were amongst the major exporters of metaphor. When Muffler claimed to possess a dirty bomb capable of hurling scenes of a gratuitously sexual nature far into Women's Fiction, the BookWorld finally took notice and the peace talks were set. Thursday Next would be the chief negotiator, and she had good form. When Scandinavian Detectives threatened to cede from Crime, it was she who brought them back.

"You seem perturbed," remarked Sprockett. "Is anything the matter?"

"I have reason to believe that the real Thursday Next might be missing," I replied guardedly. "And that's not good for all sorts of reasons."

"Has she gone missing before?" asked Sprockett.

"Many times."

"Then it's probably one of those . . . again."

I hoped he was right, but even if he wasn't, I wasn't quite sure what could be done about it. I was an underread A-8 character with no power and less influence. Besides, Jurisfiction was doubtless onto it. Commander Bradshaw, the head of Jurisfiction, was one of Thursday's closest friends.

There was a knock on the door, and Mrs. Malaprop came in.

"Miss Next? There awesome gentlemen to see you."

"Who are they?"

"They didn't give their gnomes."

The visitors didn't wait either, and strode in. They weren't the sort of people I wanted to see, but their presence might well reinforce my theories about Thursday. They were the Men in Plaid.

Several things seemed to happen at once. Sprockett's eyebrow quivered at Mrs. Malaprop, who got his meaning and knocked over an ornamental vase, which fell to the floor with a crash. The Men in Plaid turned to see what was going on, and at that very moment Sprockett grabbed Thursday's shield from the desk and threw it hard into the ceiling, where it stuck in the plasterboard. By the time the Men in Plaid looked back towards us, Sprockett was tidying my papers on the desk.

"Good afternoon, gentlemen," I said in a friendly tone. "What can I do for you?"

Like trousers, pear pips, twins and bookends, MiP always came in pairs. They were without emotion and designed to ensure that no personal ambiguity would muddy their operating parameters. MiP were designed to do what they were told to do, and nothing else.

"So," said the Man in Plaid, "you are Thursday Next A8-V-67987-FP?"

"Yes."

"Date of composure?"

"Third June, 2006. What is this about?"

"Routine, Miss Next," said the second MiP. "We are looking

for some property stolen from a leading Jurisfiction agent, and we thought you might be able to help us. I won't mince my words. We think you have it."

I resisted the temptation to look up. The shield was in plain sight, embedded in the ceiling. "Do you want me to try to guess what you're after, or are you going to tell me?"

The MiP exchanged glances.

"It has come to our attention," said the taller of the two, "that someone's been waving the real Thursday Next's Jurisfiction shield around. That person used it to get out of Poetry an hour ago. Were you in Poetry today, Miss Next?"

I wasn't supposed to be there, so the answer had to be no. "No."

They stared at me. "The officers involved told us that someone of your description had a robotic butler in the trunk of a taxi. Do you still deny this?"

I looked at Sprockett, who stared impassively ahead.

"There are probably *hundreds* of robotic manservants in Fiction," I replied, "and all of them are technically luggage. But since automata are incapable of misstatements, why don't you ask him yourself?"

They did, and Sprockett could answer without lying that he had absolutely no knowledge of the trip at all.

"Perhaps it was Thursday herself," I suggested. "Have you asked her?"

There was, perhaps, a subtle change in the Plaids' demeanor. But if she *was* missing, as I supposed, they weren't going to let on.

"How about Conspiracy?" asked the smaller Plaid. "We have a report from Elvis561 that someone looking a lot like Thursday and holding her Jurisfiction shield rescued a mechanical man from stoning."

"That was definitely me," I said. "I was on JAID business."

They both stared at me. It was highly uncomfortable.

"Then you *did* have her shield?"

"I used *my* JAID shield. Here."

I passed it across, and they stared at it. It was nothing like a Jurisfiction shield.

"The Elvis must have been mistaken," I continued. "There is a certain degree of inbuilt hyperbole to the genre that might generate outrageous claims, wouldn't you agree?"

I stared at them intently as I tried to read their expressions, but their emotionless construction made them impossible to penetrate. They probably didn't do well at singles bars but would doubtless be able to play poker at tournament level.

"Very well," said the first Man in Plaid. "We will leave you for now. One more thing: A call to Thursday Next at Jurisfiction was traced to this book not ten minutes ago. Was there a reason for this?"

"I have a new understudy," I explained. "I thought Thursday might like to give her a few tips on how to play her. If you see her, will you pass my message along?"

"We're not messengers," said the second Plaid, and they left without another word.

There followed a moment of silence. I had just lied to the Men in Plaid, which was illegal, and even if they thought I was telling the truth, my being on their radar was probably not conducive to good health. But one thing that did cross my mind was this: If Thursday was missing, the Men in Plaid had been ordered to find her, and they didn't yet know of the connection between me and the red-haired gentleman.

But I didn't have any time to muse on it further, as I heard the Read Alarm go off. Somewhere in the Outland, a reader had picked up one of my books. Luckily for us, things can happen instantaneously in the BookWorld, so I dashed through to the kitchen to find Carmine already dressed and ready to go. I half thought of taking over, but I had to let her give it a whirl sooner or later.

"It's barely teatime in the Outland," I said, glancing at the clock. "Someone must be taking a break. Are you ready?"

Carmine nodded.

I turned to Mrs. Malaprop, who was monitoring the progress of all the readings on a circular screen that plotted in word-for-word detail which readers were where, and in what book.

"It's a slope oak," she said. "*Lost in a Good Book*, page 133, SpecOps Twilight Homes. I'll contract Granny Next."

She flipped a switch on the intercom, and her voice echoed around the series on the intercom.

"*Hear this, hear this. Would Granny Next please pro-seed Toe-wads TN2, P133.*"

"An easy scene," I said, turning to Carmine. "How's your Ping-Pong?"

"Not bad."

"It doesn't matter. Granny Next will crush you anyway."

"What is a 'slope oak'?"

"She means 'a slow poke.' It's what we call readers who've been working their way through the series at a snail's pace. When they falter—which they often do—you should try to alter your dialogue for simplicity. You'll feel their ReadRate increase when you do, and we aim only to help. The reader is everything, yes?"

She looked up at me and bit her lip nervously.

"The reader is everything," she repeated. "But you'll step in if there are more then twenty concurrent reads, won't you?"

Being read simultaneously was often described as like trying to visit everywhere in Paris at the same time during rush hour. The simile was lost on me, but I made a point of never wanting to visit Paris, real or imaginary.

"Don't worry," I told her, "you'll be fine. We've got at least four hours before the other readers come onstream. Take a deep breath and repeat the first person's credo: 'Pace, Atmosphere, Plot, Prose, Character.'"

"Pace, Atmosphere, Plot, Prose, Character."

"Good. Give them hell."

And she gave me a wan smile and headed off towards the SpecOps Twilight Homes, which were cemented just between Thornfield Hall and the interior Skyrail set. With an odd feeling, I watched her go. I liked the time off, but I liked being Thursday, too—even if it was to an audience of only one.

"Here," I said, passing the Snooze access codes to Mrs. Malaprop. "Keep a close eye on her."

"This is a last resort, yes?" asked Mrs. Malaprop, who licked kittens probably more than most.

"Last resort. Call me and I'll come running."

I walked out of the kitchen. There was work to be done.

10.

Epizeuxis

Maps of the BookWorld are constantly updated as the genres snake back and forth in response to Outland trends and fads. The borders move so rapidly, in fact, that any notion of a fully updated map is considered laughable, and most maps are these days published with *average* borders that reflect recent reading trends.

Bradshaw's BookWorld Companion (3rd edition)

*D*espite the unwanted attentions of the Men in Plaid, the warnings from the red-haired gentleman and the worrying possibility that Thursday might be missing, I spent a busy and anxious afternoon going through the heap of book junk in the garage. I was, to be honest, torn. Part of me wanted nothing better than to accede to Red Herring's wishes that this be an "unrepeatable" accident, and part of me was suspicious. The closer I examined the book junk, the worse it looked. It appeared that something, while not *exactly* rotten in the state of the BookWorld, was far from fresh.

At a little after five, and with a rising sense of foreboding, I called Sprockett into my study to compare notes.

"So what do you have?" I asked, letting him air his discoveries first.

He led me across to where the *Atlas of the BookWorld* lay open on my desk. He indicated the page that depicted the southeastern part of the island and showed me where he had plotted the crashed book's debris trail by a series of black crosses. Most sections of text would have pulverized into graphemes and simply absorbed, which explains why we rarely find anything when short stories or limericks come to grief, just a hollow concussion in the distance.

Almost all the debris had been strewn across the Aviation genre, with the notable exception of the bed-sitting room already discovered inside Conspiracy and a Triumph motorcycle within Thriller (Spy) that narrowly missed George Smiley as it traveled through an early draft of *Tinker, Tailor, Soldier, Hatmaker.* The book seemed to have disintegrated somewhere above Deighton and then strewn objects in a roughly straight line north, in the direction of the Great Library and the Ungenred Zone.

"What would tigers and a macaroon be doing in an Aviation novel?" asked Mrs. Malaprop, who was cleaning with a feather duster but actually wanted to be part of the investigation.

"They might be scrambled graphemes and not actually in the book at all. Best ignored."

"There doesn't seem to be any curve to the debris trail at all," added Pickwick, who had entered unseen and jumped onto the table to look more closely. I wouldn't have minded so much if she hadn't upset the inkwell and then stood clumsily in the ink.

"You're right," I said. "Mind your feet. And that means either a rapid breakup or that the book—whatever it was—was not from the Aviation genre."

"Look here," said Pickwick as she pointed with one of her claws. "If we extend the debris-field line backwards, we come out of Aviation, across Military, and end up right here in Adventure—somewhere around *King Solomon's Mines.*"

"Which might explain the tigers."

"But not the macaroon."

"Or the box-girder bridges—and the Triumph Bonneville motorcycle."

"I didn't say it *was* Haggard," said Pickwick, "only that it came from Adventure."

Unusually, Pickwick was being helpful. Probably because she'd taken Sprockett for some cash, had already had her nap but was not yet ready for her afternoon snack and was thus in an atypically good temper.

"I have an idea," said Sprockett. "Could we try unscrambling the letters of the items we found, and thereby find tantalizing clues as to what the book might be about?"

"To an outside observer, that would seem entirely logical," I replied, "but for one thing: Anagram-related clues were outlawed six years ago by the NCU."

"NCU?"

"Narrative Clunker Unit. Villains haven't been allowed to be albinos for years, identical twins as plot devices are banned, and double negatives are a complete no-no. Forget anagrams."

"Isn't there a black box data reorder in every book?" asked Mrs. Malaprop. "We could analyze the tea lemon tree."

"Usually," I replied, "but engineering contracts have to be spread around the BookWorld, and the construction of Book Data Recorders was subcontracted to James McGuffin and Co. of the Suspense genre, so they have a tendency to go missing until dramatically being found right at the end of an investigation. It's undoubtedly suspenseful, but a little useless. Want to see what I found?"

We walked out through the French windows and the garden to my double garage, which was another example of the inverted physics of the BookWorld. The more you filled it, the emptier it appeared. But it could never be *entirely* empty, as that would require an infinite amount of stuff—or in the case of a double garage, *twice* an infinite amount of stuff.

All the sections of crashed book were laid out on the concrete floor, ostensibly so we could try to find a reason for the accident, or even to figure out a rough plot of the mystery book.

We had a few page numbers, but nothing attached to any dialogue. It was a mess. I walked past the yellow-painted back axle, pushed aside a fridge/freezer and beckoned them to one particular piece of wreckage.

"What do you make of this?" I asked.

We were standing over the bent Triumph motorcycle, and I told them to be quiet. There was a whisper in the air, and if you leaned close to the damaged motorcycle, you could hear it:

> The works that built the cycle worked;
> The cycle's labor labored on.
> And workers sought and workers bought
> The managers out and managed 'owt
> Until the cycle's cycle cycled round.
> But markets moved and markets shifted,
> To Eastern trade that Eastern made.
> Loans were pleaded, loans were needed,
> The workers' workers worked their last.
> But ruin didn't do as ruin does,
> For Triumph's collapse led to Triumph's triumph.

"I don't get it," said Pickwick, who had always favored Harley-Davidson.

"It's a poem that charts the fall and rise of the Triumph motorcycle company in the late seventies and early eighties," I said. "It's seeped out of the descriptive flux of the motorcycle—a glowing afterember of the accident."

"That's not unusual," replied Pickwick. "Poetry and prose are different facets of the same basic element. When prose breaks down, it often spontaneously rhymes. Poetry is prose in another form, and prose is simply poetry waiting to happen."

"*Epizeuxis,*" murmured Sprockett, "a rhetorical device that repeats the same word in the same sentence for increased dramatic effect. This book was almost certainly destroyed by a rhetorical worm."

I had come to the same conclusion myself. The worm would attempt to restructure sentences, and when that failed, it would take words from other sentences, leaving dangerous holes in the narrative. Once there were no more complete words to be taken, the worm would start to harvest letters to make up the shortfall, weakening the structure until the entire book disintegrated. In RealWorld terms it would be like instantaneously removing every rivet from an aircraft that was in flight.

"The problem," I said slowly, "is that rhetorical worms don't occur naturally. They're used in the demolition business to tear apart sections of scrapped books. It's cheaper and safer than chains, hooks and crowbars. A well-placed worm can burrow into prose, dissolve away tired exposition and leave description and dialogue untouched. Either the book was carrying unlicensed worms that were accidentally activated or it was—"

"*Sabotage!*" hissed Mrs. Malaprop, and I felt myself suddenly go quite cold. Such a device would require a level of sophistication utterly outside the realm of ordinary citizens. There were stories of the Council of Genres' Men in Plaid using rhetorical devices to cause injury or death, but that was mostly conjecture—drummed up by Conspiracy, no doubt.

"Okay," I said, "we have the *possibility* of skulduggery—but it's not the only explanation. Epizeuxis is often used as a rhetorical device."

"But so blatantly? And in a poem to describe the failure of a motorcycle-manufacturing cooperative?" exclaimed Pickwick. "What kind of nut would try something like that?"

"We still need to find out what the book was called," I said as we walked back into the house. "We need an ISBN. Did we check the thumb we found for fingerprints?"

"Not a single one."

"That's annoying. Those severed hands we found a few weeks ago had fingerprints all over them."

"What about DNA evidence?" asked Sprockett.

"DNA fingerprinting is still under a blanket ban," I explained. "Forensic Procedural is allowed to use it, but you know how tight the Crime genre can be."

Sadly, this was true. The Guild of Detectives had argued that although DNA fingerprinting had a use in the RealWorld, such annoyingly precise and utterly noncerebral detection methods really had no place in Fiction. And because the Crime lobby represented such a huge part of Fiction, the Council of Genres had reluctantly agreed. Mind you, detection rates hadn't suffered as a result, so everyone was happy.

I looked up at the Read-O-Meter. There were twelve simultaneous readings going on, and Carmine hadn't hit the panic button, so she was doing fine. I had a look at the clock and then went upstairs to have a bath and change. Despite all that was going on, what with sabotaged books, worms and missing Jurisfiction agents, I still had a date with Whitby Jett. I tried a call to Jurisfiction myself and was told that Thursday Next was still unavailable. I dried, then tried on several dresses but didn't like any of them. I had just dismissed the sixth and was rummaging in the bureau for a yellow top I remembered buying last time I was in Chick Lit, when I came across a photograph. It was one I had wanted to throw away but had pushed to the back of a drawer instead. It was a backstory snap of me and Landen, taken when we were in the Crimea, before Landen had lost a leg and I'd lost a brother. Happy days. I stared at it for a long time, then rang for Sprockett.

"Ma'am?"

"Is Whitby downstairs?"

"Yes, ma'am. He's waiting in the kitchen with a bunch of flowers the size of the Amazonian Basin."

"Would you send him my apologies and ask him to leave? Politely, of course."

"Ma'am?"

"I need to keep an eye on Carmine. It's her first day, and I need to stand by in case of mishaps."

"Miss Carmine is doing very well, by all accounts, ma'am, and Mr. Jett seems happily effusive over the prospect of an evening with you. I believe that his conduct has all the hallmarks of . . . love, ma'am."

"Sprockett," I said, "just do this for me, would you? Tell him I'm busy and I'll meet him for lunch tomorrow."

"Very good, ma'am. Where shall I say you will be meeting him?"

"I'll call him."

I came downstairs twenty minutes later to find the flowers on the hall table. I sighed at my own foolishness, then walked into the book and found Carmine about to play the croquet match in *The Well of Lost Plots*. I told her my date was canceled and that I'd take over from her. I think she was secretly relieved.

"Don't forget there's a party tonight at *Castle of Skeddan Jiarg*," I told her. "The queen said to drop in anytime."

"I think I might just do that," she said with a smile. "I could get hyphenated, let my hair down and chat up a goblin or something."

I didn't like the sound of this.

"I don't mean to seem judgmental. Actually, come to think of it," I said, changing my mind, "I *do* mean to seem judgmental. You mustn't bring goblins home. Quite apart from the hygiene and theft issues, Pickwick can be a real prude. She'll be plocking on about it for months, and frankly, I could do without her endless complaints."

She winked.

"I will be *most* discreet. Why don't you join me when you're done? I know goblins aren't everyone's cup of tea, but what they lack in physical beauty they make up for in endurance."

I told her I didn't really feel like going to a party or dancing all night, and she gave me a hug before skipping off.

Reading-wise, it wasn't such a bad evening. The Ph.D. student gave up pretty soon to watch *Deal or No Deal*, a popular woodworking program in the Outland, and the new readers were for the most part forgiving, with only a few of them requiring extra attention to get them over some of the more wayward plot points. As for the rereads, they pretty much looked after themselves and added a useful amount of feedback, too—the curtains had never looked brighter, and Pickwick positively shone.

11.

Plot Thickens

Minor narrative changes were often ignored, but major variations were stomped on without mercy. Perpetrators would be rounded up and banished to a copy of *Bunty* or *Sparky* until suitably contrite. Repeat offenders were suspended, and after three strikes were erased—usually without warning. Some thought it worth the risk. After all, being unread was arguably no different from erasure. Some put it this way: Better dead than unread.

Bradshaw's BookWorld Companion (7th edition)

I was up and about while everyone else in the book was still sleepily inactive. There had been no readings at all since 2:00 A.M., and I wanted to be in costume and ready on the off chance that anyone read a few pages before breakfast. It paid to keep at a state of readiness, just in case. There had been trouble inside *Captain Corelli's Mandolin* when a sudden reinterest in the book caught everyone napping—the first hundred pages or so have yet to fully recover.

I walked about the settings of the series, checking to make sure everything was ready to go. My tour wasn't just a technical housekeeping exercise either—it was about a sense of pride. Despite the lack of readers and a certain "dissatisfaction" from particular members of the cast who suggested that I might improve the readability by spicing up the prose with a bit more sex and violence, I still wanted to keep the books going as well as I could—and to win Thursday's approval, which was more important than the author's.

Once I had made sure that everything was to my satisfaction, I called Whitby to apologize for standing him up. He took it better than I had expected, but I could sense he was annoyed. I told him I would *definitely* be free for lunch, suggested the expensive and needlessly spacious Elbow Rooms, then pretended that Pickwick had broken something, so I could end the conversation.

I drew a deep breath, cursed myself for being so stupid, took a pager with me and walked down the road to Stubbs, the outrageously expensive coffee shop on the corner.

"Could I not have a coffee?" I said, meaning I wanted an empty cup. Stubbs had become so expensive that no one could afford the coffee, but since the ambience in the café was so good and the establishment so fashionable, it was always full.

"What would you not like?" asked Paul, who wore a black gown and a wig due to a syntactical head cold that made him unable to differentiate himself between a barista and a barrister.

"Better not give me a latte," I replied, "and better not make it a large one."

"How did the date with Whitby go?"

"So-so."

Paul raised an eyebrow, made no comment and handed me an empty cup. I went to a booth at the back of the store and sat down. I came here most mornings and usually read the paper over my noncoffee. I scanned the headlines of *The Word*, but if Thursday was missing, they didn't know about it. Oversize Books had gained a victory at the council. Constantly irked by snide comments about taking more than their allotted shelf space, they had sought to have their own genre and succeeded. A representative for Oversize Books had praised "common sense" and said that they looked forward to "moving to their own island as soon as one big enough was made available."

There was more about Racy Novel, with Speedy Muffler claiming that troop movements near his borders were "an act of aggression." In rebuttal, Senator Jobsworth of the Council of Genres reiterated that there would be no troop movements ahead of the peace talks on Friday.

"If Thursday is missing," I said to myself, "there won't be any peace talks."

"Mumbling to yourself?"

I looked up. It was Acheron Hades, the designated evildoer and antagonist from *The Eyre Affair*. Inside the book he was a homicidal maniac who would surgically remove people's faces for fun, but outside the book he collected stamps and wrote really bad poetry.

"Peace talks," I said, showing him the paper.

"I'm not going to hold my breath," he remarked. "Speedy Muffler is the master of brinksmanship. Any deal on the table will be unraveled the following morning—military intervention is the only thing that will stop him."

Acheron's attitude was not atypical. There were few who didn't think an all-out genre war between Women's Fiction and Racy Novel was pretty much inevitable. The more absorbing question was, Will it be broadcast live? And then, Will it involve me or damage my own genre?

"Dogma will almost certainly be dragged into the fray," I said gloomily.

"And Comedy to the south," added Acheron, "and they won't like it. I don't think they were joking when they said they would defend their land to the last giggle."

The door opened, and the king and queen walked in. They looked a little worse for wear. I nodded a greeting, and they ordered a cappuccino each, which placed Paul in something of a panic—I don't think he'd ever made one before.

"By the way," said Acheron, "I think Carmy is the best under-study yet."

"Carmy?"

"Carmine. *Great* interpretation. Are you going to keep her?"

"I've . . . not decided yet."

"Just so you know, I approve," he said. "She can vanquish me any day of the week." He stared into his empty cup for a moment. "Can I talk to you about something?"

"Is it about your poetry?"

"It's about Bertha Rochester."

"Biting again?"

Acheron showed me his hand, which had nasty tooth marks on it.

"Painful," I agreed. "I told you to keep the bite mask on until the last moment. But you do throw her to her death. She's allowed to struggle a *bit*."

"That's another thing," he said as he pulled a pained expression. "Does she have to look at me in that accusatory way when I chuck her off the roof? It makes me feel all funny inside."

Unlike Acheron, who differed wildly from his in-book persona, Bertha really *was* bonkers. She had come to us after a grueling forty-six-year stint as Anne Catherick in *The Woman in White* and was now quite beyond any form of rehabilitation. In a cruel and ironic twist, Grace Poole kept our version of Bertha Rochester locked securely up in the attic. It was safer for everyone that way.

"I'll have a word," I said, then asked after a pause, "So . . . why do you think Carmine is so good?"

"Her interpretation is respectful, but with an edginess that is both sympathetic and noir."

"And you think that's better than my interpretation?"

"Not better," replied Acheron diplomatically, "different. And there's nothing wrong with *that*," he added cautiously, finding a piece of invisible fluff on his jacket. "Carmine just plays her in a way that is . . . well, how shall I put it?"

"More readable?"

"She's an A-4—you're an A-8. You'd *expect* her to exhibit a bit more depth."

"Thanks for that."

"Don't sweat it. Carmine can't handle quantity, and when and if she can, she'll be off to the bright lights of HumDram/Highbrow. Your job is assured. Besides," he added in a lighter tone, "if it *did* come to a vote, I'd go with you."

"I'm grateful for that at the very least," I replied despondently. "So you prefer the real Thursday Next to a more marketable one?"

"Well, yes—and the free time. Poetry is a *most* absorbing pastime."

It wasn't what I really wanted to hear, and after chatting for a few more minutes he left. I finished the paper and wandered back to the book. I had a brief chat with the series prop master on the way. He was the technician responsible for all the interactive objects in the series—items that could be handled or manipulated in some way.

"We've managed to repair your car," he said, "but go easy on it during the car chase. If you could just pull up sharply rather than slewing sideways, I'd really appreciate it."

We were working to a budget these days. The remaking of the BookWorld had sneakily reorganized its budgetary systems. Instead of the "single-book payment," we now earned a "reader stipend" for every reading, with a labyrinthine system of bonuses and extra payments for targets. It wasn't universally liked. Any book that fell below the hundred-readers-a-week level could find itself hit by a double whammy: not enough funds to maintain the fabric of the novel, yet not enough Feedback Loop to hope the readers would do it for you.

I got back to the house at midmorning to find Pickwick already laying the table for lunch. She often picked up fads and trends from the BookWorld and just recently had caught the "reality bug" and insisted we sit for every meal, even though there was nothing to eat and we didn't need to. She also insisted that we play parlor games together in the evenings. This would have been fine if she didn't have to win at everything, and watching a dodo cheat badly at KerPlunk was not a happy spectacle.

I found Carmine in the kitchen looking a little green about the gills and with an ice pack on her head.

"Problems?" I asked.

"N-n-n-none at all," groaned Carmine. "I j-j-just think I hit the hyphens a little t-t-t-too hard last n-n-night."

She groaned, closed her eyes and pressed the ice pack more firmly to her head.

"If you're hyphenated while working you'll be in serious trouble," I said in my most scolding voice. "And as your mentor, so will I."

"Yeah, yeah," murmured Carmine, eyes firmly closed. "I'll be fine. B-b-but can you p-p-p-please get the b-b-birdbrain over there to shut up?"

"I'm sorry," said Pickwick haughtily, "but was the drunken tart addressing me?"

"Why, is there *another* b-b-birdbrain present?"

"Okay, okay," I said, "calm down, you two. What's the problem?"

"That b-birdbrain insists on staring at m-me and sighing."

"Is this true?"

Pickwick ruffled her feathers indignantly. "She brought a goblin home, and they're nothing but trouble. What's more, I think she is *entirely* unsuitable for carrying on the important job of being Thursday. We all like a hyphen from time to time, but consorting with pointy-eared homunculi is *totally out of order!*"

She squawked the last bit, and Carmine rolled her eyes.

"I didn't b-bring a g-goblin home."

"He followed you home. It amounts to the same thing."

"You're j-just sour because you're not g-g-getting any," sneered Carmine. "And anyway, Horace is n-n-not like other g-g-goblins."

"Hang on," I said. "So you *did* bring a goblin home?"

"He g-g-got locked out of his b-b-book. What was I supposed to d-d-do?"

I threw up my arms. "Carmine!"

"D-don't you be so j-judgmental," she replied indignantly. "Look at yourself. F-f-five books in one s-series, and each by a different g-g-ghostwriter."

"Your private life is your own," I replied angrily, "but goblins can't help themselves—or rather they *can* help themselves—to anything not nailed down."

I ran upstairs to find that my bedroom had been ransacked. Anything of even the slightest value had been stolen. Inviting a goblin to cross your threshold was a recipe for disaster, and certainly worse than doing the same with a vampire. With the latter all you got was a nasty bite, but the company, the extraordinarily good sex and the funny stories more than made up for it—apparently.

"That was dumb," I said when I'd returned. "He's taken almost everything."

Carmine looked at me, then at Pickwick, then burst into tears and ran from the room.

"Goblins!" said Pickwick with a snort. "They're just trouble with a capital G. By the way," she added, now cheerier since she'd been proved correct, "Sprockett wanted to show you something. He's in your office."

I walked through to my study, where Sprockett was indeed waiting for me. He wasn't alone. He had his foot on top of a struggling goblin, and a burlap sack full of stolen possessions was lying on the carpet.

"Your property, ma'am?" he asked. I nodded, and he took

the letter opener from the desk, held the goblin tightly by one ear and placed the opener to its throat. His eyebrow twitched. It was clearly a bluff. I decided to play along.

"No," I said, "you'll ruin the carpet. Do it outside."

The goblin opened his eyes wide and stared at me in shocked amazement, then started to babble on about an "influential uncle" who would "do unpleasant things" if he "went missing."

"Just kidding," I added. "Let him go."

"Are you sure?" asked Sprockett. "I can make it look like a shaving accident."

"Yes, I'm sure. You," I said, jabbing a finger at the goblin, "are a disgrace. Place a single toe in my series again and I'll make you wish you'd never been written."

Sprockett took his foot off the goblin, and it ran to the window, paused on the sill for a moment, made an obscene gesture and then ran off. That was the trouble with being stuck in Fantasy—too many goblins, spells, ogres, wizards, elves and warlocks. I reckoned it frightened readers off.

"So," I said, locking the window after the goblin, "what's the deal?"

"I was reappraising the condition of the wreckage from the debris field."

He showed me the Triumph Bonneville's exhaust pipe. It had been folded almost in half by the impact. He pointed to a small patch on the chrome. There was a slight mottling about four inches long and an inch wide.

"A fault in the manufacturing?" I suggested.

"But it wasn't manufactured," said Sprockett. "It was *written*. It should be perfect—better than any real motorcycle."

"You asked me in here to show me an imperfection on a Bonneville exhaust?"

"There's more. I found this orange inside the bed-sit. Here."

He tossed the orange across, and I noticed that this *also* had a slight mottling on the side. He then showed me similar imperfections on a Polaroid camera, a toaster, a half-eaten sand-wich and a plastic bath duck. Then I got it.

"The mottling," I said slowly. "They are—*were*—ISBNs. Are you trying to tell me someone has *removed* all identification marks from this book?"

He didn't answer, which was answer enough. All doubts were off. *This wasn't an accident.* Someone had hacked into the novel's source code to delete the ISBN in order to cover his tracks and ensure that no one found out which book had been destroyed or why. The epizeuxis worm and now this. We didn't have a crashed book, we had a crime scene. But it wasn't *quite* that simple.

"Only Text Grand Central or the Council of Genres would have the power to scrub ISBNs and put together a rhetorical device," I said. "And while I'm not one to use coarse idioms, someone would have to be connected up the wazoo to pull this off. Have you attempted to find out what the ISBN actually was?"

Sprockett placed a series of photographs on the desk. "I took the liberty of subjecting the marks to a complex series of photo-graphic techniques, which while appearing to have the veneer of scientific reality actually just sounded good. Do you want the full two pages of dull exposition or just the results?"

"Better just give me the results," I said, looking at my watch. "Whitby will be here any moment for a lunch date."

"Might I inquire where you are going, ma'am?"

"We thought we'd try the Elbow Rooms."

"A fine establishment. I meet up with the Hartzel chess player every two weeks there to discuss Matters of the Cog. I'd avoid the lobster."

"Food poisoning?"

"No, no, not on the menu—at the bar. *Very* opinionated and apt to lapse into unspeakably dull arthropod-related digres-sions. But see here."

He handed me a photograph that was many images superimposed on top of one another. The revealed ISBN was indistinct but legible. I jotted down the number in my notebook.

"Thank you, Sprockett. You're a star."

"Madam is most kind."

I fetched the unimaginatively titled *Cheshire Cat's Complete Guide to All Books Ever Written Everywhere* and looked up the ISBN. Our crashed book was from Self-Publishing and titled *The Murders on the Hareng Rouge*, by Adrian Dorset. I'd never heard of him. But it was Vanity, so I'd hardly be expected to. There was no other information. The ISBN database held only titles, authors, publishers' details, three-for-two offers, that kind of thing. I looked at the map we had pinned on the wall that charted the book's final journey. If you extended the line back through Adventure and past the Cliff of Notes, it made landfall in Vanity. We'd never considered such a thing. It must have lifted off there and proceeded in an almost straight line to where the Council of Genres was located, but it had come down over Conspiracy.

I sat, leaned back in my chair and ran through the likely scenarios. It was possible *The Murders on the Hareng Rouge* was a potential world beater on its way to being published. Jealousies ran deep in the BookWorld, and the possibility of someone in HumDram/Highbrow nobbling the potential competition was quite real. It had happened before; bad Vanity was universally disliked but tolerated in a condescending "yes, well done, jolly good" kind of way, but good Vanity was reviled as the worst kind of upstart.

"Blast," I said, as a more personal note added itself to the mix. "It explains why I was asked to handle the investigation. No one expected me to find anything."

Sprockett's eyebrow pointed to "Bingo."

"The thought had occurred to me, ma'am. In fact, the precise reason you were selected for this investigation, given your lack of adequacy, has been troubling me for some time."

I thought about Acheron's comments with regard to the fact that Carmine was an A-4.

"I so need that sort of comment right now."

His eyebrow clicked from "Bingo" to "Apologetic."

"Merely the facts as I see them, ma'am."

I thought carefully. Part of me—the Thursday part—was outraged over the crime, but the rest of me was more realistic. There were some things that were simply not worth meddling with, and anyone willing to engineer the destruction of an entire book wouldn't think twice about eliminating me. There were few—if any—characters who couldn't be replaced.

"Have you told anyone about this?" I asked, and Sprockett shook his head.

"Keep it that way," I murmured. "I think all we've found is what Red Herring wanted me to find: an unprecedented event that is unrepeatable."

"If asked for an opinion, ma'am," said Sprockett in an unusually forceful turn of phrase, "I should like to find out who asked Commander Herring to allocate you to this investigation."

I stared at him. I should like to know, too, but I couldn't think of a way to frame the question that wouldn't have me in the trunk of a car heading towards the traditional place to dump bodies, the New Jersey area of Crime.

"This was never meant to be reported," I said. "This was meant for looking the other way and carrying on with life as though nothing had happened. There was a good reason I was asked to do this, and I will not impugn my lack of competence by being irresponsibly accurate. I have a reputation to uphold."

It was a hopelessly poor argument, and he and I both knew it. I sat down at my desk and drew a sheet of writing paper from my stationery drawer.

"Permission to speak openly?" he asked.

I took a deep breath. "I don't want to hear what you have to say, but I should."

"It's not what Thursday Next would have done."

"No," I replied, "but then Thursday could deal with this sort of stuff. She *enjoyed* it. A woman has to know her limitations. If Herring had wanted this accident to be investigated properly, he would have given it to someone else. Maybe it's for the best. Maybe there really *are* wheels within wheels. Maybe some stuff has to be left, for the good of all of us. We leave crime to the authorities, right?"

"That would certainly seem to be the safe and conventional option, ma'am."

"Exactly," I replied. "Safe. Conventional. Besides, I have a series to look after and dignity to be maintained for Thursday. If anything happened to me, as likely as not Carmine would take over, and I'm not convinced she'd uphold the standards quite as I do, what with the goblins and the hyphenating and such."

I looked away as I said it and began to rearrange the objects on my desk. I suddenly felt hot and a bit peculiar and didn't want to look Sprockett in the eye.

"As madam wishes."

Sprockett bowed and withdrew, and I spent the next hour writing up a report for Herring. It wasn't easy to write. Try as I might, I couldn't make the report longer than forty words, and it deserved more than that. I managed at one point to write a hundred words, but after I'd taken out the bit about the epizeuxis worm and the scrubbed ISBN, it was down to only thirty-seven again. I decided to ask Whitby his hypothetical opinion and finish the report after lunch.

I called the Jurisfiction offices again to see if Thursday was available to talk.

"She's still unavailable," I reported as I trotted into the kitchen. "I might try to speak to her when I go over to deliver the report to Commander Herring this afternoon. Do you think I'm dressed okay for Whitby or should I . . ."

My voice had trailed off because something was wrong.

Sprockett and Mrs. Malaprop were looking at me in the sort of way I imagine disgruntled parents might.

"You tell her," said Mrs. Malaprop.

"It's Whitby," said Sprockett.

I suddenly had a terrible thought. This being fiction, long-unrequited romances often end in tragedy just before they finally begin, inevitably leading to a lifetime's conjecture of what might have happened and all manner of tedious and ulti-mately overwritten soul-searching. The scenario was almost as hideous as actually losing Whitby.

"He's dead?"

"No, ma'am, he's not dead. At least he was still alive two minutes ago."

"He was here? Why isn't he here now?"

Sprockett coughed politely. "I am sorry to say, ma'am, that I had to send Mr. Jett away."

I stared at him, scarcely believing what I was hearing. "Why would you do something like that?"

"I feel, ma'am, that he is *unsuitable.*"

"What?"

He showed me a newspaper clipping that was about two years old. "I exhort you to read it, ma'am, no matter how painful."

So I did.

"It is the painful duty of this journalist," went the article, "to report an act of such base depravity that it causes the worst excesses of Horror to pale into insignificance. Last Tuesday an unnamed man, for reasons known only to himself, set fire to a busload of nuns who were taking their orphaned puppies to a 'How cute is your puppy?' competition. Unfortunately, the per-petrator of this vile and heartless act is still at liberty, and . . ."

I stopped reading as a sense of confusion and disappoint-ment welled up inside me. There was a picture accompanying the article, and even though the piece did not mention Whitby by name, there was a photograph of a man whom "Jurisfiction wanted to question." It was Jett, without a doubt—holding a two-gallon gasoline can and chuckling. I didn't really know what was worse—Whitby killing the busload of nuns or me having finally plucked up the courage to have lunch at the Elbow Rooms, only for the rug to be pulled from under my feet.

"Is this true?"

"I'm afraid so. I'm sorry, ma'am. Was I wrong to send him away?"

"No, you were right."

I sighed and stared at the report I was carrying. "Better call a cab. I'm going to tell Herring what he wants to hear. At least that way someone gets to be happy today. You can come, too."

It took me twenty minutes to coax Carmine out of her bedroom. I assured her it wasn't so bad, because Sprockett had caught the goblin and recovered the swag, so he wasn't *technically* a thief. I had to tell her that he wasn't *that* unhandsome—for a goblin—and that no, I was sure he wasn't just saying nice things to her so he could be invited across the threshold. I told her she was now on book duty, as I would be out for a while, and she replied, "Yes, okay, fine," but wouldn't look at me, so I left her staring angrily at the patterned wallpaper in the front room.

12.

Jurisfiction

Budgetary overruns almost buried the remaking before the planning stage, until relief came from an unexpected quarter. A spate of dodgy accounting practices in the Outland necessitated a new genre in Fiction: Creative Accountancy. Shunned by many as "not a proper genre at all," the members' skills at turning thin air into billion-dollar profits were suddenly of huge use, and the remaking went ahead as planned. Enron may have been a pit of vipers in the Outland, but they quite literally saved the BookWorld.

Bradshaw's BookWorld Companion (16th edition)

I took the bus to Le Guin Central and then the first train to HumDram/Classics. As the train slowly steamed from the station, I sat back and stared out the window. I was mildly interested to learn that Heathcliff was on the same train, although we didn't see him—just a lot of screaming and fainting girls on the platform whenever we stopped. We halted briefly at Gaiman Junction before steaming on a wide arc to Shakespeare Terminus. There was a delay leaving the platform, as security was being taken a little more seriously than usual. A group of heavily armed Men in Plaid were scrutinizing everyone's IDs.

"Do you think this is about the Racy Novel peace talks?" I asked a French Wilkins Micawber who was there on an exchange trip.

"*Mais oui*. But I think ze CofG is being a leetle jittery 'bout

Racy Novel," he explained in a pointlessly overblown French accent. "Zey think zat zere may be fizz columnists eager to cause—'ow you say?—mischief. I'd not like to be without shirt and medallion while Barry White plays in ze background right now, I can tells you."

"Reason for visit?" asked the Plaid on guard duty.

"I have to report to Mr. Lockheed regarding a crashed-book investigation."

"Very well," said the Plaid. "And what's with the mechanical butler?"

"To lend tone to the proceedings."

This was enough for the Man in Plaid, and with a gruff "Welcome to the Classics, have an eloquent day," I was allowed to pass. On our way out of the station, I noticed a small group of characters who had been pulled aside. Some of the women wore miniskirts, tube tops and stilettos, and the men had shirts open to the navel. It seemed as though anyone even remotely resembling someone from Racy Novel was immediately under suspicion. They were protesting their innocence and complaining bitterly about the unfair character profiling, but to little avail.

We took a tram along Austen Boulevard and got out just outside the gates to *Sense and Sensibility*. This was a large compound, and a high wall topped with barbed wire surrounded the many settings that made up the book. On each corner were watchtowers, from which armed Plaids kept a constant lookout. Such tight security wasn't just to protect the Dashwoods—the residence of Norland Park within *Sense and Sensibility* was also the headquarters of Jurisfiction, Fiction's policing agency.

Waiting at the gates was a group of characters with day passes, ready for the tour. For some reason those in Sci-Fi had a thing about the classics, so of the twenty or thirty characters waiting, at least two-thirds were aliens. Since most of them hailed from the poor end of the genre, they had a lot of tentacles and left sticky trails after themselves, which caused no end of cleaning up.

"No clockwork automatons," said one of the guards on duty. "You should know better than that, Miss Next."

I had to explain that I wasn't *that* Miss Next, and the guard peered closer at me, grunted and then explained that a Duplex-4 had suffered a mainspring failure several months before and killed eight bystanders, so all cog-based life-forms below the Duplex-6 had been banned.

"The Six has been released?" asked Sprockett, who had a vested interest in the competition. To sentient machines the primary cause of worry was obsolescence, closely followed by metal fatigue and inadequate servicing.

"It was launched just after the remaking," said the guard, "but I've not seen one yet."

"They must have rushed them into production," murmured Sprockett. "A risk, if they're still at the beta-test stage."

I suggested to Sprockett that he nip into the local Stubbs and not have a coffee or two until I returned, to which he gratefully acquiesced.

After signing the visitors' book and a risk assessment that included "erasure, swollen ankles and death by drowning," I was issued a visitor's pass and allowed to walk up the graveled path towards the house. Since we were now actually *within* the backstory of *Sense and Sensibility*, the view upwards was not of the rest of the BookWorld—the curved inside of the sphere and books moving about—but of clouds and a clear blue sky. The trees gently rustled as though in a breeze, and the herbaceous borders were alive with a delicate symphony of color. This was one of the better attributes of the Reader Feedback Loop. When readers imbue a book with their own interpretations, the weather always comes first, then colors, symmetry, trees, architecture, fixtures and fittings and finally texture. Birdsong, however, is generally not something brought alive by the reader's imagination, so the birds still have to be provided. Since we were now in the unread zone of the novel, the birds were either off-duty or populating another book elsewhere. There is a certain degree of economics within the BookWorld; Austen birds are the same as Brontë ones—listen carefully and you'll hear.

I stopped at the front door to Norland Park and gave my name to the footman, who looked as much like a frog as you can without actually being one. He gazed at me for a long time and opened his eyes so wide I thought for a moment they might fall out, and I readied myself with a pocket handkerchief in case they did. But they didn't fall out, and after another minute's thought he relaxed and said, "You do look like her, don't you?"

I thought of telling him that he looked very much like a frog but thought better of it.

"You're the first person not to confuse me with her for a while," I remarked. "How did you know?"

"The real Thursday always ignored me," he replied, "walked past without a word. But never in a bad way—she always did it respectful like."

"Do you get ignored a lot?"

"I do, and not just by ordinary citizens. I've been ignored by some of the greats, you know." He then proceeded to list twenty or so major characters who hadn't acknowledged his existence on a regular basis. He had a particular fondness for David Copperfield, whom he had escorted almost three hundred times "without a glance in my direction."

"That must be quite upsetting."

"I'm a footman," he explained. "We're trained to be notthere-but-there. Being ignored is the yardstick of a footman's professional abilities. My father was sixty-seven years in the employ of the first Lord Spongg and wasn't acknowledged once. He went to his grave a fulfilled man. If you want to be ignored by the movers and shakers of the BookWorld," concluded the frog-footman proudly, "this is the place to do it."

"You've very fortunate," I said, humoring him. "Some people don't get to be ignored at all."

"Don't I know it," he replied, licking the end of his pencil and consulting his clipboard. "Now, reason for visit?"

"I'm to see Mr. Lockheed at Accident Investigation."

"Correct. This way."

The entrance hall was large and empty except for a round mahogany table in the middle, upon which stood a vase of flowers. The way to Herring's office took us past the ballroom, from which Jurisfiction's agents were given their instructions and posted to all corners of the BookWorld to face adversaries so dangerous that it was truly astonishing that anyone ever survived. I had been in there a few times when I'd been a trainee of the real Thursday, but I hadn't visited since I failed my training day. I slowed my pace as we passed, for the door was open and I could see Jurisfiction's elite talking and laughing. I recognized Emperor Zhark and a large hedgepig that could only be Mrs. Tiggy-winkle. The Red Queen was there, too, and several others.

The frog-footman coughed his disapproval, and we made to move on. But at that moment a short man in late middle age and dressed as a big-game hunter stepped out of the open door. He was wearing a pith helmet and a safari suit, and across his body was slung a Sam Brown belt and holster, with the outfit finished off by a pair of brown leather riding boots. Since Thursday's disappearance, he was probably the third-most-important person in the BookWorld after Senator Jobsworth and Red Herring. His name was Commander Bradshaw, and his expert guidance at Jurisfiction had kept the agency at the top of its game for almost as long as anyone could remember—his exploits ensured that he was hardly ever off the front page of *The Word*, and his much-updated *BookWorld*

Companion was the definitive work on the BookWorld, both before and after the remaking.

He was deep in conversation with a youngish agent. I felt out of place, so I looked straight ahead and quickened my pace. But he noticed me and without pausing for a second took me firmly by the arm and steered me to an alcove.

"Thursday," he hissed in an agitated manner, "why are you dressed in those ridiculous clothes, and where in heaven's name have you been?"

"I'm not her, sir. I'm the one who looks after her series. I'm actually A8-V-67987-FP."

He frowned, then stared at me for a moment. "You're telling me you're the *written* one?"

I nodded, and he burst into laughter.

"Well, strike me pink!" he said. "You gave me a turn and no mistake. I was . . . ah, expecting Thursday to be here any moment," he added, looking at his watch in an unsubtle manner. "I suspect she has been delayed."

His explanation didn't ring true at all. Thursday was *definitely* more missing than he would like me to know. We returned to where Bradshaw's companion was waiting for us. He was studiously ignoring the frog-footman, who for his part was accepting the snub with quiet dignity.

"I'd forgotten just how identical you looked," he said. "Are you keeping well?"

"I am, sir," I managed to mumble. "I trust you are well read?"

It was a stupid gaffe; Bradshaw's brand of jingoistic Imperialist fiction hadn't been read for a half century. But he took no offense.

"Not read anymore, and quite right, too," he said laughingly, then stared at me for a while before saying to his companion, "You've met the other Thursday, the real one?"

"Sure have," he replied. "One helluva goddamn fine operative."

"Look alike, don't they? Apart from the clothes, of course."

"Like two peas in a pod."

Bradshaw thought for a moment. "Has Thursday been down to see you recently?" he asked me with an air of feigned nonchalance.

"Not since the remaking, sir," I replied. "May I ask a question?"

"Of course."

"Am I to understand that Thursday Next is . . . *missing?*"

"She's currently on leave in the RealWorld," he said in a dismissive manner, "enjoying some time off with her family before the peace negotiations on Friday."

"Are you sure about that? I saw—"

I checked myself. I could get into big trouble for sneak-peeking the RealWorld, and the Lady of Shalott could get into bigger trouble for letting me.

"What did you see?" asked Bradshaw.

"Nothing. I must have . . . dreamt it. I'm very sorry to have wasted your time, sir."

He looked at me for a long while, trying to divine what, if anything, I knew. Finally he said, "You are keeping the Thursday Next series dignified, I trust?"

"Yes, sir—even at the expense of readability."

"Being read isn't everything. Some of the best people are hardly read at all. Listen," he said thoughtfully, staring at me with his intelligent blue eyes, "would you do something for me?"

"Of course."

Right then a man draped in the white linen robes of the most senior senatorial office walked briskly through the front doors of Norland Park and into the entrance hall in which we stood.

"Oh, crap," said Bradshaw under his breath. "Just what we need: Jobsworth."

If he was over here in person, it would be for a very good reason—probably about the Racy Novel peace talks.

I thought of dropping to one knee and averting my eyes as the frog-footman had done, but for some reason I didn't. The Thursday part of me, I suppose. Jobsworth was not alone. As well as the usual phalanx of staff, hangers-on and deputies, there was Barnes, Jobsworth's executive assistant; Colonel Barksdale, the head of the Avoiding War Department; and Commander Herring, who was busy reading a report and hadn't yet seen me.

"Good morning, Bradshaw," said Jobsworth. Bradshaw wished the senator good morning, then the same to Commander Herring and Colonel Barksdale. Barnes was too far down the pecking order to be greeted, as were all the other members of Jobsworth's staff. The senator began to speak, then saw me. His eyes opened wide.

"Great Panjandrum!" he said. "Thursday?"

Bradshaw looked at me, then at the senator. I opened my mouth to reply, but Bradshaw held up a hand. In such company it was *strictly* speak-when-spoken-to. Protocol in the Book-World was like grammatical rules—rigidly structured, arcane and fiercely defended by librarians wielding wooden rulers with painful accuracy.

"No, Senator, it's the *written* version."

"Truthfully?" asked Jobsworth. "She looks an awful lot like her."

"If she *were* the real one, do you think she would be here accompanied by that . . . that—what's your name?"

The frog-footman looked startled at being spoken to. "Wesley," he said in a quiet voice.

"Right," said Bradshaw, not really listening, "being shown around by frog guy? If this *were* the one, she'd be in the office discussing the peace talks and the metaphor crisis."

"I'll vouch that she's the written one," said Herring, who had just looked up. "Are you here on JAID business, Next?"

"I am, sir."

"Then you can take your findings direct to Lockheed."

It seemed a good moment to leave, so I bobbed politely and began to withdraw.

"Wait," said the senator. "Bradshaw, why were you speaking to her if she's just the copy?"

For a fleeting moment, Bradshaw looked uncomfortable.

"I was asking her if . . . she could ask Lorina Peabody to head up the Talking Animal Division of Jurisfiction."

"Who the hell's Lorina Peabody?"

"She's a dodo," I said.

Jobsworth stared at Bradshaw suspiciously, then me. "Introduce us," he said after a pause.

"Very well," said Bradshaw with a sigh. "Senior Senator Giles Jobsworth, head of Fiction and emissary to the Great Panjandrum, the written Thursday Next."

"Hello," he said, shaking me by the hand and giving me the smile of somebody who was considering how best one could be exploited.

"Honored, Senator, sir," I replied dutifully.

Jobsworth was perhaps sixty or sixty-five, graying at the temples and with the look of someone weighed down heavily by responsibility. He stepped forward and put a finger under my chin. I should have been more overawed in his presence, but I wasn't. In fact, I had every reason to dislike him. When the senior senator was merely a senator, he had blocked my series from having Landen in it. He had said having no Landen was "as the author intended," but that didn't really help, to be honest.

"It looks *exactly* like her," he breathed.

"Like two goddamn peas in a pod," agreed Bradshaw's companion.

"I'm mirrored with her, Senator," I explained. "The books

were built using H-29 biographical architecture before they were moved to Nonfiction, so my looks are directly linked to hers. I age at the same rate and even grow the same scars in sympath—"

"Fascinating. Does it have skills and an intellect to match, Commander Bradshaw?"

"It does not—nor any dress sense. What's your interest in an A-8 copy of Thursday Next, Senator?"

"The interests of the council are not necessarily the interests of Jurisfiction, Bradshaw."

They stared at each other for several seconds. I expect this happened quite a lot. Jurisfiction was a policing agency, working under the council, who were wholly political. I can't imagine they *ever* got on.

"Sir?" said Barnes, gently coaxing the senator to stick to his schedule. "You have a meeting."

"Very well," said the head of Fiction, and he strode off into the Jurisfiction offices with Herring, Barksdale and his entourage. Bradshaw stared at me for a moment, then told me I was excused. I needed no further bidding, and curtsied politely before hurrying off with the frog-footman.

"Well, thanks for that," said the frog-footman sarcastically. "You just ruined my six-year 'being ignored by Commander Bradshaw' record."

"He didn't remember your name," I said, trying to be helpful, "and was horribly insensitive when he called you 'frog guy.'"

"Well, okay," said the frog-footman, "that does take the sting out a little bit. But tell me," he said, staring at me with his large, protruding eyes and broad mouth, "why did he call me 'frog guy'?"

"I was up for Jurisfiction once," I said, quickly changing the subject, "but it didn't work out."

"Me, too," sadly replied the frog-footman, whose mind

didn't seem to pause on any one subject for long. "I didn't make it past the 'What is your name?' question. You?"

"Training day. Froze when the going got tough. Nearly got my mentor killed."

"To fail spectacularly is a loser's paradise," said the frog-footman wistfully. "This way."

14.

Stamped and Filed

Distilling metaphor out of raw euphemism was wasteful and expensive, and the euphemism-producing genres on the island were always squeezing the market. Besides, the by-product of metaphor using the Cracked Euphemism Process liberates irony-238 and dangerous quantities of alliteration, which are associated with downright dangerous disposal difficulties.

Bradshaw's BookWorld Companion (9th edition)

*W*e walked down the seemingly endless corridors, every door placarded with the name of the department contained within. One was labeled OLD JOKES and another NOUN-TO-VERB CONVERSION UNIT. Just past the offices of the Synonym Squad and the Danvers Union headquarters was a small office simply labeled JAID.

"Right. Well," I said, "I'll see myself out when I'm done."

"I'm afraid not," replied the frog-footman. "I am instructed to escort you both in *and* out."

So while the frog-footman sat on a chair in the corridor opposite, I knocked on the door.

"Commander Herring told me you would be stopping by," said Lockheed as I entered. "Do come in. Tea?"

"No thank you."

I looked around. The office was roomy, had a large window and was paneled in light pine. The pictures that decorated the walls all depicted a book disaster of some sort, mostly with

Lockheed featured prominently in the foreground, grinning broadly. There was little clutter, and the single filing cabinet probably contained nothing but a kettle and some cookies. Jurisfiction had finally managed to commit itself to a paperless office—all files were committed to the prodigious memory of Captain Phantastic, just down the hall.

"Impressive office, eh?" said Lockheed. "We even have a window—with a view. Come and have a look."

I walked over to the window and looked out. All I could see was a brick wall barely six feet away.

"Very nice," I murmured.

"If you lean right out with someone hanging on to your shirttails, you can almost see the sky, but not quite. Would you like to try?"

"No thanks."

"So," said Lockheed, sitting down on his swivel chair and motioning me to a seat, "something to report to Commander Herring about the accident?"

I swallowed hard. "It was simply that," I said, an odd leaden feeling dropping down inside me. "An accident."

Lockheed breathed a visible sigh of relief. "Commander Herring will be delighted. When he hears bad news, he usually likes to hit someone about the head with an iron bar, and I'm often the closest. Are you *sure* there is nothing to report?"

I wondered for a moment whether to report the epizeuxis worm, scrubbed ISBN and the Vanity roots of *The Murders on the Hareng Rouge*. Not necessarily because it was the right thing to do, but simply to watch the eye-popping effect it might have on Lockheed.

"Nothing, sir."

"Unprecedented and unrepeatable?"

"Exactly so."

I felt the curious leaden feeling again. I didn't know what it was; I patted my chest and cleared my throat.

"Little cog, big machine," said Lockheed as he filled out a form for me to sign. "We are here to facilitate, not to pontificate. If we can sew this whole incident shut, the sooner we can get on with our lives and maintain our unimpeachable hundred-percent dealt-with rate. Wheels within wheels, Thursday."

"Wheels within wheels, sir."

"Did you find out what the book was, by the way?"

"Not a clue," I lied. "I didn't find a single ISBN, so I thought 'Why bother?' and decided to simply give up."

I didn't know why I was suddenly being sarcastic. It might have been something to do with the odd leaden feeling inside. Lockheed, however, missed the sarcasm completely. Most D-3s did.

"Splendid!" he said. "I can see that you and Commander Herring will be getting on very well. You can expect a few more incidents heading your way with this kind of flagrant level of inspired disinterest. Sign here . . . and *here*."

He handed the form over, and I paused, then signed on the dotted line. This isn't what Thursday would have done, but then I wasn't Thursday.

"Excellent," he said, rising from his seat. "I'll take this along to Captain Phantastic for memorizing."

"Why don't I take it?" I suggested. The odd leaden feeling in me had released a sense of purpose, but of what I was not sure. "You can stay here and have some tea and cookies or something."

I nodded my head in the direction of the filing cabinet.

"Goodness me, that is so *very* kind," replied Lockheed, condemning the lost souls in the unknown book to eternal anonymity with a ridiculously large rubber stamp before handing me the form. "Fourth door on the left."

"Right you are."

I opened the door, thanked him again and found the frog-footman waiting for me in the corridor. I told him I had some filing to do, and he led me past the doors marked PIANO DIVISION,

ITALICS, and PEBBLES (MISCELLANEOUS) before we got to a door marked RECORDS. The frog-footman told me he'd wait for me there, and I stepped inside.

The room was small and shabby and had a half dozen people waiting to be seen, so I sat on a chair to wait my turn.

"Thursday Next," I said to the gloomy-looking individual sitting next to me, who was reading a paper and appeared to have a toad actually *growing* out of the top of his head. The pink skin of his balding pate seemed to merge with the browny-green of the toad. "The copy," I added, before he asked. But the man ignored me. The toad growing out of his head, however, was more polite.

"Ah," said the toad. "A good copy?"

"I do okay."

"Humph," said the toad before adding, "Tell me, do I look stupid with a human growing out of my bottom?"

"Not at all," I replied politely. "In fact, I think it's rather fetching."

"Do you really?" said the toad with a smile.

"Who are you talking to?" asked the man, looking up from his paper.

"The toad."

The man looked around. "What toad?"

"What did the man just say?" asked the toad.

"I like your books," said the woman on the other side of me. "When are we going to see some more?"

"Five is all you'll get," I said, happy to get away from the man-toad. "What are you seeing Captain Phantastic for?"

"I'm head of the Metaphor Allocation Committee," she explained. "Once we move to the Metaphor Credit Trading System, those books with excess metaphor will be able to trade it on the floor of the Narrative Device Exchange. Naturally, more complex figurative devices such as hypothetical futures and analogy and simile trust funds will have to be regulated; we can't have hyperbole ending up as overvalued as it was—the bottom dropped out of the litotes market, which, as anyone will tell you, was most undesirable."

"*Most* undesirable," I remarked, having not understood a word. "And how will Captain Phantastic help with all this?"

She shrugged. "I just want to run the idea past him. There might be a historical precedent that could suggest collateralized metaphor obligations might be a bad idea. Even so," she added, "we might do it anyway—just for kicks and giggles. Excuse me."

While we'd been talking, Captain Phantastic had been dealing with each inquiry at lightning speed. This wasn't surprising, as the Records Office relied on nothing as mundane as magnetic storage, paper filing or even a linked alien supermind. It had in its possession instead a single elephant with a prodigiously large memory. It was efficient and simple, and it required only buns, hay and peanuts to operate.

When it was my turn, I walked nervously into his office.

"Hello," said the elephant in a nasally, trumpety, blocked-nose sort of voice. I noticed he was dressed in an unusual three-piece pin-striped suit, unusual in that not only did it have a watch fob the size of a saucepan in the waistcoat pocket, but the pinstripes were running horizontally.

"So how can I help?"

"Jurisfiction Accident Investigation Department," I said, holding up my shield. I paused as a sudden thought struck me. Not about elephants, or even of a toad with a man growing out of its bottom, or of the volatile metaphor market. I suddenly thought about *lying*. Of subterfuge. It was wrong, but in a *right* kind of way, because I had finally figured out what the leaden feeling was. It was a deficiency of Right Thing to Do—and I needed to remedy the shortfall, and fast.

"We're investigating a crashed book out in Conspiracy," I said, tearing up the accident report behind my back, "and we need some background information on *The Murders on the Hareng Rouge* by Adrian Dorset."

"Of course," trumpeted the elephant. "Take a seat, Miss . . . ?"

"Next. *Thursday* Next. But I'm not—"

"It's all right," he said, "I know. I know everything. More even than the Cheshire Cat. And that's saying something. I'm Captain Phantastic, by the way, but you can call me 'the Captain.' You and I haven't met, but the real Thursday and I go back a ways—even partnered together during the whole sorry issue surrounding *The Cat in the Hat III—Revenge of the Things*. Did you hear about it?"

"I'm sorry, I didn't."

"No matter." And he sniffed at me delicately for a moment with his trunk.

"Do you have a chicken living in your house?"

"A dodo."

"Would that be Lorina?"

"We call her Pickwick these days, but yes."

"Tell her that Captain Phantastic is still waiting for that date she promised."

I wasn't aware that Pickwick dated elephants—or anyone, come to that.

"Did she promise you recently?"

"Eighty-six years, three months, and two days ago. Would you like me to relate the conversation? I can do it word for word."

"No thanks. I'll give her the message."

The Captain leaned back on his chair and closed his eyes.

"Now, *The Murders on the Hareng Rouge*. I try to read most books, but for obvious reasons those in Vanity I delegate. So many books, so little time. Listen, you don't have a bun on you, do you? Raisins or otherwise, I'm not fussy."

"I'm afraid not."

"Shame. Okay, well, there's not much to tell, really. *The*

Murders on the Hareng Rouge was a junker on its way to be scrapped."

I wasn't expecting this. "I'm sorry?"

"It was a stinker. One of the very worst books ever written. Self-published by one Adrian H. Dorset, who as far as we know has not written anything else. He printed two copies and spiral bound them in his local print shop. Semiautobiographical, it was the story of a man coming to terms with the death of his wife and how he then immersed himself in work to try to take revenge on the person he thought responsible. Flat, trite and uninspiring. The author burned it as a form of catharsis. By rigid convention, the version here in the BookWorld has to be scrapped before sundown. Did it hurt anyone?"

"Only the people in it."

"It should have been empty," said the elephant. "Scrapped books always have the occupants reallocated before the book is torn apart."

"We found the remains of *someone*."

"How much?"

"A thumb."

The elephant shrugged. "A hitchhiker, perhaps? Or reformed graphemes?"

"We thought the same."

"In any event," concluded Phantastic, "that's all I have."

"You're sure it was a junker?" I asked, trying to figure out why anyone would risk almost certain erasure by deleting the ISBN and then using demolition-grade epizeuxis to destroy an unreadable book from Vanity that was destined to be scrapped anyway.

"Completely sure."

I thanked Captain Phantastic for his time, promised to bring some buns next time and walked out of his office, deep in thought.

"You were in there a while," said the frog-footman as he escorted me from the building.

"The Captain likes to talk," I said. "'Hannibal said this, me and Dumbo did that, Horton's my best friend, I was Celeste's first choice but she took Babar on the rebound'—you know what it's like."

"After Madame Bovary," said the frog-footman, rolling his eyes, "the Captain is the worst name-dropper I've ever been ignored by."

I went and found Sprockett in the local Stubbs. He had got chatting to a Mystical Meg Fortune-Telling Automaton and discovered that they were distantly related.

"I've got you a fortune card, ma'am," said Sprockett. "Archie was a great-great-uncle to us both, and Meg's father-in-law is Gort."

"Nice chap?"

"So long as you don't get him annoyed."

I looked at the small card he had given me. It read, "Avoid eating oysters if there is no paycheck in the month," which is one of those generic pieces of wisdom that Mechanical Mystics often hand out, along with "Every chapter a new beginning" and "What has a clause at the end of the pause?"

Sprockett hailed a cab, and we were soon trundling off in the direction of Fantasy.

"Did all go as planned, ma'am?" he asked as we made our way back out of the genre on the Dickens Freeway.

I paused. It was better if Sprockett didn't know that the investigation was covertly still running. Better for me, and better for him. Despite being a cog-based life-form, he could still suffer at the hands of inquisitors, and he needed deniability. If I was going to go down, I'd go down on my own.

In ten minutes I had told him everything. He nodded sagely, his gears whirring as he took it all in. Once I was done, he suggested that we not tell anyone, as Carmine might tell the goblin and Pickwick was apt to blurt things out randomly to strangers. Mrs. Malaprop we didn't have to worry about—no one would be able to understand her. Besides, she probably already knew.

"The less people who know, the better."

"Fewer. The *fewer* people who know, the better."

"That's what I meant."

"That's what *who* meant?"

"Wait—who's speaking now?"

"I don't know."

"You *must* know."

"Damn. It must be me—you wouldn't say 'damn,' would you?"

"I might."

We both paused for a moment, waiting for either a speech marker or a descriptive line. It was one of those things that happened every now and again in BookWorld—akin to an empty, pregnant silence in the middle of an Outland dinner party.

"So," said Sprockett once we had sorted ourselves out, "what's the plan?"

"I don't know our next move," I said, "but until I do, we do nothing—which is excellent cover for what we should be doing—nothing."

"An inspired plan," said Sprockett.

The taxi slowed down and stopped as the traffic ground to a halt. The cabbie made some inquiries and found that a truckload of "their" had collided with a trailer containing "there" going in the opposite direction and had spread there contents across the road.

"Their will be a few hiccups after that," said the cabbie, and I agreed. Homophone mishaps often seeped out into the RealWorld and infected the Outlanders, causing theire to be all manner of confusion.

"I know a shortcut through Comedy," said the cabbie, who

was, purely as an irrelevant aside, an anteater named Ralph. "It shouldn't be too onerous—the risibility is currently at thirty yards and the mirthrate down to 1.9."

"What about puns?"

"Always about, but they're not funny, so the chance of unbridled hysteria is low."

Trips through Comedy were usually avoided, as the giggling could be painful and sometimes fatal, but the comedy in Comedy had been muted of late. I told him to go ahead, and we pulled out of the traffic and drove off in the opposite direction.

"What kind of man sets fire to a busload of nuns?" I asked, Whitby still annoyingly on my mind.

"I cannot answer that, ma'am, but I suspect one who is neither kind nor considerate."

There was a pause.

"May I ask a question regarding the subject of empathy, something I am at a loss to understand?"

"Of course."

"Since I have set neither a nun nor a puppy on fire nor gleefully pushed an old lady downstairs, does that make me kind and compassionate?"

"Not really," I replied. "It makes you normal, and respectful of accepted social rules."

"But not compassionate?"

"To be compassionate you have to demonstrate it in some sort of act that shows you care for someone."

"Care for someone? Care as in how a butler cares for someone?"

"More than that."

"I'm not sure I can envisage any greater care than that which a butler can offer."

And he sat and buzzed to himself in such deep thought that I had to give him two extra winds, much to the cabbie's sniffy disapproval.

"Don't anyone move. . . . I think we've driven into a mimefield."

We entered Comedy a few miles farther on by way of the Thurber Freeway, then took a funny turn at Bad Joke and bumped along a back road of compacted mother-in-law one-liners. We passed the Knock-Knock? Quarry, where we were held up for a few minutes while they did some blasting, then continued on past Limericks, Amusing Anecdotes and Talking-Horse Gags to the empty wilderness known as the Burlesque Depression. The huge influx of stand-up comedians in the RealWorld had overjoked the stocks of natural glee, and the stony comedic landscape was now almost barren. As an emergency measure, unfunny comedy sneakily branded "alternative" was now flooding the RealWorld until the natural stock of jokes had replenished itself. The lack of comedy in Comedy was no laughing matter.

Almost from nowhere a car shot past us at speed and, as it did so, swerved violently. The cabbie attempted to avoid a collision and spun the wheel hard to the left. He overcorrected, slewed sideways and hit the fence at the side of the road. There was a crunch as splintered wood flew everywhere, the windscreen crazed, and the taxi thumped down the short embankment, ran across some rough ground and came to rest with a clatter and a hiss against a tree.

"Are you okay?" I asked.

Sprockett nodded, even though I could see he had a crack in his porcelain face. The cabbie looked a bit shocked and was about to open his door when I placed a hand on his shoulder.

"Wait. Don't anyone move. . . . I think we've driven into a mimefield."

15.

The Mimefield

Books' moving from Nonfiction to Fiction was uncommon, but it did happen. The most recent immigrant was *I Got Beaten Every Day for Eight Years by My Drunken Father* from Misery Memoirs, when it was discovered the author had made most of it up. By all accounts *Eight Years* had to leave in disgrace, tail between bruised legs, but I think secretly delighted. There is nowhere more depressing than Misery Memoirs, and the few visitors it has are usually characters-in-training who have a tricky scene to do in Human Drama and need some inspiration.

Bradshaw's BookWorld Companion (10th edition)

*S*prockett and the cabbie looked outside. Surrounding the car were five hundred or so mimes, all dressed uniformly in tight black slacks, a stripy top, white greasepaint and a large hat with a flower stuck in the crown. They were miming in the most terrifying fashion, their hideous faces contorted with exaggerated expressions, their bodies moving in a frighteningly sinuous movement that defied written description. The cabbie panicked and started the engine. It burst into life, and he popped the car into reverse.

"Hold it," I said, looking out the rear window. "You can't go backwards—there's a mime stuck inside a pretend glass cube just behind you. Wait—he's out. No, hang on, there's another, bigger pretend glass cube outside the smaller one."

The cabbie started to sob.

"Calm down," I said. "Panic is the mind killer. We can get out of this alive if we keep our heads straight. Turn the engine off."

We glanced around as the mimes, now curious, moved closer. I almost cried out as one peered into the car while doing a routine with a balloon that was heavy, then light, then immovable.

"What are they doing?" asked the cabbie, his voice tremulous with rising fear. "I don't understand."

Comedy was one of those genres that while appearing quite jolly was actually highly dangerous. In order to generate new jokes, the custodians of the genre had tried to use nonwritten and nonverbal comedy as a growing medium. Mimes had no real home in a written or spoken canon, but some of their movements and actions could cross-pollinate with others that did. Slapstick was used for the same effect, as was as a well-timed look, a comical pause and silly expressions, voices and walks.

"Don't move," said Sprockett. "Mimes don't generally attack unless they are threatened."

"How do you threaten a mime?"

"By sighing during a performance, looking away, rolling your eyes—that sort of thing. Mimes hate being ignored or having their performance interrupted. In that respect they're almost as touchy as poets."

We did as I suggested and watched as the mimes continued their strange movements, and we laughed and applauded at the right moments. Some of the mimes appeared hardly to move at all and adopted poses like statues, and others seemed to be walking against the wind. There was also a lot of going in and out of doors that weren't there, canoeing and pretending to walk up and down stairs. It was all *very* mystifying. Mind you, I was worried just how long we could laugh and applaud. Every moment we paused, they became dangerously aggressive once more.

After another five minutes of this odd posturing, the cabbie couldn't take it anymore. He flung open his door and made a run for it. We watched with growing horror as the unfortunate taxi driver was suddenly copied in his every movement and expression. Two mimes walked close behind him, while another engaged in some curiously expressive banter. Within half a minute, it was all over, and the cabbie's tattered clothes were all that remained upon the ground.

I looked at Sprockett, whose eyebrow flicked up to "Doubtful," which meant he was out of ideas. Now that they had been blooded, the mood of the mimes seemed to have changed. A minute ago their features had been ridiculously smiley, but now they wore doleful expressions of exaggerated sadness. They also seemed to be approaching the car. Once they got in, it would be all over. Or at least it would be for me.

"Lean forward."

"Might I inquire as to why, ma'am?"

"I'm going to press your emergency spring release," I said. "You'll be nothing but an inert box of cogs to them—they'll not touch you. Someone will chance across you in a few months, and you can be rewound. You can tell them what happened."

He looked at me and buzzed for a moment. "Would that be a compassionate act on your behalf, ma'am?"

"I suppose so. Only one of us need die."

Sprockett thought about this for a moment. "I'm sorry, ma'am, but I may have to politely decline your offer. A butler never leaves his position and is loyal until death."

I made a grab for the access panel on the back of his left shoulder, but he caught my hand with surprising speed.

"In this matter, ma'am," he said firmly, "my cogs are made up."

I relented, and Sprockett let go of my arm as several mimes improvised a trampoline routine on the back bumper.

"Okay," I said as a sudden thought struck me, "here's the plan: I need you to act like a robot."

"How do I do that?"

"You tell me. *You're* the robot, after all."

"Agreed. But the whole point of the Duplex series is that we *act* human in order to function more seamlessly with our masters. 'More human than the dumbest human' is the Duplex Corporation's motto. I don't know the first thing about actually *being* a robot."

"You're going to have to give it your best shot."

Sprockett raised his eyebrow as a shower of broken glass erupted from the rear window. The mimes had become markedly more aggressive when we weren't laughing and applauding hard enough during a not-very-amusing routine where they pretend to sculpt a statue out of clay.

"Very well," said Sprockett. He opened the car door and stepped out. His gait was sporadic and clumsy, and at the end of each movement there seemed to be a slight "spring" to his actions that gave the impression of increased mass. The effect upon the mimes was instantaneous and dramatic. They all took a step back and gazed in wide-eyed astonishment as Sprockett lumbered from the car with me close behind. A few of them dropped to their knees, and others fell into paroxysms of exaggerated crying.

"What do I do?" whispered Sprockett. "I can't keep this up for long."

"Head back towards the road."

So he did, and I followed him. The mimes stayed with us, their grief and sadness changing to anger and surprise. Sprockett continued his overblown movements, but it wasn't working. The mimes closed in, and just when their white gloves were upon us, they suddenly paused and exhibited the sort of mock surprise you can feign by opening your mouth wide and placing both hands on your cheeks.

The reason for this was soon apparent. One of their number had started to *copy* Sprockett in a series of similar robotic moves. Uncertain at first, the moves soon gained fluidity until his gestures exactly matched Sprockett's. Within a few seconds, the "robot" idea had spread amongst them like a virus, and the field was full of five hundred or so mimes acting like robots. As soon as they were all distracted in this fashion, I yelled "Run!" and we sprinted back to the road.

"Well," said Sprockett, stretching the barbed-quip wire back across the hole in the fence to keep the five hundred or so mimes from escaping, "I think that was a close-run thing, ma'am. Might I congratulate you on your quick thinking?"

"Let's just say it was a team effort."

He bowed politely, and I sat on a rock by the side of the road to regain my composure. I looked around. The dusty track was empty in both directions, and aside from the books drifting silently overhead and the now-robotic mimes, the only signs of life were corralled Jokes of Questionable Taste sitting silently in fenced-off areas a little way distant.

"Did you get a good look at that car that passed us?" I asked.

"Yes, ma'am. I believe it was a 1949 Buick Roadmaster."

"Men in Plaid?"

"So it would appear. Their capacity for causing us harm and annoyance seems not to be abating."

I saw it simpler: *They had just tried to kill us.* The only question that remained was, Why? And more worryingly, How much longer before they succeeded?

Just then a rattly pickup stopped opposite us. The bearded driver was staring at us with an amused twinkle in his eye. He was a Funnster, one of a hardy breed of crusty old men and women who spent their days trapping gags and taking them to market.

"Have an accident?" he asked.

It was the height of bad manners in Comedy to decline a feed line when offered, so I had to think quickly.

"No thanks," I replied, "I've already had one."

The Funnster laughed, took off his hat and mopped the sweat from his brow. He looked awhile at the mimes, who had evolved their new robot idea into robots going downstairs, robots canoeing, robots getting stuck inside glass cubes and robots walking against the wind.

"Looks like you may have started something," said the Funnster with a chuckle, climbing out of the cab and rummaging for a net and a baseball bat in the flatbed. "Wait here."

A few moments later, we were bowling down the road towards the local railway station, sitting in the back of the flatbed. On one side of us there was a mime who was miming a robot being trapped inside a net while *actually* being trapped inside a net, and on the other side of us a mature Austrian gentleman with a beard, a small hat and the look of someone who was trying to figure out what we were thinking and why we were thinking it.

After considering us for a moment, he leaned forward and said, "How many Sigmund Freuds does it take to change a lightbulb?"

"I don't know," I said. "How many?"

"Penis," said the Freud, then quickly corrected himself. "I mean father. No, wait! One. One Sigmund Freud. All it takes. Yes. *Verflucht und zugenäht!*" He added gloomily, "*Wenn ich nur bei der Aalsektion geblieben wäre!*"

16.

Commander Bradshaw

Perils for the Unwary #231: literalism. Usually a result of substandard wiring in the synonym-distribution box or a ripple in the contextual flux, the literalism can appear randomly, without warning. Example: One of the loan sharks inside *Get Shorty* turned out to be a three-ton great white with HERTZ SHARK RENTAL stamped on the side, and it was all the cast could do to keep a straight face and carry on as though nothing had happened. Peril Rating: medium-high. Action: walk away.

Bradshaw's BookWorld Companion (5th edition)

*W*e were dropped off at Cooper Central, thanked the Funnster and said farewell to Freud, who had become all wobbly and tearful. We bought some tickets and then gave them to the fez-wearing inspector who hailed us with the customary "Just like that" before directing us to our carriage. Within a few minutes, the train was steaming out of the station and towards Fantasy.

We weren't the only people in the compartment eager to get out of Comedy. A small man who wore the off-duty fatigues of a foot soldier enlisted in the Clown Army was looking about anxiously and sweating. You could tell he was off-duty because he wasn't wearing his bright red nose and his long shoes were carefully strapped to his duffel bag.

"What's your unit?" I asked.

"Sixth Clown," he said nervously, "Supply and Gigglistics.

We deploy next week to Bawdy Romp, the buffer zone between Comedy and Racy Novel. Purely as a precaution, you understand. I'm on leave and certainly not stealing military equipment, no, ma'am."

And he stared at his feet, leaving Sprockett and me to wonder what he *was* stealing and whether it was hazardous. The Clown Army's Supply division was notoriously porous, and sneeze and itching powder often found its way into the wrong hands, such as Blyton separatists—always an angry mob.

"I hope your deployment goes well."

"Thank you," said the clown, staring out the window.

We sat in silence for a while.

"Ma'am?" asked Sprockett, who had been buzzing quietly to himself in the corner.

"Yes?"

"Why do you think we were attacked?"

"Because of what we know."

"But who knows what we know? Others have to *know* that we know. Just *us* knowing it isn't enough—unless we attacked ourselves, which isn't likely."

I thought carefully. There were at least half a dozen people who might have had an idea that the investigation wasn't totally open and shut, all the way from Captain Phantastic to Pickwick/Lorina. But it was also possible we were being silenced for some other reason entirely, an accident or even a textual glitch, such as happens from time to time in the BookWorld.

"The attempt on our life *might* have been a lexicographical literalism," I said. "After all, comedians often 'kill' their audiences or 'die' onstage, and the phrases 'You'll be the death of me' or 'It was so funny I could have died' might all have colluded to cause us harm."

I was fooling myself. Although Buick Roadmasters *did* exist independently of the Men in Plaid, it seemed too suspicious to ignore. Besides, running people off the road was something that occurred in Crime, where it would be unusual to drive five miles without having it happen at least twice. It was much more unlikely in Comedy. Or at least not without a punch line. But then again, maybe my "No thanks, I've already had one" *was* the punch line. Comedy was never straightforward. When all the good jokes had left, only the dubiously amusing stuff remained. Was the mimefield funny or not? To us I think not. But it might have been funny to *someone*.

I stared out the window, thinking about my current predicament. I had a junker on its way to the scrap yard from Vanity that someone had destroyed and then tried to cover his tracks in case of discovery. The accident had been handed to the least skilled accident investigator for a quick and easy resolution, and I had almost been murdered by the Men in Plaid. I had compounded my difficulties by lying to Lockheed, gaining intelligence from Captain Phantastic on false pretenses, and I had not only failed to deliver a legal accident report but destroyed it. If I was found out, I would be confined to my series and as likely as not lose Carmine and possibly Sprockett, too. It was a good moment to pack it all in, accept the level of my own incompetence and start concentrating on what should be my primary goal: increasing readership in the Thursday Next series. Thursday, after all, could take care of herself—she had done so on numerous occasions. If I shared my plans with Sprockett, I reasoned, it would be an affirmation of my resolve, and harder to go back on.

"Sprockett?"

He started out of standby mode with a buzz.

"A cocktail, ma'am?"

"No thank you. It's just that I've decided to . . ." I sighed and rubbed my temples.

"Decided to what, ma'am?"

"Nothing."

And I slumped down into my seat, cursing the Thursday in me.

The train slowed to a halt at the border between Fantasy and Comedy and the off-duty clown started fidgeting.

"Identification, please." One of the border guards was standing at the doorway, and we all rummaged for our identification papers.

"I'll deal with this," said a familiar voice, and Commander Bradshaw appeared in the corridor. He flashed his own ID at the border guard, who saluted smartly and moved on.

Sprockett and I both stood up politely, as did the clown, who didn't want to be left out.

"Please," said Bradshaw, "sit down. What's this, a joke?" he asked, indicating the clown once we had all sat and Sprockett had offered Bradshaw a cocktail.

"A lance corporal in the Sixth Clown," I said, "Supply and Gigglistics."

"Oh, yes?" said Bradshaw with a smile. "And what would you be smuggling across the border?"

The clown sighed resignedly and opened his duffel bag to reveal boxes of military-grade custard pies. He wasn't a very good smuggler. Few were.

"It's jail for you, my lad," said Bradshaw sternly. "CPs are banned in every genre outside Comedy. I'd turn you in, but I'm busy. If you can dispose of them all before we get to Gaiman Junction, I'll overlook it."

"How would I do that?"

"Do you have a spoon in your bag?"

So while the off-duty clown began to eat his way through four dozen custard pies, Bradshaw explained what he was there for.

"*Please* don't ask Lorina to contact me," he said. "That was just for Jobsworth to hear."

"I figured."

"Is she still a colossal pain in the butt, by the way?"

"Getting worse, if anything."

Bradshaw looked at Sprockett, who took the cue and shimmered from the compartment with the clown, who was already on his ninth custard pie and groaning quietly to himself. Sprockett returned momentarily with the Chicago Fizz he had mixed for Bradshaw, then departed again.

Bradshaw leaned forward, looked left and right and whispered, "Are you her? The real one, I mean?"

"No."

He stared at me for a while. "Are you sure? You're not doing some sort of deep-cover double bluff or something?"

"Yes, quite sure. I think I know who I am."

"Prove it."

"I can't. You'll have to take my word for it. Believe me, I wish I were."

Bradshaw seemed satisfied with this and stared at me some more for quite some time. He wasn't here on a social visit.

"What can I do for you, sir?"

"The thing is," he began, taking a sip from his Chicago Fizz, "we're in a bit of a pickle here in the BookWorld, what with Speedy Muffler and the whole Racy Novel debacle. Add to that the dwindling metaphor issue, the e-book accelerators using a disproportionate amount of Text Grand Central's throughput capacity and all the other day-to-day whatnot we have to handle, and I'm sure you'll appreciate that we need the real Thursday now more than ever. Do we agree?"

"We do."

He sighed and ran his fingers through his hair. "She was due to be the Jurisfiction delegate at the Racy Novel peace talks on Friday. I'll have to send Emperor Zhark instead, and his negotiating skills are more along the lines of annihilate first, ask questions later, but without the 'ask questions later' part."

"She may turn up."

He shook his head. "I knew she was going undercover, but she said she'd check in two days ago without fail. She didn't.

That's not like her. She might be stuck in a book somewhere, lost in a book somewhere—even held against her will. The possibilities are endless."

"If she *was* lost, wouldn't she have a TextMarker™ homing beacon on her?"

"True—but Textual Sieve coverage is patchy even in Fiction, and absent entirely across at least two-thirds of the BookWorld. We've sent unmanned probes into the most impenetrable tomes at Antiquarian and dispatched agents into almost every genre there is—nothing. The BookWorld is a big place. We've even considered that she might be in the DRM."

I raised an eyebrow. If they were considering this, they really were desperate. The DRM was the Dark Reading Matter—the unseeable part of the BookWorld.

"It's been almost two weeks," continued Bradshaw, "and I fear that something dreadful might have happened."

"Dead?"

"Worse—retired back to the RealWorld."

He stopped and stared at me. It wasn't just Thursday's absence from Jurisfiction that he was worried about; he had lost a good friend, too. Thursday trusted Commander Bradshaw implicitly. I thought I should do likewise.

"I sneak-peeked the Outland yesterday," I said. "I realize it was wrong. But it seemed to me that Landen was missing her, too."

Bradshaw raised an eyebrow. "Truthfully?"

"Yes, sir."

He took a sip of the cocktail, set it down and strode about the compartment for some minutes.

"Look here," he said, "desperate situations call for desperate measures. I want you to talk to Landen and see if you can find out anything. Perhaps locate her in time for the peace talks."

"Talk to Landen? How can I do that?"

"By traveling to the RealWorld."

My heart nearly missed a beat.

"You're joking."

"No joke, Miss Next. In fact, I'll *tell* you a joke so you'll know the difference. How many Sigmund Freuds does it take to change a lightbulb?"

"I've heard it."

"You have? Blast. In any event, you look *exactly* like Thursday—the best cover in the world. And what could possibly go wrong?"

There was actually quite a lot, but before I could itemize the first sixteen, Bradshaw had moved on.

"Splendid. All transfictional travel has been strictly banned this past eighteen months, so you'll be doing this covertly. If anyone finds out, I'll deny everything. Most of all, you can't tell anyone from the Council of Genres. If Jobsworth or Red Herring finds I've been breaking the transfictional travel embargo, they'll want to send their own. And I can't have that. Do you understand?"

"Yes, but—"

"Then that's all agreed," said Bradshaw, rising from his seat and handing me a signed authorization. "This will give you access to Norland Park to see Professor Plum on the pretext of adding e-book accelerators to your series. He'll know why you're there. I'll also contact my deep-cover agents to offer you every assistance in the Outland. Any questions?"

I had several hundred, but didn't know where to start. Bradshaw took my silence to mean I didn't have any, and he shook me by the hand.

"Good to have you on board. Twelve hours in the RealWorld isn't long, but enough to at least get an idea of what's happened to her. I could send you out for longer, but Thursday has many enemies in the RealWorld, and they'll be onto you pretty quick. If you die in the RealWorld, you die for real, and I'm not having that on my conscience. Shall we say tomorrow morning? Oh, and officially speaking, I was never here."

"You were never here."

"Good show. Appreciate a girl who knows she wasn't somewhere. Oh, and thank your man for the Chicago Fizz, will you? But next time a little less gherkin. Cheerio."

And without another word, he opened the outside door, a motorcycle drew alongside the train, Bradshaw hopped onto the pillion and was gone.

"Might I inquire of madam what that was all about?" asked Sprockett, who returned with a very ill-looking clown.

"A little too much gherkin in the Chicago Fizz."

"He came all the way over here just to tell you that?"

"No—I'm going to the RealWorld to look for Thursday so we can get her to the peace talks on Friday."

"In that case," said Sprockett, "I'd better lay out your things. Will madam be staying long?"

"Twelve hours."

"I'll pack you a toothbrush, a scrunchie and some clean socks."

"I'd be grateful."

I spent the rest of the journey fretting about my trip to reality. It was only a twelve-hour trip—barely a flash in and out—but that wasn't important. What *was* important was that I would meet Landen in person, and although the notion of that filled me with a tingly sensation of anticipation, his rejection of me when he found out I wasn't his wife would be . . . well, not pleasant—for him and for me. I almost thought of not going. Bradshaw couldn't exactly punish me for not doing something he hadn't told me to do. But then there was the possibility that I might help to find Thursday, and that filled me with the same sense of purpose I'd felt when I lied to Lockheed and Captain Phantastic. I sighed inwardly. Life was easier when I was just a character in a book, going from Preface to Acknowledgments without a care in the world. Within another twenty minutes, the train steamed into Gaiman Junction, and we took the bus home.

"You're back," said Pickwick, who liked to open any conversation by pointing out the obvious.

"Yes indeed," I replied. "What's the news?"

"My water dish is empty."

"That's because you just trod in it."

Pickwick looked at her foot. "I have a wet foot . . . and my water dish is empty."

"Anything else?"

"I saw Carmine with that goblin again. Sitting in the *niche d'amour* at the bottom of the garden, they were."

"As long as she doesn't invite him over the threshold again, I'm not bothered."

"You should be. Goblins. *Nasty.* Full of diseases."

"That's Carmine's problem. I told you, I'm not bothered."

Actually, I was. I had tried to give Carmine a dressing-down for her poor choice in men, but she'd just stared at me and retorted that yes, Horace *might* be a thief, but at least he hadn't set fire to a busload of nuns.

"Any news of Whitby?" I asked.

"Being questioned in custardy," replied Mrs. Malaprop, who had walked in with a clipboard full of reports that all needed my signature. "His pasta is catching up with him. How were things at Jurisfiction?"

I didn't tell them what had happened as it was safer that way.

"Captain Phantastic mentioned you owed him a date," I said to Pickwick.

"The Captain?" she said with a fond smile. "I'm amazed he remembers—it was a long time ago. We were both young and foolish, and I'd do anything for a dare. Ah, Frederic—so many cats, so little recipes."

"*Few* recipes."

"What?"

"So many cats, so *few* recipes," I said, pleased that I had figured out who'd been talking earlier.

Pickwick looked at me disdainfully, muttered "amateur" and marched out.

"The investigation is still on," I said to Mrs. Malaprop as soon as Pickwick had gone, "but keep it under your hat, will you?"

"Squirtainly, ma'am. I found this note pinned to the newel post."

> Gone to find Horace, back in half an hour.
> P.S.: I don't care what Pickwick thinks.

"Horace?"

"The goblin."

I wasn't particularly annoyed with Carmine for chasing after the goblin—as long as he wasn't invited back in again—but I *was* very annoyed that she had gone AWOL. It meant that for the past ten minutes there'd been no one here to play Thursday. If word had gotten out, there might have been a panic from the other characters, and it was against at least nine regulations that I could think of.

"Do we report her as absinthe without leaf?" asked Mrs. Malaprop.

I scrunched up the note. Reporting her as missing would get Jurisfiction involved, and Carmine would probably be shipped off to spend the next decade in *Roger Red Hat*.

"No," I said, "but let me know the moment she gets back so I can give her a ticking off."

Sprockett knocked and entered, his eyebrow pointing firmly at the "Worried" mark.

"Excuse me, ma'am, but the Men in Plaid are back."

"So soon? You better admit th—"

"Thursday Next?" said the first of the MiP as he walked in the door.

"Yes?"

"You're coming with us," said the second.

"I can't leave the series," I said. "My understudy is at lunch."

"That's not what the board says," observed the first, pointing at Carmine's status on the indicator board, which was now blinking an orange "at readiness" light, despite the fact that she was out looking for Horace. "Is she AWOL?"

"No," I lied.

"Then she's in?"

"Yes," I lied again.

"Then you can come with us."

I looked at Malaprop and Sprockett. They knew what needed to be done—find Carmine at the earliest opportunity.

The Man in Plaid who seemed to be in charge jerked a thumb in the direction of the front door, and we walked outside. Predictably, there was a Buick Roadmaster, but that wasn't the end of the story. The left-hand mudguard was dented and streaked with yellow paint—the sort of yellow paint that taxis are finished in. This was the car that had forced us off the road and into the mimefield.

"Am I in some sort of trouble?"

"You are if you don't come with us."

17.

The Council of Genres

The Council of Genres is the administrative body that looks after all aspects of BookWorld regulation, from policy decisions in the main debating chamber to the day-to-day running of ordinary BookWorld affairs, supply of plot devices and even the word supply coming in from the Text Sea. It controls the Book Inspectorate, which governs which books are to be published and which to be demolished, and also manages Text Grand Central and Jurisfiction.

Bradshaw's BookWorld Companion (11th edition)

I sat between the Men in Plaid in the back, which was uncomfortable, as they seemed to have a plethora of weapons beneath their suits, all of which poked me painfully in the ribs.

"So," I said brightly, doing what I hoped Thursday would do—showing no fear. "How long have you been in plaid?"

"It's not plaid. It's tartan."

"Right," said the second one, "tartan."

And despite more questions of a similar nature, they declined to talk further. I hoped to goodness that Mrs. Malaprop and Sprockett managed to hunt down Carmine in time for the early-evening readers.

We drove past Political Thriller on the Ludlum Freeway and made our way towards the towering heights of the Great Library, and I guessed where we were headed. On the twenty-sixth floor would be the Council of Genres and Senator Jobsworth, the man from whom the Men in Plaid ultimately drew their authority. Like Bradshaw, he must have figured out a way in which a Thursday Next look-alike could be used.

The security was even tighter here, and the Roadmaster slowed to negotiate the concrete roadblocks and high anti-bookjump mesh. We were waved through with only a cursory glance and drove across a narrow bridge and into the Ungenred Zone. This was an area of independent, narrative-free space where the governing body of the BookWorld could exist free from influence and bias. Or at least that was the theory. I'd been a few times to the Council of Genres, but only with the real Thursday. Ordinary citizens didn't come here unless strictly on business. If we wanted to pretend we had influence, we could take any grievances to our genre representatives, and they would intercede on our behalf—or so the theory went.

"Where are you taking me?" I asked.

"Right to the very top."

"That high, huh?"

Having the Great Library and the Ungenred Zone on Fiction Island was not without problems. Theoretically speaking, if it was located here, then it must be potentially readable by the RealWorld population, something about which the CofG was not happy. If it became common knowledge that there was a text-based realm on the other side of the printed page, hacking into the BookWorld would be a far bigger problem than it was already. The Outlander corporation known as Goliath had been attempting to find a way in for decades, but aside from their transfictional tour bus, quaintly named the Austen Rover and the occasional bookhacker, the independent existence of the BookWorld remained secret.

Even so, council officials were taking no chances, and the entire Ungenred Zone was rendered invisible to potential bookhackers by the simple expedient of not being written about. At least not directly. The adventures in my own series hinted at a BookWorld but these were heavily fictionalized, since the ghostwriter had no collaboration from Thursday when writing them. There was only the vaguest reference to the Great Library, and nothing about Jurisfiction or the Council of Genres. Despite this, some of the more talented readers in the Outland had managed to hack into the zone by exploiting a hole in the defenses that allowed one to "read between the lines." To counter this, the CofG had all the borders covered in soporific paint the shade of young lettuces, which worked like a charm. Every attempted incursion into the Ungenred Zone was met by drowsiness followed by an almost instantaneous torpor on the part of the potential hacker. It had exactly the same effect as the emergency Snooze Button, except that no kittens were ever hurt or injured.

The Roadmaster drove up to the BookWorld's main port, where the Metaphoric River joined the Text Sea by a series of locks, weirs, traps and sluices. The port was large, and several hundred scrawl trawlers rode gently in the swell, grammasites wheeling above the mast tops, hoping to dart down and snatch a dropped article. On the dockside was the day's catch. Most scrawlers simply netted the words that basked upon the surface for a quick and easy sale to the wordsmiths, while others deep-trawled for binary clause systems, whereby a verb and a noun had clumped together in a symbiotic relationship to form a protosentence. But even these hardened scrawlers were in awe of those who hunted fully formed sentences. These weather-beaten sea dogs would sail far across the Text Sea in search of an entire paragraph, a descriptive zinger or even an original comedy monologue—the elusive Moby-Shtick that legends speak of.

Facing the docks and beyond the coils of ropes, nets, harpoons and infinitive splitters were several rows of single-story workshops where the words and letters were crocheted, knitted, sewed, glued, riveted or nailed together into sentences, depending on the softness of the prose to which they were destined. The completed sentences were either rough-sorted into bundles and sold direct to the Well of Lost Plots or woven into standard paragraphs on power looms, the nouns, verbs and adjectives left loose so the end users could make their own choices.

The Buick pulled to a stop outside the main entrance of the Great Library, and we climbed out. The library was housed in a towering Gothic skyscraper that stood as a reminder of the BookWorld before it was remade. Back then the area below the Great Library had been simply unexplored jungle. All that was swept away in the nine minutes of the remaking. The Book-World may be slow when it comes to changing fashions and storytelling conventions, but it can rebuild itself in a flash if required.

I paused for a moment. It was impossible not to be impressed by the Great Library, and this in a world noted for its superlative structures, settings and depth. Just by way of example, the landscape inside *Lord of the Rings* was *so* stunning and *so* stupendous that it could be absorbed as a form of nourishment. The huge tourism opportunities within the trilogy had been long understood and exploited, and even though the battles were exciting and fun to watch, most people went only for the valleys, rivers, waterfalls, crags, trees and moss.

I stepped into the lobby of the library and paid my respects to those names on the Boojumorial—a marble tablet that commemorated Jurisfiction agents from both the RealWorld and the BookWorld who had lost their lives in the protection of the written word. They may have been carbon- or text-based, but here they were equal; no preference was given to the real over the imaginary. My companions, however, due either to indifference or to long acquaintance with the "Honored Erased," paid it no heed at all. We walked towards the circular void that ran through the building, and I looked up. Twenty-six floors above us, the glazed roof was just visible. Twenty-six floors of every book that had ever been written, and here logged faithfully in alphabetical order for mostly serial-continuity purposes. It wasn't necessary to have the library anymore, but it paid to have a backup in case something went wrong. And something always *did* go wrong. Although infuriating, it was unavoidable. With all the drama at hand, it was inevitable that the BookWorld would spontaneously erupt into intrigue, which would then set off a chain reaction of unexpected consequence. If the Book-World were itself a book, it would be self-writing.

I glanced down. Below me were the twenty-six basements that made up the Well of Lost Plots—the place where all books are built. As I looked, I could see flashes of light as inspiration fired off in small bursts of energy. A really good idea could burn brightly for many months and give nearby books-in-progress much-needed warmth.

We entered the elevator, and I felt myself grow increasingly apprehensive as the ancient lift slowly clanked its way to the top. The senator's summons might have been related to Bradshaw's recent request, to our chance meeting in Norland Park or to something else entirely—I had no idea. The lift doors opened, and the CofG spread out in front of us, a seething mass of offices, desks, meeting rooms and people scurrying back and forth in a ceaseless quest to keep the BookWorld running as efficiently as possible. The chamber was bigger in here than it appeared from the outside, but nothing was particularly linear or even logical within the BookWorld; the fabric of imagination is elastic, and that reflected itself within the Council of Genres.

I passed the big viewing windows, where I had stood with the real Thursday when she was my mentor, and peered out at a BookWorld that appeared deceptively orderly. Because I was quite high and the island dished to fit snugly on the inside face of the sphere, I could clearly see every part of it, from the volcanoes in the far north all the way down to Vanity Island off the southern tip. I could even see my own series as a dark smudge in the distance.

I was escorted away from the viewing windows and walked past the public gallery above the debating chamber. There was a session in progress, and although it was being conducted in **Courier Bold,** the antiquated yet universal language of the BookWorld, I could make out that it was a discussion about the possibility of Text Sea levels rising due to the advent of e-books. I'd heard about this issue. The argument went that because e-books were composed almost entirely of electrons and barely any ink and paper at all, the scrawl trawlers' work would be cut by 90 percent overnight, and there was a possibility for inundation of the low-lying areas of the BookWorld—essentially Maritime and Disaster. This argument was countered by a delegate who maintained that e-books were the way of the future, and since the power of a book is undiminished irrespective of the carrier medium, no such panic was necessary. Still another delegate suggested that the advent of e-books might actually *increase* the demand for new material and thus cause a shortage of words—something for which the BookWorld must be prepared by the construction of more scrawl trawlers and the training of extra scrawlermen. All three were experts, and all three had conflicting views. I was reminded of Clarke's Second Law of Egodynamics: "For every expert there is an equal and opposite expert."

"Come on," said one of the Plaids. "We're not bleeding tour guides."

We walked down a corridor, past more security, then arrived at an opulent antechamber with expansive views across the BookWorld.

"Miss Next?" said a friendly clerk holding a clipboard. "The senator will see you now."

18.

Senator Jobsworth

Dark Reading Matter: the hypothetical last resting place of books never published, ideas never penned and poems held only in the heart by poets who died without passing them on. Theoretical bibliologists have proved that the Background Story Radiation was appreciably more than the apparent quantity of STORY in the BookWorld. No one had any idea where it might be or how you could reach it. DRM's existence remained theoretical, at best.

Bradshaw's BookWorld Companion (4th edition)

The senator was sitting behind his desk as I was ushered into his office. Several men and women dressed in the uniform of almost every military conflict there was were in attendance, as well as a couple of high-ranking generals, Colonel Barksdale and Commander Herring, the chief of staff.

"Would you excuse us?" said the senator, and everyone except Red Herring and Colonel Barksdale filed out, looking at me suspiciously as they did so. I stood in front of Jobsworth's desk while he finished what he was doing. I didn't know which book he had come from, but wagging tongues suggested he was an illegal immigrant from Quackery, a subgenre within Lies & Self-Delusion, just off the north coast. I don't think anyone ever raised it with him, or if they did, no answer was forthcoming. It didn't really much matter, since Jobsworth had been the overall leader of the Council of Genres for as long as it had been in existence, and his unassailable position as head of the council looked set to continue far into the future. He had the ear, apparently, of the Great Panjandrum himself, who could fix almost everything when he had a mind to.

"They say she's dead, you know," said Jobsworth, striding to the large window in his office that looked out over the Book-World, the islands of the various categories of books patches of verdant green against the dark slatey gray of the Text Sea. "Killed in the Outland, killed in the BookWorld—who knows? What do you think?"

"I have no opinion on the matter, sir. I just play her in the series."

"You must have *some* idea."

I looked across at the chief of staff, who was gazing at me intently. "No."

Jobsworth stared at me for a long while, then grunted and looked outside his office again. Yet this time he wasn't looking at the larger BookWorld, but rather at the island of Fiction below him. The Ungenred Zone was on the west coast about halfway up. Crime was just to the north, but the areas I knew best—Adventure, Fantasy and Sci-Fi—were situated in the southeast, out of sight. It was Herring who spoke next.

"Ever been up-country?"

"I've been to Crime."

"Farther. Towards Racy Novel."

"No."

"So there is a good chance they haven't seen you up there? Or even know about you?"

I suddenly had a very unpleasant feeling and turned back to Jobsworth. "What is it you want me to do, Senator?"

"A small favor. I wouldn't ask you if it wasn't important. And if you do this for us, I'm sure it will be to your benefit if you reapply to join Jurisfiction."

I was right. If that was the carrot, I could be in for some serious stick.

"It's nothing too onerous," added Colonel Barksdale, who had so many campaign medals on his chest that he was probably bulletproof. "It simply requires you to take Thursday's place at the peace talks on Friday."

I was momentarily at a loss for words. I should have tried to extricate myself, but I had paused too long.

"Splendid," said Jobsworth, crossing to a scale model of the island that was built upon a large oak table. "Let me give you some background."

"Would you excuse me?" said Herring. "I have to revise the upcoming Linguistic Hygiene Bill if we're to have any chance of rejecting it."

"Thank you, Red."

Herring wished me good day, thanked me for my selfless adherence to duty and walked from the room. Jobsworth beckoned me closer to the large model of the island, where the topography was perfectly realized in miniature, including the individual genres along with their borders, railway networks, major rivers and capital novels. He swept his hand in the direction of the Northern Genres.

"You've heard about Speedy Muffler's threats and the peace talks on Friday?"

I said that I had.

"Speedy Muffler claims to have developed a dirty bomb," announced Jobsworth with a grimace, "a loosely bound collection of badly described scenes of a sexual nature. The detonation of such a bomb could cause untold damage, flinging wholly gratuitous sex scenes as far as *Mrs. Dalloway*."

"But has he really?" I asked, since the possession of the bomb was only conjecture, much like Comedy's claim to be experimenting with a fifty-megaton-yield deep satire device.

"Do you know," said Jobsworth, "it doesn't matter. Feminism and Dogma are taking the threat seriously and are massing armies on the border ready to take preemptive action ahead of the peace talks. And we can't have that."

"Invasion?" I said. "What would Feminism and Dogma do with Racy Novel?"

"They'll simply push the rogue genre up north towards Porn and De Sade. *Fanny Hill, The Story of* O and *The Adventures of Tom Jones* will be annexed back into Classics, and the territory shared between them. Comedy will still insist upon the buffer zone of Bedroom Farce, and since Comedy is regarded with a certain sense of reluctant admiration by Romance and Dogma, they'll not want to go any farther."

He took a deep breath.

"But we can't risk that kind of disruption. The genres might take months to rebuild to current strength, and the prose will suffer terribly. With the advent of e-books in the Outland, this is not a good time to have a cross-genre war. The battle between Sci-Fi and Horror all those years ago has still left its mark; their reputations as serious literature have still to recover completely—and the civil war inside Fantasy has left the reading public with an entirely unwarranted dismal view of the genre. I can't have Romance and Female Crime marginalized in the same way—they're 43.9 percent of our readership."

"I'm not sure what I can do," I said. "I'm not much good at negotiating. I tend to want everyone to simply hug and make up."

"I'm not asking you to *do* anything, you little fool. We're putting it about that you—the *real* Thursday—has irritable vowel syndrome and can't speak, so Emperor Zhark will be doing the talking. You'll just sit there and nod and look serious. Muffler might be a troublemaker, but even he will knuckle under if he thinks Thursday Next might be annoyed if he shouts too loudly. How about it?"

He was asking too much. No, it was more than that—*insane,*

even by Council of Genre standards. If Muffler found out I wasn't her, things might get even worse, and I wasn't going to have a cross-genre war on my conscience.

"I may have to politely decline," I said.

He stared at me for a moment, then opened a manila folder on his desk.

"Hmm," he said, "looks like we have a lot of illegal narrative flexations in your series, doesn't it?"

"I'm playing Thursday as Thursday wants me to."

"We have only your word for that. There is also a possible charge of your understudy consorting with undesirables and, most seriously, your harboring an illegal alien from Vanity."

He meant Sprockett.

"We call it Self-Publishing these days."

"Immaterial. We'll be taking the Metaphoric River route up-country via paddle steamer. I'll have a car pick you up Friday morning at 0700. Are we agreed?"

I took a deep breath. "Yes, sir."

"Excellent!"

He pressed a button on his desk.

"Miss Next, you must also understand that in matters of BookWorld politics like this, it is essential you do not speak of this to anyone, *especially* that busybody Bradshaw. Jurisfiction has a twisted vision of the good work we do at the council, and I don't want him to get the wrong idea. Do you understand?"

If there was any lingering doubt that the CofG and Jurisfiction distrusted each other, it was dispelled. Neither wanted the other to know what it was asking me to do. The clerk came back in, and I was escorted from the building by the same two Men in Plaid who had brought me there.

In a very short time, I was deposited back at my front door, and the Roadmaster pulled silently away. Sprockett was waiting for me in the hall, his single eyebrow pointer clicking alternately between "Quizzical" and "Uncomfortable."

But he knew what to do.

"Can I interest ma'am in a Ludlow Scorcher?"

I told him a cocktail would go down very well so long as he went easy on the parsley, and then I related what had just happened with Jobsworth. I decided not to mention the threats he'd made regarding Sprockett and Carmine, but I *did* mention that I would be going up-country on Friday—and also the dent and the streak of yellow paint on the Men in Plaid's Buick Roadmaster.

"The fact that they haven't tried to kill us again tends to indicate that they believe we have abandoned the investigation," said Sprockett, handing me the cocktail. "Are you sure it was *our* yellow paint on the side of their Roadmaster?"

"What else is painted yellow in the BookWorld?"

As soon as I said it, I suddenly remembered something. I stood up and quickly walked to the garage at the bottom of the garden, Sprockett close behind.

"Ma'am?" he said as I swung up the double doors and started to poke amongst the book junk for what I was looking for. I found it easily enough: the back axle that had once been painted yellow. There was no sign of an ISBN, scrubbed or otherwise.

"It wasn't from *The Murders on the Hareng Rouge*," I said excitedly. "It's from a TransGenre Taxi. I rode back from Poetry stuck onto the side of an ocean tanker, part of a book about the Bermuda Triangle. There was a taxi attached to *Murders* when it went down, piggybacking from one part of the BookWorld to another. The sabotage might not have been aimed at the book at all—*it might have been aimed at whoever was in the cab!*"

"Or both," said Sprockett, annoyingly muddying the waters.

"Or both," I agreed.

"Where *is* the rest of the cab?" asked Sprockett.

"Who knows? Either vaporized or embedded somewhere in the unread backwaters of Thriller. Here's the deal: You're going to call the TransGenre Taxi offices and find out about any missing cabs, and I'm going to find out more about *The Murders on the Hareng Rouge* and Adrian Dorset."

"But where, ma'am? If Captain Phantastic doesn't know, it's unknowable."

"In the RealWorld, Sprockett. Cheers."

I tried the Scorcher. It wasn't too bad. A bit loamy for my taste, but otherwise good.

I went upstairs and packed a small tote bag. A few clothes and some spare underwear—I'd heard all the scare stories—then worried about taking my pistol or not, but eventually I did. After that I dithered over taking ammunition and decided to, but only one cartridge and of the armor-piercing variety. I argued to myself that I would be too scared to use it, so I wouldn't. I gave Carmine some last-minute instructions in case of emergencies, ignored her protestations about "having to face more readers than she was happy with" and then ordered a cab. "If I have to press the Snooze Button," said Mrs. Malaprop as I waited, "it's on your conch séance, not mine."

"Agreed."

"Where to?" asked the cabbie when he pulled up ten minutes later.

"Norland Park," I said, "*Sense and Sensibility*. Any route you like."

But at that moment someone else got into the cab by way of the opposite door. He was wearing a large floppy hat that partially obscured his features.

"Sorry," I said, "cab taken."

The other passenger lifted the brim of the hat so I could see his face. It was Whitby.

"It's okay," I said to the cabbie, and we moved off.

"Holy cow!" I said, turning to Whitby, "you've got a nerve. When were you going to tell me about setting fire to that busload of nuns? Two years I spent building myself up to a date, and then I find that you're a homicidal maniac."

"*Lots* of people are homicidal maniacs," he replied. "Throw a stick into Crime and you'll hit six of them."

"But we're not in Crime, are we?"

He stared at me for a moment. "I've done lots of good in my life, Thursday—helped people to narrative independence, coached Generics through entrance exams, was EZ-Read's Employee of the Month three months running, and I even helped little old ladies across the road—some when they actually wanted to go. Do I get credit for that? No. All you want to think about is the nuns."

"*Orphaned* nuns," I reminded him.

"Actually, it was the puppies who were orphaned," he said petulantly. "Let's stick to the facts here."

"Does it matter?"

"Not really. But I don't think that one teensy-weensy incident with a small busload of nuns and puppies should taint a man's life."

"I think it does, Whitby. You might have told me."

"I couldn't."

"Why?"

He sighed. "You remember Dermot McGruber? EZ-Read's rep over in HumDram?"

"Yes."

"He wanted to impress a girl. But he'd done some seriously bad shit when he was a character in Crime."

"The nuns?"

"Right. With a backstory like that hanging around his neck and guilt consuming his every moment, he couldn't even *begin* to get a date. So I said I'd look after his backstory for the weekend so he could ask her out, guilt-free and with an easy heart."

"That was generous of you."

He shrugged. "He helped me out once when I over-ordered some EZ-Read PlotHoleFiller. I owed him. A weekend of all-consuming guilt seemed easy enough. I could keep myself to myself, get totally hyphenated, and no one need ever know."

"Let me guess," I said. "He's legged it."

Whitby nodded as the cabbie changed down a gear and moved onto the Dickens Freeway.

"I don't know where Dermot's gone. In fact, I think he might have been planning this for a while. I feel such an idiot—and what's more, I think he put Jurisfiction onto me. You won't tell them, will you?"

"Not yet, but I will. You can't set fire to people—nuns or otherwise—and expect to get away with it."

"I know," he said sadly. "It weighs heavily on my conscience. The yapping, oh, the *yapping*."

I sat in silence for a moment. The thing about backstories is that once you've taken one on, they're true and real, irrespective of who owned them before you. You could pass it on, of course, but it was understandably tricky. Who wants a busload of burning nuns and puppies on his conscience?

"So what do you want?" I asked.

"I just wanted to see you," he said simply, "and hear your voice."

"Well, now you have," I replied, a bit more harshly than perhaps I should have. "Maybe we should say good-bye."

"I'm living over in Hemingway if you need anything," he said, not wanting to give up on the slimmest chance a date was still possible. "Page 127, *To Have and Have Not*. If you need anything, just whistle. You can drop me on this corner, driver."

The cabbie pulled up, and Whitby got out. He told me to take care and then hurried off around a street corner. The taxi moved on, and I slumped back into my seat as we turned onto Austen Boulevard. I thought of turning him in, then of not turning him in. It was a tricky call, but luckily the least of my worries.

I wasn't feeling that good about the trip, to be honest. A

nervy, sickly feeling was festering in the pit of my stomach—and not just from the difficulty of making the move across, or what I might find there or the truth about *The Murders on the Hareng Rouge*. Notwithstanding the recent developments with Whitby, I was most worried about meeting Landen. He was the man I was written to love and never meet. And now I was going to meet him.

19.

JurisTech, Inc.

The JurisTech Museum is open Monday to Friday, a half day on Wednesday. A whole range of technologies both past and present is on display, including an impressive array of BookWorld weaponry, grammasite traps, word dams, Eject-O-Hats, TextMarkers, grapheme splitters and noun-to-verb alchemical technologies. On Tuesdays there is a technical demonstration of the Textual Sieve (not to be missed).

Bradshaw's BookWorld Companion (3rd edition)

I turned up at the front gate of *Sense and Sensibility* and showed the guards the authorization given to me by Bradshaw. The guards rang through and spoke briefly to JurisTech before I was once more issued a docket and ushered in. I met the frog-footman at the front door, who was surprised to see me again so soon.

"You again?" he said, staring at the docket. "What do you want with JurisTech?"

Fortified by the mission entrusted to me by Bradshaw, I was no longer so frightened of him.

"None of your business," I replied, and his face lit up. This was more how he liked it.

"Labs or office?"

"Labs."

He guided me though the long corridors of Norland Park, down several flights of steps and an elevator or two before we stopped outside an inconspicuous door with a pair of milk bottles outside.

"The JurisTech Labs," announced the frog-footman. "My instructions are to wait for you."

"It'll be a long wait. Pick me up in twelve hours. Here," I said, handing him a Rubik's Cube. "See if you can figure this out."

The frog-footman stared at the cube curiously. All six faces were quite naturally the same color, and all was orderly and neat.

"You have to try to make it random," I said, "by twisting the faces."

The frog-footman twisted the faces in a fairly haphazard manner, but try as he might, every face remained the same color. For a BookWorld puzzle, it was a classic. The lack of randomness within the orderly structure of the BookWorld tended not to permit disorder. As far as I knew, no one had yet managed to scramble a Rubik's, but I thought it might pass the time for him.

"Thank you," replied the frog-footman, and he sat cross-legged on the floor, twisting the cube this way and that as he tried to scramble the faces.

I knocked on the door, and it was soon answered by a small man in a brown boiler suit that was liberally covered in oil stains, food and science merit badges.

"Good Lord!" he said when he saw me. "Thursday? Come inside quick."

Once safely away from the prying ears of the frog-footman, I explained who I was—or, more important, who I wasn't—and showed Professor Plum the authorization from Bradshaw.

"Did he give you a code word?"

"What?"

"A code word."

"The commander didn't say anything about a code word."

"Correct. There is no code word—but only Bradshaw would know that. Follow me."

The basement was twice the size of a cathedral and quite full to capacity with machinery. An army of technicians scurried around looking purposeful while lights blinked on and off as arcs of electricity discharged into the air at regular intervals.

"That's mostly for effect," explained Plum as we moved among the machines. "It's sometimes of equal importance to have a machine's form and function in equilibrium. Who wants an italicizer that can be carried around in the pocket? Much better to have a large device that flashes lights randomly and occasionally goes bzzz."

I agreed, even if I'd never *seen* an italicizer, much less *used* one.

"All this technology," I mused. "Is there any limit to what you can do?"

"If there is, we haven't found it," replied Plum. "We can figure out most technologies, and those that we can't are subcontracted to Technobabble™ Industries, which can usually cobble something together. The good thing about being in the BookWorld is that we aren't hampered by anything as awkward as physical laws. The RealWorld must be hideously annoying to do science in, but given how difficult it is, I suppose breakthroughs are of greater value. In here, for example, perpetual-motion machines are quite feasible."

"What's stopping us from using them?"

"Finding a way to make them *stop*. Once we've figured that out, we'll have perpetual engines in every minicab and bus in the BookWorld."

He paused while I stared at a machine that could transform dark humor to sarcasm and then back again with no loss of narrative mass.

"As you know," continued Plum, "the Council of Genres permits us to suspend the rules of physics in order that we can develop the somewhat unique technologies that the BookWorld requires. See this?"

We had stopped next to a large machine that seemed to be nothing but a riveted tube about a yard thick running through the entire length of the workshop. It appeared through one wall and then vanished out the other. If I hadn't known any better, I would have thought it a throughput pipe or a footnoterphone conduit.

"This is just a small part of the Large Metaphor Collider."

"What does that do?"

Professor Plum stopped for a moment at the control panel. "You know we've got a serious metaphor deficit at present?"

I nodded. The problem was well documented. Most of Fiction's rhetorical power, dramatic irony and pathos were brought naturally by the mighty Metaphoric River that snaked about the island. But the huge influx of novels in the past century had exacted a burden on the waterway as the much-needed metaphor was abstracted on a massive scale, and these days it was no longer considered possible that the river could supply all of Fiction's requirements, hence the trade in raw metaphor and JurisTech's attempts to synthesize it.

"This collider," continued Professor Plum, "will take depleted metaphor—simile, in effect—and accelerate it in a circular trackway over eighteen miles long to a velocity approaching ninety-five percent of absurd, at which point it will be collided with indisputable fact. There is a brief flash of energy as the two different modes of communication are fused together and then explode in a burst of high-energy subcomprehension particles. We then record the event as traces on a sheet of onionskin paper."

"The flimsy blue variety?"

"*Exactly.* In this manner we hope not only to figure out the individual building blocks of STORY in order to have a better understanding of how it all works but also to use it as a way of extracting usable quantities of metaphor from even the most prosaic, tired or clumsily constructed simile."

"Does it work?"

"I was just about to test it. You can help if you want."

I said I would be delighted, and Plum pointed me in the direction of a lidded crucible that was steaming gently to itself.

"You'll find some tongs and gloves over there—I need that simile in the accelerator chamber."

He carried on with his measurements. The crucible was steaming not from heat but from cold. Liquid nitrogen was keeping a raw simile in an inactive state. So much so that I couldn't tell what it was, as the meaning and allusion were all contracted and frozen into one lump. I put on the glove and, using the wooden pincers, placed the simile in the acceleration chamber.

"Excellent," said Plum, who closed the door and spun a wheel on the front to effect a secure lock. He then pressed a button, and there was a low humming noise, which gradually increased in pitch as the simile started to move around the accelerator. There was a dial marked "Absurd Velocity," and the needle began to rise as the simile zipped round at ever-increasing speeds.

"The Council of Genres is very keen to have this up and running as soon as possible," he said, staring at the dials carefully. "Synthesizing metaphor is the holy grail of the BookWorld, if you don't count finding the Holy Grail, which confusingly is *also* the holy grail of the BookWorld."

The Large Metaphor Collider had by now wound itself up to a whine so high-pitched that I couldn't hear it, and all the equipment on the desk was vibrating. As the needle nudged up to .95 Absurd, Plum took a deep breath and pressed the red button, which instantaneously brought indisputable fact into the path of the absurdly fast simile.

It is difficult to describe what happened next. The machine

changed from being something akin to an engine with a throttle stuck wide open to that of a Brave New Dawn. I saw the Clouds Open and the Rain Stop. The Lark Ascended, and I saw Saint John on the island of Patmos, and a New Heaven and a New Earth. I saw— But in another second, those feelings had vanished, and all we were left with was the collider, humming down to speed.

"What was that?" I asked.

"A sudden flash of pure metaphor," replied Plum excitedly. "This kind of event usually liberates about a hundred and twenty PicoMets."

"Is that safe?"

"Don't worry," he said with a smile. "The background metaphor level is about fifty PicoMets, and a fatal dose is up around the forty-MilliMet mark. You'd have to do something daft for that to happen, although there have been accidents. A few years ago, a colleague of mine was experimenting with a few grams of dead metaphor when it went critical. He was bathed in almost a hundred MilliMets and started barking on about Prometheus stealing fire from the gods before he exploded into a ball of fire and ascended into the night sky, where he could be seen for many weeks, a salutary lesson of the dangers of playing with metaphor. Wrecked the laboratory, too. Let me see."

Professor Plum pulled the single sheet of onionskin from the annihilation chamber and looked at it, brows knitted. The paper had recorded the subword particles. Some were dotted, others colored, some hatched. There was even a legend at the bottom explaining what each one meant. Fiction has no time for lengthy and potentially confusing data analysis, so experimentation is always followed by easily interpretable and generally unequivocal results.

"That's alliteration," said Plum, tracing the various paths with his finger. "Anaphora, epistrophe, epanalepsis, analepsis, hyperbole and polyptoton."

In all, he could list twenty-nine submeaning particles, but of pure metaphor there was no evidence at all.

"You felt it, though, didn't you?"

I answered that I had. A feeling of a new dawn and old things being swept away.

Plum stared at the paper for a long time. So long, in fact, that I thought he might have gone to sleep standing up and might need catching when he fell over.

"Well," he said at last, "back to the drawing board."

"But we felt something, didn't we?" I said.

"Without proof we've got nothing," he said in a resigned voice. "Perhaps metaphor has no mass. If so, I'm very surprised—although it might explain why Dark Reading Matter is undetectable. It could be mostly metaphorical. Come on. Let's get you real."

The professor led me to the back of the workshop, past the entrance to a scrubbing device for declichéing otherwise healthy idioms and down a corridor to a door obscured by several discarded packing cases and a stack of unread copies of the almost fatally dull *JurisTech Review*.

"We haven't used the Jumper for over eighteen months," he explained, struggling with a padlock that had grown rusty with age. "Not since the imaginatively titled 'RealWorld Travel Ban' banned all travel to the RealWorld."

"Why the ban?"

"I didn't ask, and neither should you. If anyone at the CoG gets wind of this, you and I are nothing but text."

I didn't like the sound of this.

"But Bradshaw—"

"Bradshaw is a good man," interrupted Plum, "but in matters like this he'd deny he even knew you. And me. And himself, it it came to that. I agree with him. To maintain the integrity of Jurisfiction, I would accept being reduced to a bucket of graphemes. And so should you."

He left me thinking about this and pulled open the door. He paused, the interior of the lab a dark hole.

"You can leave now if you want to."

"No, I'm okay," I said, even if I wasn't. "Let's just get on with it, yes?"

He turned on the light to reveal a large room that was musty and hung with cobwebs. Occasionally there was a low rumble, and dust trickled from the ceiling.

"The Carnegie Underpass," explained Plum. "It runs directly overhead."

In the middle of the room was a large machine that looked like a collection of sieves, each lined up one in front of the other. The sieves began with one that might have been designed to make chips, so long as you could hurl a potato at it fast enough, and the rest were of rapidly decreasing mesh, until the penulti-mate was no more than a fine wire gauze. The last of all was a thin sheet of silver that shimmered with the microscopic cur-rents of air that moved around the workshop. Beyond this was the wide end of a copper funnel with the sharp end finishing in a point no bigger than a pin—and beyond this a small drop of blue something-or-other within a localized gravitational field that kept it suspended in the air. Around the room was an array of computers covered with more dials, levers, switches and meters than I had ever seen before.

"What exactly is it?" I asked, not unnaturally and with a certain degree of trepidation.

"It's the Large Textual Sieve Array," he explained. "Although the construction and methodology of Textual Sieves remain generally unexplained, they can be used for a number of func-tions. Cross-triangulation searches, the 'locking' of text within books—and, more controversially, for making fictional people real, even if for only a short period."

"How long?"

"I can send you out for forty-eight hours, but Bradshaw insisted you go for only twelve. As soon as that time is up, you'll spontaneously return. We'll send you in at midday, and you'll be out at midnight—pumpkin hour. If you want to stay longer, you'll have to Blue Fairy, but then you're there for good and you'll have to suffer the worst rigors of being real—aging, death and daytime television.

The twelve-hour pumpkin option suited me fine, and I told him so. I'd heard many stories about the RealWorld, and although it sounded an interesting place to visit, you'd not want to live there.

"So how does it work?" I asked.

"Simplicity itself. You see this howitzer?"

He pointed at a large-caliber cannon that was pointed directly at the sieves. It was mounted on a small carriage and was gaily decorated with red stars and had THE FLYING ZAMBINIS painted on the side.

"You are placed in this cannon and then fired into the array at .346 Absurd speed. The mesh of the first sieve is quite broad, to break down your base description into individual words. The next breaks the words down into letters, and then the letters are divided further into subcalligraphic particles, until you hit the silver sheet, which has holes in it one-tenth the size of a polyptoton. After that," he concluded as he tapped the large funnel, "your descriptive dust is compressed in the Pittmanizer to a concentrated pellet of ultradense prose, where the several thousand words of your description take up less space than one-millionth of a period. Put it another way: If all Fiction were compressed to the same degree, it would take up the space of an average-size rabbit."

"I like comparative factoids like that."

"Me, too. This tiny speck of you is then injected at speed into a drop of AntiBook, where your essence is rebuilt into something closely resembling human. By controlling the Sieve Array, I can drop you wherever you want in the RealWorld."

"Does it hurt?"

"Quite a lot, actually," he admitted, "but only fleetingly. You'll barely have enough time to scream before it will be over. The return is not so dramatic. You'll simply find yourself in our arrivals suite, which is just behind that door."

"Do you have any advice?"

"I've never been there myself," confessed Plum, "but they say if you can handle the first ten minutes, you're good for the whole twelve hours. If you can't hack it, then just find a quiet wardrobe in which to hide until the free return brings you back."

I found his comments disconcerting.

"What is there that one might not be able to handle?"

Professor Plum made a clicky noise with his tongue. "It's highly disorderly," he explained, "not like here. There is no easily definable plot, and you can run yourself ragged wondering what the significance can be of a chance encounter. You'll also find that for the most part there is no shorthand to the narrative, so everything happens in a long and painfully drawn-out sequence. Apparently the talk can be confusing—for the most part, people just say the first thing that comes into their heads."

"Is it as bad as they say it is?"

"I've heard it's worse. Here in the BookWorld, we say what needs to be said for the story to proceed. Out there? Well, you can discount at least eighty percent of chat as just meaningless drivel."

"I never thought the percentage was *that* high."

"In some individuals it can be as high as ninety-two percent. The people to listen to are the ones who don't say very much."

"Oh."

"There are fun things, too," said Plum, sensing my disappointment. "You'll get used to it in the end, but if you go out there accepting that seventy-five percent of talk is utter twaddle and eighty-five percent of people's lives are spent dithering around, you won't go far wrong. But above all don't be annoyed or distracted when random things happen for absolutely no purpose."

"There's always a purpose," I said, amused by the notion of utter pointlessness, "even if you don't understand what it is until much later."

"That's the big difference between here and there," said Plum. "When things happen after a randomly pointless event, all that follows is simply unintended consequences, not a coherent narrative thrust that propels the story forward."

I rolled the idea of unintended consequences around in my head. "Nope," I said finally, "you've got me on that one."

"It confuses me, too," admitted Plum, "but that's the RealWorld for you. A brutal and beautiful place, run for the most part on passion, fads, incentives and mathematics. A *lot* of mathematics."

"That's it?" I asked, astonished by the brevity in which Plum could sum up the world that had, after all, made us.

"Pretty much," he replied glumly. "And some very good cuisine. And the smells. You'll like those, I assure you. And real sex—not like the oddly described stuff we have to make do with in here."

"I assure you I'm not going to the RealWorld for the sex."

"When tourism was permitted, many visitors used it for little else. Anything that is impossible to describe adequately in the BookWorld was much sought and, coincidentally, usually beginning with *c*: cooking, copulation, Caravaggio, coastlines and chocolate. Will you do me a favor and bring some back? I adore chocolate. As much as you can carry, in fact. And none of that Lindt or Nestlé muck—Cadbury's the thing."

I promised him I would, and he opened the hatch at the back of the cannon.

"Good luck," he said. "Don't worry if it seems a bit odd to

begin with. You're made in the image of the flesh-and-bloods, so there's nothing you can't figure out as long as you keep your wits about you. It helps if you crouch tight, like a hedgehog. It's why Mrs. Tiggy-winkle was so good at moving across."

I crawled inside and crunched myself up into the fetal position. Plum instructed me to hold my breath when he reached the count of two, as it helped to have a breath in you when you arrived, since breathing out can give a good indication of how breathing actually works. I thanked him for the advice, and he closed the hatch. I looked along the barrel of the cannon to the muzzle, and beyond that to the series of textual sieves that would chop me into the smallest component parts imaginable. I admit it, I was nervous. I waited for about a minute in the gloom, and then, when nothing had happened, I called out.

"Sorry!" came Plum's voice. "I'm just winding her up to speed. If I don't get you to *exactly* .346 of Absurd Speed, all you'll be is a tattered mass of text caught in the sieves. If I fire you too fast, you'll be embedded in the back of the laboratory."

"What would happen then?"

"Paper over you, I suppose."

I wasn't particularly reassured by this but waited patiently for another half minute until I heard a faint whine that grew in pitch as Plum counted down from ten. When he got to five, the whine had grown so loud I could hardly hear him, so I guessed when two would be and took a deep breath. I was just thinking that perhaps this wasn't such a great idea after all and I should really be getting back to my series and staying there for a sensible period of time—such as forever—when there was a noise like a thousand metallic frogs all croaking at the same time and my body was suddenly skewered by a thousand hot needles. Before I could cry out, the pain passed, and after a low hum and a sensation of treacle, Klein Blue and Wagner all mixed together but not very well, there was a brilliant flash of light.

20.

Alive!

The "Alive" simulator at the BookWorld Conference is one of those devices that all characters should try at least once. The experience of being real has two purposes: firstly, to assist characters in their quest for a greater understanding of people and, secondly, to discourage characters from ever attempting to escape to the Real-World. Most customers last ten minutes before hitting the panic button and being led shaken from the simulator.

Bradshaw's BookWorld Companion (8th edition)

I heard a gurgling sound, a heavy thumping and something odd in my nose that generated backstory memories I hadn't had for a while—something about going for walks in the park when I was small. It was dark, too, and I felt a pain in my chest. I didn't know what it was until, with a sound like a tornado, a hot gush of foul air erupted from within me and blew out of my mouth. Before I could recover from this shock, I spontaneously did the opposite and drew in an equally fast gush of air that cooled my teeth and tasted of pine needles.

"It's called breathing," came a voice close at hand. "It's very simple, and everyone does it. Just relax and go with the flow."

"I used to 'take a breath' and 'exhale uneasily' at home," I managed to say, "but this is quite different."

"Those were merely descriptive terms intended to suggest a mood," came the voice again, which sounded how I imagined a cheese straw might sound. "Here you are doing it to stay alive. Can you hear a thumping and a gushing noise, and a few rumbles, grunts, squeaks and growls?"

"Yes."

"It's your body. The thumping is your heart. It's all new to you, so it will fit oddly, like a new pair of shoes, but you'll get used to it. Feel your wrist."

I did so and was surprised to note that my skin was warm, soft and ever so slightly tacky. It was also thumping. It was my pulse, and I was sweating. Not for any descriptive reasons but because I was *alive*. After a few minutes of doing nothing but breathing, I spoke again.

"What's that random sensation of memories I keep getting?"

"It's smells. They have a way of firing off recollections. No one knows why."

I didn't understand and moved rapidly on. "Why can't I see anything?"

"You need to open your eyes."

So I did. I sat and blinked for some minutes. The view was quite astonishing, not only in range but in *detail*. I had been used to seeing only what was relevant within a scene. Back home, anything extra would have been unnecessary and was a pasty shade of magnolia with the texture of uncooked dough. Here there was *everything*, in all directions, in full color and in full detail. Several books' worth of description was just sitting there, with no one except me to revel in its glorious detail. The trees swayed ever so gently in the breeze, and the clouds moved slowly across the heavens. It was summer, and the flower beds had erupted in a sumptuous palette of color, while on the air were delicate tastes of cooking and garbage and rain and earth. I could hear stuff, too, except not one thing at a time, but all things at all times. The delicate symphony of sounds that reached my ears so heaped together that it was difficult to separate anything out at all, and I sat there quite numbed by the overload of sensations.

"How do they filter it out?" I asked.

"Humans filter well," said the voice. "In fact, they can filter out almost anything. Sound, vision, smells, love, anger, passion, reason. Everything except hunger and thirst, cold and hot. No need to hurry. Take your time."

I sat there for an hour, attempting to make sense of the world, and I did reasonably well, all things considered. In that time I managed to figure out I was sitting on a bench in a small and well-kept park hemmed in by redbrick houses on every side. There was a children's play area, a pond, a flower bed and two trees, both silver birch. A main road was to one side, and on a building opposite were two billboards. One was advertising the Goliath Corporation's supposed good work on behalf of the community, and the other promoted "Daphne Farquitt Day" on Friday, which began with a celebration of her works and ended with a Farquitt Readathon. It was a name I recognized, of course. The popularity of the romance author dictated that she had a genre all her own.

"It's beautiful!" I said at last. "I could stay here and watch the clouds for the whole twelve hours alone!"

"Many do," came the voice again.

I looked around. Aside from an impertinent squirrel foraging on the grass, I was entirely alone.

"Who are you?" I asked. "And why can't I see you?"

"Bradshaw asked me to keep an eye on you," came the voice. "The name's Square—Agent Square. If you want to know why you can't see me, it's because I'm from *Flatland* and bounded in only two dimensions. At the moment I'm presenting my edge to you. Since I have no thickness, I am effectively invisible. Watch."

A line a half inch thick and two feet long appeared in the air quite near me. The line separated and opened out into a thin rectangle, which broadened until it was a square, hanging in the air.

"How do you do?" I said.

"Oh, can't complain," said Square. "A spot of trapezoidism in this chill weather, but hey-ho. I worked with the real Thursday several times. Do you really look like her?"

"You can't see, then?"

"Since I am only two-dimensional," said Agent Square, "I can see the world only as a series of infinitely thin slices, like a ham. May I approach and have a look?"

Square moved closer. Out of curiosity I put my hand inside the area bounded by his vertices, and a soft bluish light gave me four rings around my fingers.

"Four disks is all I can see," said Square. "Viewing one dimension up is always a bit confusing. Mind you, for you people bounded in three dimensions, it's no different."

"I don't understand."

"Time," said Square, "is your next dimension, so to anyone in the RealWorld it appears as your third spatial dimension does to me—a thin slice in plain view but with the abstract notions of 'forward' and 'beyond' unseeable. May I?"

Square approached me and then tilted to a narrow rectangle, again became a line, vanished and then reappeared again. It was as though he were tilting in front of me in order, I assumed, to allow his two-dimensional frame of reference to scan my features. Once satisfied, Square withdrew.

"Spooky!" he said. "You *do* look just like her. What's the mission?"

"To find Thursday."

"Nothing hard, then."

I moved to stand up, but everything felt funny, so I sat down again.

"Why does my face feel all draggy?" I asked. "The underneath of my arms, too, and my boobs—everything feels all . . . well, *weighted down.*"

"That'll be gravity," said Square with a sigh.

"We have gravity in the BookWorld," I said. "It's not like this."

"No, we just talk as though gravity existed. There's a huge difference. In the BookWorld, gravity is simply useful. Here it is the effect of mass upon space-time. It would be manageable if it were constant, but it isn't. Acceleration forces can give one a localized gravitational effect that is quite disconcerting. If you're here for only twelve hours, I'd stay well clear of trains, elevators, airplanes and cars. Very odd, I'm told, although I don't notice it myself. By the way, do you have a timer on your watch? You're here for just twelve hours, remember."

I looked at my watch, which had nothing but hands and a face. "No."

"You'll get used to that, too. If this were the BookWorld, you'd have one of those watches that counts down from twelve hours to add some suspense. Believe me, the plot in this world takes a bit of getting used to. I've not done anything for Bradshaw for six months. That's nothing in the BookWorld, barely half a dozen words. Out here it really *is* six months. Hell's teeth! The boredom. There's a limit to how much reality TV one can watch, although it's become a lot easier for me since they brought in flat-screens. Now, what do you want to know first?"

"Walking would be a good start."

Agent Square was a good teacher, and within the space of twenty minutes I had mastered the concept of mass and the ticklish practical considerations of coping with momentum. Though easy to someone who'd been doing it for years, being able to lean back when negotiating a sharp stop to avoid falling over was an acquired skill.

"Bipedal movement is the skill of controlled falling," said Square. "If it weren't so commonplace, it would seem miraculous—like much out here, to be truthful."

I found the "walking straight" part fairly easy to master, but learning to conserve momentum while doing a right-hander at speed was a lot harder, and I was flailing my arms for balance until Square patiently taught me how angular velocity, centripetal forces and shoe/ground friction coefficients all worked together.

"Outlanders must be very good at math," I said, struggling with the vast quantity of complex equations necessary to recover after a stumble.

"So good they do it without thinking," he said. "Wait until you see someone riding a unicycle—it's math to die for."

The physical walking I soon got the hang of, but the rapidly moving pavement beneath me I found disconcerting—not to mention the highly constricting pull and drag of my clothes. Square told me to keep my eyes on the horizon and not look down, and after ten or so laps around the small park I was ready to venture farther.

We walked out of the park and down the street, and I stared at the intricate detail with which the RealWorld was imbued. The stains, the corrosion, the reflections—none of it could be adequately explained or described, and I became fascinated by every facet.

"What's that?"

"A spider."

"And that?"

"A dog turd."

"So *that's* what they look like. Who's that person over there?"

"Which one?" asked Square, tilting his body so his infinitely thin frame of reference sliced in the direction I was pointing. "I don't see anything."

But there *was* something there—a wispy humanlike form, through which I could see the wall and hedge beyond. I had met Marley's Ghost once when he was doing one of those tedious grammasite-awareness talks, and it was like him—transparent. I'd queued up for autographs afterwards, but when I'd asked him for a personalization, his agent told me to sod off. He wouldn't sign memorabilia either.

"What did you expect?" Marley's Ghost had said when I protested. "Albert Schweitzer?"

"Ghosts?" said Square when I explained what I could see. "Perhaps. There is much unexplained in the world. It behooves one to be wary at all times. Just when you think you've got the hang of it, along comes string theory, collateralized debt obligations or Björk's new album, and bam! You're as confused as you were when you first started."

We arrived at the Clary-LaMarr Travelport soon after. As in fiction, this was the main transportation hub in Swindon, where the Skyrail and mainline bullet services met. From here you could travel off to the west and Bristol and the steamer ports or east to London and the Gravitube. This was the business district, and the impressively high glassy towers disgorged a constant stream of people, all working together to make Swindon the powerhouse it was, deservedly known as "the Jewel of the M4." My Swindon was pretty similar, even if it lagged behind by eight years, the time that had elapsed since my series was written.

"What's that?" I asked, pointing towards a steel latticework tower that was being built on a hill to the south of the city. It was only half built but looked large enough to dwarf the skyscrapers when complete.

"It's part of the Anti-Smite Strategic Defense Shield that will one day protect a sinful citizenry from God's wrath—a series of force fields supported by steel pylons. Not even the most powerful smiting by the angriest or most vengeful God will make it through—or so it is claimed."

"That sounds pretty daft."

"That's the whole point," he said. "It's *meant* to be daft. The Commonsense Party's unswervingly sensible management of the country has left the nation with a woefully high stupidity surplus that needs to be safely discharged. It's hoped that the extraordinarily pointless and ridiculously expensive defense shield will be enough to deplete the stupidity quickly enough to allow time to more sensibly deal with a bigger problem that's coming up."

"What could be a bigger problem than God's wrath upon his creations and a cleansing fire falling from the heavens?"

"I'm not sure. Something to do with polar bears."

I sighed. "It's been a while since I had any concept of current affairs," I said. "All of this was barely thought of when I was penned."

"I keep abreast of things," said Square. "It's the closest thing to STORY they have out here. Makes me feel less homesick. You've been here an hour and you can walk pretty well, so you're doing okay. The next thing you need to learn is *interaction* and how humans all manage to live together without descending into chaos. The best place for appreciating this is crowds."

"Crowds?"

"Right. Humans are more or less identical except for a few peculiar habits generally delineated by geographic circumstances and historical precedent. But essentially they're all the same and reading from the same rule book. To get along you have to appreciate the rules but also know that other people know the rules— and that *they* know that *you* know the rules. Get it?"

"No."

"You will. Observe the crowds for a moment."

I watched as the thousand or so individuals milled around the Skyrail port, all of them heading in one of six directions and moving on their own yet as one. Astonishingly, *without* bumping into one another and falling over. It was a most remarkable sight. The wispy Marley-like ones had it even easier, since they could go *through* the pedestrians just as easily as around them.

"I'm still seeing the transparent humans."

"How insubstantial are they?"

"Pretty smoky. And they all look so *sad*."

This was true. They all wandered about looking very dejected, as if the world were pressing heavily on their shoulders. I had tried to catch the eye of one or two, but they'd steadfastly ignore me and, it seemed, everyone else. I knew about "ghosts" but always thought they were a fictional construct, like some of the odder facets of Japanese culture. However, Square was uninterested in my transparent people and wanted to carry on with my education.

"If you can manage crowd work, you can handle almost anything," said Square. "You know about flocks of starlings and schools of fish, how they all seem to move at the same time?"

I told him that I had heard of this but not witnessed it.

"Humans are exactly the same when they get into crowds. By using subtle sensory cues and working to a set of basic rules, you can enter a crowd full of people all heading in different directions and come out the other side without touching anyone or causing an accident."

"How?" I said, looking suspiciously at the swirling mass of humanity.

"Think of it as a subtle dance, where you have to avoid touching anyone. You have to jog and dodge your way around but also have to know when people are going to dodge and jink round *you*. Give it a whirl."

I stepped into the crowd, and almost immediately a woman stopped dead in front of me.

"Sorry," I said, and walked on. I could sense I was disrupting the smooth liquidity of the crowd, and based on the noises people were making, it wasn't appreciated. I got to the other side of the street without bumping into anyone, but only just.

"Not so easy, is it?" said Square, and I had to admit he was right. I had thought being in the RealWorld would be simple, or at least a lot like home, but it wasn't. Nothing here was assumed; everything had to be actually *done*, and witnessed.

Weirder still, once something *was* done, it was gone, and the knowledge of it faded almost immediately into memory. Once or twice I found myself attempting to move backwards or forwards in time before realizing that that's not how it worked. If I wanted to be five minutes in the future, I had to laboriously *run* the five minutes in real time, and if I wanted to go back, I couldn't. It was how I imagined the narrator in *À la Recherche du Temps Perdu* spent most of his life—trapped in a noisy, brightly colored cage barely two or three seconds wide.

After twenty minutes I could walk through the crowd without too much difficulty, but once or twice I found myself in the situation where the people I was trying to avoid met me head-on, and I moved left, and they did, so I moved right, and they did, too, and so on, for up to five times, which elicited nothing more than a chuckle from my dancing partner.

"The old 'back and forth' happens a lot when real and fictional people meet," said Square when I'd returned to where he was waiting for me. "If the Outlanders had any idea we were amongst them, it would be the surest way to tell. That and a certain confusion when it comes to everyday tasks. If you see someone unable to boil a kettle, open a sash window or understand he has an appalling haircut, it probably means he's fictional."

"Hmm," I said, "why is that woman in the annoyingly flamboyant clothes staring at me?"

"Probably because she recognizes you."

"Don't I have to know who she is before she can recognize me?"

"It doesn't work that way."

"Thursday?" said the woman, bounding up to me with a huge grin and a clatter of beads. "Is that really you? Where have you been hiding these past few months?"

I recognized her from the vague approximation that had

made it through to my series. It was Cordelia Flakk, ex–SpecOps publicity guru and now . . . well, I had no idea what she did.

"Hello, Cordelia."

"How are Landen and the kids?"

"Apparently they're very well."

"Did you hear about Hermione? Went to the slammer for trying to fiddle her taxes and then tried to escape. She was caught between the wire with two saber-toothed tigers. They didn't know what had happened to her until a bangle and parts of her synthetic kidney turned up in one of the sabers' . . . well, I don't want the story to get too gruesome."

"Too late."

"You old wag, you! Will you be coming to Penelope's for the Daphne Farquitt reading party Friday afternoon? She wants us all to come round to her place for the readathon, and she's dying to show off her new man." She leaned closer. "A *neanderthal*, you know. Frightfully polite, of course, but likes to sleep in the garden shed. She has a few stories about matters south, I should warrant—a few glasses and she'll spill the beans, if you know what I mean."

The woman laughed.

"Goodness, is that the time? How I prattle so!" She suddenly lowered her voice. "By the way, are you still dealing in cheese?"

"Not really—"

"A pound of Limburger would set us straight. Just a taster, then—anything, in fact. I mean, it's not like we're asking for any X-14. Oh. Sorry, is that still a sore point? Why not bring a taster of cheese to Penelope's do on Friday? We can enhance them with some pineapple chunks. Cheese and Farquitt! Naughty us! Ta-ra!"

And she tossed her head and moved off.

"Did you understand any of that?" asked Square.

"About one word in eight."

"That many?"

I stood there, stunned by the fact that I had no idea what Thursday actually *did* in the RealWorld, nor what had happened and what hadn't. The recent exchange told me that she *had* been involved in the illegal cheese market, and we had walked past the abandoned Special Operations Division headquarters earlier, so I knew that at least some of her SpecOps adventures had been real. But what else had happened in her life I had no idea. If anyone asked me anything specific, I was going to have to wing it, or simply grin stupidly. Best of all, stay well away from anyone who might know me.

"Was that meeting at all relevant?" I asked Square. "In the grand scheme of things, I mean?"

"Probably not," replied Square. "Just a chance meeting that means nothing. If this were a book, Cordelia wouldn't have survived the first draft."

I spent the next two hours walking around trying to figure out how the world worked. It was confusing and tiring, and it seemed that much energy was expended for very little outcome. I had my first real pee, which was pretty bizarre, then ate some chocolate, which was hugely enjoyable. Mostly I listened in on conversations and was dismayed to note that Professor Plum had been correct. A lot of what was said was superficially very banal. Less of a sense of communication and more to do with being comfortable and secure amongst members of one's own species—the modern equivalent of being huddled together in the dark.

"There seems to be a tremendous fear of being alone," I said once we had stopped for a break in the graveyard of the Blessed Lady of the Lobster.

"My theory is that it's all misdirection."

"From what?"

"The depressing certainty that one day all of us will die."

"Speak for yourself. What's your story, Square?"

"I used to work in *Flatland* but was fired after 'artistic

differences' with Circle. After that I was recruited by Bradshaw for deep-cover operations in the Outland. I was here on assignment when the RealWorld travel ban came down, so I took Blue Fairy, became real and volunteered to stay."

He sighed deeply, in a thin, two-dimensional sort of way. "Blue Fairy" was the term used to describe the only way in which fictional people could become real, and unsurprisingly, the Blue Fairy from *Pinocchio* was the only person who could do it. She used to do it for free if you asked nicely and had a chit from the CofG, but now she is not permitted to conduct any realizations at all and is paid handsomely by the council for the honor of doing nothing. Nice work if you can get it.

"When do you get to go home?" I asked.

"I don't get to return home. The only good thing about this place is that it's fantastically roomy. Are you ready?"

I said I was, and we walked the three blocks to Landen and Thursday's house, situated in a quiet part of the Old Town. I asked Square to keep a low profile, took a deep breath, walked up the garden path and stared at the front door, heart beating furiously. This time for real.

21.

Landen Parke-Laine

The manufacture of robots, automatons and assorted mechanical people is undertaken by the Duplex Corporation, situated on the border of Sci-Fi and Fantasy. Most automata are energy cell powered these days, but the factory still produces a "Classic" line of clockwork men to satisfy clients who require something more retro. Despite problems with emotion, adverse wear and the continual windings, the Duplex range of robots (currently in its fifth incarnation) remains popular. Tours of the factory by arrangement.

Bradshaw's BookWorld Companion (6th edition)

I knocked twice. There was the sound of noises from within, and the door opened. It was Landen, and we stared at each other for a few seconds.

"Hello," I said.

"Hello," said Landen.

"Hello," I said again.

"Are you her?" he asked.

"No, not really."

"Then you'd better come in."

He moved aside, and I stepped into the hallway that was familiar to mine, but only in layout. Thursday's real house was more real, more worn, more lived in. The banisters were chipped, the newel post was draped with discarded clothes, and a tide mark of children's fingerprints ran along the wall and up the staircase. Pictures hung askew, and there was a small cobweb around the lampshade. Landen led me through to the kitchen, which was a big extension at the back of the house, partly consuming the garden and covered with a large glazed roof above the junk-strewn kitchen table. It was packed with the chaotic assortment of the minutiae of life being lived—not the sanitized shorthand we get in the BookWorld, even with the Reader Feedback Loop set to max. Life seemed to be a lot messier than people wanted fiction to be. Feedback reflected hopes, not realities. I looked around carefully and sat in the seat he had indicated.

"Tea?" he asked.

"Do I drink it?"

"Gallons of it, usually."

"At a single sitting?"

"No, generally one cup at a time."

"Then I'd love some, thank you."

He went to put the kettle on.

"You look a lot like Thursday," he said.

"I'm often mistaken for her," I replied, feeling less nervous around familiar questions. "In fact, I'm surprised you needed so little convincing I wasn't the real Thursday."

"I don't know that for certain," he replied. "Not yet anyway. I'd like you to be her, naturally, but there have been others who looked a lot like her. Not quite as much as you do, but pretty similar. Goliath is keen to know what Thursday gets up to when she's not at home, and they've sent one or two to try to trick me into giving information. The first was just a voice on the phone, then one who could be seen only from a distance. The last one almost took me in, but up close she didn't pass muster. Her texture was all wrong, the smell was different, the smile lopsided and the ears too high. I don't know why they keep sending them, to be honest—nor where they end up. After I booted the last one out the door, someone from Goliath's Synthetic Human Division came round demanding to know what I'd done with it. Then, after I asked about the legality of such a device, he denied there had been any, or even that he was from the Synthetic Human Division. He then asked to read the meter."

"So how can they lose two synthetic Thursdays?"

"They lost three. There was *another* that I hadn't even seen. They said it was the best yet. They dropped it off two weeks ago near Clary-LaMarr and haven't heard anything since. Are you that one?"

"No."

"Are you sure?"

"Yes," I replied, vaguely indignant. "I'm not a Goliath robot."

"Not a robot—a *synthetic*. Human in everything but name."

I took a deep breath. I had to lay my cards on the table. "She's missing, isn't she?"

There was a flicker of consternation on Landen's face. "Not at all. Her absences are quite long, admittedly, but we're always in constant communication."

"From the BookWorld?"

He laughed. "That old chestnut! It was never *proved* she could move across at will. I think you've perhaps spent a little too much time listening to deranged theories."

It sounded like a cover story to keep the real nature of the BookWorld secret. I didn't expect him to tell me anything. He didn't know who or what I was, after all. But he had to know.

"I'm the *written* her," I told him. "She may have spoken to you about me. I was the tree-hugging version in the Great Samuel Pepys Fiasco, who then took over from the evil Thursday who was deleted with Pepys. I run books one to five now— less along the lines of the old Thursday, but more how the real Thursday wanted them to be. Less sex and violence. It explains why we're out of print."

If I thought he would be surprised or shocked, however, I was mistaken. I guess when you're married to Thursday, the nature of weird becomes somewhat relative. Landen smiled.

"That's a novel approach. Mind you, there's nothing you've told me that I couldn't find out by rereading *First Among Sequels*. Goliath has access to that book, too, so if you *were* one of the synthetic Thursdays, I'd expect you to come up with something like that."

"Commander Bradshaw of Jurisfiction sent me."

He stared at me. The relevance wasn't lost on him. Jurisfiction and Bradshaw were never mentioned in the books.

"I'm not yet convinced," he said, giving nothing away, "but let's suppose Thursday *is* missing—you want my help to find her?"

"If she's missing, then you and I can help each other. I'll be going home in less than twelve hours. Any information learned out here might be helpful."

He took a deep breath. "She's been gone four weeks, that much is common knowledge. Everyone wants to find her. It's a national obsession. *The Mole*, *The Toad*, Goliath, SO-5, the police, the Cheese Squad, the government, the NSA—and now you claim the BookWorld, too."

"Do you have any idea where she is?"

He poured the boiling water into the teapot.

"No. And the thing is," he added, looking at the clock, "we need to resolve this one way or another pretty soon."

"Because of the police and the NSA and whatnot?"

Landen laughed. "No, not *them*. The kids. Friday won't get away from his shift at B&Q until six, but Tuesday will be home in two hours, and although my mind has been rendered as supple as custard when it comes to things Thursday, the kids are still at an impressionable age—besides, I don't think the doors in the house will take much more slamming."

And he smiled again, but it was sadder, and more uncertain.

"I understand."

"Do you? *Can* you?"

"I think so."

"Hmm," he said, pondering carefully, "does anyone else know you're here?"

"Cordelia Flakk's the only one we need to worry about."

"That's bad," he murmured. "Flakk's the worst gossip in the city. I've a feeling you've less than forty minutes before the press starts to knock at the door, two hours before the police arrive with an arrest warrant and three hours before President van de Poste demands you hand over the plans."

"What plans?"

"The *secret* plans."

"I don't have any secret plans."

"I'd keep that to yourself."

He poured out the tea and placed it in front of me. He was standing close to me, and I felt myself shiver within his proximity. I wanted to take him in my arms and hug him tightly and breathe in great lungfuls of Landen with my face buried in his collar. I'd dreamed of the moment for years. Instead I did nothing and cursed my restraint.

"Does Thursday know the president?"

"He often seeks her counsel. Thursday?"

"Yes?"

"How like her are you?"

I rolled up my sleeve to reveal a long scar on my forearm. "I don't know how I got that one."

"That was Tiger."

"Was Tiger a tiger?"

"No, Tiger was a leopard. Your mother's. Only Mrs. Next would name a leopard Tiger. May I?"

"Please do."

He looked at my scalp where there was another scar, just above my hairline.

"That was Norman Johnson at the close of the 1989 Super-Hoop," I said. "*Something Rotten*, page 351."

He went and sat at the other end of the table and stared at me for a while.

"You even smell like her," he said, "and rub your forehead in the same way when you're thinking. I have a lot of respect for Goliath, but they never got synthetics this good."

"So you believe I'm the written one?"

"There's another possible explanation."

"Who would I be if not Goliath or the written one?"

He looked at me for a long time, an expression of concern on his face. I understood what he was trying to say.

"You think I might *be* Thursday, but suffering some sort of weird delusion?"

"Stranger things have happened."

"I've spent my entire life in books," I explained. "I'm really only five years old. I can remember popping out of the character press as plain old D8-V-67987, and my first day at St. Tabularasa's. I did well, so I was streamed into the First-Person fast-track program. Long story short, I look after the Thursday books one to five but also work for JAID—that's the Jurisfiction Accident Investigation Department. I can tell you about Sprockett and Carmine, and how Lorina/Pickwick doesn't approve of her bringing goblins home and likes to bore us stupid by quoting Latin mottos, and the new book that arrived in the neighborhood. And there's Bradshaw, and the metaphor shortage, and Jobsworth wanting me to go up-country to help deal with Speedy Muffler in the peace talks on Friday. That's me. I'm *not* Thursday. I'm nothing like her. Show me a frightening situation and I'll run a mile. Square will vouch for me."

And I called his name, but there was no answer.

"Right," I said, wondering where he'd gone. "That makes me look stupid."

We both fell silent, and Landen stared at me for a long time once more. I saw his eyes moisten, and mine spontaneously did the same.

"I so want to be her," I sniffed as my eyes blurred with tears. "But I'm not."

Before I knew it, I had discovered what crying actually means when you do it for real. He gave me his handkerchief and hugged me, and I responded by wrapping my arms around his neck. It felt *wonderful*. Natural—like two parts in a jigsaw. When I had calmed down, he gently took my hands from around him and held them in his, gazing into my eyes.

"Here's the thing," he said at last. "If you're *not* the real Thursday, we must come clean to the kids and explain that you're not. I can't have them being disappointed again. But if you *are* the real Thursday, you must stay so we can look after you. It's possible that you just *think* you're not Thursday. All that stuff about the BookWorld—it could be Aornis up to her tricks again."

"Aornis, sister of Acheron?"

He raised an eyebrow. "How many children do Thursday and I have?" he asked.

"Two."

"That's in your favor as the written Thursday. Aornis gave the *real* Thursday a mindworm so she thought she had a third child—another daughter—and Thursday was always worrying about her. We helped her by pretending there was, and occasionally, in lucid moments, she would realize what was going on. Then she'd forget and was worrying about her missing daughter again."

I tried to imagine what it might be like having a child who was a figment but could not. If Aornis was anything like the written Acheron, she was pretty unpleasant. Still, I was kind of glad I didn't know about the extra daughter. I had an idea.

"T minus pumpkin in ten hours," I said, consulting my watch. "If you see me vanish in front of your eyes will you believe I'm from the BookWorld?"

"Yes," he said, "I'll believe you. But if you don't vanish, will you believe that you *might* be Thursday except . . . well, nuts?"

"I could be the missing Goliath *synthetic* Thursday," I said, "with a well-researched cover story."

Landen smiled. "Being married to you has never been boring."

I was pondering over the consequences of being either mad or synthetic when Thursday's mother arrived.

"Thursday!" she squealed, having let herself in. "You naughty girl! Where have you been?"

The real version of my mother was quite different from the written one. The real one was a lot older—at least seventy, by my guess, but didn't seem to have lost any of her youthful vigor. She was a little gray, a little hunched and a little odd.

"Here for long?" she asked.

"Only until midnight," I managed to mutter.

"Shame!" she said, then turned to Landen. "Is this one of the synthetics?"

"The jury's still out."

Mrs. Next walked up close and peered at me through her spectacles, as one might regard a stubborn stain on the carpet.

"It's very lifelike. Does she have the scars?"

Landen nodded.

"I know how to check," she said, and cut me a slice of Battenberg cake. "Here," she said, and handed it over. "Your favorite."

I took a large bite, and even though it had some yellow coating on the outside that was almost indescribably nasty, I smiled politely and tried to eat it as quickly as I could.

"Very nice," I managed to say.

"Hmm," said Mrs. Next, "that doesn't sound like her at all. Thursday *hates* marzipan."

"Is that what it was?" I said, running to the sink to spit it out. I knew I didn't like it, I just didn't know what it was. I had thought Marzipan was the name of a boy band.

"Hmm," said my mother, "this doesn't really help. Hating it

does make her Thursday, but pretending to like it to spare my feelings definitely does *not* make her Thursday."

"It's a tricky one," agreed Landen.

They eyed me for a long time as they tried to figure out what to do and how best to tell if I was the real one or the written one. Nothing I could say would convince them of either alternative, and the only way to truly know—if I vanished at pumpkin hour—was a bit pointless, since by then I would no longer be around for them to answer any questions I might have, which was a bit like devising a 100 percent destructive test for counterfeit tenners.

The doorbell rang.

"That will be the first of your fan club," said Landen, and he went off to answer it.

"So," said Mrs. Next, "loopy, fictional or synthetic. Which would you prefer?"

"Loopy, I guess," I said sadly.

"Me, too. But the shitstorm that will be unleashed when you get back is not something I'd like anyone to face. President van de Poste won't be able to make his Anti-smite Shield without you and the secret plans, and as a key witness in the Stiltonista cheese-smuggling trial, you'll need round-the-clock protection. And that's before we get into the fun Goliath has in store for you."

"She made a few enemies, right?"

"Only a few thousand. Start causing trouble amongst the criminal fraternity and no end of unfair retribution starts coming your way. Would you excuse me? I must avail myself of the facilities. The bad plumbing needs to meet the bad plumbing, so to speak."

And she tottered off in the direction of the downstairs loo.

I sat there for a moment unsure of what to think or do. I called out to Square but to no avail, then heard a noise. I looked up and noticed that the broom-cupboard door was ajar. Looking at me through the crack were two bright eyes. The door opened a little farther, and a small girl aged about eight stepped out. She was like the spirits I had seen around the place—that is to say, mildly transparent. I could see the bottle of Brasso on the shelf directly behind her.

"You're the last person I want to see," I said as my heart fell.

"That's not a very nice thing to say," said the girl.

"Let me guess," I said. "You're the mindworm."

"I prefer Jenny," said Jenny indignantly. "Who are you?"

"If I can see you, I guess I'm the real Thursday—just insane. Still, at least this way I don't have to worry about Carmine and the goblin anymore."

"You're not insane," said Jenny, "and you're not Thursday either."

"I could be making you up," I remarked, "and making up your denial, too."

She shook her head.

"Creating figments like me takes a serious amount of effort, and you're not that good."

"Thanks. Insulted by someone's else's delusion."

"Jenny."

"Jenny, then. So how can I see you?"

"You're not seeing just *me*, are you?"

"No," I said, "there are others. Lots of them."

"Then you see what I mean. What does Landen think you are?"

I shrugged. "The real Thursday mad, I think."

"Don't upset him," said Jenny. "Thursday wouldn't like it."

"Thursday could be dead."

"I know for a fact that she isn't."

"How?"

But at that moment Landen came pacing down the corridor, and Jenny jumped back into the broom cupboard.

"That was your old buddy Lydia Startright, wanting to get an exclusive before the network vans turn up. I told her you weren't here and I had no idea where you were."

"Did she believe you?"

"She's an excellent journalist—of course not."

We sat in silence for some moments. I didn't think I would tell him I'd just seen Jenny, but the seeds of doubt had been sown. I *could* be the real Thursday. And even though the ramifications of being someone suffering bizarre delusions were *not* good news, the possibility that I would be with the man I loved was some consolation.

"Ask me some questions," I said finally. "I want to convince myself I'm not her."

"What's my middle name?" he asked.

"Is it . . . Whitby?"

"Not even close. Where was our first date?"

"At the Alhambra. The Richard III thing."

"No, that was later. Where did I lose my leg?"

"You've lost a leg?"

Mrs. Next came back into the room. "You never told me you'd bought a gold-plated toilet."

Landen frowned. "We don't have a gold-plated toilet."

"Oh, dear," said Mrs. Next. "I think I've just peed in your tuba."

She then muttered something about "the shocking price of dodo feed" and went out without saying good-bye to either of us.

"Daft as a brush," said Landen, "and just a teeny-weeny bit repulsive."

"Plock."

I turned. A dodo stood at the open door. It was nothing like the Pickwick/Lorina back home. This dodo was *old*. Her beak was worn and scaly, she had no feathers, and her left foot had a tremor. She was dressed in an all-over body warmer made of fleecy material and was regarding me curiously.

"Pickwick?"

"Plock?" said the dodo, cocking her head to one side. She walked unsteadily up to me and looked very closely at me for a long time.

"Plock, plock," she said, and rubbed her beak affectionately on my trouser leg before walking over to her water dish.

"Pickwick thinks you're real."

"Pickwick has a brain the size of a *petit pois*."

"True."

The doorbell went again.

"That will be the Toad News Network."

As soon as he had gone, the broom-cupboard door opened again.

"Has he gone?" asked Jenny.

I nodded.

"Right, then. I'll show you what I mean about Thursday not being dead. Come with me."

22.

Jenny

Places to Eat #15: Bar Humbug, 68 *Christmas Carol*. Very cheap food served in an authentically austere and utterly miserable Dickensian atmosphere. Waifs wait at tables, and portions are notoriously small. People with silly names particularly welcome, and those with an archaic job title (beadle, proctor, sexton, etc.) can eat for free.

Bradshaw's BookWorld Companion (5th edition)

*J*enny opened the back door and checked to make sure the coast was clear.

"Why do you do that?" I asked. "Check that no one's coming? Only I can see you, right?"

Jenny looked at me and raised an eyebrow. "When you're illusory like me," she said, with great clarity, "it pays to keep an eye out for imaginary foes."

She checked again and beckoned me out. I followed her down to the end of the garden and opened the door that led into the garage behind. I knew that my car would be kept here, but Thursday's figment had no time to waste and hurriedly led me down the rear access road until we came back out onto the same street. Landen had been correct. Parked outside the house was a large Toad News Network van, complete with transmitter dish ready for bouncing a live feed to a handy airship.

"Landen will be surprised to find me not there."

"Nothing could surprise Landen. This way."

"Miss Next?" asked a man who had just gotten out of a car opposite. "May I have a word?"

I looked around, but Jenny seemed to have vanished. "I suppose so."

"I just heard about your return. I'm a *huge* fan of your work. Adrian Vole of the Wapcaplit and Vole Advertising Agency. We understand you travel in Fiction, and we were wondering if you wanted to do a bit of product placement around the written world."

"I hardly think that's appropriate, do you?" I said, adding quickly, "Even if there is a BookWorld, which is by no means proven."

"Thirty grand to plug the Toast Marketing Board in the Thursday Next series. You can introduce it how you want."

"I've never even *heard* of the Toast Marketing Board."

"You wouldn't. It's new. What do you say?"

"What do you think I'm going to say?"

"Yes," said Vole unhappily, "we thought you'd tell us to stick it in our ear. Here's a check. If you cash it, we know you're on board."

I took the check and moved on. Oddly enough, as soon as Vole turned away, Jenny was back.

"What's going on?" asked Square, who had suddenly reappeared. "It's not like the BookWorld, where I can be five or six places at once."

"Landen thinks I might actually *be* Thursday," I said, "and if I can see Jenny, then he might be right."

"Who's Jenny? I don't see anyone."

"She's one of the wraiths I've been seeing. And if I *am* Thursday, then I'm simply imagining you."

"Who are you talking to?" asked the figment Jenny, which seemed a bit impertinent given her less-than-definite existence.

"Agent Square," I said, "in Jurisfiction deep cover."

"Who are you talking to?" asked Square.

I sighed. This was getting more and more complex, but in a way I was heartened that they couldn't see or hear each other. If they were *both* in my head, they should be able to converse— unless I was more insane than I thought possible.

"I'll tell you about it later," I said as we crossed another road, walked through the graveyard of the Blessed Lady of the Lobster, took a right down the hill and then an immediate left, where we found a small apartment building. Jenny led us into the lobby, and we paused while she consulted the names on the mailboxes.

"Fifth floor."

We took the stairs, as neither I nor Square wanted to get into the elevator, and arrived at the upstairs corridor, from which four apartments could be accessed. As I walked along the corridor, one of the doors opened and a nurse walked out, glanced at me and moved off towards the elevators. As the door closed on the apartment, I could see that other medics were in attendance, clustered around a bed.

"You brought me here to see a guy dying?"

"Sort of," replied Jenny, "but not him in there—him out here."

She pointed. At the far end of the corridor were five more of the wraithlike figures I had seen earlier. They all stood around looking solemn, trying to comfort one of their number, who flickered in and out like a badly tuned TV set. They all spoke in a low growl that I couldn't really understand, and as I walked closer, I noticed that they were dressed rather oddly.

"You brought me here to see some spooks?"

"They're not spooks," said Jenny. "They're like me and you, Thursday—made up. Figments, inventions. Created in the white-hot heat of a child's imagination, they linger on even when redundancy renders them invisible to their creators. Sometimes people catch a glimpse of them, but for the most part they're invisible. You can see them because you're fictional.

So can I. You, them, me—we're all one and the same. A living fiction that needs no book."

I looked closer at the figures. They were partially dressed as clowns, had bold, large features and spoke in a simple dialect of basic verbs and a limited number of nouns.

"They're . . . imaginary childhood friends, aren't they?"

Jenny smiled. "Bravo, Thursday—a chip off the old block. They follow their creators about, an echo of a vibrant childhood imagination."

She indicated the one who was flickering.

"Pookles here is about to leave—they can have no independent existence without their creator."

As we watched, the flickering imaginary friend started shaking hands with the others, hugging them and thanking them, and then, with a final bright burst, it vanished. Almost immediately we heard a cry of grief from the bedroom behind us, and one by one the ethereal figures took their leave, walking through us and along the corridor, leaning on one another for support and shaking their heads sadly.

"So where does Thursday come into all this?"

"This is how I know she's still alive. *I'm still here.* Unlike you, who are the figment of a ghostwriter and are now carved into a textual matrix, a part of Thursday is all I am. If she were dead, I wouldn't be around to be thought of. I'm bound to her, like a dog on a leash."

"Right," I said, "I get that. But it doesn't tell us where she is. Any ideas? The Dark Reading Matter, for instance?"

"That was one of her interests, certainly, but the whole Racy Novel stuff had taken over her life. The last time we spoke, she said something about Lyell being boring."

"Lyell? Boring?"

"Yes. I don't know who Lyell was or why he should be boring, but boring he was—and Thursday didn't like it. Not one little bit." Jenny shook her head and took me by the hand. "I miss her, Thursday. It's lonely not being directly imagined on a day-to-day basis."

We walked back towards Landen's house.

"I'm confused," said Square. "What, precisely, is going on?"

"I'm not really sure. I feel like I'm following in Thursday's footsteps, only several hundred yards behind, and—hello, that's odd."

I looked around. Jenny, who'd been with us just a second ago, was nowhere to be seen. I twisted this way and that to see where she'd gone, and as I was doing so, a black van screeched to a halt in front of me. Within a few moments, the sliding door had opened and I'd been bundled inside in a less-than-polite manner, a sack put over my head. With another screech of tires, the van set off, and to make matters worse, I was then immediately sat upon by someone who smelled strongly of Gorgonzola.

23.

The Stiltonista

The most cost-effective way to tour the BookWorld is by bus. A BookWorld Rover is the preferred method, giving you unlimited travel for a month. Delays might be expected at the borders between islands, but for the discerning tourist eager to see the BookWorld at a leisurely pace, the Rover ticket is ideal. Next page: working your passage on a scrawl trawler. Not for the fainthearted.

Bradshaw's BookWorld Companion (5th edition)

*A*ny attempt to describe the journey would have been futile, as the varying degrees of gravitational flux that I encountered during the trip were unpleasantly distracting. Suffice it to say that all the lurches, bumps, swerves and twists made me feel quite peculiar, and I wondered how anyone could undertake journeys on a regular basis and not only become ambivalent but actually enjoy them. Fortunately, this journey ended after not too long, and once the van came to a stop and I was rather impolitely hauled from the back and placed on a chair, the sack was pulled off.

I was in a deserted warehouse. There were puddles of water on the floor and holes in the ceiling—which probably accounted for the puddles on the floor. The windows were broken, and green streaks of algae had formed on the walls. In several places brambles had started to grow, and the odd pile of rubble and twisted metal sat in heaps. I wasn't alone. Aside from the four men who had brought me in the van, there was a Rolls-Royce motorcar and three other men. Two of them seemed to be bodyguards, and the third was undoubtedly the leader. He was dressed in a mohair suit and greatcoat, and his features were drawn and sunken—he looked like a skull that someone had thrown some skin at.

"I am Keitel Potblack," he said in the tone of someone who felt I should know who he was and not fail to be impressed, "head of the Wiltshire Stiltonista. Your failure to remain properly dead is becoming something of an inconvenience."

I laughed at the ridiculousness of the situation. This guy dealt in cheese, and he was acting as though he were a Bond villain.

"You're kidding, right?"

"I don't kid," said Mr. Potblack.

"Oh," I said, "right."

I looked at him, then at the men standing next to him, one of whom was carrying a spade. "Going gardening?"

They exchanged glances, as though this were the sort of comment they expected.

"It's up to you. Now, are you the real Thursday or just another copy?"

"I'm not her," I said, "so if you can take me home, I'd be really grateful."

"If you're not her," said Potblack, "I have no further need of you."

"Good. If you could tell your driver to go easy a bit on the way back, that would be—"

"Mr. Blue? Would you do the honors?"

The man with the spade walked towards me, and all of a sudden I realized that if he was digging anything over today, it would be me.

"You want to talk?" I said, the ease with which I stayed calm surprising even me. "Then let's talk."

"So you are Thursday?"

"Yes," I replied, which was no lie—I was *a* Thursday.

The man with the spade walked back to his position to the left of his boss. I noticed as he did that one edge of the spade had been sharpened.

"Okay," said Potblack, who seemed annoyed that I wasn't more frightened than I was. Perhaps if I'd known who he was, I would have been. But this was Thursday's life, not mine.

"In the past," began Potblack in a slow, deliberate speech, "we may have had an 'understanding' over who deals what cheese where. Perhaps you think I was being too harsh when I started dealing in really strong cheeses, but I am a businessman. The stronger the cheese, the more people will pay. Business is good, and we want to keep it that way. If the government lifts the cheese ban as threatened, then it could be very bad business for all of us. The last thing we want is legal cheese."

I vaguely knew what he was talking about, but not the details. I'd heard that cheese in the Outland was subject to a swingingly large amount of duty, but it seemed the government, in an attempt to control the burgeoning illegal-cheese market, had tried cheese prohibition. Judging from Potblack's jewelry, car and ability to supply, the ban didn't seem to be working.

"So what do you want me to do?" I asked. "It's not like I have the ear of the president, now, is it?"

The Stiltonista looked at his henchman with the spade, who picked it up again. I was wrong—I *did* have the ear of the president. Landen had said so earlier.

"Anymore. I don't have his ear *anymore*. But I'm sure I could give him a call and advise him to keep the prohibition in place."

Potblack stared at me and narrowed his eyes. "You're being uncharacteristically compliant."

"But characteristically *realistic*," I said cheerfully. "You're the one with the sharpened spade."

"Hmm," said the Stiltonista, "very well. But I want to offer an incentive to make sure that once released you don't 'forget' your part of the bargain."

"Bargain?" I echoed. "You mean I get something from this?"

"You do. You get to keep your life, your husband gets to keep his, and your children get to keep their fingers."

The man with the spade tapped it on the ground as if to emphasize the point, and the steel rang out with a threatening *ting-ting-ting-ting* sound. I stared at the Stiltonista for a moment, and when I spoke, I tried to convey as much menace as I could—surprisingly easy, for I *was* angry—and it wasn't the sort of anger I get when I fluff my lines or my father misses a cue and comes in late. Or even the sort of anger I felt when Horace the goblin nicked all my stuff or Carmine went AWOL. This was *real* anger. The sort of "don't shit with me" stuff that mothers feel when you threaten their children.

"Dear, oh, dear," I said, sadly shaking my head, "and we were getting on so well. I said I'd help you out, and you respond by threatening my kids. That's not only insulting, it's impolite. There's a new deal: You let me go right now and promise never to even *look* at my husband or children, and I will let you live to see tomorrow's dawn."

The Stiltonista bit his lip ever so subtly. It was clear that I had a reputation, and it moved in front of me like a bulldozer. Despite the fact that I was outnumbered six to one, the Stiltonista obviously considered that at the very least I should not be underrated. Thursday, it seemed, was a formidable foe—and highly dangerous if you got on the wrong side of her.

"You're not in any position to be doing deals."

"I don't want anyone to think me unfair," I said. "I'll give you until the count of three. One."

There was the sound of safety catches being released from the men behind me. They were quite obviously armed and, from the sound of it, heavily.

"I'm sorry we couldn't do any sort of deal, Miss Next," said Potblack with renewed confidence. "Perhaps you would like to reconsider. My men will finish you before you get to three, and you'll end up with all the others—six feet under the Savernake Forest, a feast for the worms. I apologize if I have been impolite, but as you understand, a lot rides on a lifted prohibition, and I speak not only for myself but for many cheese suppliers up and down the country. We can make this work to the best advantage for all of us, I'm sure—and perhaps even offer up some sort of compensatory payment."

"Two."

"You really don't understand, do you?" said the Stiltonista in a voice that now carried an echo of uncertainty. "It doesn't have to end for you like this."

I didn't have a plan of action, but that didn't seem to be a problem, for the plan of action had *me*, and before I knew what had happened, I had the barrel of my pistol pressed hard against the Stiltonista's throat and the man with the spade was flat on his back unconscious. The goon next to me had managed to get his hand to the butt of his automatic, but no farther. The rest were just blinking stupidly. Oddly, I didn't feel nervous in the least. It felt like I was someone else. Someone else *inside* me.

"You see what happens when you're impolite?" I said. "And don't struggle. This an armor piercer. Once it's gone through, only Exxon will be able to retrieve it—or you."

He stopped struggling.

"Tell them to drop their weapons."

He did, and they did.

"Right," I said, unsure what to do next. "This is the plan. . . ."

If there was a plan, I never found out what it was, for a voice rang out from one corner of the warehouse.

"*Armed police!* You are surrounded. Do *exactly* as we tell you. Carefully and slowly, put your hands behind your heads."

The Stiltonista's goons did as the voice asked and seemed to know the drill, as they also lay flat on their faces without being asked.

"And you, Next."

I set my pistol on the floor, kicked it away and then obediently placed my hands on the back of my head and lay on the ground quite close to where Potblack now lay.

"I'll get you for this if it's the last thing I do, Next."

He said it without looking at me, his voice a low growl.

"Really?" I replied evenly. "Try to get me or my family and I'll happily ensure that it is."

He grumbled and faced the other way.

I heard the patter of feet, and within a few seconds I felt my arms pulled behind me and bound with a plastic tie. They weren't rough, though—they were almost gentle.

"Got a weapon here," said a voice, quickly followed by, "Got several weapons here."

"Thursday, Thursday," came the voice that had been behind the bullhorn. It was deep and earthy and was exactly how I expected Spike to sound. He was one of Thursday's SpecOps pals—someone who had been more than happy to feature in the series. It was the only recognition he'd ever got.

"Spike?"

"Hello, old friend," he said. "What have you got for us?"

"Keitel Potblack, head of the Swindon Stiltonistas," I said, "threatened to kill me, wanted to bribe me to block the repeal of prohibition and is also guilty of putting three of Goliath's synthetic Thursdays under the Savernake Forest."

"You've nothing to connect me with the Stiltonistas," said Mr. Potblack. "I happened to be here pursuing a potential property development when I was set upon by this madwoman."

"We've got a trunkful of Gorgonzola here," said one of the armed officers. "At least fifty kilos."

"For personal use," said Potblack in an unconvincing tone of voice.

"And your armed associates?"

"I employed them as decorators this morning. I am shocked, *shocked* to discover they are armed."

Spike helped me to my feet and walked me across to the front of the Rolls-Royce.

"It's good to see you again, Thursday. The Cheese Squad will have a field day with this lot. How in heaven's name did you nail Potblack of all people? We've been after him for years."

"Let's just say I have a magnetic personality."

Spike laughed. "Still the same. Tell me, do you want to do some moonlighting? The undead are about to be culled again, and there aren't many with Class IV zombie hunters' licenses about—or at least none who don't drool a lot and mumble."

I thought carefully. "If I'm around tomorrow, I'm totally up for it."

It was quite fun being her. I had a sudden thought.

"Spike, if you weren't here to arrest Potblack, what were you here for?"

"We've been trailing you for the past hour, Thursday."

"Why?"

"Because if *we* know you're here, so will *they*."

"'They' being . . . ?"

"Who else? Goliath."

"I can handle them."

"I don't think so," said Spike. "You've been gone a month, right?"

"In a manner of speaking."

"Three weeks ago SpecOps announced it had been privatized. The Goliath Corporation now runs not only SpecOps but the police as well. Almost the first thing Goliath did was charge you with crimes against humanity, murder, theft, illegal possession of a firearm, the discharge of a weapon in a public place, murder, impersonating a SpecOps officer, cheese smuggling, assorted motoring offenses and murder. It's quite a list. They must *really* hate you to dream up so many spurious charges."

"I think the feeling's pretty much mutual. Does that mean I'm under arrest?"

"We tried to, but you escaped." He smiled and removed the plastic cuffs with a flick knife. "Now go before Flanker gets here."

It was too late. A group of blue-suited individuals had arrived, brandishing Goliath IDs and a lot of attitude. Their leader I recognized from the description I had in the series—Commander Flanker, once head of SO-1, the police who police the police, now presumably answering to Goliath.

"Thank you, Officer Stoker," said Flanker, "for securing our prisoner."

"You can have her once we're done," said Spike, pulling himself up to his full height—he was well over six feet six. "Miss Next is charged with the illegal possession of a firearm, and I need to process her."

"The charge of crimes against humanity has precedence, Stoker."

"Your bullshit charge is bigger than my bullshit charge?"

"We could argue this all night, but the outcome remains the same. She is coming with me to be interrogated at Goliathopolis."

"Over my dead body," said Spike.

"I'm sure that can be arranged."

They growled at each other, but there was little, it seemed, that Spike could do. Within a half hour, I was in the back of a large automobile being driven to the Clary-LaMarr Travelport to be put on a private bullet train to Goliathopolis.

I took a deep breath. Being Thursday was exciting and was certainly distracting. I'd hardly thought about Whitby at all.

24.

Goliath

Perils for the Unwary #16: Big Martin. A large catlike beast who is never seen but always leaves a trail of damage and mayhem in its wake. A Big Martin event can always be avoided, due to the ample warning given by a series of cats that gradually increase in size. The universal Rule of Three should be adopted: Simply put, the third Big Martin warning should be considered the last, and it is time to leave.

Bradshaw's BookWorld Companion (2nd edition)

Well," said Flanker as we sat in the plush interior of the bullet train, "we'll be at Goliathopolis in an hour, and your debrief can begin."

"Mr. Flanker, sir," said one of the accompanying heavies, a small man with a rounded face and a crew cut like a tennis ball, "have you checked she's not one of ours?"

"Good point," said Flanker. "Would you be so kind?"

The two heavies needed no extra encouragement, and while one held me down, the other clasped my upper eyelid and peered underneath. It wasn't painful, but it *was* undignified. Plus, the agent looking at my eye had been eating an onion sandwich not long before, and his breath was pretty unpleasant.

"She's not one of our Thursdays," said the agent, and they released me.

"I'm delighted to hear it," I said—and I was. There were now only two possibilities for who I was: me or Thursday. "Potblack killed them all," I added, "and had them buried in the Savernake."

"I don't know what you're talking about," replied Flanker airily. "Goliath no longer conducts experiments into synthetics. It's against the law. Oh," he added, "I forgot. We *are* the law. Shall I come straight to the point? We've been contracted to complete Phase One of the Anti-Smite Strategic Defense Shield by the end of the year, and the penalties are severe for noncompliance. We're not in the business of paying out severe penalties, so tell us where the secret plans are and we can release you and drop all the charges."

It felt like covering for a character in a book without being told what the book was about, who was in it or even what your character had been doing up until then. I'd done it twice in the BookWorld, so I had some experience in these matters. But at least I was beginning to understand what was going on.

"The plans are in a safe place," I replied, assuming they were, "but if you think you can simply ask questions and I'll simply answer them, you've got another think coming."

"Oh, this is just the preamble," said Flanker in an unpleasant tone, "so I can tell the board that I did ask you and you refused. We can cut the information out of you, but it's a very messy business. Now, where are the plans?"

"And I said somewhere safe."

Flanker was quiet for a moment. "Do you have any idea how much trouble you have caused Goliath?"

"I'm hoping it's a lot."

"You'd be right. Just getting you off the streets is a small triumph, but we have other plans. The Goliath Advanced Weapons Division has been wanting to get hold of you for a long time."

"I won't help you make any weapons, Flanker."

"It's simpler than that, Thursday. Since you have been so devastatingly destructive to us over the years, we have decided that *you* would make the ideal weapon. We can create excellent visual copies, but none of them have the unique skills that make you the dangerous person you are. Now that we have you and that precious brain of yours, with a couple of modifications in your moral compass our Thursday Mark V will be the ultimate killing machine. Of course, the host rarely survives the procedure, but we can replace you with another copy. I'm sure Landen won't notice. In fact, with a couple of modifications we can improve you for him—make the new Thursday more . . . compliant to his wishes."

"What makes you think that I'm not already? If he were only a quarter of the man he is, he'd still be ten times more of a man than you."

Flanker ignored me, and the bullet train moved off. We were soon zipping through the countryside, humming along thirty feet above the induction rail. When another bullet train passed in the opposite direction, we gently moved to the left of the induction wave, and the opposite train shot past us in a blur.

I stared at Flanker, who was sitting there grinning at me. If he could have started to laugh maniacally, he would have. But the thing was, this didn't sound like the Flanker in my books. Pain in the ass he might have been, but Goliath lackey he most certainly wasn't. His life was SpecOps, and although a strict rules man, that's all he was. I had an idea.

"When did they replace you, Flanker?"

"What do you mean?"

"This isn't you. Shit you might have been, evil-toady Goliath-lackey shit you most definitely weren't. Ever had a look at your own eyelid? Just to make sure?"

He laughed uneasily but then excused himself to the bathroom. When he came back, he looked somewhat pale and sat down in silence.

"When was I replaced?" he asked one of the heavies.

I'd not really given them much thought, but now that I

looked at them, they also seemed to be vaguely familiar, as though they'd been described to me long ago. There were plenty of Goliath personalities in my book, but the litigious multinational had always insisted that no actual names could be used, nor realistic descriptions—they went further by denying that anything in the Thursday Next books ever took place, something that Thursday told me was anything but the truth.

"This morning," said one of the heavies in a matter-of-fact tone, "and you're due for retirement this evening. You're what we call a day player."

Flanker put on a good face of being unperturbed and picked up the phone that connected him to the central command for the bullet train. Before he could speak, the other heavy leaned forward and placed his finger on the "disconnect" button.

"Even if I am only a day player," said Flanker, "I still outrank you."

"You're not the ranking officer here," said the other heavy. "You're just the friendly face of Goliath—and I say that without any sense of irony."

Flanker looked at me, then at the heavies, then out the window. He said nothing for perhaps thirty seconds, but I knew he was going to make a move. The trouble was, so did the heavies. Flanker reached for his gun, but no sooner had he grasped the butt than he suddenly stopped, his eyes rolled upwards into his head, and he collapsed without a noise. It was as though he'd been switched off. The Goliath heavy showed me a small remote with a single button on it.

"Useful little gadget," he said. "All our enemies should have one. Boris? Get rid of him and then fetch Miss Next a cup of tea."

The synthetic Flanker was unceremoniously dragged from the compartment by Boris, and the first heavy came to sit in Flanker's old place.

"An excellent move," he said with the air of authority, "to pit one of your foes against another. Worthy of the real Thursday. Now, where is she?"

"I'm her," I said, suddenly realizing that while this whole Goliath adventure was kind of amusing, it wasn't helping me find out where Thursday had actually gone. The sum total of my knowledge was that she'd been gone a month, was not dead, and had said that Lyell was boring. Goliath didn't have her, so I was wasting my time here. I needed to get back to Swindon.

"Are you a day player as well?" I asked.

"No," said the man, "I'm real. I check every morning. I know better than most that Goliath can't be trusted. Now, where are you from and where's Thursday?"

"I'm her. You don't need to look any further."

"You're not her," he said, "because you don't recognize me. It surprised me at first, which was why I had to make sure you weren't one of ours gone rogue. They do that sometimes. Despite our best attempts to create synthetics with little or no emotions, empathy tends to invade the mind like a virus. It's most troublesome. Flanker would have killed you this morning if I'd told him to, and by the afternoon he dies trying to protect you. It's just too bad. Now, where's Thursday?"

Finally I figured it out. The one person at Goliath who had more reason to hate me than any other.

"You're Jack Schitt, aren't you?"

He stared at me for a moment, and smiled.

"By all that's great and greedy," he said, staring at me in wonder, "what a coup. You're the written one, aren't you?"

"No."

But he knew I was lying. Unwittingly, I had revealed everything. Jack Schitt wasn't his real name—*it was his name in the series.* I didn't know what his real name was, but he would certainly have known his fictional counterpart. He pulled the phone off the hook and punched a few buttons.

"It's me. Listen carefully: It's not Thursday, it's the *written* Thursday. . . . Yes, I'm positive. She could melt back any second, so we need to get her Blue Fairyed the second we're on Goliath soil. . . . I don't care what it takes. If she's not real by teatime, heads will roll. And no, I'm not talking figuratively."

He hung up the phone and stared at me with a soft, triumphal grin. "When are you due back?"

I stared at him, a feeling of genuine fear starting to fill me. My actions so far had been based on the certainty that I would return. The idea of staying here forever was not in the game plan.

"What happened to the Austen Rover, Next?"

"The what?"

"The Austen Rover. Our experimental transfictional tour bus. The real Thursday traveled with it on its inaugural flight and never returned. Where is it?"

"I don't know what you're talking about, and besides, the Blue Fairy is fictional and lives inside *Pinocchio*. She doesn't do any actualizing these days. The Council of Genres forbade it."

"Better and better," he said, waving away the second heavy, who had returned with my tea, and closing the compartment door. "So you *are* from the BookWorld. And I was bluffing—we don't have a Blue Fairy. But we have the next best thing: a *green* fairy."

"I've never heard of the Green Fairy."

"It's a concoction of our own. It's not so much a fairy—more like a magnetic containment facility designed to keep fictional characters from crossing back. I understand that the first few hours can be *excruciatingly* painful, and it gets worse from there. You'll talk—they always do. How do you suppose we managed to get the inside information necessary to even begin research into the Book Project? Perhaps we can't make you real, but we can keep you here indefinitely—or at least until such time as you can't bear it any longer and agree to help us. Make it easy for yourself, Thursday: Where is the Austen Rover?"

"I have no idea."

"You'll tell us eventually. A few hours of Green Fairy will loosen your tongue."

"Goliath wouldn't last twenty minutes inside fiction," I said, but I wasn't convinced. If this "Jack Schitt" was even half as devious as the one written about, we were in big trouble. Thursday had spent a great deal of time and effort ensuring that the Goliath Corporation didn't get into fiction, either to dump toxic waste, use the people within it as unpaid labor or even just to find another market to dominate and exploit.

I said nothing, which probably was all he wanted to know. It was rotten luck that he'd been the one to figure me out. The real Thursday had once imprisoned the so-called Jack Schitt within Poe's "The Raven," so here was a man with some experience of being in the BookWorld.

"What's your name, then?" I asked. "If not Jack Schitt?"

"It was a ridiculous name, not to mention insulting," he snorted. "I'm Dorset. Adrian Dorset."

25.

An Intervention

Places to Eat #28: Inn Uendo, 3578 Comedy Boulevard. Made famous as the meeting place of the Toilet-Humor Appreciation Society, most of whose motions are passed while members are seated at the bar. The Double Entendre Bar and Grill is also highly recommended, and if you require satiating, the friendly waitstaff will be able to offer relief at the table.

Bradshaw's BookWorld Companion (5th edition)

Adrian Dorset?" I said. "Are you sure?"

"No, I'm not sure at all."

"What's your name, then?"

"You're not as smart as her, are you? Of *course* it's Dorset. I think I know my own name."

"The Adrian Dorset who wrote *The Murders on the Hareng Rouge?*"

He looked surprised for a moment. "The worthless scribblings of a man who was fooling himself that he could write. It was following the death of Anne, but I don't expect you'd know anything about that, do you?"

I shook my head.

"Anne was my wife," he said. "Head of the Book Project. She was on board the Austen Rover's inaugural journey. Thursday told me what had happened to her and what she'd done before she died. I don't blame Thursday. Not anymore. Revenge is for losers, cash is the winning currency. I burned the book a month ago. I didn't need it anymore. I'm over her."

He looked down at his feet, and I suddenly felt sorry for him.

"I'm sorry for your loss."

"Thank you."

He said very little for the rest of the journey, and I watched out the window as the English countryside zipped beneath us at breathtaking speed; we had nothing as fast as this in the BookWorld—not even in Sci-Fi, where they were a lot more conservative than they made out. As we approached Liverpool and the Tarbuck International Travelport, the traffic became more intense as other bullet gondolas joined the induction rail and clumped around for a while before moving off in separate directions. At all times the small, bullet-shaped craft, each no bigger than a bus, kept well spaced from one another, moving apart and together as congestion dictated.

The intercom buzzed, and Dorset picked it up, looked at me, then said, "Security override seventeen," before listening for a while and then saying, "*Bastards.* Very well."

"Problems?"

"Nothing to worry your sweet fictional head about."

We glided to a halt on Platform 24 at Tarbuck International. The doors hissed open, but we didn't move, and a few minutes later a small, meek-looking man arrived. He was wearing a dark suit and a bowler hat, and he was carrying a small briefcase. When he spoke, his voice was thin and reedy, and his nose was red from a recent cold.

"Good afternoon, Mr. Meakle," said my captor, without getting up.

"Good afternoon," said Meakle, who looked strikingly similar to someone who had played a bit part early on in my series. "You will release Miss Next to the custody of a federal marshal."

He indicated several marshals who were all standing on the platform outside the bullet.

"I'm afraid not, old chap," said Dorset or Schitt or whoever he was. "Miss Next is under arrest for crimes against humanity, which effectively trumps anything you might have in store for her."

"You're right *and* wrong," said Mr. Meakle. "She is under arrest, but *house* arrest, and will remain there until the government decides the best course of action. National heroes are not treated as common prisoners, Mr. Dorset."

"I have the authority of the police and SpecOps," replied Dorset coolly, "an authority given to us under mandate from the minister of justice."

The bureaucrat opened his case and took out a sheet of paper. "I repeat, Miss Next is to be taken into custody by a federal marshal. Here is an executive order signed personally by President Redmond van de Poste. Need I say more?"

Dorset took the document and stared at it minutely. I could tell from his expression that all was very much in order. He handed it back, looked at me and told me the game "was far from over."

I was taken across the concourse to where Meakle had his own private bullet with the presidential seal painted upon it, and within a few moments we were skimming back south across the countryside.

"Thank you."

Mr. Meakle seemed distracted, as though this were just one of many jobs he had to do in a single day. It looked, in fact, as though he worked from the bullet.

"My pleasure," said Mr. Meakle. "Where can we drop you?"

I asked for Swindon, and he relayed the instructions through the phone.

"I know I speak for the president when we say how fortunate it is to see you back," he added. "NSA officials and SO-5 will be briefed to protect you from Goliath. Can I schedule a meeting with the president anytime soon? We are eager to receive the secret plans as soon as we can, and we hope that the security arrangements are to your satisfaction."

I told him I'd meet with them tomorrow. Meakle nodded solemnly and returned to his work.

I sat back in my seat and ran the events of the afternoon through my head. I had just gotten to the bit where Spike had rescued me from the Stiltonista when I began to feel very peculiar. I started to have odd thoughts, then couldn't figure out why I'd thought of them. The world would soften around the edges, and I could feel myself almost lose consciousness. I thought for a moment I might be dying, as I could feel my conscious mind nearly close down. Before I knew it, I had closed my eyes and an overwhelming darkness stole over me. I might indeed have died, but I didn't, and I slept quite soundly until Mr. Meakle woke me when we arrived back at Clary-LaMarr.

26.

Family

Places to Visit #7: Poetry Island. Although this is at first glance a wild and powerful place, by turns beautiful, wayward, passionate and thought provoking, any visit longer than a few hours will start to have an *exaggerating* effect on the senses. Upbeat poems will tend to have you laughing uncontrollably, while somber poems will have you questioning your own worth in a most hideously self-obsessed manner. Early explorers of Poetry spent weeks acclimatizing in Walter de la Mare and Longfellow before daring to explore the Romantics.

Bradshaw's BookWorld Companion (12th edition)

*W*here did you get to?" asked Landen as soon as I tapped on the back door to be let in. "I was thinking you'd gone missing again."

"I brought down the Stiltonista, was arrested for crimes against humanity, found out where the other Thursdays are buried, was almost kidnapped by Goliath and was then rescued by the attorney general."

"Is that all?"

"No. I found out what ghosts are. They're childhood memories. Oh, and the president wants to see me tomorrow to discuss the Anti-Smite Strategic Defense Shield—I think it's what the whole 'secret plans' deal is all about."

"Are you sure you're not Thursday?"

"Positive. Hey, listen: Jack Schitt's real name is Adrian Dorset. How weird is that?"

"Not weird at all. You and I have known for years. Jack Schitt is a daft pseudonym—not to mention actionable."

"Perhaps so—but he wrote *The Murders on the Hareng Rouge*, the book I was asking you about."

"And the significance of this is . . . ?"

"I don't know, but the RealWorld's kind of wild with all this strange stuff going on, although it's a good thing this isn't Fiction—it wouldn't really make *any* sense."

I was becoming quite animated by now—randomness has an intoxicating effect on the preordained.

"By the way," I added, "do you want thirty grand?"

Landen raised an eyebrow in surprise. "You earned thirty thousand pounds this afternoon . . . *as well?*"

"From a Vole."

"What the . . . ? No, I don't want to know. But yes, we could do with the cash, so long as it's not illegally earned."

"Here you go," I said, handing him the crumpled check.

I'd have to make good on my side of the bargain, but I felt sure I could drop some Toast Marketing Board references into the series without much problem.

"Oh, and if you see anyone who looks like NSA or SpecOps watching the house, don't be alarmed. The president is protecting us—I don't think Goliath is too keen on me right now."

"Were they ever?"

"Not really. But I know what they're up to, and it's particularly unpleasant. In fact, I shouldn't really hang around. I'll only make things dangerous for you."

"Until we prove you're not my wife," he said, "you're staying."

It seemed like a generous sentiment, so I accepted gracefully.

"Listen," he said, "just in case I'm wrong and you really *are* written, you should know something."

"Yes?"

"You know I said I didn't know where she was?"

I nodded.

"That's not *strictly* true. I didn't know whether I could trust you. You see, when Thursday went to the BookWorld, she *always* came and went via her office at Acme Carpets. Bowden is the manager over there, and when she went missing, I asked him to go and look for her."

"She wasn't in her office?"

"No—*and the door was locked from the inside.*"

He let this information sink in. She had gone to the Book-World four weeks ago—and not returned.

"So," he said, "if you're *not* her, it's where you need to be looking. If you *are* her, it's where you need to go to find out what has happened to you."

I stared at him and bit my lip. Thursday was definitely somewhere in the BookWorld. Lost, alone, perhaps hurt—who knows? But at least I had somewhere to start. My mission, such as it was, was at least a partial success.

"Well, then," said Landen, clapping his hands together, "you'd better meet Tuesday."

So I sat down at the kitchen table and felt all goose-bumpy and hot. I'd been less nervous facing down Potblack, but this was different. Landen and the children were everything I'd ever wanted. Potblack was just a jumped-up cheesemonger.

Tuesday wandered shyly into the room and stared at me intently.

"Hello," I said. "I'm not your mother."

"You look like her. Dad says that you might be Mum but you don't know it."

"That's possible, too," I said, "and I'd like to be."

"Could she be?" asked Tuesday of Landen.

"It's possible, but we won't know until later."

"Oh, well," said Tuesday, sitting next to me at the kitchen table. "Do you want to see what I'm working on?"

"Sure."

So she opened her exercise book and showed me a sketch of an idea she'd been having.

"This is a sundial that works in the overcast—or even indoors. This is a method of sending power wirelessly using music, and what do you make of this?" She showed me several pages of complex mathematical notation.

"Looks important."

"It's an algorithm that can predict the movement of cats with ninety-seven percent accuracy," she explained with a smile. "I'm presenting it to Nuffield College the day after tomorrow. Do you want to come?"

Over the next few minutes, she explained her work, which was far-ranging in its originality and depth. The real Thursday's inventor uncle Mycroft was dead now, and his intellect had crossed to Tuesday. If at age twelve she was working out the complex mathematics required to accurately predict random events, her work when she was an adult would be awe inspiring. She spoke to me of her latest project: a plausible method to crack one of the most intractable problems in modern physics, that of attempting to instill a sense of urgency in teenagers. After that she explained how she was designing daylight fireworks, which would sparkle darkness in the light, and then finally mentioned the possibility of using beamed electron fields as a kind of impermeable barrier with such diverse applications as enabling people to go underwater without need for an Aqua Lung or to protect one from rockfalls or even for use as an umbrella. "Especially useful" remarked Tuesday, "for an electron-field umbrella wouldn't poke anyone in the eye and never needs shaking."

After Tuesday had gone off to fetch a photograph album, I turned to Landen. "*She's* the secret plans, isn't she?"

He looked at me but said nothing, which I took to mean she

was. Tuesday's intellect would be the driving force behind the government's Anti-Smite Strategic Defense Shield.

"I guess we're just about to find out if you're the Goliath Thursday," said Landen. "If you are, you'll be contacting them straightaway."

I wouldn't, of course. "How long do you think before they figure it out?"

"I don't know," replied Landen, scraping the carrots he'd been chopping into a saucepan, "but know this: I'll die to protect my daughter."

"Me, too."

Landen smiled. "Are you sure you're not her?"

"I'm sure."

Tuesday came back with the photograph album, and I joined her as she leafed through the family holidays of which I had no knowledge. I stared at the Thursday in the pictures and tried to figure her out. She never looked totally relaxed—not as much as Landen and the kids anyway, but clearly loved them all, even if she seemed to be glancing around her as though on the lookout for anyone wishing to do them or her harm. There were very few pictures in which she was smiling. She took life seriously, but her family kept her anchored, and probably as sane as she could ever hope to be. Tuesday reached for my hand and held it tightly without really thinking, and as we chatted, it crossed my mind that I could *become* Thursday, if the real one never showed up. I could go Blue Fairy, and all this would be mine. For a fleeting moment, it seemed like a good, worthy and attainable idea, but reality quickly returned. I was fooling myself. The longer I listened to Tuesday, the more I realized just how much she needed her mother. Not any mother, but *her* mother. I would never be anything more than a pale reflection.

"Landen," I said when Tuesday had gone off to watch *Bonzo the Wonder Hound, Series Twelve*, "I shouldn't have come."

"Nonsense."

"No, really. It was a huge mistake. I can't be her, no matter how much I want to."

"You sell yourself short—I'm more convinced by the minute. The way you sat with Tuesday."

"Yes?"

"That's how Thursday used to do it. Proud, loving—but not understanding a single word she said."

"Land, I'm not her. I've got no idea what's going on, I didn't recognize Adrian Dorset, I didn't know that you'd lost a leg and, and, and . . . I can't see Jenny. I should just go and hide in a large cupboard somewhere until I'm whisked back into Fiction."

He stared at me for a moment. "I never said her name was Jenny."

"*Damn.*"

He took a step closer and held my hand. "You saw her?"

I nodded. "Jenny mentioned Thursday saying 'Lyell was boring.' Does that make any sense to you?"

"Thursday didn't discuss her BookWorld work with me. She pretended it was a secret, and I pretended I didn't know about it. Same as the SpecOps work. But I don't know anyone called Lyell, and she *hated* boring people. Except me."

"You're not boring."

"I am, but I'm okay with it. I'm the anchor. The shoulder."

"And you're all right with the support role?"

He laughed. "Of course! It's my *function*. Besides, I love her. More than anything on the planet—with the possible exception of Tuesday and Friday. And I'm actually quite fond of Jenny, too, even though she doesn't exist."

"You're a good man."

He smiled. "No, I'm an average man . . . with a truly extraordinary wife."

I rubbed my temples with the frustration of it. I so wanted to be her and have all this—Landen, the kids. There was a dull throb in my head, and I felt hot and prickly. It was a lot easier being fictional—always assuming that I was, of course.

"That's another reason I should leave," I said in a harsher tone than I might have wished. "This morning I knew who I was and what I was doing. Now? I've got no idea."

And I started to sob.

"Hey, hey," he said, resting a hand on mine, "don't cry. There's four hours to go before you vanish or not, and I'm not sure I can wait that long. I'm pretty confident you're her. You called me 'Land,' you saw Jenny, you're a bit odd, you love the kids. But there's one simple way I'll be able to tell."

"And what's that?"

"Kiss me."

I felt myself shiver with anticipation, and my heart—my real heart, that is, not the descriptive one—suddenly thumped faster. I placed my hand on his cheek, which was warm to the touch, and leaned forward. I felt his breath on my face, and our lips were just about to touch when suddenly I once more felt the hot needles and Klein-Blue Wagnerian treacle, and I was back in the arrivals lounge at JurisTech. As Plum had promised, there was a glass of water and some cookies waiting for me. I picked up the water glass and threw it at the wall.

27.

Back Early

Plot 9 (Human Drama) revolved around a protagonist returning to a dying parent to seek reconciliation for past strife and
then finding new meaning to his or her life. If you lived anywhere but HumDram, "go do a Plot 9" was considered a serious insult, the Outlander equivalent of being told to "go screw
yourself."

Bradshaw's BookWorld Companion (3rd edition)

I found Professor Plum working on his Large Metaphor
Collider. As soon as he saw me, he pressed a couple of buttons
on his mobilefootnoterphone, uttered a few words and smiled
at me.

"Oh!" he said in some surprise. "You're back."

"What happened? I wasn't meant to come back for another
four hours!"

"Transfictional travel isn't an exact science," he replied with
a shrug. "Sometimes you'll pop back early for no adequately
explained reason."

"Can you send me out there again? I was right in the middle
of something important."

"If Bradshaw allows it, I'll be more than happy to."

"Please?"

"There are safety issues," he explained. "The more you stay
out there, the less time you can spend there. Bradshaw used to

travel across quite often, but these days he can barely stay out for ten minutes before popping back."

I thought about the excitement I'd felt just as I was about to kiss Landen and the potential chain of events that might have occurred from there on in.

"I *really* need to get back, Professor. Lives . . . um, depend on it."

"Whose lives?"

Commander Bradshaw had appeared in the laboratory. But he didn't walk in, he had *bookjumped* in. I hadn't seen that for a while; it was considered very common and was actively discouraged. The Ungenred Zone and Racy Novel, to name but two, even had antijump sieves set up on their borders—large sails of a fine mesh that snagged the punctuation in one's description and brought one down to earth with a thump.

"I'm very busy," he said, glancing at his watch. "Walk with me."

So I walked with Bradshaw out of the labs, past the frog-footman, who followed at a discreet distance and up the stairs.

"So," said Bradshaw, "how did you get on?"

"Not very well. *Lots* happened, but I've got no way of knowing which of the facts were significant and which weren't."

"The RealWorld is like that. It's possible that nothing was significant or that everything was. It scares the bejesus out of me, I can tell you—and I don't scare easily. Anything on Thursday's whereabouts?"

I told him about the locked room at Acme.

"Hmm," he said, "*definitely* in here somewhere. I'll ask Professor Plum to attempt another Textual Sieve triangulation." He thought for a moment. "How were Landen and the kids?"

"As good as might be expected. Permission to speak honestly, sir?"

"I welcome nothing else."

"Is it possible that Thursday is alive and well but just suffering some bizarre mental aberration?"

He stared at me. "You think you might be Thursday?"

I shrugged. "Landen seems to think so. I saw Jenny, and I could do things—fight, think on my feet and disarm a man in under a second. Things I never knew I could do."

He smiled and patted my arm. "It's not uncommon to have feelings of elevated status after visiting the RealWorld. It'll soon pass."

"But *could* I tell if I were real? Could anyone tell?"

"There are lots of signs," said Bradshaw, "but here's the easiest: What am I doing now?"

"I don't know."

"How about now?"

"As far as I can tell, you're not doing anything at all."

Bradshaw took his finger off my nose and smiled. "I suppressed my action line. The real Thursday could have seen what I was doing, but you had to rely on the description. You're fictional, my dear, through and through."

"But I could be just *thinking* you did that—the same as I *thought* I saw Jenny, and all my backstory about being the written Thursday. I could be . . . delusional."

"And part of this delusion is you *thinking* you might be delusional? And me here right now talking to you?"

"I suppose so."

"Pull yourself together, girl," he snapped, "and don't be such a bloody fool. If you *were* Thursday, you'd be saving the Book-World, not blundering around the Outland like a petulant bull in a china shop. This is Fiction, not Psychology."

"I'm sorry, sir."

"That's okay. Now, is there anything else to report?"

I told him about Jenny, the comment about Lyell and how Goliath had developed a Green Fairy and wanted to know where the Austen Rover had ended up.

"Goliath is an ongoing thorn," said Bradshaw grimly, "but we're dealing with the problem. Anything else?"

I thought for a moment. If I couldn't trust Bradshaw, I couldn't trust anyone.

"This morning Jobsworth and Red Herring asked me to pretend to be Thursday and go to the peace talks on Friday."

"We thought they might."

"Should I go?"

"It would be my advice that you shouldn't. Don't be insulted by this, but civilians are ill equipped to deal with anything beyond that which is normally expected of them. The Book-World is fraught with dangers, and your time is best served bringing as many readers as you can to your series, then keeping them."

"Can I go back to the RealWorld?"

"No."

"I have unfinished business. I did go on a somewhat risky mission for you—I could have ended up erased or dead—or both."

"You have the gratitude of the head of Jurisfiction," he said. "That should be enough. He's not *your* husband, Thursday. He's Thursday's. Go back to your book and just forget about everything that's happened. You're not her and never can be. Understand?"

"Yes, sir."

"Excellent. Appreciate a girl who knows when to call it a day. The frog guy will see you out. Good day."

And so saying, he turned on his heel and walked into the ballroom. The door closed behind him, leaving me confused, drained and missing Landen. I thought of going to find Whitby to cry on his shoulder, but then I remembered about the nuns.

"Damn," I said, to no one in particular.

The frog-footman saw me to the front door, then handed me the Rubik's Cube I'd lent him.

"Here," he said. "It's got me flummoxed, I can tell you."

Despite his working on the puzzle during my absence the cube had remained resolutely unsolved—all six sides were still the same unbroken colors.

28.

Home Again

There are multiple BookWorlds, all coexisting in parallel planes and each unique to its own language. Naturally, varying tastes around the Outland make for varying popularity of genres, so no two BookWorlds are ever the same. Generally, they keep themselves to themselves, except for the annual BookWorld Conference, where the equivalent characters get together to discuss translation issues. It invariably ends in arguments and recriminations.

Bradshaw's BookWorld Companion (2nd edition)

I climbed out of the Porsche, slammed the door and leaned against the stone wall. We'd just done the "bad time" section within *The Eyre Affair*, which was always tiring and a bit spacey. Despite our best endeavors, our sole reader had simply given up and left us dangling less than a page before the end of that chapter—the Outlander equivalent of letting someone reach the punch line before announcing you'd heard the joke before.

Bowden climbed out to join me. I got on better with him than I did with the character who played my father, but that wasn't saying much. It was like saying sparrows got on better with cats than robins. Bowden had a thing going on with the previous written Thursday, and when he tried to hit on me at the Christmas party, I'd tipped an entire quiche in his lap. Our relationship on and off book had been strained ever since.

"That was just plain *embarrassing*," said Bowden. "You were barely even trying."

I'd taken over from Carmine the second I got home, so I couldn't blame her. I should have let her just carry on—she was doing fine, after all, but . . . well, I needed the distraction.

"So we had a bit of wastage," I said. "It happens."

Reader "wastage" was something one had to get used to but never did. Most of the time it was simply that our book wasn't the reader's thing, which was borne with a philosophical shrug. We'd lost six readers at one hit once when my brother Joffy went AWOL and missed an entire chapter. It had never been more tempting to hit the Snooze Button. Mind you, in the annals of reader wastage, our six readers were peanuts. *Stig of the Dump* once lost seven hundred readers in the early seventies when Stig was kidnapped by *Homo erectus* fundamentalists, eager to push a promegalith agenda. Unusually, terms were agreed on with the kidnappers and a new megalith section was inserted into the book. It messed slightly with the whole dream/reality issue but never dented the popularity of the novel. On that occasion the Snooze Button *was* pressed, which accounts for the lack of a sequel. Kitten death—even *written* kitten death—carries a lot of stigma. Barney eventually handed over the reins to a replacement and works these days at Text Grand Central; Stig is now much in demand as an after-dinner nonspeaker.

"So what's up?" asked Bowden. "I've seen more dynamic performances in *Mystery on the Island*."

I shrugged. "Things aren't going that well for me at the moment."

"Man trouble?"

"Of a sort."

"Do you want some advice?"

"Thank you, Bowden, I would."

"Get your ass into gear and act like a mature character. You're making us the laughingstock of Speculative Fantasy. Our readership is in free fall. Want to go the way of *Raphael's Walrus*?"

It wasn't the sort of advice I was expecting.

"So you'd prefer the old Thursday, would you?" I replied indignantly. "The gratuitous sex and violence?".

"At least it got us read."

"Yes," I replied, "but by whom? We want the *quality* readers, not the prurient ones who—"

"You're a terrible snob, you know that?"

"I am not."

"You should value *all* readers. If you want to mix in the rarefied heights of 'quality readership,' then why don't you sod off to HumDram and do a Plot 9?"

"Because," I said, "I'm trying to do what the real Thursday wants."

"And where is she?" he asked with a sneer. "Not been down this way for ages. You keep on banging on about the greater glory of your illustrious namesake, but if she *really* cared for us, she'd drop in from time to time."

I fell silent. There was some truth in this. It had been six months since she'd visited, and then only because she wanted to borrow Mrs. Malaprop to put up some shelves.

"Listen," said Bowden, "you're nice enough in a scatty kind of way, but if you try to add any new scenarios, you'll just make trouble for us. If you're going to change anything, revert to the previous Thursday. It's within the purview of 'character interpretation.' And since she was once that way, there's a precedent. More readers and no risk. Who the hell is the Toast Marketing Board anyway?"

"It's a *secret* plan," I remarked defensively, "to improve readership. You're going to have to trust me. And while I'm in charge, we'll do it my way, thank you very much. I may even decide," I added daringly, "to add some more about the Book-World in the stories. It would make it more realistic, and readers might find it amusing."

It was a bold statement. The CofG went to great expense

to ensure that readers didn't find out about the inner workings of the BookWorld. I left Bowden looking shocked and opened a door in the Yorkshire Dales setting, then took a shortcut through the SpecOps Building to find myself back home. Carmine and Sprockett were waiting in the kitchen and sensed that something was wrong.

"I met Mr. and Mrs. Goblin," said Carmine, "and they seem very—"

"I'm really not that bothered, Carmine. You're taking over. I've added something about the Toast Marketing Board. It'll require line changes on these pages here and an extra scene."

I handed her the additional pages, and she looked at me with a quizzical expression. Making up scenes was utterly forbidden, and we both knew it.

"I'll take responsibility. Now, get on with it or I'll have Mrs. Malaprop stand in for me—she'd kill for some first-person time in her logbook."

Carmine said no more and hurried from the kitchen.

"I'm hungry," said Pickwick, waddling in from the living room.

"You know where the cupboard is."

"*What* did you say?"

"I said you know where the cupboard is."

Pickwick opened her eyes wide in shock. She wasn't used to being talked to that way. "Don't use that tone of voice with me, Miss Next!"

"Or else what?"

Pickwick waddled up and pecked me as hard as she could on the knee. It wasn't remotely painful, as a dodo's beak is quite blunt. If she'd been a woodpecker, I might have had more reason to complain. I held her beak shut with my finger and thumb and then leaned down so close that she went cross-eyed trying to look up at me.

"Listen here," I said, "try to peck me again and I'll lock you in the toolshed overnight. Understand?"

Pickwick nodded her beak, and I let go, and she very quietly sidled from the room. There was a mechanical cough from behind me. It was Sprockett, and his eyebrow pointer was indicating "Puzzled."

"How did the trip to the RealWorld go?" he asked.

"Not great."

"So I observe, ma'am."

I sat down at the kitchen table and ran my fingers through my hair.

"Perhaps if ma'am would like to change out of her work costume? I could run a bath—perhaps a long soak might help."

I looked down at the clothes I was wearing. It was classic Thursday: Levi's, boots and a shirt, faded leather jacket and a pistol in a shoulder holster. I felt more at home in these now than I felt in my Gypsy skirts and tie-dye top. In fact, I would be happy never to see a sandal again, much less wear one.

"You know," I said as Sprockett brought me a cup of tea, "I thought it was odd in the BookWorld. Out in the RealWorld it's positively *insane*."

"How was Landen?"

"Dangerously perfect."

I told him all that had happened. Of Jack Schitt being Adrian Dorset, of Goliath, the Toast Marketing Board and the contention from Jenny that Thursday couldn't be dead. I also told him my suspicions that I might actually be her, despite what Bradshaw had said and much evidence to the contrary.

"And then I lost a reader and got pissed off with Bowden, Carmine and Pickwick," I added.

"Any clues as to Miss Next's whereabouts?" asked Sprockett as he attempted to keep me on the task at hand.

"Only that Lyell is boring. How many Lyells are there in the BookWorld?"

Sprockett buzzed for a moment. "Seven thousand, give or take. None of them particularly boring—that's a trait generally attached to Geralds, Brians and Keiths—or at least, here in the BookWorld it is."

"Interviewing every Lyell would take too long. Friday and the peace talks are not getting any further away."

"Did you speak to the Jack Schitt here in the series?"

"First thing when I got back."

"And . . . ?"

"He knew nothing about Adrian Dorset or *Murders*. Didn't even know that Jack wasn't his real name."

"But it's a bit of a stretch, isn't it?" said Sprockett, his eyebrow pointer clicking down to "Thinking." "I mean, it can't be a coincidence. Jack Schitt's book being the accident book?"

"In the Outland there *are* coincidences. It's only in the Book-World they're considered relevant. What about you? Come up with anything?"

"I went and spoke to TransGenre Taxis. To see if they were missing anyone."

"And?"

"They wouldn't give me any information. I think it was a mixture of corporate policy, laziness and overt coggism."

"Really?" I replied. "We'll see about that."

I went into the study, fetched a chair and pulled Thursday's shield from where it was still embedded in the ceiling. I turned the shiny badge over in my hand. It was encased in a soft leather wallet and was well worn with use. It could get me almost anywhere in the BookWorld, no questions asked.

"Why would the red-haired gentleman have given this to me?"

"Maybe he was asked to," said Sprockett. "Thursday has many friends, but there is only one person she knows she can truly trust."

"And who's that?"

"Herself."

"That's what the red-haired man told me," I said, suddenly

realizing that recent events might have had some greater purpose behind them. "Something happened. Thursday must have left instructions for him to get out of his story, find me and ask me to help."

"Why didn't he say so directly?" asked Sprockett, not unreasonably.

"This is Fiction," I explained. "The exigency of drama requires events to be clouded in ambiguity." I placed Thursday's badge in my pocket.

"Is using the shield wise?" asked Sprockett. "The last time you used it, the Men in Plaid were onto us within the hour."

"It opens doors. And what's more, I don't *care* if the Men in Plaid arrive. We'll do as Thursday would do."

"And what would that be, ma'am?"

I opened the bureau drawer, retrieved my second-best pistol and emptied all the ammunition I had into my jacket pocket.

"We kick some butt, Sprockett."

"Very good, ma'am."

29.

TransGenre Taxis

The TransGenre Taxi service has been going for almost as long as the BookWorld has been self-aware, and has adapted to the remaking with barely a murmur. TGTs are clean, the drivers have an encyclopedic knowledge of the BookWorld that would put a librarian to shame, and they can be relied upon to bend the rules when required—for a fee. Traditionally, they rarely have change for a twenty.

Bradshaw's BookWorld Companion (2nd edition)

*T*he TransGenre Taxi head office was housed over in Nonfiction within the pages of the less-than-thrilling *World Taxi Review*, published bimonthly. But traveling all the way to Nonfiction would take a needlessly long time and would alert the Men in Plaid before we'd even gotten as far as Zoology. Luckily for us, there was a regional office located within *The First Men in the Moon*, located over in Sci-Fi/Classic. It was rumored that the propulsion system used by the taxis was based upon a modified Cavorite design, but this was poohpoohed by Sci-Fi purists as "unworkable." Mind you, so was the "interior of a sphere" BookWorld, but that seemed to work fine, too.

The dispatch clerk was a small, deeply harassed individual with the look of someone who had unwisely conditioned his hair and then slept on it wet.

"No refunds!" he said as soon as we entered.

"I'm not after a refund."

"You wouldn't get one if you were. What can I do for you?"

"We're looking for a missing taxi. Took a fare from Vanity early yesterday morning."

The dispatch clerk was unfazed. "I'm afraid to say that company policy is quite strict on this matter, madam. You'll need a Jurisfiction warrant—"

"How's this?" I asked, slapping Thursday's shield on the counter.

The dispatch clerk stared at the badge for a moment, then picked up a clipboard from under the counter and started to flick through the pages. There were a lot of them.

"You're fortunate we still have them," he said. "We file with Captain Phantastic in an hour."

He searched though them, chatting as he did so.

"We lose a couple of taxis every day to erasure, wastage, accidental reabsorption or simply to being used in books. For obvious reasons we're keen to hide the actual number of accidents for fear of frightening people from our cabs."

"Most thoughtful of you."

"You're in luck," he said, staring at his notes. "The only taxi missing that morning was Car 1517. Its last-known fare was a pickup from Sargasso Plaza, opposite the entrance to Fan Fiction."

"On Vanity Island?"

"Right. The driver departed Sargasso Plaza bound for the Ungenred Zone at 0823, and that was the last we heard."

"You didn't think about reporting it?"

"We usually wait a week. Besides, search parties are expensive."

"Do we have a passenger name?"

"Tuesday Laste."

Sprockett and I looked at each other. We seemed finally to be getting somewhere.

"And the name of the driver?"

"Gatsby."

"The Great Gatsby drives taxis in his spare time?"

"No, his younger and less handsome and intelligent brother— the Mediocre Gatsby. He lives in Parody Valley over in Vanity. Here's his address."

We thanked him and left the office.

"*Tuesday Laste?*" repeated Sprockett as we hailed a cab.

"Almost certainly Thursday."

Sprockett's eyebrow pointer switched from "Puzzled" to "Bingo," paused for a moment and then switched to "Worried."

"Problems?" I asked as we climbed into the cab.

"In the shape of a Buick," replied Sprockett, indicating a Roadmaster that had just pulled up outside the TransGenre Taxi office. It was the Men in Plaid, and they were following the same trail we were. I leaned forward.

"Vanity Island," I said to the driver, "and step on it."

Vanity wasn't a place that conventionally published people liked to visit, as it was a bizarre mixture of the best and worst prose, where descriptive passages of exceptional beauty rubbed shoulders with dialogue so spectacularly poor it could make one's ears bleed. We skimmed low across the narrow straits that separated Vanity from the mainland and circled the craggy island, past sprawling shantytowns of abandoned novellas, half-described castles and ragged descriptions of variable quality before coming to land in a small square just outside Parody Valley.

"You can wait for us," I said to the cabbie, who gave me a sarcastic, "Yeah, right," and left almost immediately, which made me regret I'd paid up front and tipped him.

We took a left turn into Cold Comfort Boulevard and made our way past unpublished pastiches and parodies of famous novels that were only on Vanity at all due to their being just within the law. If they had used the same character names from the parodied novel, they were removed to the copyright-tolerance haven of Fan Fiction. This was situated on a smaller island close by and joined to Vanity by a stone arched bridge a half mile long, and guarded by a game show host.

"How long before the Men in Plaid follow us here?" asked Sprockett.

"Five or ten minutes," I replied, and we quickened our pace.

Given that parodies—even unpublished ones—have a shelf life governed by the currency of the novel that is being parodied, the small subgenre was dominated by that year's favorites. We walked on, and once past the still-popular Tolkien pastiches we were in the unread Parody hinterland, based on books either out of print themselves or so far off the zeitgeist radar that they had little or no meaning. We took a left turn by *When Nine Bells Toll; Hello, My Lovely* and *I, Robert* before finding the book we were looking for: an outrageously unfunny Fitzgerald parody entitled *The Diamond as Big as the South Mimms Travelodge.*

Mediocre's apartment was above a set of garages. There was a brand-new taxi parked in an empty bay beneath, and we carefully climbed the rickety stairs. I knocked on the screen door, and after a few moments a woman of slovenly demeanor stood on the threshold gnawing a chicken drumstick. She wore heavy eyeliner that had run, and she looked as though she'd just had a fight with a hairbrush—and lost.

"Yes?" she asked in a lazy manner. "Can I help?"

I flashed Thursday's badge. "Thursday Next," I announced, "and this is my butler, Sprockett. Your name is . . . ?"

"Gatsby."

This was unexpected.

"The Mediocre Gatsby?"

"No, the *Loser* Gatsby, the youngest of the three Gatsbys. I haven't seen Great for a while. How did it turn out with crazy Daisy? She looked like trouble to me."

"Not . . . *terrific*, as I recall."

"Did they let Mia Farrow play her in the movie?"

"I'm not sure. Is Mediocre here?"

"I've not seen the miserable fart for three days," she sniffed, picking her nose. "How did you know he was missing? I didn't call you."

"May we come in?"

"I guess," said Loser Gatsby with a shrug, and we walked into the apartment. Sprawled in the front room were a half dozen men and women who looked as though life had not been kind to them. One of the women had been crying recently, and two of the men still were.

"This is our Siblings of More Famous BookWorld Personalities self-help group," explained Loser. "That's Sharon Eyre, the younger and wholly disreputable sister of Jane; Roger Yossarian, the draft dodger and coward; Brian Heep, who despite admonishments from his family continues to wash daily; Rupert Bond, still a virgin and can't keep a secret; Tracy Capulet, who has slept her way round Verona twice; and Nancy Potter, who is . . . well, let's just say she's a term that is subject to several international trademark agreements."

"She's a Muggle?"

"Pretty much."

They all nodded a greeting.

"We meet twice daily to try to iron out the feelings of low self-worth we experience, given our more famous family members. It's quite hard, I assure you, being a nobody when an elder sister or brother is iconic for all time. Tracy Capulet was telling us what it was like living in Verona."

"It's 'Juliet this, Juliet that' all day long," said Tracy petulantly. "Juliet's on the balcony, Juliet's shagging a Montague, Juliet's pretending to be dead—blah, blah, blah. I tell you, I'm totally sick of it."

Sprockett moved to the window and peered out. The Men in Plaid would be here soon.

"This is a matter of some urgency," I said. "Does Mediocre have a room?"

Loser pointed to a door, and before she could explain that it was locked, Sprockett had wrenched it off its hinges.

The room was grubby and the floor scattered with discarded pizza containers and empty hyphen cans. The TV was still on and was tuned to a shopping channel, and his record collection contained *Hooked on Classics* and *Footloose*. Mediocre lived up to his name.

"What do you make of this?" asked Sprockett, who had come across a large model of the Forth Rail Bridge. It had large spans that in reality would have thrust boldly across the Forth Estuary, not just to connect two landmasses separated by a barrier that was also an arterial trade route but to demonstrate man's technological prowess in the face of natural obstacles.

"It's not a bridge," I whispered, "it's *metaphor*."

We started opening boxes and found three more bridges, two rivers and a distant mountain range, swathed in mist with a road leading to unknown valleys beyond. Loser Gatsby was at the door, mouth open.

"Tell me," I said, "where did your brother get all this?"

"I don't know."

"Truthfully?"

"I'm a loser," she said. "If I'd known about this little lot, I would have sold it all, gone on a bender and had a dolphin tattooed on my left boob."

Her logic was impeccable. I questioned her further, but she knew nothing.

"In two minutes the Men in Plaid will be coming through that door," I told her. "Believe me, you don't want to be here when they do."

I didn't need to say it twice, and she and the rest of the loser literary siblings made a hasty exit down the stairs.

"So," said Sprockett, staring at all the metaphor, "stolen?"

"Not if Mediocre was as his name suggests," I replied. "How much do you think this is all worth?"

"Twenty grand," said Sprockett. "People will pay good money to get hold of raw metaphor. There's enough here to keep a man comfortable for a long time."

"Or even enroll at character college," I said holding up a prospectus from St. Tabularasa's. "Looks like Mediocre was trying to better himself and shed his epithet. A cabbie couldn't earn this much in a decade of Octobers." I added, "I reckon we're looking at a bribe."

"To do what?"

"I don't know."

I picked up Mediocre's account book. It outlined all the trips he had done and which needed to be billed. The last day was not there, of course, but the previous day *was*.

"Well, well," I said, "looks like Thursday went on a trip to Biography the day before she vanished. And that's not all," I added. "Every single fare Mediocre accepted was picked up from the same place—Sargasso Plaza, just outside the entrance to Fan Fiction. Coincidence?"

"We have company," murmured Sprockett, who'd been standing at the window.

I joined him and noted that a 1949 Buick Roadmaster had pulled up outside the building. Two Men in Plaid got out and looked around.

"Time we weren't here."

We crossed to the other side of the room and exited though the French windows, which opened onto a veranda. From there we climbed down onto the roof of a garden shed, then let ourselves out into an alley beyond. We walked back around the house and watched as the Plaids went into the building.

"What now, ma'am?"

I handed him a set of keys I'd found in Mediocre's room and nodded towards the brand-new taxi parked outside. "Can you drive one of those?"

"If it has wheels, I can drive it, ma'am. Are we heading for Biography?"

"We are."

"And what will we do when we get there?"

"Find out if Lyell is as boring as Thursday said he was."

30.

High Orbit

Sooner or later a resident of the BookWorld will start to question what is *beyond* the internal sphere that we call home. Stated simply, what would happen if one burrowed directly downwards? In pursuit of an answer, noted explorer Arne Saknussemm entered a disused metaphor mine to see if a way through could be found. As this edition went to press, he has not yet returned.

Bradshaw's BookWorld Companion (3rd edition)

*S*prockett reversed the cab out of the garage, engaged the Technobabble™ Swivelmatic vectored-ion plasma drive and powered vertically upwards from Parody Valley and Vanity. I was pressed back into my seat by the acceleration and the ascent angle, and I might have been frightened had my mind not been tumbling with what we'd discovered so far—or even with what we had still yet to find out. Within a few minutes, we were hanging in the heavens a couple of thousand feet from the surface, right at the cruising altitude of local books that were being moved around Fiction. Below us the islands that made up the Fiction Archipelago were laid out in precise detail.

"Would it be impertinent to point out that visiting another island in the BookWorld without transit papers is strictly forbidden?"

"What does Thursday Next care for transit papers?"

"I would politely point out that you're not her, ma'am."

"I might as well be. I have a shield and I look like her. Who can say I'm not?"

"Who indeed, ma'am?"

I looked behind us and out to sea. Biography was situated beyond Artistic Criticism, and it was unlikely that any books would be going that way at this lower level. I wound down the window, poked my head out and looked up. Several miles above us, I could see the high-level books crisscrossing the sky, their journey made less arduous by traveling at the precise altitude where the force of gravity from below cancels the force of gravity from above—the gravopause. At that height you could usually find someone going your way—so long as you could get up there. The Technobabble™ drive on the cab would get us to local traffic height, but after that we were on our own.

We had to wait a nail-biting two and three-quarters minutes, every second worrying that the Plaids would spot us.

"Buckle up, ma'am," said Sprockett. "Looks like someone's been discovered."

As we watched, an entire section of Vanity Island seemed to fall away. A book had been accepted into the mainstream and was rising from the flanks of Mount Sleeper, trailing the debris of a ramshackle group of shameless Zadie Smith rip-offs that had been unwisely built on top of it.

The settings—mostly of a winter scene in London, it appeared—rotated slowly about its axis as it rose vertically to meet us, and just as it transitioned into forward flight, Sprockett stepped on the throttle and accelerated to meet the book, which loomed as large as eight cathedrals in the windscreen. As soon as we were close enough, Sprockett slewed the vehicle to a stop on the side of a dream sequence—a picnic the family had once spent on a grassy hill in spring, where a silver pond alive with bulrushes lay within the dappled glade of beech trees.

"Congratulations on the publication," I said to a small boy who was playing with a tin train, and he waved shyly in return. We weren't there for long. Piggybacking around the BookWorld was a dark art that needed calm nerves and good timing; within a few minutes, Sprockett lifted off again and made the short hop to a historical novel that was moving up to join the High Stream in order to make its way to History for fact-checking. They looked less friendly in this book, so Sprockett simply fired one of the vehicle's two grapnels into the soft intratextual matrix to which the book's settings were bolted, and we began the tow into the high orbit dangling on the end of a slender length of steel cable.

"Okay," I said as we moved steadily upwards, the cab's altimeter winding around like a top, "how's this for a scenario? Thursday is investigating something that requires her to stay out of sight. She hides out in Vanity, somewhere near Sargasso Plaza. The Mediocre Gatsby always hangs out there, waiting for fares. He takes her to Biography and the following day picks her up to go to the Council of Genres. He piggybacks *The Murders on the Hareng Rouge*, which is heading—ISBN already scrubbed—towards the Ungenred Zone to be scrapped. Somewhere above Aviation the rhetorical device is activated. The book explodes into a zillion fragments within a fraction of a second, taking with it Thursday, Mediocre, and the TransGenre Taxi. It's just another book coming to grief that would be swiftly investigated, and then as swiftly dismissed as an accident."

"Barmouth Blaster?" asked Sprockett, offering me a cocktail.

"Thank you."

"So we were right—it wasn't an attack on the book at all," murmured Sprockett, adding the ice and lemon to the cocktail shaker along with half a can of Red Bull, a Mucinex and two onions. "It was a hit on the taxi—with Thursday Next inside. Which means that Mediocre must have been bribed to take the particular book—"

"But knew nothing of the reason. He was tricked into attending his own execution, as well as Thursday's."

We sat in silence for some minutes as we were towed ever upwards, thinking about what we had just uncovered. In the RealWorld such a convoluted method of murder would be faintly ridiculous, but in the BookWorld all murders happened this way.

"Your Barmouth Blaster, ma'am."

"Thank you."

"Ma'am?"

"Yes?"

"Why was Ms. Next murdered?"

There were at least seventy-two people who had tried to kill her over the years, and narrowing it down was going to be tricky. I decided to head for the most obvious.

"Without Thursday the Racy Novel peace talks might well fail. Who would benefit most from a genre war in the north of the island?"

"Men in Plaid," said Sprockett.

"Hardly likely," I replied. "They're probably mopping up for someone else—or simply want to find Thursday—or are just being wicked for the hell of it."

"You misunderstand me, madam," he said politely. "I mean Men in Plaid—*behind us*!"

I turned and looked out the cab's rear window. Sprockett was right. Far below was not one Buick Roadmaster but three. They would also have Technobabble™ Scramjamcious Gravitational Flux Throb-O-Tron Torque Converter drive systems and, knowing the Men in Plaid, ones considerably more advanced than ours and twice as nonsensical.

"How far to the gravopause?" I asked.

"We're almost there."

Despite the gravopause's usefulness for getting about, one had to be careful. If you had the misfortune to move *above* this altitude and had insufficient thrust to escape, you could be caught in the dead center of the sphere forever. There was a small moon in the gravitational dead spot made from accreted book traffic that had accidentally fallen in and been unable to escape. From the dizzying heights we had now reached, I could actually see the moon above us, no bigger than a pea.

Within a half minute more, we had reached the gravopause. Sprockett cast off the towline, and we drifted onwards, safely in orbit. All that was required now was to coast along until we were above Biography and then dip the cab into a downwards trajectory and let gravity take over.

"Ma'am, would you wind me up?" said Sprockett. "I can see fun and games ahead, and I wouldn't want to risk spring depletion at an inopportune moment."

I leaned forward and wound him until his indicator was just below the red line. I felt his bronze outer casing flex with the increased tension.

"The Men in Plaid are gaining," I said, looking behind us.

The three Roadmasters were in V formation about a half mile away and had just reached the gravopause. At the rate they were going, they would be upon us in under five minutes.

"I'm going to head for that cluster of book traffic," announced Sprockett, opening the throttle and accelerating towards a loose gaggle of several hundred books that all appeared to be heading in the same direction. As we drew closer, I could see that they were mostly nonfiction and of considerable size. It was the renegade Oversize Books section, on their way to their new home.

They grew dramatically in size as we approached, and as we passed between *John Deere Tractors* and *Clarice Cliff Tableware*, they towered over us like skyscrapers.

"Hold tight," said Sprockett, and he pulled the cab hard over and darted behind *Lighthouses of Maine*.

"They're still behind us!" I barked, peering out the rear

windshield as the Monhegan Island Light Station flashed past on our left-hand side, foghorn blaring. "Or at least one is."

"They only attack one at a time," replied Sprockett, his eyebrow flicking past "Indignant" to "Peeved," "and in that respect they're very like baddies in seventies martial-arts movies. Hold tight."

Sprockett skimmed past *Best of National Geographic* so close I could taste the hot dust of the Serengeti, then pulled up sharply in front of *Chronicle of Britain*. I felt myself pressed hard into my seat. My vision grew gray, then faded out entirely. My arms and head felt intolerably heavy, and a second later I was unconscious as Sprockett—his body designed to tolerate up to 17.6 Gs—pulled the cab into an almost vertical climb. I came around again as soon as he reached the top of the book, and he immediately plunged the cab into a near-vertical dive.

"Still behind us?"

They were. I could see the emotionless features of the Plaids as they edged closer. Sprockett corkscrewed around *Knitting Toy Animals for Pleasure and Profit* as the passenger in the Road-master leaned out the window and fired a shot, which flew wide to blow a ragged hole in *Knitting Toy Animals* as we sped on, and a blue knitted giraffe named Natalie began a long, slow fall to the Text Sea, sixteen miles below.

"These Men in Plaid are made of stern stuff," said Sprockett, his eyebrow pointer clicking from "Peeved" to "Puzzled" to "Indignant," then almost to "Severely Peeved" before settling on "Peeved" again. "Hold tight."

The Oversized Books were now moving in a more random fashion as they tried to avoid us, and Sprockett dived to get more speed, then pulled up and headed towards where *What Do People Do All Day?* and *ABC with Dewin the Dog* were about to collide, cover to cover. There was barely a ten-foot gap on either side as we flew between them, and the gap narrowed as we moved on. I barely had a chance to wave a cheery hello to

. . . the passenger in the Roadmaster fired a shot, which flew wide to blow a ragged hole in Knitting Toy Animals, and a blue knitted giraffe named Natalie began a long, slow fall to the Text Sea, sixteen miles below.

a worried-looking Lowly Worm as the covers closed together a split second before we shot out the other side. The Roadmaster was less fortunate, and there was a tremendous detonation as the car was crushed between the two books, the worried shouts of Scarry's folk mixing with Dewin the Dog's furious barking.

"Do you see the others, ma'am?" asked Sprockett as he swerved hard to miss the Greatest Oversize Book of All Time but the abrupt sideways movement caused a ventral compressor stall on the Technobabble™ drive, and we went spiraling downwards out of control until Sprockett achieved an emergency relight.

"On the left!" I yelled as the second Roadmaster swept past, a shot from an eraserhead removing half the rear bumper and a fender. Sprockett jinked hard, spiraled up for a second, then shot past *Cooking for Fusspots* and *Helmut Newton Nudes*.

"Rewind me again, ma'am, if you please," said Sprockett, hauling sideways on the wheel to avoid the *Times Atlas*. The exertions on his frame had depleted his spring at a furious rate—I'd have to remain conscious, if only to rewind him.

"Watch out!"

It was too late. We had taken a hard left at *The Titanic Revisited* and were met by a group of Oversize Books that had bunched together tightly for self-protection. There was no time to avoid them and all we could see was a saber jet fragmenting in front of us as we loomed ever closer to *Lichtenstein Prints*. But just when I thought we were dead for sure, Sprocket pulled the wheel hard over and we entered *The Works of Thomas Gains-borough* through a small thermal-exhaust port near the preface.

I stared wide-eyed as Sprockett drove the cab through the paintings of Gainsborough at over a hundred miles per hour. We shot through early landscapes, dodged past *Cornard Wood* and then burst into portraiture at *John Plampin*, then twisted and turned past a dozen or so well-dressed dignitaries, who for their part looked as startled and horrified as we did. We went between the knees of Mr. Byam and at one point nearly knocked the hat off Mrs. Siddons. But still the Roadmaster stuck to us like glue, not able to fire at us with the constant movement but awaiting the opportunity with a certain calm detachment. We doubled back around *The Blue Boy* as Sprockett searched for the exit.

"Can you see a way out, ma'am?"

"There!" I said, having heard a lowing in the distance, "behind the third cow from the left in *The Watering Place*."

We passed *The Harvest Wagon* for a second time as Sprockett lowered the nose and accelerated across the painted landscape, the Roadmaster still close behind. We turned sharp left as the Duchess of Devonshire loomed up in front of us, and there was a thump as we collided with something. The Roadmaster behind us had misjudged the turn and struck the duchess on the shins, the resulting explosion scattering metal fragments that hit the back of the cab with a metallic rattle.

In another second we were clear, none the worse for our rapid traverse aside from a brace of partridge that had jammed in the wipers and cracked the screen.

"What did they hit?" asked Sprockett.

"The Duchess of Devonshire—took off both legs."

"She'll be a half portrait from now on. Whoops."

The third Roadmaster had appeared in front of us, and another eraserhead had taken the "taxi" light off the roof and blasted a hole into *Classic Bedford Single-Deckers*, releasing several Plaxton-bodied coaches to tumble out into the void.

"We're causing too much damage," I said, catching sight of the now-chaotic movement of the Oversize Books, some of them on fire, others locked in collision and one, *Detroit's Muscle Cars*, falling to earth in a slow death spiral, the huge forces breaking apart the book and spilling 1972 Dodge Chargers across the BookWorld. "We need to leave the Oversize Books section."

"Logically, it places us in grave danger, ma'am."

"But we are endangering *others*, Sprockett."

"I place our chances of survival in open orbit at less than 1.7 percent, ma'am."

"Nevertheless," I said, "we are causing more destruction and death than we are worth."

His eyebrow pointer clicked to "Puzzled." "I do not understand."

"It's the right thing to do, Sprockett. Not for us but for *them*."

"Is this *compassion*, ma'am? The following of the correct course irrespective of the outcome?"

The Duplex-5s were never great at this sort of stuff.

"You should always place others before yourself."

"Even if it means certain destruction?"

"Yes, Sprockett, that's *exactly* what it means."

He buzzed to himself for a moment in deep thought.

"Thank you for explaining it to me, ma'am," he replied. "I think I understand now."

He peeled away from the Oversize Books and headed off into clear air. The last Buick Roadmaster was close on our tail, and with no books to take cover behind, the end didn't seem far off. I pulled out my pistol and attempted to load it, but all the cartridges had spilled out of my pockets and into the foot well, and with Sprockett's constant bobbing and weaving they were proving almost impossible to pick up.

But just then the car stopped moving about and all was calm. I seized the opportunity to grab an armor-piercing round and flick it into my pistol.

"Sprockett?"

He wasn't moving. I thought at first he might have run down or been hit, but then I noticed that his eyebrow pointer was stuck firmly on "Thinking." He had committed his entire mainspring to his thought processes and had shut down all motor functions to enable him to think faster. When I looked at his spring-tension indicator, I could see it visibly moving—Sprockett was thinking, and thinking *hard*.

The Buick Roadmaster gained ground until it was no more than ten yards away. The Man in Plaid in the passenger seat leaned out the window, took careful aim and fired.

The eraserhead is one of a series of special-function cartridges that can be chambered within the large-caliber pistol common among BookWorld law enforcers. A long history of implausibly survivable bullet wounds in Thriller and Crime had rendered characters in the BookWorld invulnerable to small-caliber weapons, so the Textual Disrupter was designed to instantly break the bonds that hold graphemes together. A well-placed eraserhead can reduce anything in the BookWorld to nothing more than text—titanium, diamond, Mrs. Malaprop's sponge cake—anything. The effective range in the pistol was limited to less than forty feet, but the shoulder-mounted, rocket-propelled eraserhead was effective up to a hundred yards, though highly inaccurate.

The eraserhead struck the back of the cab, and the entire trunk section, spare tire, bumper, jack and wheel brace burst into a cloud of individual letters, leaving only the rear part of the chassis and the back axle. One more shot and they would erase me and half of the cab. Two more shots and we would be nothing but a few thousand scrap letters, orbiting at the gravopause until nudged up to the moon or down to the BookWorld.

I fired my own pistol in reply, but the armor-piercing round simply passed through the Roadmaster's windshield and left-side rear door pillar, doing no lasting damage at all. I watched with detached fascination as the passenger reloaded, took aim and fired.

The cab dodged sideways, and the eraserhead flew wide.

"Sprockett?"

"I was thinking, ma'am. I was *calculating*."

I noticed then with a sense of horror that we were climbing. We were moving *above* the gravopause.

"Sprockett," I said nervously, "if we get too high, we'll be pulled into the gravitational dead spot. We'll *never* get out."

"As I said, ma'am, I was calculating. Do as I instruct and there is an 18 percent probability that we will survive."

"Those aren't good odds."

"On the contrary, ma'am. Next to the 98.3 percent possibility of being erased, they're staggeringly good."

"They may not follow," I said, looking around.

"They're Men in Plaid," replied Sprockett, "and painfully dogged. They'll follow."

I watched the Roadmaster, and after pausing momentarily it was soon following our slow fall towards the moon. Although not gaining, it was certainly keeping pace.

"Do you have any armor-piercing rounds left, ma'am?"

I said that I did.

"Have them at hand, and use them only when I say."

The long fall towards the moon was conducted at a greatly increased velocity. I peered over Sprockett's shoulder and noted that the speedometer went only as fast as .5 Absurd, and we exceeded that speed within half a minute. The glass on the instrument shattered. The moon went from the size of a pea to an orange and to a soccer ball, and as we moved ever closer, I could see that the small moon was about a quarter of a mile in diameter and was indeed made of accreted junk—bits of books that had been nudged from the gravopause and lost. Pretty soon the moon was the biggest object in the sky, and just when we were less than five hundred feet from the surface, Sprockett rolled inverted and pulled the cab into a tight orbit. I felt a lurch as we accelerated rapidly, had time to see several people on the surface waving at us desperately, and then we were off and around and away again, flung out back towards the gravopause in a slingshot maneuver.

"Now we will see if my calculations are correct," murmured Sprockett, his eyebrow pointer clicking to "Doubtful," then

"Apologetic," then back to "Doubtful" again before settling on "Worried."

I looked around. The Roadmaster was gaining, perhaps as a result of its greater mass, but we were still out of range of the eraserhead. We cannoned on, still at speeds in excess of Absurd, but all the while slowly decelerating. Sprockett had hoped we would be able to reach the gravopause again, but if he had miscalculated and we fell short by even a few feet, we would fall inexorably back towards the moon and end our days playing cribbage and I Spy with the unfortunate souls who were already there.

"Fire at the Roadmaster, ma'am."

"They're out of range."

"It doesn't matter."

So I did, and the shot missed by a mile, and Sprockett nodded and pointed towards a lone copy of *World Hotel Review* that was orbiting at the gravopause and thereby offering us a convenient yardstick of where safety lay.

I could feel ourselves slow down, and the needle from the shattered speedometer was now reading .25 Absurd and slowing by the second. *World Hotel Review* was less than half a mile away, and it seemed doubtful we would make it.

"Fire at them again."

So I reloaded and did as he asked, and at his insistence I continued to fire.

"Is there a point to this?" I asked after firing five times and managing only to clip a wing mirror.

"If we can make them angry and act irrationally, there is every point to it, ma'am. The cab has no power remaining. I am relying on our momentum to reach the gravopause."

I realized then what his calculations had been for, although I failed to see what we had gained, aside from twenty extra minutes, and a never-before-seen view of the moon. The Men in

Plaid would simply wait until we were once more within range and then finish us off.

The gravopause was barely one hundred yards distant when they fired again. We were now moving at less than a fast walking pace and had drifted sideways. The last armor piercer I'd fired had sent us in a gentle end-over-end spinning motion, which, while not unpleasant, was certainly disconcerting.

The first eraserhead took away the front left side of the car and the second the back axle. I returned fire at Sprockett's request, and an odd sight we must have seemed, two helplessly drifting cars less than thirty feet apart, trading shots.

"I hope this was part of your plan, Sprockett. That was my last round, and I missed them again. I think my poor marksmanship has squandered our chances."

"*Au contraire*, ma'am. Every shot you fire pushes us farther towards the gravopause—and every shot they fire stops them from reaching it."

I frowned and stared out the window. The passenger in the Roadmaster pointed his weapon and fired straight at us, but the disrupting power of the eraserhead evaporated a few feet short of the battered cab in a sparkle of light. The Men in Plaid had acted irrationally, and as we drifted behind *World Hotel Review* and safety, the Roadmaster hung in space for a moment and then started to fall away in a slow trajectory that would eventually find it, a few weeks hence, adding permanently to the moon's mass.

I breathed a sigh of relief, rewound Sprockett—who had redlined without my realizing it—and sat back in my seat.

"Well done," I said. "You've just earned yourself an extra week's paid holiday."

"I seek only to serve," said Sprockett, his eyebrow clicking from "Nervous" to "Contented."

He fired the last remaining grapnel into the back of *World*

Hotel Review, then hailed a distress signal, and we were taken on board.

"The name's Thursday Next," I said to the duty book officer, a frightfully dapper individual who was also manager of the Hotel Ukraina in Moscow, a place that we soon learned "offers a wide range of modern conveniences to suit both the business and leisure traveler."

"I'd like to use your book-to-Fiction footnoterphone link," I added, flashing Thursday's badge. "And after that I'll need to requisition a small family-run guesthouse in Ghent to take me all the way to Biography."

"Certainly," said the manager, eager to help someone he thought was a Jurisfiction agent in distress. "How about the Hotel Verhaegen? It provides elegant guest rooms in the heart of historic Ghent and offers contemporary style in an authentic eighteenth-century residence."

"It sounds perfect."

"This way."

As we made our way to the Belgium section of the book, we caught a glimpse of the Roadmaster, now a tiny speck in the distance.

31.

Biography

Although Outlander authors kill, maim, disfigure and eviscerate bookpeople on a regular basis, no author has ever been held to account, although lawyers are working on a test case to deal with serial offenders. The mechanism for transfictional jurisdiction has yet to be finalized, but when it is, some authors may have cause to regret their worst excesses.

Bradshaw's BookWorld Companion (16th edition)

The Hotel Verhaegen landed on the lawn outside one of the biographical tenements. I sat for several moments in silence in the lobby. For some odd reason, my left leg wouldn't stop shaking, and when I tried to speak, it sounded like I was hyphenated. I'd been fine on the trip down, but as soon as I started to think about the Men in Plaid who'd tried so hard to kill us, I suddenly felt all hot and fearful. I thought for a moment it might have been a virus I'd picked up from the RealWorld until I realized I was in mild shock.

I rested for ten minutes, and after downing one of Sprockett's restoratives and writing *"Very nice"* in the guest book, I stepped from the Verhaegen, which lifted off behind us. The manager wasn't going to hang around—the Pay and Display fees in Biography were ridiculous.

"Sp-Sprockett," I said as we walked across the car park, "where d-d-did you learn to d-drive like that?"

"My cousin Malcolm, ma'am."

"He's a r-racing driver?"

"He's a racing *car*. Is madam all right?"

"Madam is surprised she didn't scream, vomit and then pass out. I owe you my life, Sprockett."

"A good butler," intoned Sprockett airily, "should save his employer's life at least once a day, if not more than once."

Luckily for us, the island of Biography had elected to maintain parts of the Great Library model during the remaking, so while the Geographic model gave it the appearance of a low-lying island mostly covered with well-kept gardens, exciting statuary and dignified pavilions of learning, the biographical subjects themselves lived in twenty-six large tower blocks, each designated by a single letter painted conveniently on the front. The lobby of the apartment building was roomy and bright and was connected to a game room, where D. H. Lawrence was playing H. P. Lovecraft at Ping-Pong, and also a cafeteria, where we could see Abraham Lincoln and Martin Luther discussing the struggles of faith over conscience. In the lobby were eight different Lindsay Lohans, all arguing over which biographical study had been the least correct.

Even before I'd reached the front desk, I knew we were in luck. The receptionist recognized me.

"Hello again, Miss Next," he said cheerfully. "How did the peace talks go?"

"They're not until Friday."

"How silly of me. You can go straight up. I'll ring ahead to announce you."

"Most kind," I replied, still unsure whom Thursday had seen. "Remind me again the floor?"

"Fourth," said the receptionist, and he turned to the telephone switchboard.

We took the brass-and-cast-iron elevator, which was of the same design as the one in the Great Library—the two buildings shared similar BookWorld architecture. Even the paint was peeling in the same places.

"How long do you think before the Men in Plaid catch up with us?" asked Sprockett as the elevator moved upwards.

"I have no idea," I replied, opening my pistol and chambering my last cartridge, a disrupter that was nicknamed "the Cherry Fondue," as it was always the last one in the box, and extremely nasty, "but the Hotel Verhaegen won't give them any clues— you signed the register as 'Mr. and Mrs. Dueffer,' yes?"

"Y-e-es," said Sprockett, his eyebrow pointer clicking to "Apologetic."

"Problems?"

"Indeed, ma'am. In an unthinking moment, I may have written 'choice of oils open to improvement' in the comments section of the visitor's book."

"We'll just have to hope they're not curious."

I replaced the weapon in my shoulder holster, and the lift doors opened on the fourth floor. We walked out and padded noiselessly down the corridor. We walked past Lysander, Lyons, Lyndsay, Lynch and Lynam before we got to the Lyells.

"Charles Lyell, Botanist," read Sprockett on the first door, "Is botany boring?"

"I suspect that it isn't given there is an entire island committed to little else."

The next door was for "Sir James Lyell, Politician."

"Boring, ma'am?" inquired Sprockett.

"Politicians' lives are never boring," I assured him, and we moved to the next.

"'Sir Charles Lyell, Geologist,'" I read. "Is geology more or less boring than politics or botany?"

Sprockett's pointer flicked to "Bingo."

"I believe, ma'am, that as regards boring, geology is less to do with tediousness and more to do with . . . drilling."

"Genius," I remarked, mildly annoyed that I hadn't thought of it myself. Sir Charles Lyell was the father of modern geology. If Thursday had come to him, she was after the finest geological advice available in the BookWorld. I knocked on the door in a state of some excitement, and when I heard a shrill "Enter," we walked in.

The room was a spacious paneled study, the walls covered with bookcases and a large walnut desk in the center. It was not tidy; papers were strewn everywhere, and a chair was over-turned. The pictures were crooked, and a plant pot lay on its side. The wall safe, usually hidden behind a painting of a rock, was open and empty.

A man of considerable presence was standing in the middle of the chaos. He had a high-domed head, white sideburns and somewhat small eyes that seemed to glisten slightly with inner thoughts of a distracting nature.

"Thursday?" he said when he saw me. "I have to confess I am not pleased."

"Oh?"

"Yes. You told me that my assignment with you would be of the utmost secrecy. Look at my study—ransacked!"

"Ah," I said, glancing around, "I am most dreadfully sorry, Sir Charles. This was done after we came back from . . . ?"

"An afterlifetime's work *ruined*," he said in a much-aggrieved tone. "I am most displeased. Good Lord. Who is that mechanical man with the curiously emotive eyebrow?"

"My butler, Sir Charles. You have no objection?"

He stared at Sprockett curiously. "When I was alive, I pursued the advancement of scientific truth with all passion—I am afraid to say that I am at odds to explain Fiction, which often seems to have no basis in logic at all."

"Some enjoy it precisely for that reason."

"You may be right. Can he tidy?"

"We can both tidy, Sir Charles."

And we started to pick up the papers.

"It is most unfortunate," remarked Sir Charles, "after we had done all that work together. *Most* unfortunate."

I suddenly felt worried. "Our work together?"

"The report!" he muttered. "All the maps, notes, core samples, graphs, analysis—stolen!"

"Sir Charles," I said, "this might seem an odd request, but can you go over what was in the report?"

"Again?"

"Again."

He blinked owlishly at me. "Over tea, Miss Next. First we must . . . tidy."

"Sir Charles," I said in a more emphatic tone, "you must tell me what was in the report, and *now*!"

He frowned at me. "As you wish. All that metaphor—"

He didn't have time to finish his sentence. With a tremendous crash, the door was pushed off its hinges, and two Men in Plaid entered. From door to death was scarcely less than fifteen seconds, and much happened. Sprockett was between us and the MiP, and he valiantly made a lunge for the intruders. The first Plaid was quicker and before we knew it had popped Sprockett's inspection panel and pressed his emergency spring release. In an instant the butler fell lifeless. Before Sprockett hit the floor, the Plaid had advanced, knocked my pistol from my grasp and pushed me sideways. As I lay sprawling, the second Man in Plaid picked up Sir Charles and threw him bodily out the window, while the first Plaid moved towards me, his expressionless eyes boring into mine like a pair of gimlets. We'd just killed six of their compatriots; I didn't think there was much room for negotiation.

I quickly scrambled across the floor and was grabbed by my foot. I wriggled out of my boot, and it was this, I think, that saved us. The Man in Plaid was put off balance and gave me the split second I needed to find my pistol. Without hesitation

I turned and fired. There was a *whompa* noise, and the air wobbled as the Cherry Fondue hit home. With an agonizing scream of pain, the Man in Plaid exploded into not graphemes but the infinitely more painful *words*, many of which embedded themselves into the woodwork like shards of glass. The blast caught the second Man in Plaid and cut him in two. He fell to the floor with a heavy thump, the lower half of him spilling cogs, springs and brass actuating rods onto the floor.

"You're robotic?" I said, moving closer. The Man in Plaid was moving his arms in a feeble manner, and his eyes followed me as I approached. He was still functioning, but it was clear he was damaged well beyond economic repair. He looked as though he was out of warranty, too.

"You are impressive, Miss Next," he managed to say. "A worthy adversary."

"Who sent you?"

"I don't answer questions. I ask them."

I noticed I was shaking. I retrieved my boot and walked to the broken window. Lying on the grass four stories below was Sir Charles. The heavy impact had caused the binding matrix of his body to become fused to the ground, and he was beginning to merge with the lawn. I could see several people staring up and pointing, first at me and then at the remains of Sir Charles. We didn't have long before someone called Jurisfaction. Lyell could be rewritten, but these things take time and money, and Biography's budget was tighter than ours.

Sprockett was lying flat on his face in an undignified manner, and I quickly rewound him. As soon as his gyros, thought cogs and speech diaphragm were back to speed, he sat up.

"I've had the most peculiar dream," he told me, his eyebrow clicking through each emotion in turn and then back again, "about being caught by my mother oiling a Mark III Ford Capri in an 'inappropriate' manner."

"I didn't know you had a mother."

"I don't—that's what was so peculiar."

"See what you can get out of him," I said, pointing to the damaged Man in Plaid. "I'm going to have a look around."

I didn't waste any time and hunted through the remains of Lyell's study to see what—if anything—had been left behind. The short answer was not much, until I went through the waste-paper basket and came across a pencil sketch of Racy Novel with WomFic on one side and Dogma on the other. A rough outline of the geology had been sketched in, and for the most part the strata were more or less identical beneath all the genres, except for a shaded patch the shape of a tailless salmon that seemed to be mostly beneath Racy Novel. I returned to where Sprockett had been talking with the badly damaged Plaid.

"He's a Duplex-6," said Sprockett with a sense of deep respect. "I was wondering why they managed to stay on our tail so easily during the Oversize Books section."

"Who is he working for?"

"He won't tell us, but it's of no matter—the Duplex automaton's memories are recorded on punched tape. We can have it read."

"So remove his tape and let's get out of here."

In reply the Duplex-6 took a large brass key from his jacket pocket and inserted it into the socket in the base of his neck. We could see he was almost run down, and before we could stop him, he had started to turn the key.

"Good Lord," said Sprockett. "The Duplex-6 has a self-wind capability."

Sprockett tried to stop the damaged Man in Plaid from winding himself up, but the 6's superior strength was too much, and we watched with increased hopelessness as the Plaid's tension indicator neared the red line.

"We're leaving," said Sprockett, and without waiting for a reply he took me by the hand and we ran to the bathroom window and out the fire escape at the back of the building.

We were two flights down when the Duplex-6's mainspring finally ruptured in an almighty outburst of stored mechanical energy. There was a loud *twuuung* noise, and the shattered remains of the Man in Plaid erupted out the windows of Lyell's apartment. We were showered with minute cogs, sprockets, bevel gears, and dogs, chains, pushrods and actuators.

"A self-winding capability," said Sprockett, who was obviously deeply impressed. "I wonder if they would retrofit that feature for us Duplex-5s?"

32.

Homecoming

Islands to Visit #124: Photography. This beautifully expressive and lyrical island has been divided between Black-and-White and Color for many years, and the two factions are almost constantly at war, an event that is itself documented by resident war photographers. The recording of the war recording is also recorded, with Martin Parr photographing the ears and neckties of those who are recording the people who are recording the people recording the events.

Bradshaw's BookWorld Companion (5th edition)

$\mathcal{W}$e dodged Jurisfaction officers for two hours and eventually negotiated a ride home aboard a copy of the recently discredited *President Formby War Diaries*, which was on a one-way trip to Historical Counterfactuals.

"May I be so bold," said Sprockett once we had landed and were on the train heading back towards Fantasy and home, "as to inquire about our next move?"

"Placating an angry Carmine, I should imagine—I've been away a lot these past few days. After that we'll have to recover anything Horace has stolen again, put up with petulant huffing and tutting from Pickwick—and my dopey father will be complaining about something, I shouldn't wonder."

"I was referring to Racy Novel, ma'am. Should you call Commander Bradshaw again?"

I'd asked myself the same question on the way back from

Biography. I'd spoken to him briefly while on board the *World Hotel Review*. He had expressed surprise and alarm about the Men in Plaid and had also checked out Mediocre's address and reported back to us no sign of metaphor—in bridges or otherwise. Unwisely, I had told him we were going on to Biography, and now I didn't know if I could trust him or not.

"He might have tipped off the Men in Plaid," I said after airing my thoughts, "or he simply might be having his footnoterphone messages read in transit."

It wasn't hard, apparently. All you needed do was to sit in the footnoterphone ducts and read the messages as they flitted past.

"Even if he is on the level," I added, "it's not like we have any answers or evidence—just a geologist out to grass and a rough sketch of the strata beneath the northern part of Fiction."

Sprockett nodded agreement.

"But," I added, "we know that Thursday would have been working to avert war at the peace talks. If she *was* silenced, the attacks by the Men in Plaid would seem to implicate the Council of Genres, but the CofG want to avoid a war, not start one. It was Senator Jobsworth *himself* who wanted me to go to the peace talks tomorrow. The only person we know who seems to actually welcome war is Speedy Muffler."

"Would he have access to Duplex-6 automatons that could be made to look like Men in Plaid?" asked Sprockett.

"Duplex will sell to anyone with the cash, but the Council's strict sales embargoes are hard to circumvent. Not impossible, but hard."

"What about Red Herring, ma'am?"

"I'm not sure. Is Red Herring a red herring? Or is it the fact that we're meant to *think* Red Herring is a red herring that is actually the red herring?"

"Or perhaps the fact you're meant to think Red Herring *isn't* a red herring is what makes Red Herring a red herring after all."

"We're talking serious metaherrings here. Oh, crap, I'm lost again. Who's talking now?"

"It's you," said Sprockett.

"Right."

"Whatever is going on," I said, "it's big. *Really* big. If it's big enough to risk killing Thursday Next, destroying a book and subverting the Men in Plaid from their usual duties of frightening the citizenry to the more specific duty of frightening *individual* citizens, then there is no limit to what they might do. We need to keep our eyes open at all times."

We took a cab from Le Guin Central and, deep in thought, walked up to the house. I had my hand on the butt of my pistol, just in case. I needn't have worried. Men in Plaid were never seen without their Buick Roadmasters, and the driveway was empty. I opened the front door and found a dozen members of the cast sitting around the kitchen table.

"Hello," I said, somewhat surprised. "Have we got a cast meeting scheduled for this evening?"

"We have now," replied Carmine.

My eyes flicked from face to face, and they seemed very serious. Most of the major players were there—my father, Bowden, Hades, Jack Schitt, Braxton, Rochester, Paige Turner, Joffy, Stig, Victor Analogy, my mother and even Bertha Rochester, although she had been put in a straitjacket in the event she tried to bite anyone.

"What's going on?"

"You've been acting a bit irresponsibly recently," said Carmine, "running around the BookWorld, pretending to be her. You've been neglecting your duties. I've been covering for you far more than is written in my contract, and only yesterday you were shouting at us all."

"I've had things on my mind," I replied by way of excuse, "*important* things."

"So *you* say. To the casual outside observer, you're simply getting delusions of adequacy. Play a strong character for too long and it tends to have an unhinging effect."

"And today," said Bowden in an annoying "I told you so" sort of voice, "you were threatening to tell the Outland all about the BookWorld. There's a good reason the real Thursday never put that part of the story in her books, you know."

"I admit I might have gone too far on that point," I conceded, but I could see they didn't believe me.

"None of us are happy," said my father, "and we feel you might be leading the series into disrepute. If the book gets punished for your transgressions, then every one of us has to suffer. Punish one, punish all. You know how it works."

I did, far too well. To keep books in line, the entire cast is often disciplined for the misdeeds of one. It generated a certain degree of conformity within the cast—and a lot of ill feeling.

"So what are you saying?" I asked.

My father nudged Bowden, who nudged Victor, who nudged Acheron Hades.

"We're saying," said Hades slowly, "that we might need to make some . . . *changes*."

"Changes? What sorts of changes?"

"Changes in leadership."

"You want to have me fired? You can't do that."

"In point of fact," piped up Pickwick, "we can. Article 218 of the Textual Code states, 'If the nominated leader of a book acts in an unlawful or reckless manner that might affect the smooth operation of a book, he or she can be removed by a simple show of hands.'"

There was a deathly hush as they waited to see what I would say.

"The series is operating smoothly. It will be hard to prove recklessness on my part."

"We don't need to," replied Carmine. "We need only prove unlawfulness."

"And how would you do that?"

"The Toast Marketing Board subplot. *Totally* illegal. You wrote out the new pages in your own handwriting."

"Listen," I said, changing my tone to one of conciliation, "we have an average weekly ReadRate of 3.7 at present—remaindered, out of print and, technically speaking, unread. You need my leadership to try to turn this series around. If you want to negotiate, we can negotiate—everything's on the table. So let's talk. Who's for tea?"

They all stared at me in a stony-faced manner, and I suddenly felt that things were a lot worse than I'd thought. There had been grumblings before, but nothing like this.

"Well, then," I said, my temper rising, "who's going to lead the book? Carmine?"

"I can handle it."

"You can handle it *now*. What if the ReadRate goes above forty? How screwed will you be then?"

"There is no need to be unkind," said my father. "With our support she'll manage. At least she doesn't spend her days gallivanting around the BookWorld on arguably pointless quests for a namesake who doesn't even like her."

That hurt.

"Well," I replied in a sarcastic tone, "how does consorting with a goblin fare on the 'bringing the book into disrepute' stakes?"

"You can talk," retorted Carmine. "*Your* intended boyfriend set fire to a busload of nuns."

"And puppies," said Pickwick.

"*Orphaned* puppies," added Rochester, dabbing his eyes with a handkerchief.

"Besides," said Carmine, "Horace and I have agreed to a trial separation."

"I think we've all said quite enough," announced Bowden haughtily. "All in favor of replacing Thursday with Carmine, raise a hand."

They all raised a hand except Stig, who I know liked me, Bertha Rochester who was in a straitjacket, and Pickwick.

"Thank you, Pickwick," I said. "Nice to know some friends haven't abandoned me."

"Are we voting now?" asked Pickwick, waking with a start. "I'm in."

And she put a wing in the air.

"All right, you bunch of disloyal ingrates," I said, taking the Snooze Button's access codes and the key to the core containment from around my neck, "have the job. Who cajoled you all when you thought you were rubbish? Who made sure we rehearsed the whole way through the six weeks we were unread last winter?"

Victor looked at the ceiling, and Pickwick stared at her foot. They all knew I'd been holding things together for a while. The previous written Thursday had left the series in a terrible state. Everyone arguing with everyone else, and with a humor deficit that I had only just managed to plug.

"And a fat lot of good it did us," replied Carmine angrily. "We're the laughingstock of Speculative Fantasy."

"We're still being read. Do you know what to do if there is a flameout on the e-book throughput intensifiers?"

Carmine's blank look told me she didn't.

"Or if the metaphor depletes midscene? What about the irony injectors? How often should they be cleaned? Do you even *know* what an adjectivore looks like or what happens if you get Martha Stewarts behind the wainscoting?"

"Hey," said Horace, who had been sitting unnoticed on the top of the bureau, "why don't you go do a Plot 9 on yourself? We can muddle through. With less than twenty active readers, we've certainly got enough time."

"*We?*" I demanded. "Since when were you anything to do with this series?"

"Since Carmine asked me."

"He has some very good ideas," said Carmine. "Even Pickwick thinks they're quite good. Isn't that so, Pickers?"

"Sort of," said Pickwick, looking the other way huffily.

"We'd better get on," said Hades in a pointed fashion. "We've got some readings to attend to."

"Right," I said, lips pursed as I tried to control my temper, "I'll let you get on with it."

And without another word, I strode out of the house with as much dignity as I could muster. As soon as I was outside, I sat on the garden wall, my heart beating fast, taking short gasps of air. I looked back at the series. It was a jagged collection of settings—the towers of Thornfield Hall set among the floodlights of the Swindon croquet field and the Penderyn Hotel. There were a few airships, too, but only one-tenth scale. It was all I'd ever known. It had seemed like *home*.

"You should look on the bright side, ma'am," said Sprockett, handing me a Chicago Fizz he had conjured up seemingly from nowhere.

"There *is* a bright side? No book, no home, no one to believe in me and no real idea what became of Thursday—or what the hell's going on. And in addition I'd *really* like to punch Horace."

"Punching goblins," replied Sprockett soothingly, "while offering short-term relief, has no long-term beneficial value."

I sighed. "You're right."

"By referring to the 'bright side,' ma'am, I merely meant that the recent upset simply frees your schedule for more pressing matters. You have larger fish to fry over the next couple of days."

I stood up. Sprockett was right. To hell with the series—for the moment at least.

"So where do you suggest we go now?"

"Back to Vanity."

33.

The League of Cogmen

There are two languages peculiar to the BookWorld of which a vague understanding will help the enthusiastic tourist. **Courier Bold** is the traditional language of those in the support industries, such as within the Well of Lost Plots, and Lorem Ipsum is the gutter slang of the underworld—useful to have a few phrases in case you get into trouble in Horror or Noir.

Bradshaw's BookWorld Companion (1st edition)

*S*prockett, I learned, lived in the Fantasy section of Vanity, not far from Parody Valley. I was more at leisure to look about upon this, my second visit, and I noticed that whereas in Fiction the landscape was well maintained, relatively open and with good infrastructure, years of self-publishing into the same geographic area meant that Vanity was untidy, chaotic and overcrowded.

The resident novels with their settings, props and characters now occupied every spare corner of the island and had accreted on top of one another like alluvial deposits. Grand towers of imaginative speculation had arisen from the bare rock, and the island was honeycombed with passageways, tunnels and shafts to provide access to the scenes and settings now buried far below the surface. In some places the books were so close that boundaries became blurred—a tiger hunt in 1920s Bengal merged seamlessly with the TT races on the Isle of Man, a western with the 1983 Tour de France. Space in Vanity was limited.

"Don't let on you're published," remarked Sprockett as we arrived at his book, a badly worn tome cemented into a cliff face of similar books and supported on slender stilts that were anchored to the rock below. He needn't have—I knew the score. Vanity's beef with the rest of Fiction was long-lived and not without some degree of justification.

I wiped my feet on the doormat as we entered and noted that the novel was set mostly in the manor house that belonged to Professor Winterhope, Sprockett's creator, and was populated by a large and mildly eccentric family of mechanical men, none of whom looked as though they had been serviced for years.

"Welcome to *The League of Cogmen*," said Mrs. Winterhope once the professor had taken Sprockett off for an oil change and general service. "Would you like some tea?"

I told her I would, and we walked into the front room, which was like my kitchen back home, a command center and meeting place all in one. Mrs. Winterhope introduced me to the Cogmen, who had been wound sufficiently to converse but were under strict orders not to move, so as not to wear themselves out—quite literally, as they had a limited stock of spare parts. Despite these obvious drawbacks, they still expressed the languorous attitude of the long-unread. It didn't look as though they rehearsed much either, which was a lamentable lapse in professionalism, although I wasn't going to say so.

"We must thank you for rescuing Sprocky from that rabble in Conspiracy," said Mrs. Winterhope, putting an empty kettle onto a cold stove. "And we were delighted to hear he was employed by Thursday Next—even if not the real one."

"You're very kind."

"Has our Sprockett been serving you well?"

"He has been beyond exemplary," I told her. "A gentleman's gentleman."

"Excellent," she replied. "I can count on you to give good references?"

"I cannot see a scenario where I would let him go," I said with a smile. "He is utterly admirable in every respect."

But Mrs. Winterhope wasn't smiling.

"I understand," she said slowly, "that you have recently found yourself in diminished circumstances?"

This was true, of course. I had almost nothing except Sprockett and the clothes I was wearing.

"At present yes, that is true," I admitted somewhat sheepishly.

Mrs. Winterhope poured the contents of the empty kettle into a teapot that I noted contained no tea.

"Sprockett is the most advanced automaton we possess," she continued, "and whilst not wishing to be indelicate in these matters, I cannot help thinking that his career may not be well serviced by someone who finds herself—I'm sorry to be blunt—in a position of . . . *unreadiness*."

She stared at me with a kind yet desperate expression and handed me an empty cup.

"Would you like no milk?"

"Yes thank you," I said, not wishing to embarrass her. Not a single reader in over seventeen years had graced the Winterhopes' pages, so the reader stipend was unavailable to them, and they had, quite literally, nothing. The only possible avenue to a better life was through the one character who might conceivably find a placement in the world of wider readership. Four days ago I'd been a potential help; now I was a millstone. I knew what I had to do.

"Yes," I said to Mrs. Winterhope, "I understand."

She nodded politely and patted me on the arm. "Will you stay with us tonight?" she asked. "We have absolutely nothing, but we would be happy to share it with you."

I told her I would be honored to share in their nothing, then excused myself to go for a walk.

I left the novel and wandered down through the narrow streets to where the Tennyson Boardwalk ran alongside the beach.

The walk was full of evening strollers and traders, mostly selling book-clearance salvage from those novels that had been recently scrapped. I stopped to lean on the decorative cast-iron railings and absently watched the Text Sea lap against the foreshore, the jumbled collection of letters heaving and mixing in the swell. Every now and then, a chance encounter would construct a word, and the constituent parts glowed with the joyous harmony of word construction. Farther down, some kids were fishing these new words from the sea with hooked sticks. Three-letter constructions were thrown back to potentially grow larger, but longer ones were pulled ashore for possible sale. While I stood there watching, they caught a "theodolite," a "linoleum" and a "pumpkin," although truth to tell the "pumpkin" was actually a "pump" and a "kin" that were tickled together after being pulled from the Text Sea.

I couldn't help feeling a bit sorry for myself. I had no job, no book, no friends and no immediate prospects. The man I loved was real and wholly unavailable, the deputy man I loved was a mass murderer. More important, I was no nearer to who had killed Thursday, nor to what Sir Charles Lyell had discovered about Racy Novel that was so potentially devastating that it was worth murdering him, Thursday and Mediocre for. The truth was this: I wasn't up to scratch. I'd been trying too hard to be her, and I had failed.

I thought of Whitby, then of Landen, and what he had said about my actually *being* Thursday and not knowing it. I wasn't in agreement with him over that one, and when I'd vanished in front of his eyes, he would have known that, too. I thought for a minute as I considered putting myself in Landen's shoes. He might try to get in touch with me—after all, we both wanted Thursday back. The question was this: If I wanted to contact someone in the BookWorld, how would I go about it?

The Mediocre Gatsby had picked Thursday up in Sargasso Plaza, a stone's throw from where I was now, right on the southeast tip of Vanity. She was likely to have been hiding close by, somewhere she would have been off the Council of Genres' radar—somewhere even the Men in Plaid would fear to tread. And there it was, staring at me across the the bay—Fan Fiction. Where better to hide a Thursday than in a bunch of that? The small island was lit up by thousands of lightbulbs strung from trees and lampposts. It was a busy place, that much I knew, and given that Vanity had been unfairly shunned by the rest of Fiction, the fact that Fan Fiction was isolated still further gave one an idea how poorly it was regarded.

I walked to the entrance of the narrow causeway and approached the two game-show hosts who were guarding the entrance. One was sitting on a high stool and dressed in a gold lamé suit, while the other was holding a hunting rifle.

"Hello, Thursday!" said the first host, beaming happily at me with a set of teeth so perfectly white that I had to blink in the glare. "Back to win further prizes?"

It was Julian Sparkle of *Puzzlemania*. We had met a few years back when the real Thursday was attempting to train me up for Jurisfiction. He was what we called an "anecdotal," someone who lived in the oral tradition, ready to leap to the Outland when puzzles and brain teasers were related—usually during boring car journeys or in pubs. The last time we'd met, I would almost certainly have been eaten by a tiger if not for Thursday's brilliant intervention.

"I was actually thinking of visiting Fan Fiction," I replied.

"No problem," said Julian in his singsong voice. "Anyone can go in—but no one can come out."

As if to bring home the point, the second game-show host showed me the hunting rifle.

"Unless," said Julian Sparkle, "you want to play *Puzzlemania*?"

"What do I win?"

"A set of steak knives."

"And if I lose?"

"We destroy you with a high-powered eraserhead."

"Fair enough," I replied. "I'm in."

Sparkle smiled warmly, and I stepped to a mark on the floor that he indicated. As I did so, the lights seemed to dim, except for a bright spotlight on the two of us. There was a short blast of applause, seemingly from nowhere.

"So, Thursday Next, today we're going to play . . . 'Escape Across the Bridge.'"

He indicated the long, narrow causeway.

"It's very simple. We erase anyone we see walking towards us across the causeway. There is no way to go round the causeway, and you'll be dissolved in the Text Sea if you try to swim."

"And?"

"That's it. We check the bridge every half minute, and it takes four minutes to run across."

As if to accentuate the point, the second host noticed someone trying to sneak across as we were talking. He shouldered the rifle and fired. The unfortunate escapee exploded in a chrysanthemum of text, which was quickly snapped up by the gulls.

"Ha-ha!" said the host, reloading the rifle. "Bagged another Baggins."

And he made a mark on his tally board, which contained several hundred other Bagginses, three dozen Gandalfs, a plethora of Pratchett characters and sixty-seven Harry Potters.

"Right, then," said Sparkle, "off you toddle."

"Don't you want the answer?"

He smiled in an oddly unpleasant way. "You can figure it out for the return journey."

I walked across the causeway with a curiously heavy heart, as I had no idea how to get back, but once I arrived on the other side, it seemed a party was in full swing. Everyone was chatting to everyone else, and the mildly depressed feeling I had felt over in Vanity seemed to vanish completely.

"What's the party about?" I asked a Hobbit who had thrust a drink into my hand.

"Where *have* you been?" she said with a smile. "Fan Fiction isn't copying—it's a *celebration*. One long party, from the first capital letter to the last period!"

"I never thought of that."

"Few do—especially the authors who should really accept the praise with better grace. They're a bunch of pompous fatheads, really—no slur intended. Nice clothes, by the way."

"Thank you."

And she wandered off.

"Thursday?"

I turned to find myself staring at . . . well, *myself.* I knew she wasn't me or the real Thursday because she seemed somewhat narrow. In fact, now that I looked around, most people here were similar to real characters but of varying thickness. Some were barely flatter than normal, while others were so lacking in depth that they appeared only as an animated sheet of cardboard.

"Why is everyone so flat?" I asked.

"It's a natural consequence of being borrowed from somewhere else," explained the Thursday, who was, I noted, less than half an inch thick but apparently normal in every other way. "It doesn't make us any less real or lacking in quality. But being written by someone who might not *quite* understand the subconscious nuance of the character leaves us in varying degrees of flatness."

This made sense. I'd never really thought about it before, but it explained why the Edward Rochester and indeed *all* the borrowed characters in my series were of varying degrees of depth. Some weren't that bad, but others, like Jane Eyre herself, were thin enough to be slipped under the door and could sleep rolled up and slipped into a drainpipe.

"How's all that cloak-and-dagger stuff going?" asked Flat Thursday.

It seemed she thought I was the real one, and I wasn't going to deny it.

"It's going so-so," I said. "How much did I tell you?"

She laughed. "You never tell us anything. Landen sent another message, by the way."

"That's good," I replied, attempting to hide my enthusiasm. "Lead on."

Thursday turned, and as she did so, she almost vanished as I saw her edge on. I wondered whether perhaps Agent Square might *not* be a Flatlander as he claimed, but a hyperfiction cube or something.

"We all think Landen's totally Mr. Dreamcake," said Flat Thursday as we walked past a reinterpretation of Middle Earth that was every bit as good as the real one, only flatter, "but he won't speak to anyone except the real one."

We walked down Thursday Street, and everything started to look vaguely familiar. The characters and settings were sort of similar, but the situations were not. The combinations were unusual, too, and although I had not personally supposed that Thursday might battle the Daleks with Dr. Who in a literary landscape, in here it was very much business as usual.

"He's in there," said Thursday, and she ushered me into a large, square room with a stripped pine floor, a thin skirting board and empty walls painted in magnolia. In the middle of the room was Landen, and he smiled as I walked in. But it wasn't actually him; it was just a *feeling* of him.

"Hello, Landen."

"Hello, Thursday. I needed to speak to you."

"What about?"

"I'm sorry," he said apologetically, "my answers are limited."

I stared at him for a moment. Flat Thursday had said this was *another* message, so he must be communicating on a one-way basis by writing a short story—possibly with himself and his wife in conversation.

"Which Thursday do you want to talk to?" I asked.

"The written Thursday."

So far, so good.

"Do you *now* believe I'm from the BookWorld?"

"You vanished as I was about to kiss you. Thursday never did that. I'm sorry I doubted you."

"Do you know what the real Thursday was doing with Sir Charles Lyell?"

"I'm sorry," he said, "my answers are limited."

"Do you know who was trying to kill Thursday?"

"The Men in Plaid have tried to murder her on numerous occasions. At the last count, she had killed six of them. She doesn't know who orders them to do it, or why."

This was good news. Between Thursday and Sprockett and me, we'd taken out fourteen Plaids.

"Where is she now? Do you know?"

"I'm sorry," he said, "my answers are limited."

"Why did she ask the red-headed man to give me her badge?"

"She didn't—*I did*. As soon as she was out of touch for over five days, I contacted Kiki."

"Why did she ask *me* to help her?"

"She'd hoped you had evolved into something more closely resembling her. The only person she knew she could truly trust was . . . herself."

This sounded encouraging. "Can I trust Bradshaw?"

"I'm sorry," he said, "my answers are limited."

"Is there anything else I should know?"

"She told me that she would try to contact you. She said the circumstances of your confusion will be your path to enlightenment."

"What did she mean by that?"

"I'm sorry," he said, "I have no more answers for you. I won't know if you even got these. Good luck, Thursday."

He stopped talking and just stood there blinking, awaiting any possible response from me.

"Listen," I said, lowering my voice and looking around to make sure that Flat Thursday wasn't listening, "did you write in a kiss, just to make up for the one I missed earlier?"

"Good luck, Thursday," he said again. "I'm in a hurry, as I told your mother I'd help her with the Daphne Farquitt Reada-thon. Remember: *The circumstances of your confusion will be your path to enlightenment.* Four pounds of carrots, one medium cabbage, four-pack tin of beans, Moggilicious for Pickwick, pick up dry cleaning, toilet paper."

I was confused until I realized that he had probably writ-ten the short story on the back of a shopping list. I watched and listened while he went through "Tonic water, snacks and the latest Wayne Skunk album, *Lick the Toad*" before he stopped, smiled again and then just stood there blinking in a state of rest.

I walked back outside to where many Thursdays of vary-ing thicknesses were waiting to be told a story and given a few tips. It felt like I was doing a Thursday master class in a hall of mirrors, but I think they appreciated it. By the time I left two hours later, some of the thinner Thursdays were a little bit thicker.

"Might I inquire where madam has been?" asked Sprockett once I had returned to *The League of Cogmen*. "*Vanity* can be a dangerous place for those published. Brigands, scoundrels, verb artists and the Unread lurk in doorways, ready to steal the Essence of Read from the unwary."

"I was in Fan Fiction."

Sprockett's eyebrow shot to "Worried" in alarm.

"How did you get back across the causeway?"

"Quite easily. They shoot anyone trying to escape, and

they check the causeway every half minute to make sure. You can't possibly run the distance in less than four minutes, so the answer seemed quite obvious."

He diverted his mainspring to his thought cogs and whirred and clicked noisily for a full minute before giving up, and I had to tell him.

"That's quite clever."

"Elementary, my dear Sprockett. Julian Sparkle was a bit annoyed. He said that he'd have to change the puzzle. I won these steak knives. Perhaps Mrs. Winterhope would like them?"

"I think she should be delighted. May I ask a question, ma'am?"

"Of course."

"What are we going to do now?"

"I'm going to accept Senator Jobsworth's invitation to go to the peace talks tomorrow masquerading as the real Thursday Next. The paddle steamer leaves at seven A.M. Everything that has happened is to do with Racy Novel and Speedy Muffler, and unless I start getting to the heart of the problem, I'm not going to get anywhere. The Men in Plaid will think twice before doing anything while I'm in plain view, and Landen told me that this was the way to find Thursday: 'The circumstances of your confusion will be your path to enlightenment.' I don't understand that, but I *can* become more confused—going upriver with Jobsworth will *definitely* provide the extra confusion I need."

Sprockett stared at me for a moment, and I could tell by the way his eyebrow was quivering between "Thinking" and "Worried" that he knew something was up.

"Don't you mean 'we,' ma'am?"

I pulled a letter from my pocket that I'd prepared while seated at a You for Coffee? franchise just off Sargasso Plaza.

"These are glowing references, Sprockett. They should allow you to find a position in Fiction without any problem. You have been a steadfast and loyal companion whom I am happy to have known as a friend. Thank you."

I blinked as my eyes started to mist, and Sprockett stared back at me with his blank porcelain features. His eyebrow pointed in turn at all the possible emotions engraved on his forehead. There was nothing for "Sad," so it sprang backwards and forwards between "Doubtful" and "Worried."

"I must protest, ma'am. I do not—"

"My mind is made up, Sprockett. I have nothing to offer. You have a bright future. It will please me greatly if you find onward employment that I can be proud of."

Sprockett buzzed quietly to himself for a moment. "This is compassion, isn't it?"

"Yes."

"I can *recognize* it," he said, "but I am at odds to understand it. Shall we go indoors?"

We had boiled cabbage for dinner, which might have been improved had there been any cabbage to go in it. But the Winterhopes were more than friendly, and after several rounds of bezique that might have been more enjoyable had there been cards, Sprockett played the piano accordion without actually having a piano accordion, and the empty unread book didn't ring to the tune of the "Beer Barrel Polka" until the small hours.

34.

The *Metaphoric Queen*

Journeys up the Metaphoric River are hugely enjoyable and highly recommended. Since every genre is nourished by its heady waters, a paddle steamer can take even the most walk-shy tourists to their chosen destination. As a bonus there is traditionally at least one murder on board each trip—a "consideration" to the head steward will ensure that it is not you.

Bradshaw's BookWorld Companion (1st edition)

*T*he steamer was called the *Metaphoric Queen,* and when I arrived, it was lying at the dockside just above the lock gates that separated the river from the Text Sea. The *Queen* was built of a wooden superstructure on a steel hull, measured almost three hundred feet from stem to stern and was the very latest in luxury river travel. A covered walkway ran around the upper deck, and behind the wheelhouse on the top deck was a single central stack that breathed out small puffs of smoke. As I approached, I could see the crew making ready. They loaded and unloaded freight, polished the brasswork, checked the paddle for broken vanes and oiled the traction arm that turned the massive sternwheel.

The *Queen* had docked only an hour before, and the cargo was being offloaded when I arrived: crude metaphor, sealed into twenty-gallon wooden casks, each stenciled PRODUCT OF RACY NOVEL. I watched as the casks were taken under guard and moved towards the Great Library, where they would be distilled into their component parts for onward trade.

"Welcome aboard!" said the captain as I walked up the gangplank. "The senator will be joining us shortly. The staterooms are the first door on the left—tea will be served in ten minutes."

I thanked him and moved aft to the rear deck, which afforded a good view of the docks and the river. The other passengers were already on board and were exactly the sort of people one would expect to see on a voyage of this type. There was a missionary, a businessman, a family of settlers eager to make a new home for themselves, two ladies of negotiable affection and, strangely enough, *several* odd foreigners who wore rumpled linen suits and looked a bit mad.

"I think someone made a mistake on the manifest," came a voice close at hand.

I turned to find an adventurer standing next to me. He looked as though he had argued with a rake at some point as a teenager and come off worse; three deep scars showed livid on his cheek and jaw. He was quite handsome in an understated sort of way, with a plain shirt, grubby chinos and a revolver on his belt. He was wearing a battered trilby with a dark sweat stain on the band, and he looked as though he hadn't shaved—or slept—for days.

"A mistake on the manifest?"

"Three eccentric foreigners on a trip like this rather than the mandatory one. Mind you, it could be worse. I was on a similar jaunt last year, and instead of a single insultingly stereotypical Italian, all fast talking and gesticulating—we had six. Hell on earth, it was."

As if in answer to this, the three eccentric foreigners started to jostle one another in an infantile manner.

"It's Thursday Next, isn't it?"

I looked at him, trying to remember where I'd seen him

before. I stared for a little too long at the scars on his face, and he touched the pink marks thoughtfully.

"I don't know how I got them," he confessed, "but they're supposed to make me look like I'm a man with an adventurous past."

"Aren't you?"

"I'm really not sure. I was given the scars but no backstory to go with them. Perhaps it will be revealed to me later. It's an honor to meet you, I must say. My name's Foden. Drake Foden."

We shook hands. I didn't want to deny I was Thursday, given my reason for being here, so I decided to hit him with some pseudo-erudition I had picked up in HumDram.

"You're kind," I replied, "but last Thursday and next Thursday are still a week apart."

"Deep," he said with a smile. "Where are you headed?"

"Upriver a bit," I said, giving little away. "You?"

"Beyond Racy Novel," he said, "and into the Dismal Woods."

"Hoping to find the source of the Metaphoric?"

"Is there one?" He laughed.

Most people these days agreed that the river couldn't actually have a source, since it flowed in several directions at once. Instead of starting in one place and ending in another using the traditionally mundane "downhill" plan, it would pretty much go as the mood took it. Indeed, the Metaphoric had been known to bunch up in Horror while Thriller suffered a drought, and then, when all was considered lost, the river would suddenly release and cause a flood throughout Comedy and HumDram. Not quite so devastating as one might imagine, for the Metaphoric brought with it the rhetorical nutrients necessary for good prose—the river was the lifeblood of Fiction, and nothing could exist without it.

The puzzle, therefore, was how the river replenished itself. It had long been known that the river flowed up into the Dismal

Woods a tired and stagnant backwater and emerged four hundred miles to the west reinvigorated and fizzing with a heady broth of creative alternatives. Quite what mechanism existed to make this happen was a matter of some conjecture. Many adventurers had been lost trying to find out. Some said the secret was guarded by a Mysteriously Vanished subplot that would devour all comers, while others maintained there existed a Fountain of Bestsellerdom that could grant eternal life, and no one troubled to expend a further word in consequence.

"No," said the adventurer, "better men than me have been lost searching for the source of the Metaphoric. That's next year. *This* year I'm in training: I'm going to attempt to uncover the legendary Euphemasauri graveyard."

"Good luck," I said, knowing full well that he would doubtless be dead in a week—the Euphemasaurus was a fearsome beast and not conducive to being tracked. It would perhaps be a safer, easier and more productive quest to look for his own refrigerator.

"Who is that?" I asked as a man with his face obscured by a large pair of dark glasses hurried past and went belowdecks, followed by a porter carrying his suitcases.

"He's the mandatory MP-C12: Mysterious Passenger in Cabin Twelve. All sweaty journeys upriver have to carry the full complement of odd characters. It's a union thing."

"Hence the foreigners?"

"Hence the foreigners. Mark my words, there'll be a mixed-race cook with a violent streak who speaks only Creole, a cardsharp and a man from the company."

"Which company?"

"A company with commercial interests upriver. It doesn't really matter what."

"You must have done this many times."

"Actually, it's my first. I graduated from St. Tabularasa's only this morning."

"You must be nervous."

The adventurer smiled confidently. "I'm running around inside screaming."

I excused myself, as Red Herring, Colonel Barksdale and Senator Jobsworth had just arrived. They were accompanied by an entourage of perhaps a dozen staff, most of whom were simply faceless bureaucrats: D-grade Generics who did nothing but add background and tone to the general proceedings. Try to engage them in conversation and they would just blink stupidly and then stare at their feet.

"Good morning, Miss Next," said Herring affably. "A moment of your time, if you would?"

He was dressed in a light cotton suit and was overseeing the arrival of a riveted steel box that had been placed on the foredeck by four burly rivermen and was now being lashed in place.

"Gifts for Speedy Muffler?"

"Two dozen plot lines and some A-grade characterization to show willingness," replied Herring, tipping the rivermen and checking the cords. "Racy Novel doesn't have much of either, so it should go down well."

I thought of saying that this was because of Council of Genres sanctions but thought better of it.

"So," he said, mopping his brow with a handkerchief, "good to see you could make it."

"All BookWorldians have a duty to avert war whenever it presents itself," I said pointedly.

"Goes without saying. Your series is in good health, I trust?"

"Nothing a reissue in the Outland wouldn't fix."

He steered me to the rail and lowered his voice.

"Have the Men in Plaid been bothering you?"

"Why do you ask, sir?"

"Speedy Muffler has . . . *friends* within government. Some people are sympathetic to his cause. They feel that he has been unfairly treated and may try to work against the peace."

I didn't know whom to trust on this boat, so I decided to trust no one.

"I have seen a few Roadmasters following me over the past few days," I replied cagily.

"Not that unusual," said Herring. "Fantasy is a hotbed of Imaginative Fundamentalism; if we didn't keep a Plaid presence on the streets to rein in Fantasy's worst excesses, we'd be in cross-genre anarchy before we knew it. We'd regulate it more than we do if it weren't so damn readable."

Herring was nothing if not conservative in his opinions, but that only reflected the dominant politics of Fiction. The opposition called for more deregulation and even the banning of genres themselves, dubbing them "an affront to experimentation" and "the measles of the BookWorld," while others called for greater formulaicism—if for nothing better than to appease publishers. A noise made me turn.

"Miss Next," said Senator Jobsworth. "I am most grateful for your attendance. Will you join me in the captain's cabin in twenty minutes?"

I told him I would, and he disappeared off towards his private rooms with his entourage. Red Herring looked at his watch nervously.

"Are we late leaving?" I asked.

"We're waiting for the official Jurisfiction delegate."

We were kept waiting another ten minutes until a sleek spaceship that seemed to have been carved from a single block of obsidian approached from the south, circled twice, lowered its landing gear and, with a rolling blast from its swiveling thrusters, landed on the dockside. The entrance ramp descended, and two imperial guards hurried down it while one blue-skinned valet spread rose petals on the ground and two more played a brief alarum on trumpets. After a dramatic pause, a tall figure swathed in a high-collared black cloak strode menacingly down the ramp. He had a pale complexion, high cheekbones and a small and very precise goatee. This was His Mercilessness the Emperor Zhark, tyrannical ruler of a thousand solar systems and undisputed star of the Emperor Zhark novels. He was also a senior Jurisfiction agent and by all accounts quite a sweetie—if you didn't consider his habit for enslaving entire planets to be worked to death in his spice mines.

"Good morning, Your Mercilessness," said Red Herring, stepping forward to greet him. "No entourage today?"

"Hello, Herring old chap. Where's my cabin? I've a splitting headache. I was up all night dealing with Star Corps—bloody nuisance, they are. What am I doing here again?"

"You're the Jurisfiction delegate to the Racy Novel peace talks."

"Who are we fighting?"

"No one yet—that's why we call them 'peace talks.'"

"Couldn't we just lay waste to the entire region and put everyone to the sword? It would save a lot of boring chat, and I can go back to bed."

"I'm afraid not, Your Mercilessness."

"Very well," he said with a sigh, "just don't expect me to bunk in with the cook again. He frightens me."

"You have your own cabin this time, Emperor. We are already behind schedule. Steward?"

A steward stepped forward to take the emperor's bag, which I noticed was made out of the skin of the uncle he had murdered in order to seize the Zharkian throne. Despite appearances, Zhark was a skilled negotiator; it was he and he alone who had brought Forensic Procedural to the table and averted a potential fracturing of the Crime genre.

"Good Lord," said Zhark when he saw me. "Thursday?"

"The written one, Your Mercilessness," I said, bowing low. "We last met six months ago at the Paragon Tea Rooms."

He stared at me for a moment. Sometimes he was slow on the uptake. "You're the written one?"

"Yes, sir."

He moved closer, looked to left and right and lowered his voice.

"Do you remember that waitress at the Paragon? The perky one who answered back a lot and was wholly disrespectful?"

"I think so."

"You didn't get her number, did you?"

"I'm afraid not."

"Never mind. Written Thursday, eh? Know where the real one is?"

"No, sir."

"Bummer," he said, and walked off towards his cabin.

35.

We Go Upriver

For those with adventure on their minds, a trip watching the never-seen Euphemasaurus might be considered. For a fee, intrepid holiday makers will be taken into the Dismal Woods in the far north of the island where they will spend a pestilential four days being eaten alive by insects and bled white by leeches. Recovery is said to be three to six months, but the blurry pictures of "something in the distance" can be treasured forever.

Bradshaw's BookWorld Companion (7th edition)

*W*ithin a few minutes, the captain ordered the mooring ropes cast off, and with a blast of the whistle, a shudder from the deck and the venting of steam from the pistons, the sternwheel began to rotate and the boat pulled slowly away from the dock.

For a moment I watched the Great Library recede, and I suddenly realized that I was very much here on false pretenses. I wasn't Thursday, and I was here on the coattails of a mystery that I had singularly failed to uncover. It was frustrating because, this being Fiction, most of the relevant facts would already have been demonstrated to me but safely peppered with enough red herrings to ensure I couldn't see the true picture. Thursday would have spotted it all and indeed, given her "absent" status, had done so long ago. I still had no clear idea as to what was going on, but I was fortified by the simple fact that I was here, not cowering in a cupboard back home being bullied by Pickwick.

Luckily, my thoughts were interrupted by the adventurer, who asked me to meet him in the bar in an hour, and after that I went to find my cabin—a cozy wood-lined cubbyhole with the sink bolted to the ceiling to save room. There was no electricity, but a single porthole gave ample light. I unpacked the small case I had brought with me, and after freshening up I stepped outside, then stopped. I was next door to Cabin 12, where the mysterious passenger was staying. I heard raised voices from within.

"*. . . but I won't take your place at the talks,*" came the voice. I leaned closer, but the conversation was muted and indistinct from then on, and I hurried off towards the captain's quarters, which were situated just behind the wheelhouse, two decks up.

The senator was already there and had ensconced himself in a large and very worn wicker chair, from which spot he contemplated the river traffic that floated past as we made our way out of the Ungenred Zone and into Comedy. The captain and the helmsman were also present, and they expertly steered a path around the many underwater obstructions, islands and sandbars. I decided to try to act as much like the real Thursday as I could.

"Do you expect a clear run up the river, Captain?" I asked.

The captain chuckled.

"It's always eventful, Miss Next. Someone will doubtless be murdered, there will be romantic intrigue, and after that we'll pass a deserted village with a lone survivor who will ramble incoherently about something that we don't understand but has relevance later on. Did you meet the adventurer? Youngish chap. Handsome. He's probably met you before."

I said that I had, and both he and the senator laughed.

"What's the joke?"

"He's the fodder. There's always at least one on a trip like this. Someone for you to get attached to, probably sleep with, but who then dies on the journey, probably saving your life. You won't tell him, will you? It'll ruin his day."

"I'll try to keep it under my hat."

"Do you have the route all planned, Captain?" asked Jobsworth, who was sipping on a pink gin handed to him by a steward dressed in starched whites.

"We'll stay on the Metaphoric until we've entered Comedy and moved past Sitcoms," replied the captain, pointing to a map of the river, "and after that we follow a tributary past Mother-in-Law Jokes and then to Edgy Rapids before cruising the flat plain of Bob Hope and Vaudeville. At the foothills of the Scatological Mountains, we'll enter the subgenres of Bedroom Farce and Bawdy Romp. Twenty minutes after that, we stop at Middle Station, which marks the border into Racy Novel."

"Emissaries from Speedy Muffler will meet us at Fanny Hill," added Senator Jobsworth, "and they will accompany us to Pornucopia, the capital."

The conversation fell off after that, and once I'd mustered some courage, I spoke.

"Did you want to speak to me, Senator?" I asked.

"Yes," he replied. "I want you to understand that you are here simply as a face—nothing more. As already explained, we have been putting around the story that you have irritable-vowel syndrome and are mute. You will not be party to talks, or to preparations for talks. You will not express an opinion by gesticulating or written notes unless we decide and are fully briefed. You'll be told where to appear and when. Is that clear?"

"As a bell, sir."

"Good. Off you toddle, then. Ah!" he added, much relieved, "Come in, gentlemen."

Red Herring, Colonel Barksdale and Zhark had just appeared at the doorway. I was no longer needed. I thought for a moment of voicing my concerns over what Thursday might have been up to, but I didn't know for certain what she *had* been up to, so I said nothing, bowed and withdrew politely from the cabin.

I walked down the companionway to the main deck and

found my way to the bar. I wasn't particularly bothered by the senator's attitude. It was what I was expecting—a friendly welcome, then being put firmly in my place.

The bar was elegantly paneled in light wood with inlaid etched mirrors to give the the illusion of greater space. The furniture was of leather but had worn badly, and the horsehair stuffing was beginning to sprout at the seams. One of the mad-looking foreigners was asleep in an armchair, and at the bar was the adventurer. He looked handsomer than he had earlier, and his hat was placed on the bar next to him.

"Enjoying the trip?" I asked as I sat down.

"I thought it would be funnier steaming through Comedy."

"It's less funny the closer you get."

"Hmm. Would you permit me to buy you a drink?"

"I buy my own drinks," I told him, doing as Thursday would. It wasn't like it was a real drink anyway. Alcohol doesn't do anything in the BookWorld, except act as narrative furniture in scenes such as these. If you wanted to get off your head, you'd hit the hyphens, but I needed my wits about me.

"A beer for me," I said. "Drake?"

"Scotch."

The barman placed our drinks on the counter, and I took a sip. The beer was a light, amber-colored liquid, but it tasted like warm tea. This wasn't unusual, since everything in the BookWorld tasted like warm tea—except warm tea itself, which tasted of dishwater. But since dishwater tasted of warm tea, warm tea actually might have tasted like warm tea after all.

"Are you part of the diplomatic mission?" asked Drake.

I told him that I was, and he grunted noncommittally. Since the senator said he was fodder and unlikely to last the next few hours, I though it a safe bet to trust him.

"I overheard something odd outside the mysterious passenger's cabin."

"That's entirely normal. You'll probably hear odd noises in

the night, too, and if we've got time, someone will be found shot dead with a cryptic note close by."

"Do you want to know what I overheard?"

"Not really. There'll be an impostor on the boat, too—and a shape-changer."

"What, of the alien variety?" I asked, looking nervously about.

"No," he replied, smiling at my naïveté. "Someone or something who is not what it seems."

"Isn't that the impostor?"

"There's a subtle difference." Drake mused for a moment, staring at the ceiling. "But I'm not sure *precisely* what it is. I was born yesterday, you know."

"My name is Florent," announced a new bar steward who had just come on duty. "May I mix you a Tahiti Tingle?"

I frowned, then turned. It was Sprockett, dressed as a bar steward and sporting a ridiculous false mustache on his porcelain features. Since he didn't greet me, I assumed he wanted to remain incognito, so I merely said I already had a drink and resumed my conversation with Drake.

"Are journeys upriver usually like this?" I asked.

"Apparently so. How do they think they're going to stop Speedy Muffler anyway?"

"By telling him that massed armies on the borders of WomFic and Dogma are waiting to invade if he so much as hiccups."

"What makes you think Speedy Muffler is doing anything but rattling his saber? The only people who stand to gain by a war are the neighboring genres who get to divvy up the spoils."

"I knew Speedy Muffler in the old days," said one of the foreigners who had joined us, "long before the BookWorld was remade—even before Herring and Barksdale and that idiot Jobsworth were about."

"What do you know about Speedy Muffler?"

"That he wasn't always the leader of Racy Novel. He was

once a minor character in Porn with delusions of grandeur. Muffler was up here in the days before Racy Novel, when the Frowned-Upon Genres were clustered in the north beyond Comedy. His name came to prominence when he quite suddenly started sending large quantities of metaphor downriver. He wasn't licensed to do so, but because his supplies were consistent, the rules were relaxed. Pretty soon he was taking more and more territory for himself, but he kept on sending down the metaphor, and the CofG kept on turning a blind eye until he publicly proclaimed the area as Racy Novel, which was when the CofG started to take notice."

"By then it was too late," added Drake. "Speedy Muffler's power was established, his genre large enough to demand a chair at the Council of Genres."

"I guess WomFic/Feminism were none too happy?"

"Not overawed, no. Especially when he used to turn up at high-level summits with his shirt open and declaring that feminists needed to 'loosen up' and should groove with his love machine."

"Is he still shipping metaphor downriver?" I asked.

"Not as much as before," said Drake, "but still more than WomFic and Dogma. The area is rich in metaphor, and whoever can send the most downriver is the wealthiest. Put simply: Whoever controls the Northern Genres controls the metaphor supply, and whoever controls the supply of metaphor controls Fiction. It's not by chance that WomFic and Crime have forty-three percent of the Outland readership. If Squid Procedural had been positioned up here, everyone would be reading about Decapod Gumshoes, and loving it."

"So why isn't Racy Novel read more than Women's Fiction? If he sends more metaphor downriver, I mean?"

"Because of *sanctions*," said Drake, looking at me oddly, "imposed by WomFic and Dogma—and pretty much everyone else. Like it or not, Racy Novel isn't very highly thought of."

"Is that fair?"

"You're asking a lot of *basic* questions," said Drake. "I thought Thursday Next would be well up on all this—especially if she's here for the peace talks."

"I need to gauge local opinion," I said quickly. "This is Fiction, after all—interpretation trumps fact every time."

"Oh," said Drake, "I see."

I excused myself, as Sprockett had just left the bar, and I caught up with him farther down the steamer, just outside the storeroom.

"Good afternoon, ma'am," he whispered. "How is it going?"

"What are you doing here?"

"I'm the bar steward."

"I can see that."

"I knew you couldn't *actually* let me go," he said. "I'm too good a butler for that. So I simply assumed you were being compassionate and thought this trip too dangerous for you to take staff. So I came anyway. What do you want me to do?"

I took a deep breath. It seemed as though butlers were like flat feet, dimples and troublesome aunts—you've got them for life.

"There's a mysterious passenger in Cabin Twelve. I want you to find out what he's doing here."

"He doesn't *do* anything—he's simply the MP-C12. Have you figured out who the fodder is yet?"

"It's Drake."

"Ooh. Will he be eaten by a crocodile? A poison dart in the eye?"

"Just find out what you can about the mysterious passenger, would you? I overheard him say, 'I won't take your place at the talks,' and it might be significant."

"Very good, ma'am. I'll make inquiries."

36.

Middle Station

For those of you who have tired of the glitzy world of shopping and inappropriate boyfriends in Chick Lit, a trip to Dubious Lifestyle Advice might be the next step. An hour in the hallowed halls of invented ills will leave you with at least ten problems you never knew you had, or even knew existed.

Bradshaw's BookWorld Companion (7th edition)

*I*t took us an hour to steam through Comedy, and whilst mostly light and airy and heard-it-beforeish, the atmosphere became more strained and intimidating as we chugged slowly through Mother-in-Law Jokes and Sexist Banter. Despite being advised to remain out of sight, I elected to stay on deck and brazen out the worst abuses that came shouted unseen from the thick trees that covered the riverbank. The two ladies of negotiable affection had no difficulty with the comments, having heard much worse before, and simply retorted with aplomb—delicately countering the more vulgar insinuations with amusing attacks on the male psyche and various aspersions on their manhood or ability.

We came across the Middle Station at noon. The small trading town was right on the point where the Double Entendre River becomes the Innuendo, and although we had been traveling through the buffer genre of Bawdy Romp, replete with amusing sketches of people running in and out of each other's bedrooms in a retro-amusing manner, we were now very much within the influence of Racy Novel, and we all knew it. The first part of the journey had been a pleasing chug up the river, but now we were here for business, and a sense of brooding introspection had fallen upon the boat.

The arrival of the paddle steamer at the Middle Station was welcomed not by sound but by silence. The constant *tramp-tramp-tramp* of the engines, for five hours a constant background chorus, made things seem deafeningly quiet when the engines were stopped. I stood on the foredeck as the steamer drifted towards the jetty. The Middle Station, usually a throbbing hub of activity, seemed deserted. Drake stood next to me, his hand on the butt of his revolver.

"I'm going ashore to check this out," I said, "and I think it would be better if you stayed here."

"*Au contraire*, Miss Next. It is *you* who will be staying here."

There seemed no easy way to say this, so I came right out with it.

"Drake," I said in a quiet voice, "you're the fodder, due for a tragic yet potentially heroic end."

He looked at me for a moment. "It's very good of you to warn me, but that's not how I see it."

"You think it's someone else?"

"I think the fodder is *you*, Thursday."

"No it's not."

"What are you if you're not the fodder?"

"I'm the impostor."

"You . . . could be the impostor *and* the fodder."

"The unions would never allow it."

"They might."

"Look," I said, "we could argue this all day, but here's the thing: You graduated only this morning with a minimal backstory. I've been working the BookWorld for over three years—who's most likely to cop it in the next few hours?"

"You might just *think* you've been working the BookWorld for three years. It could be *your* backstory."

"Okay," I said, beginning to get angry, "we'll both go out there and see who gets eaten by a crocodile or gets a poison dart in the eye. *Then* we'll know."

"Deal."

The rest of the peace delegation had joined us on deck, and they were staring silently towards the Middle Station. As we drew closer, we could see that the houses had been recently burned, for wisps of smoke hung in the air with the faint smell of scorched custard. We waited for the steamer to drift towards the jetty, until it touched with a faint bump. The crew made the steamer fast before jumping back onto the boat, and we watched and waited as the steamer slowly swung around in the current. There was not a single sign of life anywhere in the station.

"Well," said Colonel Barksdale after a few minutes, "I've seen enough—doubtless skirmishers from Racy Novel causing trouble. Let's steam on deeper into the genre and start getting some face time with this lunatic."

"We're not going anywhere until we load some coal," said the captain.

I stepped off the steamer and onto the rickety old jetty, Drake at my side. We walked slowly into the town. Drake looked about anxiously, but not, I realized, about the deserted Middle Station.

"You'll keep an eye out for crocodiles, won't you?" I asked.

"As long as you watch my back for poison darts."

We came across the first body near the mailbox on the corner. There was an ugly wound in the middle of his chest, and the small letters and words that made up his existence had been caught by the breeze and blown into the fishing nets set up to dry. We looked around and noticed more bodies and the detritus of conflict: discarded rubber chickens, feather dusters, strings of silk flags, spinning bow ties and custard-pie shrapnel that somehow seemed sadder and less funny than usual.

"Is this a garrison town?" I asked.

"No," replied the adventurer.

"Then what's a lance corporal of the Fourteenth Motorized Clown doing up here?"

The corpse was indeed a member of Comedy's frontline troops. He had orange hair, a bulbous red nose, and he was wearing camouflage battle dress, along with a pair of size-twenty-eight shoes. Not much good for marching and a hangover from their days as an Alpine regiment.

Drake placed his hand on the clown's bright red nose.

"Still warm," he said, "probably been dead less than an hour. Any thoughts?"

"I don't know," I said, picking up a nurse's hat from the ground. A little farther on, a stethoscope was lying broken in the dust. "But it wasn't just clowns who died here today."

We walked some more and came across a dozen or so other bodies. All clowns, all dead and none meant to be here. Bawdy Romp was within Racy Novel's control and officially a demilitarized zone.

"This doesn't make sense," said Drake. "Comedy never had any beef with Racy Novel. Quite the reverse—they actually got on very well. Without Racy Novel, Comedy would be very poor indeed—especially for the stand-ups."

"Let's not hang around. Where did the captain say the coal was?"

We walked deeper into the station and saw more evidence of a pitched battle having taken place not long before. We found the remains of several burned-out clown cars; despite their being able to drive in either direction and having a device for shedding all the body work in order to lighten the vehicle for a speedy getaway, it hadn't done any good. There was evidence of atrocities, too. Medical staff had been killed. I noted several pretty nurses and a handsome doctor lying in a doorway, and several crash carts were strewn about. There were a few dead rustic serving wenches, too, a ripped bodice and a couple of horses with ruggedly handsome and now very dead riders lying in the road amidst scorched brickwork and smoking rubble. We came across more dead clowns; it seemed as though an entire company had been wiped out.

"Looks like someone was making sure Comedy couldn't come to Racy Novel's aid," observed Drake.

"It makes me wonder why we're bothering with peace talks. Crocodile."

"What?"

"Behind you."

Drake jumped out of the way as the crocodile's jaws snapped shut. "Thank you."

"Now do you believe you might be the fodder?" I asked.

Drake thought for a moment. "He could have been trying to eat his way through me to get to you."

"Sure," I said with a smile, "and while we're on the subject: If I were the fodder, why didn't you warn me? I warned you."

"Because I . . . didn't want to ruin your day?"

"How very generous of you."

We found the coal heap amidst a few more civilians—this time pretty secretaries who had died in the arms of their bosses. We filled a couple of wheelbarrows with coal before returning to the steamer. As soon as we were aboard, the crew slipped the moorings and the captain ordered, "Astern slow," and swung the bows into the limpid river. We took the left branch up the tributary known as the Innuendo, and pretty soon the steamer was at full speed once more. Despite others' misgivings, Jobsworth seemed adamant that the peace talks should go ahead.

It seemed as though an entire company had been wiped out.

37.

Revision

Amongst all the genres on Fiction Island, Comedy is the only one that still demands compulsory military service and a bucket of water down the trousers for every citizen. Conscripts are trained in the clown martial art of slapstick and do not graduate from military academy until they can kill silently with a frying pan and achieve fatal accuracy with a custard pie at forty yards. It's a bit like Sparta, only with jokes.

Bradshaw's BookWorld Companion (7th edition)

*W*e convened in the bar soon afterwards and related everything we had seen at the Middle Station. Colonel Barksdale, Herring, Zhark and Senator Jobsworth listened carefully to all we had to say but didn't seem to have any better idea of what was going on than we did.

"There is no reason for the Fourteenth Motorized Clown to be this far north," declared Colonel Barksdale angrily. "It is a flagrant breach of numerous peace agreements and specifically the 1996 Clown Army Proliferation Treaty."

"Shouldn't you have known about it?" asked Emperor Zhark, who knew better than most the value of intelligence.

"The Textual Sieve network is patchy up here," replied Barksdale in a sulky tone. "We can't know everything. I can only think the Fourteenth Clown must have been massing in the demilitarized zone as the potential allies of Racy Novel."

"Then who killed them and all the civilians?" asked the

adventurer, to which question there didn't seem to be much of an answer. They all fell silent for a moment.

"When do we meet with the other delegates?" asked Jobsworth.

"In an hour," replied Herring. "Aunt Augusta of WomFic and Cardinal Fang of Outdated Religious Dogma are meeting us at Fanny Hill. Would you excuse me? We're out of footnoterphone range, and I'm going to have to send a message to the council via the shortwave colophone."

Drake and I were dismissed, as Jobsworth, Barksdale and Zhark had decided to discuss the finer points of the peace talks, something to which we could not be privy.

"I'm going to freshen up before we get there," said Drake, "and maybe rub on some crocodile repellent."

I laughed, saw he was serious, turned the laugh into a cough and said, "Good idea."

We were now well within Racy Novel, and the rustling of bushes, the groans and squeaks of delight echoed in from the riverbanks, where large privet hedges were grown to afford some sort of privacy for the residents. Every now and then, a slip in the riverbank allowed us a brief glimpse of what went on, which was generally several scantily dressed people running around in a gleeful manner—usually in a bedroom somewhere, but occasionally in the outdoors and once on the top deck of a London bus.

I made my way forward, where I was met by Sprockett, who beckoned me into a laundry cupboard.

"I took the opportunity to go through the mysterious passenger's belongings, ma'am."

"And?"

"I came across some shoulder pads, knee pads, a chest protector and a gallon of fire retardant."

"*What?*"

"Shoulder pads—"

"I heard. It just doesn't make any sense."

"What doesn't?"

"All of it. From beginning to end. We reach Fanny Hill in half an hour, and the peace talks begin as soon as we are escorted to Pornucopia. It's time to go over what we've found. I feel the answer is staring me in the face."

"Shouldn't we gather all the suspects in the bar?" asked Sprockett, who was fast becoming infected by the *Metaphoric Queen*'s capacity for narrative formulaicism.

"No. And another thing—"

I was interrupted by a cry from outside, and the engine went to slow ahead. We stepped out of the laundry cupboard to see several crewmen run past, and we followed them to the upper rear deck, from where we could see across the top of the stern-wheel. Behind us in midstream was a figure in one of the riverboat's four-man tenders. The man was rowing in a measured pace away from the boat, and given our forward speed, the distance between the two craft was rapidly increasing.

"Who is it?" asked Herring.

"It looks like the mysterious passenger from Cabin Twelve," replied Drake, who had a small telescope, as befits an adventurer. "He's even taken his luggage with him."

"What's the meaning of this?" asked Jobsworth, who had just arrived.

Herring explained, and Jobsworth looked at us all in turn. "Let me see."

He peered through the telescope for a moment. "He's taken his luggage with him."

"That's what I said," remarked Drake.

"Mr. Herring," said Jobsworth, "what's going on here?"

"I've no idea, Senator."

"Advice?"

"Um . . . carry on?"

"Sounds good to me. Captain?"

"Sir?"

"Carry on."

But the captain, long a riverman, knew more of the perils that can be found on the Metaphoric.

"We can't leave him out here, sir. The forests are full of Sirens eager to . . . well, how can I put it? He'll be captured and made to . . . Listen, he'll be killed."

"Will it be quick?"

"No—it will be long and very drawn out. He might enjoy it to begin with, but he will eventually be discarded, a shriveled husk of a man devoid of any clothes, humanity or moisture."

But the senator was made of sterner stuff.

"This mission is too important to delay, Captain. The mysterious passenger formerly of Cabin Twelve will have to remain exactly that. In every campaign there are always casualties. Full ahead."

"Yes, sir."

And they all walked away. The engines ran up to full speed again, and after a few more minutes the small boat was lost to view behind an overhanging tree on a bend in the river.

"I guess that's what mysterious passengers do," said Drake with a shrug. "Be mysterious. Drink?"

"I'll see you down there," I replied. "I must admonish this bar steward for the lamentable lack of quality in his Tahiti Tingle."

Drake nodded and moved off, and Sprockett and I sat on the curved bench on the upper rear deck to discuss recent events. From the epizeuxis to the mimefield to the Men in Plaid to Sir Charles Lyell and the bed-sitting room.

"What had Thursday discovered that was so devastating to the peace process?" asked Sprockett.

"I don't know. I wish to Panjandrum I were more like her."

I took the sketch I had found in Sir Charles's office out of my pocket. It was a map of Racy Novel with WomFic to one side and Dogma on the other. There was a shaded patch the shape of a tailless salmon that was mostly beneath Racy Novel.

As I stared at the picture, I felt a sudden flush of new intelligence, as though a jigsaw had been thrown into the air and landed fully completed. Everything that had happened to me over the past few days had been inexorably pointing me in one direction. But up until now I'd been too slow or stupid to be able to sift the relevant facts from the herrings.

"By all the spell checkers of Isugfsf," I said, pointing at Lyell's sketch. "It's *metaphor*. A trillion tons of the stuff waiting to be mined, lying beneath our feet!"

"Yes?" said Sprockett, his eyebrow pointing at "Doubtful."

"That's what Lyell and Thursday had discovered," I said excitedly. "It's as Drake said: 'Whoever controls the supply of metaphor controls Fiction.'"

"If so," said Sprockett carefully, "Racy Novel would be sending more metaphor downriver than anyone else. And they're not."

I thought about this for a moment. "Maybe Speedy Muffler isn't bad at all. Perhaps he's defending the metaphor against greedy genres intent on mining it to exhaustion. Metaphor should be controlled—a glut on the market would make Fiction overtly highbrow, painfully ambiguous and potentially unreadable. The new star on the horizon would be the elephant in the room that might lead the BookWorld into a long winter's night."

"That would be frightful," replied Sprockett, recoiling in terror as the overmetaphorication hit him like a hammer. "But how does that explain the Fourteenth Clown's destruction? Or even who's responsible for all this?"

"I don't know," I said, "but Senator Jobsworth needs to hear about it."

I jumped up and ran down the companionway to the captain's cabin, nearly colliding with Red Herring on the way.

"Sorry," he said, "I'm just going to find a doughnut—do you want one?"

"No thank you, sir."

I found Senator Jobsworth discussing the talks with Emperor Zhark and Colonel Barksdale.

"Have you seen Herring?" asked Jobsworth. "He should really be going through the final details with us."

"He went to get a doughnut."

"He did? Leave us now. We're very busy."

"I have important information. I think I know why Thursday was assassinated."

Jobsworth stared at me. "Thursday's dead?"

"Well, no, because her imagination is still alive. It was an assassination *attempt*—in a crummy book written by Adrian Dorset."

"Adrian Dorset?"

"Jack Schitt, if you must. It was the epizeuxis that got her. And Mediocre."

"Who's Mediocre?"

"Gatsby."

"He's anything but mediocre, my girl."

And both he and Zhark laughed in a patronizing sort of way.

"Seriously," I said hotly, "Thursday was attacked, and the reason—"

"Whatever it is, I'm sure it's *fascinating*," said Jobsworth, "but it's going to have to wait. We enter the subgenre Racy Classics in five minutes and meet with the other delegates in forty-five. We have much work to do. If you really want to be helpful, make me a cup of tea or go find Herring."

"But—"

"GO!"

I mumbled an apology and backed out the door, cursing my own weakness.

"That could have gone better," said Sprockett. "I'll try to find Herring for you."

And with a mild buzz, he disappeared. I walked down to the lower deck feeling hot and frustrated. I didn't like to be talked to that way, but this could indeed wait. I'd leave it until Jobsworth had a quieter moment and then tell him—or perhaps speak to Speedy Muffler's people in private and see if my suspicions were correct. Perhaps it was better *not* to talk to Jobsworth.

I went down to my cabin to wash my face but stopped at Cabin 12, next door to mine. The mysterious passenger's escape from the steamer still made no sense, so I pushed open the door and went in.

The bed was made up, as I might have suspected—we weren't due to return until tomorrow. I searched through the missing passenger's baggage and found none of the shoulder or knee pads that Sprockett had described, although the fire retardant was still there, unopened. There was a change of clothes and nothing else. I was about to close the door when I remembered—*the mysterious passenger had his luggage with him when we saw him rowing away.*

A flurry of unpleasant thoughts went through my head, and I suddenly realized not only why the mysterious passenger would have knee pads, but who had attacked the Fourteenth Clown and what was going on in the Outland that made the whole thing possible. This was a complex plot of considerable dimension, and I was now certain who was behind it all. My first thought was to go and tell Jobsworth exactly what was happening, but I stopped as a far worse realization dawned upon me. The plan would work only if everyone on board the *Metaphoric Queen* were to be assassinated.

I grabbed a fire ax and ran up the companionway to the deck.

38.

Answers

Off the coast lies Vanity Island, and off Vanity lies Fan Fiction. Beyond Fan Fiction is School Essays and beyond that Excuses for Not Doing School Essays. The latter is often the most eloquent, constructed as it is in the white-hot heat of panic, necessity and the desire not to get a detention.

Bradshaw's BookWorld Companion (2nd edition)

*O*ne of Jobsworth's D-3 minions had been given the task of keeping an eye on the riveted box that contained the valuable plot-line gifts for Speedy Muffler, and he noticed me only when I was halfway across the foredeck, my intention already clear to those present. He dropped his copy of *The Word* and took a pace towards me. I caught him on the solar plexus with the ball of my hand, and he reeled over backwards. The foredeck would have been in plain view from the wheelhouse, and the captain pulled on the steam whistle and sent a deafening blast echoing across Racy Novel, temporarily quenching the sounds of the enthusiastic moans that echoed over the water.

The whistle also drowned out the sound of the padlock being smashed off, and I had the lid open and was looking at the contents when Zhark and Jobsworth arrived beside me. They stopped, too, and stared inside the box.

"Those aren't plot lines," said Jobsworth.

"No," I replied, looking up the river to where I could just see *Lady Chatterley's Lover* appear around the next bend, less than five hundred yards away, "and you need to stop the boat before we get to Racy Classics."

"Captain!" yelled Jobsworth, who knew how to act properly when evidence presented itself. The captain opened the wheel-house window and leaned out, cupping a hand to his ear.

"Turn the *Queen* about and get us downstream. If we go up, I want to be taking only Racy Pulp with us!"

The captain needed no further bidding, and he ordered the helm hard over to turn midriver.

I leaned in and examined the contents of the box. It was a classy job. There was a single glass jar that contained, as far as I could see, a lot of foam. This was attached to a funnel and a time switch, and wrapped around all this was a series of embarrassingly bad descriptions of sexual congress. Emperor Zhark moved closer and put on his glasses.

"By the seven-headed Zook of Zargon," he breathed. "It's full of antikern."

"It's full of what?"

"Kerning is the adjustment of the white spaces between the letters," he explained, "in order to make the letters seem proportionally spaced. What this does is remove the white spaces entirely—within an instant this entire boat and everyone in it will implode into nothing more than an oily puddle of ink floating on the river."

I pointed to the poorly written descriptions of sexual congress wrapped around the device.

"With a few telltale descriptions of a sexual nature to point the finger toward Speedy Muffler."

"So it would appear. *Blast!*"

Emperor Zhark had been examining the device carefully.

"What's up?" I asked.

"No blue wire. There's usually a choice of wires to cut, and by long convention it's always the blue one. Without that there's no way we can know how to defuse it."

I glanced at the timing device, which also by long convention was prominently featured—and had two and a half minutes to go.

"Can we throw it overboard?" asked Jobsworth.

"Not unless you want to see the entire Metaphoric River vanish in under a second."

"We could abandon the steamer."

"It'll be a tight fit in the one tender remaining—and those high privet hedges along the riverbank won't make for an easy escape."

"I'll take it in a boat with me."

It was Drake Foden, adventurer.

"I don't want any arguments," he said. "This is my function. I'm the fodder."

"I told you he was," said Barksdale, jabbing Jobsworth on the shoulder with his index finger.

There was no time to do anything else, and at a single word from the captain the second tender was lowered over the side and the riveted box placed inside. Drake turned to me and took my hands in his.

"Good-bye, Thursday. I'm sorry we didn't get to sleep together and perhaps have a few jokes and get into a couple of scrapes and thus make this farewell more poignant and mournful, which it isn't."

"Yes," I replied. "I'll always regret not knowing you at all or even liking you very much. Perhaps next time."

"There won't be a next time."

"I know that. Drake?"

"Yes?"

"You have something stuck in your teeth."

"Here?"

"Other side."

"Thanks."

And without another word, Drake clambered aboard,

cast off the mooring and began to row quickly away from the steamer.

"Hey!" I yelled across the water. "Aren't you glad it wasn't a poison dart in your—"

But I didn't get a chance to say any more. Drake, the tender and the iron box suddenly imploded with a sound like a cough going backwards, accompanied by a swift rush of air that sucked in to fill the void and made our ears pop. I'd never seen text destroyed so rapidly—even an eraserhead takes a half second to work.

"Slow ahead," ordered Jobsworth, "and wire the delegation that we have been 'unavoidably delayed.'"

He turned to me.

"Just what in Wheatley's name is going on here, Next?"

My mind was still racing. There was the fate of the Fourteenth Clown to think of, and the broader implications of regional stability, pretty nurses, handsome doctors and fire retardant.

"Time is of the essence. Senator, I need you to do something without question."

"And that is?"

"Shut down every single Feedback Loop north of *Three Men in a Boat.*"

"Are you mad?" he said. "That's almost three hundred million books!"

"Mad? Perhaps. But if you don't do what I ask, you'll have a genre war on your hands so devastating it will turn your blood to ice."

"My blood is already ice, Miss Next."

The senator paused, then looked at Zhark, who nodded his agreement.

"Very well."

Jobsworth instructed Barnes to get the message to Text Grand Central in any way he could—and to expedite, code puce.

"And you," said Jobsworth, pointing a finger at me, "have some serious explaining to do."

We convened in the bar almost immediately. Jobsworth was there with Herring, Barksdale, the captain and Emperor Zhark—as well as all of Jobsworth's D-3s and Sprockett, who had divested himself of his bar-steward disguise and was once more in full butler regalia.

"Where would you like me to start?" I asked.

"At the beginning," said Jobsworth, "and don't stop until you get to the end."

I took a deep breath and showed them the map Lyell had drawn.

"We won't find out exactly *how* she knew until we find her, but the real Thursday Next became aware that there might exist a huge quantity of raw metaphor under the Northern Genres. Such a state of affairs would throw the entire power balance of Fiction on its head, so she needed to make sure. She took leading geologist Sir Charles Lyell up-country to conduct some test drilling, and it seems she was right. Buried beneath Racy Novel are the largest reserves of untapped metaphor the BookWorld has ever seen."

I had everyone's attention by now—you could have heard a pin drop.

"It was potentially explosive news, and Thursday knew that she would be in severe danger if this got out—so she hid among the flat Thursdays out in Fan Fiction. Despite her precautions, her activities were being scrutinized without her knowledge, and Thursday—reliably touted as 'the second-hardest person to kill in the BookWorld'—had to be gotten rid of. A cabbie named the Mediocre Gatsby was bribed to hang around Fan Fiction on the off chance she would want picking up. A previously scrapped book called *The Murders on the Hareng Rouge* was being kept in Vanity and as soon as she was in the cab, the book was dispatched to the Council of Genres. Mediocre piggybacked the book for the trip as instructed, and a second later a rhetorical device was detonated, leaving the book, the cabbie and, it was hoped, Thursday herself little more then textual confetti—a million graphemes littered all over Fiction."

There was silence, so I carried on. "That might have been the end of it. Most of the book was just small, tattered remnants not dissimilar to the usual detritus that flutters occasionally from the heavens and is absorbed into the ground, except that for some reason, Adrian Dorset described a bed-sitting room so well that it survived the sabotage intact and came to rest in Conspiracy, and JAID had to be alerted. This was tricky, because a diligent investigator might start to ask awkward questions, so Lockheed was ordered to employ his most useless investigator to look into it. Me. And that's not a coincidence. Why would that be, Sprockett?"

"There are *no* coincidences in the BookWorld—so long as you don't count the last chapters in some of Charles Dickens's books."

"Exactly. But we *do* find problems—the fact that someone scrubbed off the ISBN to avoid discovery, and the epizeuxis device. And as we look, we find ourselves one step behind the Men in Plaid, who are silencing anyone who had anything to do with the attempted hit on Thursday Next."

"Rogue Men in Plaid?" said Emperor Zhark in an accusatory tone, staring at Jobsworth and Herring—the two who were responsible for them.

"Scrubbed ISBN?" demanded Jobsworth. "Dead geologists? Epizeuxis devices? Who is responsible for this outrage?"

"One of us present here."

They all looked at one another.

"It was little things to begin with—things that didn't click until later. I learned from Adrian Dorset that he destroyed *The Murders on the Hareng Rouge* a month back, yet it was still floating around Vanity waiting to intercept Thursday. The rules state that it has to be scrapped immediately—on Red Herring's signature."

They all looked at Herring, who had started to go pale.

"He controls the Book Transit Authority, and also the Men in Plaid. He's the second-in-command to the BookWorld, but he wanted more. He was after the top job and, what's more, control of the vast stores of metaphor that are lying under Racy Novel. He knew that whoever controlled the metaphor would control Fiction."

"But how could he control Speedy Muffler and Racy Novel?" asked Zhark.

"That's the clever bit. He planned to invade—using an army mustered from one of the most powerful genres on the island."

"Women's Fiction?" said Colonel Barksdale with a smirk. "Not possible. They have neither the manpower nor the inclination."

Emperor Zhark and Jobsworth nodded their heads vigorously; WomFic was wholly against any sort of warfare and had agreed to sanctions only as a last resort.

"Not WomFic," I said. "A smaller subgenre with enough shock troops to take on the Fourteenth Clown and win. A genre that has for many years been the buffer zone between WomFic and Racy Novel. A genre that has successfully blended raciness and euphemism to create an empire that sells books by the billion—Daphne Farquitt. More readers than almost any other writer, and eighteen percent of total global readership."

"They don't have any troops," scoffed Barksdale. "You're mistaken."

I chose my words carefully. Despite recent events, I'd be pushing my luck if I admitted I'd been in the RealWorld.

"Today is Daphne Farquitt Day in the Outland. As we speak, a massive readathon is in progress. At even conservative estimates, there must be upwards of two hundred million readers making their way through Farquitt's three hundred seventy-two novels. There will be speed-reading events, trivia quizzes and read-ins. The power of the Feedback Loop will be astronomical—and easy enough to create an unstoppable army of ditzy romantic heroines and their lantern-jawed potential husband/lovers."

"The nurses, secretaries and medical equipment you saw at Middle Station?"

"*Exactly*," I replied. "Not civilians at all—but the romantically involved honored dead. The Farquitt Army was working against Racy Novel by taking a preemptive strike and eradicating any possible threat from Speedy Muffler's allies in Comedy. With members of the peace envoy all assassinated in an apparent Muffler attack, there would be no opposition to the total and complete invasion of Racy Novel by the Farquitt Army and, with it, control of the vast stocks of metaphor beneath our feet."

There was silence in the room. They all looked stunned. Barksdale was the first to speak.

"That explanation," he said in admiration, "was of a complexity that would gather plaudits from even the most intractable of political thrillers. With all of us dead in an attack that could be blamed on Speedy Muffler, Red Herring would step into the top slot, direct his allies to annex Racy Novel, secure the metaphor and set himself up as supreme dictator of Fiction."

"It's a brilliant scheme," murmured Zhark in admiration. "I'll *definitely* be using it on the Rambosians next week. The little devils. They love a good subjugation. Senator?"

"A plan of titanic proportions. If he weren't going to be erased for treason, I'd offer him a job."

Red Herring was starting to shake when he heard this. He tried to speak, but only a strangled squeak came out.

"Might I make an observation?" asked Sprockett.

"Go ahead," replied Jobsworth, who was now in a generous mood.

"Mr. Herring is here with us now—how could he seize power if he was assassinated along with the rest of us?"

Barksdale's and Zhark's faces fell, and even Jobsworth's smile dropped from his face. They looked at me.

"Simple," I said, placing my hand on Herring's shoulder. "This *isn't* Red Herring. Figuring that out was the key to the whole thing."

"That's absurd," remarked Jobsworth. "We were discussing the minutiae of the peace talks on the way in. He can't be anything but."

"I assure you," said Faux Herring, who had finally managed to find his voice. "I'm *not* Red Herring."

"He's right," I said. "This is Herring's stunt double, Fallon Hairbag. He took Herring's place when Red Herring made his escape in the boat's tender."

"You're the mysterious passenger?" asked Zhark, and the Herring-that-wasn't nodded unhappily.

"Mr. Herring promised me the pick of all the stunt work in the BookWorld if I did this for him. He said it was for a prank. That it would be funny."

"I overheard Herring and his stunt double talking in the cabin—about 'not doing the talks'—and my butler discovered knee and elbow pads as well as a gallon of fire retardant."

"Whatever for?" asked Barksdale.

"Just in case I had to set myself on fire and leap out a window waving my arms," replied Fallon wistfully. "It always pays to be prepared."

"The switch was subtly done," I said, "but when I met the replaced Herring later on, he was polite and asked me if I wanted a doughnut—the real Herring would never have been so accommodating."

"I've heard enough," announced Senator Jobsworth, rising to his feet. "Send word that the peace talks are postponed. I want an emergency meeting of everyone in the debating chamber this evening, a press conference at five and the WomFic and Farquitt senators in my office the minute we get back. Barnes?"

"Yes, sir?"

"Implement Emergency Snooze Protocol 7B on the whole Farquitt canon *immediately*. I want every Farquitt reader yawning and nodding off in under ten minutes. We need to not only close down their feedback but send Daphne Farquitt a clear message that we will not be trifled with."

"What about the kittens?" asked Zhark in a shocked tone.

"It's a feline-compliant executive order," replied Jobsworth grandly. "No kittens will be harmed in the great Farquitt Snooza-thon."

While Barnes and the rest of the D-3s scurried off to do Jobsworth's bidding, the senator and the others put their heads together. I told Fallon to go hide in his cabin until we got in, by which time he would doubtless be forgotten. He thanked me and gave me his card in case I needed someone to attempt to leap fourteen motorcycles in a double-decker bus or something, and Sprockett and I went and sat on the foredeck to watch the riverbank drift slowly past. Despite keeping a careful eye out for Herring, we saw only the upturned tender he had escaped in and figured that he was either making his escape to Farquitt or had been eaten by a crocodile who had mistaken him for fodder.

"Well," said Sprockett, "that denouement went very well. Your first?"

"Did it show?"

"Not at all."

I was glad of this. "I think Thursday might have been proud."

"Yes," agreed Sprockett, "I think she might."

39.

Story-Ending Options

To finish off your Character Exchange Program break, Thomas Cook (BookWorld) Limited is offering tourists the option to choose how they would like to end their holidays. The "Chase" or "Scooby-Doo" endings remain popular, as do the "Death Scene" and "Reconciliation with Sworn Enemy." Traditionalists may be disappointed, though. The ever-popular "Riding Off into the Sunset" option has recently had to be withdrawn owing to irreconcilable cliché issues.

Bradshaw's BookWorld Companion (15th edition)

*T*he trip back downriver was uneventful and over in only twelve words. By the time the *Metaphoric Queen* had docked, the senator for Farquitt had already denied that her genre had anything to do with Herring's plan and expressed "great surprise" and "total outrage" that someone had "faked Romantic Troops" in order to attack the Fourteenth Clown. For its part, Comedy had mobilized its Second and Sixth Clown divisions to its borders and was demanding reparations from Farquitt, at the same time bringing pressure to bear on WomFic by threatening to withdraw all humor. Not to be outdone, Speedy Muffler had declared that the "presence of untapped metaphor" within his territory was "unproven and absurd," and he had so far refused all offers of commercial extraction contracts, further commenting that individual senators were welcome to see him personally in his "love train."

"Looks like it's business as usual," I said to Commander Bradshaw.

We were in the Jurisfiction offices at Norland Park, and I was having a lengthy debrief that same afternoon. I had entered the offices not as a bit player nor an apprentice but on my own merit. Emperor Zhark had awarded me a gift of some valuable jewelry that he said had been buried with his grandfather, Mr. Fainset doffed his cap in an agreeable manner, and Mrs. Tiggy-winkle had kindly offered to do my laundry. It felt like I was part of the family.

"So what are you going to do now?" asked Bradshaw, leaning back in his chair.

"I had a small mutiny in my series," I explained. "My own fault, really—I was thinking of Thursday and not my books. It'll need a lot of tact and diplomacy to win it back."

Bradshaw smiled and thought for a minute. "The Book-World is falling apart at the seams," he said, waving his hand at the huge pile of paperwork in his in-tray. "We've got a major problem with e-books that we'd never envisioned. The Racy Novel–Farquitt affair will rumble on for years, and I'm sure we haven't heard the last of Red Herring. Ten Duplex-6s have gone missing, and everyone has escaped from *The Great Escape*."

"How is that possible?"

"There was a fourth tunnel we didn't know about—Tom, Dick, Harry and *Keith*. There's a serial killer still at large, not to mention several character assassins—and that pink gorilla running around inside *A Tale of Two Cities* is really beginning to piss me off."

He took a sip of coffee and stared at me.

"I'm down to only seven agents. You've proved your capacity for this sort of work. I want you to join us here at Jurisfiction."

"No, no," I said quickly, "I've had quite enough, thank you. The idea that people actually do this because *they like it* strikes me as double insanity with added insanity. Besides, you've already got a Thursday—you just have to find her. That reminds me." I dug Thursday's shield from my pocket and pushed it across the desk.

Bradshaw picked it up and rubbed his thumb against the smooth metal. "Where did you get this?"

"The red-haired man. I think Thursday knew she was compromised before she set off on her last trip and wanted me to carry on her work."

"So that's why he was out of his book," muttered Bradshaw. "I'll see him pardoned at the earliest opportunity."

Bradshaw looked at the badge, then at me.

"So how do you think this story's going to end?"

"I don't know, sir."

"Are you sure you're not her?"

"It's a tricky one," I replied after giving the matter some thought, "and there's evidence to suppose that I am. I can do things only she can do, I can see some things that only she can see. Landen thought I was her, and although he now thinks I'm the written one, that might be part of a fevered delusion. His or mine, I'm not sure. It's even possible I've been Owlcreeked."

Bradshaw knew what I was talking about. "Owlcreeking" was a Biercian device in which a character could spend the last few seconds of his life in a long-drawn-out digression of what might have happened had he lived. I might be at this very moment spiraling out of control in Mediocre's cab, Herring's coup still ahead of me and perfect in its unrevealed complexity.

"Carmine might actually be the Thursday I think I am," I added. "It's even possible I'm suffering the hallucinatory aftershock of a recent rewriting. And while we're pushing the plausibility envelope, the BookWorld might not be real at all, and maybe I'm simply an Acme carpet fitter with a vibrant imagination."

I shuddered with the possibility that none of this might be happening at all.

"This is Fiction," said Bradshaw in a calm voice, "and the truth is whatever you make it. You can interpret the situation in any way you want, and all versions could be real—and what's more, depending on how you act now, any one of those scenarios could *become* real."

I frowned. "I can be Thursday just by thinking I am?"

"More or less. We may require you to undergo a short narrative procedure known as a 'Bobby Ewing,' where you wake up in the next chapter and it's all been a dream, but it's pretty painless so long as you don't mind any potential readers throwing up their hands in disgust."

"I can be Thursday?" I said again.

He nodded. "All you have to do is *know* you are. And don't deny that you've had some doubts over the past few days."

It was tempting. I could be her and do Thursday things and never have to worry about falling ReadRates, keeping Bowden in line or dealing with Pickwick. I could even have Landen and the kids. I looked around at the Jurisfiction office. The Red Queen was hopping mad as usual, Mr. Fainset was attempting to figure out why Tracy Capulet had locked her sister in a cupboard, Lady Cavendish was drafting an indictment against Red Herring for "impersonating a red herring when you're not one," and Emperor Zhark was putting together an interim peace deal for the Northern Genres. It looked enjoyable, relevant and a good use of anyone's time.

Commander Bradshaw smiled and pushed Thursday's shield back across the table, where I stared at it. "What do you say?"

"I can be Thursday," I said slowly. "I can work at Jurisfiction. But at a *fictional* Jurisfiction. I want to depict the real Thursday doing everything she really did. I want her series to feature the BookWorld and you and Miss Havisham and Zhark and all the rest of them. *That's* where I'd like to be Thursday. That's the Thursday I can be. A *fictional* one. I'd like to help you out, but I can't."

Bradshaw looked at me for a long time.

"I *reluctantly* respect your decision to stay with your books," he said at last, "and I understand your wanting to tell it like it is. Naturally we're very grateful for everything you've done, but even if Jobsworth and I sign off on a Textual Flexation Certificate to change your series, I must point out that you can't truly be Thursday without Landen, and even if you get his permission, you still have to get Thursday's approval before you even begin to *think* about trying to change your series. And as far as we know, she may already be . . . dead."

He had trouble saying the final word and had to almost roll it around in his mouth before he could spit it out.

"She's not dead," I said firmly.

"I hope not, too. But without any leads—and we have none—it's going to be an onerous task to find her. Here in Fiction we have over a quarter of a billion titles. That's just one island in a BookWorld of two hundred and twenty-eight different and very distinct literary groupings. Most of those islands have fewer titles but some—like Nonfiction—have more. And then there are the foreign-language BookWorlds. Even if you are right—and I hope you are—Thursday could be anywhere from the Urdu translation of *Wuthering Heights* to the guarantee card on a 1965 Sunbeam Mixmaster."

"But you're still looking, right?"

"Of course. We rely on telemetry from our many unmanned probes that move throughout the BookWorld, all Textual Sieves have been set to pick her up if she makes a move, and Text Grand Central is keeping the waste gates on the imaginotransference engines on alert for a 'Thursday Next' word string. There's always hope, but there's a big BookWorld out there."

"If she's alive," I said in a resolute tone, "I can find her."

"If you do," said Bradshaw with a smile, "you can change whatever you want in your book—even introduce the Toast Marketing Board."

I started. "You heard about that?"

He smiled. "We hear about *everything*. Take the shield. Use her rights and privileges. You might need them. And if you change your mind and want to be her, call me."

I picked up the badge from the table and put it in my pocket.

"Commander?" said the Red Queen, who had been hovering and stepped in when she saw that our conversation was at an end. "Text Grand Central has reported a major narrative flexation over in Shakespeare. It seems Othello has murdered his wife."

"Again? I do wish that trollop Desdemona would be more careful when she's fooling around. What is it this time? Incriminating love letters?"

The Red Queen looked at her notes. "No, it seems there was this handkerchief—"

"Hell's teeth!" yelled Bradshaw in frustration. "Do I have to do everything around here? I want Iago in my office in ten minutes."

"He's doing that spinoff with Hamlet," said Mr. Fainset from across the room.

"*Iago v. Hamlet*? They got the green light for that?"

"Shylock bankrolled their appeal and got Portia to represent them. They were seriously pissed off about the mandatory European directive of 'give me my .453 kilo of flesh'—hence the anti-European subplot in *Iago v. Hamlet*."

"Get him to see me as soon as he can. What is it, Mr. Fainset?"

"The Unread, sir."

"Causing trouble again?"

"They're all over Horror like cheap perfume."

I moved off, as tales of the Unread gave me the spooks. Most characters who were long unread either made themselves useful like Bradshaw or went into a downward spiral of increased torpidity. Others, for some unknown reason, went bad and became the Unread. They festered in dark alleys, in holes in the ground, the crevices between paragraphs—anywhere they could leap out and ensnare characters and suck the reading light out of them. Even grammasites, goblins and the Danvers avoided them.

I moved away. Bradshaw was busy, and my debrief was over. Thursday was missed, but Jurisfiction's work couldn't stop just so it could utilize its full resources to find her. It would be the same for any one of them, and they all knew it.

I walked across to Thursday's desk and rested my fingertips on the smooth oak surface. The desk was clean and, aside from a SpecOps mug, a picture of Landen, a stack of messages and a goodly caseload in the in-basket, fairly tidy. I looked at the worn chair but didn't sit down. This wasn't my desk. I opened the drawers but could find little of relevance, which wasn't hard—I didn't know what would *be* relevant.

I stepped outside the Jurisfiction offices and found the frog-footman dozing on a chair in the lobby.

"Wesley?"

He started at hearing his name called and almost fell off the chair in surprise. "Miss Next?"

"Where do I requisition a vehicle?"

His eyes lit up. "We have a large choice. What would you like?"

"A hover car," I said, having always wanted to ride in one. "A convertible."

I picked up Sprockett, who had been waiting outside, and soon we were heading west out of HumDram/Classics in a Zhark-ian Bubble-Drive Hovermatic. We arrived over Thriller within a few minutes and flew slowly over the area in which *The Murders on the Hareng Rouge* had come down almost a week ago. If Thursday had survived the sabotage, she would have landed somewhere within the half million or so novels along the debris trail.

If Thursday had survived, I reasoned, the cab had come down more or less intact. No one had reported the remains of a taxi falling to earth, and I wanted to know why. We flew up and down the area of the debris trail for a while, searching for even the merest clue of what might have happened but seeing nothing except an endless landscape of novels. We were yelled at several times by cabbies annoyed that we were "hovering about like a bunch of numpties," and on one occasion we were pulled over by a Thriller border guard and made to explain why we were loitering. I flashed Thursday's badge, and he apologized and moved on.

"What are we looking for, ma'am?"

"I wish I knew."

I had a thought and took out my notebook to remind me what Landen had told me when I spoke to him in Fan Fiction.

He had stated that in an emergency, Thursday would try to contact me. As far as I knew, she hadn't. She had also said, *The circumstances of your confusion will be your path to enlightenment.*

I stared at the sentence for a long time, then took my *Bradshaw's BookWorld Companion* from my bag and flicked to the map section at the back. And then all was light. She *had* been contacting me, and my confusion was indeed the answer.

"Bingo," I said softly.

40.

Thursday Next

A trip to Text Grand Central is a must for the technophile, and a day spent on one of the main imaginotransference-engine floors is not to be missed. A visit will dispel forever the notion that those at TGC do little to smooth out the throughputting of the story to the reader's imagination. Tours around the Reader Feedback Loop are available on Tuesday afternoons, but owing to the sometimes hazardous nature of feedback, exposure is limited to eighteen seconds.

Bradshaw's BookWorld Companion (15th edition)

*I*t took nearly an hour to find what we were looking for. Sandwiched between Political Thriller and Spy Thriller and well within the condemned book's debris trail was Psychological Thriller. The whole "Am I really Thursday?" stuff I'd been laboring through over the past few days had all the hallmarks of a PsychoThriller plot device and made total sense of Thursday's obscure "confusion enlightenment" sentence.

Finding the genre, however, was harder. It was difficult to spot from the air, as a sense of ambiguity blurred the edges of the small genre, and with good reason. Psychological was another "rogue genre" where nothing could be taken at face value, trusted or even believed, a genre whose very raison d'être was to confuse and obfuscate. Often accused of harboring known felons and offering safe haven to deposed leaders of other rogue genres, PsychoThriller could never be directly indicted, as nothing was ever quite what it seemed—a trait it shared with others that also had a tenuous hold on reality, such as Creative Accounting and Lies to Tell Your Partner When S/He Finds Underwear in the Glove Box.

We found it by using our small onboard Textual Sieve to home in on a trail of confused reader feedback, and Sprockett expertly brought us in for a landing at the corner of Forsyth and Ludlum. We walked across a vacant lot to the unfenced border of Psychological Thriller. The weather, naturally, was atmospheric. On the Thriller side of the border, the skies were clear, but across into Psychological there seemed to be an impenetrable wall of rain-soaked air. Jurisfiction had considerately posted signs along the border at regular intervals, warning trespassers to stay away or potentially suffer "lethal levels of bewilderment." Only fools or the very brave ventured into Psychological Thriller alone.

"Ma'am?" said Sprockett, his eyebrow flickering "Alarm."

"Problems?"

"You find me hugely embarrassed."

"What is it? You need winding?"

"No, ma'am. It's the damp. Humans might fear viruses and old age, two things with which cog-based life-forms have very little issue. But when it comes to corrosion, honey, magnets and damp, I'm afraid to say I must warn you that a rebuild might be necessary, and spare parts are becoming scandalously expensive."

"It's all right," I said. "Just wait for me here."

I stepped across. Inside Psychological Thriller it was raining, and night. The cold wind lashed my face and drove the rain into every crevice of my clothes, until within a very short period I was soaked through. The tops of the trees swayed dangerously in the wind, and every now and then there was a flash of lightning followed by a splintering crack and the sound of a tree falling with a muffled crash somewhere in the dark.

I moved on, occasionally sinking ankle-deep in the marshy ground. After a few hundred yards, I came to a small clearing of tussock grass, pools of brackish water and a scattering of broken branches. On the far side, partially immersed in ooze, were the remains of a TransGenre Taxi. The front had been staved in, the engine torn out and the bodywork rippled and bent. Scraps of tree had been caught in the side mirrors as the taxi tore through the foliage on its way down. While I stared at the mangled wreck, the lightning flashed, and on the side was painted NO TIPS and, farther along, 1517. It was Thursday's cab.

I hurried round to see if anyone had survived. I was perhaps in too much haste and swiftly sank up to my thighs in the fetid waters. I extricated myself with a considerable amount of grunting and swearing and finally made my way to the taxi and peered in. The rear door was open and the empty backseat scattered with papers, mostly about the geology under Racy Novel. The Mediocre Gatsby was still sitting in the front seat, impaled on the steering column. He had been killed by a bad case of selective nostalgia. For some peculiar reason, all Trans-Genre Taxis were modeled on the 1950s yellow Checker Cab design, at a time when safety standards were nonexistent and fatal accidents embraced by Detroit with an alarming level of indifference. The "hose down the dash and sell it to the next man" attitude pervaded all the way into the BookWorld, and not without good reason. In here there was always a battle between nostalgia and safety, and nostalgia usually won.

I stood up, pushed the wet hair out of my eyes and tried to think what might have happened. As I stared in turn at the taxi, the empty backseat and the remains of Mediocre Gatsby, I suddenly had a thought: The rear door had been open when I got here. I looked around to see where I might have gone if I'd found myself unceremoniously dumped in the middle of a rainy swamp at night, possibly injured and very alone. I took the most obvious way out of the marsh and managed to find a path to higher ground. I followed the trail as best as I could, and after stumbling through the forest for a few hundred yards in a generally uphill direction I came across a doorway in a high brick wall, upon the top of which were the remains of a corroded electrified fence. Attached to the brick wall was a weathered wooden board telling me to keep away from THE WILFRED D. AKRON HOME FOR THE CRIMINALLY INSANE.

If I had been real, I would doubtless have been more nervous than I was, but this was Psychological Thriller, and secure hospitals for the criminally insane were pretty much a dime a dozen, and rarely secure. I found myself in a small and very overgrown graveyard, the lichen-encrusted stones leaning with a frightening level of apparent randomness. I moved through the graveyard towards a mausoleum built of brick and stone but in an advanced state of decay. If I had crash-landed here in the taxi, this is where I would have sought shelter.

The double doors were bronze, heavy and streaked green with age. There was a hole about three feet wide in the middle, so both doors looked as though they had a semicircle cut from each. My foot knocked against something. It was Thursday's well-worn pistol, her name engraved on the barrel—the hole in the locked doors had been blasted out for access. I was getting close. I carefully climbed through the hole and pushed my rain-soaked hair from my face. It was light enough to see, and below the broken skylight was a table that had once held flowers but was now a collection of dirty vases. There were a few personal items scattered about—a picture of Landen and the kids, a five-pound note, an Acme Carpets ID.

"It's difficult to know sometimes who you are, isn't it?"

I turned to see the small figure of a girl aged no more than eight standing in a shaft of light that seemed to descend vertically from the roof.

"Hello, Jenny," I said.

"Did anyone figure you out?" she asked. "Hiding in plain

sight as the written version of you. How did the written Thursday feel about taking a backseat for a while? And where is she, by the way?"

"I'm really Thursday?" I asked.

"Oh, yes," replied Jenny with a chuckle. "Doesn't it all seem so obvious now?"

Two days ago I might have believed her.

"No," I replied. "You see, I spoke to Landen, and he told me I vanished from the RealWorld as a good bookperson might do, so don't give me any of your Psychological Thriller bullshit."

"O-o-o-kay," said Jenny, thinking quickly, "how about this: You're actually just witnessing—"

"Don't even *think* to try Owlcreeking me. And while we're at it, you're not Jenny."

"Is she giving you any trouble?" said another voice I recognized.

"A little," said Jenny, and Sprockett—or a reasonable facsimile of him—appeared from out of the shadows. I sighed. My mother would be appearing next, and then probably myself. It was all becoming a little tedious.

"Did you try her on the *You really are Thursday* twist ending?" asked Sprockett.

"She didn't buy it. I tried the *It's all in your last moment before dying* gambit, too."

Ersatz Sprockett thought for a moment. "What about the *You're actually a patient in a mental hospital and we've been enacting all this to try to find out if you killed Thursday?* That usually works."

"Goodness," said Faux Jenny, "I'd clean forgotten about that one."

"And now that you've told me," I said, "I'm hardly likely to go for it, am I?"

"Well done, Einstein," said Faux Jenny to her partner in a sarcastic tone. "Any other bright ideas?"

Ersatz Sprockett looked at me, then at Faux Jenny, then tried to telegraph an idea across to her in a very lame portrayal of someone being in a shower.

"Oh!" said Faux Jenny as she twigged to what he was talking about. "Good idea."

But I had figured it out, too.

"You wouldn't be thinking about pulling a Bobby Ewing on me, would you?"

And they both swore under their breath.

"Well," grumbled Ersatz Sprockett with a shrug, "that's me, clean out of ideas."

And as I watched, they reverted to the strangely misshapen shape-changers who skulked around Psychological Thriller, hoping to trap unwary travelers into thinking they had once been homicidal maniacs but now had amnesia and all their previous visions depicted in horrific nightmares were actually recovered memories. In a word, they were a pair of utter *nuisances*.

"Thank heavens for that," I said. "Let's get down to business. Where is Thursday, and why didn't you report her presence here to Jurisfiction?"

"We send so many conflicting and utterly bizarre plot lines out of the genre that everyone ignores us," said Shifter Once Jenny sadly. "I think Jurisfiction set our messages to 'auto-ignore.'"

"For good reason," I replied. "You're only marginally less troublesome than Conspiracy."

"That's why Thursday asked us to transmit all those ambiguities direct to you. We were hoping you'd get here sooner than this. We peppered you with as much confusion as we could, but you didn't pick it up."

If I'd been Thursday, I would have. Being confused over identity had been a mainstay of Psychological Thriller for years. I had a lot to learn.

"I'm new to this."

"You'll get the hang of it."

"I hope not. Where is she?"

"In that antechamber."

I turned and followed a short corridor to where there was a small room off the main mausoleum. It was obviously where the shape-changers usually lived, as there were posters of Faceache on the wall. They had given over the one bed to Thursday, who was lying on her back. The room was lit by a gas lantern, and by its flickering jet I could see that she was in a bad state. There was an ugly bruise on her face, and one eye was red with blood. She moved her head to look at me, and I saw her eyes glisten.

"Hey," I said.

"Hey," said Thursday in a weak voice.

I placed my hand on her forehead. It was hot.

"How are you feeling?" I asked.

She gave a faint smile and shrugged, but she winced when she did it.

"Landen?" she whispered.

"He's fine. Kids, too."

"Tell them—"

"Tell them yourself."

I stood up. I had to get her to *Gray's Anatomy* as soon as possible. There was an umbrella in a stand at the door, and I picked it up.

"Thursday? I'm going to fetch someone who can carry you out of here. My butler. I'll be ten minutes."

"You have a butler?" she managed.

"Yes," I replied in a chirpy voice in order to hide my concern. "*Everyone* needs a butler."

41.

The End of the Book

About the author: Commander Bradshaw has been one of the stalwarts of Jurisfiction for over fifty years and has been the Bellman an unprecedented eight times. Hailing from a long-unread branch of British imperialist fiction, he now divides his time between Jurisfiction duties, his lovely wife, Melanie, and continually updating the *BookWorld Companion*, which remains the definitive work on the BookWorld and everything in it.

Bradshaw's BookWorld Companion (17th edition)

I flew the Hovermatic home from *Gray's Anatomy* two hours later, but Sprockett and I said nothing on the trip. I was quiet because I was thinking about Thursday, and what a close call it had been. She had a fractured skull, a broken femur and eight breaks to her left arm and hand. There were multiple lacerations, a loss of blood, fever and a concussion. Henry Gray himself took charge and whisked her into surgery almost the moment I arrived. Within ten minutes the waiting room was full of concerned well-wishers, Bradshaw and Zhark amongst them. I knew she was in good hands, so I'd quietly slipped away as soon as I heard she was out of danger.

I was quiet also because I had averted a war and saved many lives today, and that's a peculiar feeling that's difficult to describe. Sprockett was quiet, too—but only because I had inadvertently allowed his spring to run down, and he had shut off all functions except thought, and he was thinking mildly erotic thoughts about bevel gears and how nice it might be to have a flywheel fitted in order to give him a little more oomph in the mornings.

The first thing I saw when I got back to my house was Bowden, dressed up as me.

"This isn't how it appears," he said in the same tone of voice he'd used when I found him looking through my underwear drawer the year before. He told me then that he'd "heard a mouse," but I didn't believe him.

"How *should* it appear if you're dressed up in my clothes?"

"Carmine's goblin ran off with a goblinette, and she locked herself in the bathroom again. I'm standing in for her. *You.* I've just done a scene with myself. It was most odd."

"How many readers we got?" I asked.

"Six."

"You can handle it."

"Oh!" said Bowden, in the manner of one who is pretending to be disappointed but is actually delighted. "If I must. But who will play me?"

"I will," came a voice from the door. I turned to find Whitby Jett standing there.

"Whitby?"

"How's my little Thursday?"

"She's good. But . . . what about the nuns?"

"A misunderstanding," he said. "I hadn't set fire to any of them, as it turned out."

I stepped forward and touched his chest. I could feel that the guilt had lifted. He'd managed to move the damaging back-story on.

"I'm going to mix some cocktails," announced Sprockett, and he buzzed from the room.

"Make mine a Sidcup Sling, Sprocky old boy," said Jett. "Bowden—where are my lines?"

"Here!" said Bowden, passing him a well-thumbed script.

"Whitby?"

"Yes, muffin?"

"Are you busy right now?"

"Only selling useless rubbish for EZ-Read. Why?"

"Nothing." I smiled, but there *was* something. Whitby could play Landen beautifully.

He and Bowden both went off to play a scene in the Spec-Ops Building, leaving me to sit at the kitchen table trying to figure out if I could have found Thursday earlier. If I'd had more experience, probably.

Pickwick stuck her head around the door and looked relieved when she saw me.

"Thank goodness!" she said. "I can't tell you what a disaster it's been. They threatened to tape my beak shut if I didn't join them. Your father was the ringleader—along with Carmine, of course. She'll come to a sticky end, I can tell you."

"She'll be fine," I said, feeling magnanimous. Carmine had problems, but so did we all. "Make the tea, will you?"

"Isn't that why we have a butler?"

I stared at her and raised an eyebrow.

"So . . . milk and one sugar, right?"

And she waddled into the kitchen to try to figure out which object was the kettle.

"May I come in?"

It was the character who played my father. He was quite unlike his usual abrasive self and seemed almost painfully eager to be friendly.

"Hello, Thursday," he said. "Is . . . that chair comfortable?"

"Don't sweat it," I said, almost embarrassed to see him like this. "I'm going to make some radical changes to your character. It's very simple: Do the new scenes or you can have a transfer. Take it or leave it."

He thought about it for a moment, mumbled something about how he would "look forward to seeing his new lines" and made some excuse before departing.

Pickwick came back in. "The tea is in the jar marked 'tea,' right?"

"Right."

The doorbell rang. It was Emperor Zhark.

"Good evening, Your Mercilessness," I said, opening the door wide. "Come on in and have a cocktail. My man does a Gooseberry Flip so strong it will make your toes swell."

"That's a figure of speech, right?"

"Not at all. Your toes really do swell—to the size of apples."

"I won't, thank you. I'm actually here on business. Do you have an automaton living here, name of Sprockett?"

I think my heart might almost have stopped.

"What is it?" I asked. "What's going on?"

"I am ready, sir."

It was Sprockett. He had his overcoat on and had packed his oils and a spare knee joint, just in case.

"Wait a minute," I said, "you can't take him away. He has a job with me. I'll sign any papers you want."

"Ma'am," said Sprockett, "I am no longer in your employ. If you recall, you gave me glowing references and relieved me of my duties. Emperor, may we go?"

The emperor moved to the door, but I wasn't done.

"Emperor," I said, "I don't wish to appear above my station, but I do feel that a simple work-permit violation could be overlooked on this occasion."

Zhark told Sprockett to get into his car and turned back to me.

"Miss Next," he said in a firm voice, "your butler might be the perfect Thursday's Friday, but he is far too dangerous to allow to remain at liberty. All those laws of robotics you've heard of are pretty much baloney. Good evening, Miss Next, and I'm sorry."

And he turned in a sweep of black velvet and strode up to his waiting limousine, leaving me shaking with frustration until I had a thought.

"Wait!"

I ran up to the limousine's window.

"This crime," I said, "did it have anything to do with nuns?"

"And puppies," said Zhark with a shudder. "Frightful business."

"You stay right here. Don't move. Understand?"

I think Emperor Zhark started to respect me just then. Not just as a Thursday but as a person. Either that or he was used to taking orders from angry women.

Whitby and Bowden were in the SpecOps office, talking about Hades. I'd found Carmine looking in the fridge for something to eat, and she did a mid-read changeover with Whitby. I took him by the hand and pushed him into an adjoining room. I'll admit it. I was angry.

"What the hell do you think you're doing?" I demanded.

"A scene with Bowden. You told me to."

"Not *that*. I'm talking about Sprockett and the incident with the nuns. What were you doing?"

He shrugged. "Listen, muffin, he approached *me*. Said he'd take on my backstory so you'd be happy. What am I going to do? Turn him down? I want you and me to be happy, pumpkin, and we'll always be thankful to it for such a selfless act."

"Not 'it'—*him*."

I stared at him and shook my head, and he knew then that however much I liked him, I couldn't let it happen this way, and neither could he. He leaned forward and kissed me on the cheek, and I could feel my eyes fill with tears.

"Listen, Whitby, you'll find a way of getting rid of it."

"Yes," he said, "and when I do—"

"You'll know where to find me."

He smiled a wan smile and walked out the door. I wiped my eyes and went and sat down in the kitchen to stare at the wall.

"Here," said Pickwick, panting with the exertion, "your tea."

She pushed it across the table with her beak, and I picked it up.

"Oh," I said, "it's gone cold."

"It was supposed to be hot?"

"No, actually, this is good. Thank you, Pickers."

"That's a relief. What's for dinner? I'm starving after all that tea making. It really takes it out of you."

"Mrs. Malaprop suggested a macarena cheese," came a voice from the doorway. I turned to see Sprockett standing tall and as straight as a poker, every bit the perfect butler.

I ran across and gave him a hug. He was hard and cold, and although he was outwardly emotionless, deep within him I could hear his cogs speed up as I squeezed.

"Madam, *please*," he said, faintly embarrassed.

"Thank you, Sprockett," I said. "For everything."

The automaton inclined his head politely, but my eyes were fixed on his eyebrow to see what it would do. I wanted to see what loyal friendship meant to him—whether a man of cogs, dials, chains and sprockets could *really* feel as humans feel.

But I was to be disappointed. He pressed a white-gloved finger to his eyebrow, blocking any movement. All I could see in his face was blank molded porcelain, two lenses for eyes and a slot through which he spoke.

"May I ask a question, ma'am?"

"Of course."

"Was it a compassionate act to take over Whitby's backstory to enable you to be together?"

"Yes."

"I believe I have learned something of value here today, ma'am. But what made Whitby retake the backstory?"

"He knew it was the right thing to do."

Sprockett buzzed briefly to himself. "Does that sort of thing happen out there in the RealWorld, or is it just in books?"

I thought for a moment. Of the untidy chaos I had seen in the RealWorld; of not knowing what was going to happen; of not knowing what, if anything, had relevance. The Real-World was a sprawling mess of a book in need of a good editor. I thought then of the narrative order here in the BookWorld, our resolved plot lines and the observance of natural justice we took for granted.

"Literature is claimed to be a mirror of the world," I said, "but the Outlanders are fooling themselves. The BookWorld is as orderly as people in the RealWorld *hope* their own world to be—it isn't a mirror, it's an aspiration."

"Humans," said Sprockett, "are the most gloriously bizarre creatures."

"Yes," I said with a smile. "They certainly are."

Acknowledgments

First, my thanks to Carolyn Mays and Josh Kendall and all the team at Hodder and Viking for their steadfast support and understanding during the final stages of the book, where events of a daughtering nature conspired to render the manuscript past the ideal delivery time.

My thanks to Dr. John Wooten for his valuable contributions to the understanding of Nextian Physics, and for being at the end of an e-mail if I had a query with regard to the best way to mangle physics while still looking vaguely correct.

The illustrations were drawn by Bill Mudron and Dylan Meconis of Portland, Oregon, and they have, as usual, surpassed themselves in their depiction of the Nextian Universe. Bill can be found at www.excelsiorstudios.net and Dylan at www.dylanmeconis.com.

My apologies to the many, many authors who have used the "hollow earth" notion as the setting for a book. It *must* have been done before, and I would expect the mechanics of how it functions would be universal, as the concept has a tendency to write itself. In case of unavoidable parallels, my apologies.

BookWorld cartographers. My thanks to the following for submitting wonderful ideas to me about the possible shape and layout of Fiction Island: Alex Maunders, Robert Persson, Laura, Catherine Fitzsimons, Geoffrey Elliot-Howell, Michael O'Connor, Ellie Randall, Steve James, Elizabeth Walter, Derek Walter, Theresa Porst, Sarah Porter, Dhana Sabanathan, Alex

Clark, Loraine Weston, Elisabeth Parsons, Jane Ren, Birgit Prihodko and Helen Griin-Looveer.

I am also indebted to my new agents, Will Francis and Claire Paterson, who have filled Tif's recently vacated shoes with an aplomb and unswerving professionalism of which I know she would approve.

No thanks would be complete without special mention of Mari, whose constant and overwhelming support allows me to function as a vaguely sentient creature rather than a mass of quivering jelly. I would also like to thank Ingrid and Ian for much support when we needed it, and finally thanks to my in-laws, Maggy and Stewart, for help and assistance on occasions too numerous to mention.

This book took 108 days to write between December 22, 2009, and September 3, 2010. It was written on a Mac Pro using Pages software. I've been Mac since 1995, when it was OS 7.9.2, and I have used Apple writing software on all my projects. During the writing I consumed thirty-two gallons of coffee, eighteen gallons of tea, and I walked 192 miles. The filing backed up to a depth of seven and a half inches, and I received 1,672 e-mails and sent 380. The average daytime temperature was 9.2 degrees Celsius and I burned 1.2 tons of logs in my wood burner. In that time I lost a faithful hound but gained a fourth daughter.

Jasper Fforde
September 2010

GOWER
PENINSULA

Socialist Republic of Wales

Not <u>always</u> raining.

See your local tourist office for details.

TransGenreTaxis
AS USED BY THURSDAY NEXT

* GENERALLY SAFE *
* USUALLY CLEAN *
* MOSTLY POLITE DRIVERS *
* ALL CARS NOW WITH SEATS *
* BRIBES READILY ACCEPTED *
* OVERCHARGING RARE *
* NO EXTRA FEE FOR WINDOWS *
* AIRCON WHEN FUNCTIONING*
* HASTILY TRAINED DRIVERS*

TransGenreTaxis
CALL FOOTNOTERPHONE 7177 CASH - ACCOUNT - BARTER

AVAILABLE FROM PENGUIN

The Eyre Affair
In the first Thursday Next adventure, the renowned literary Spec Op must protect Jane Eyre from a villain set upon kidnapping her from the pages of Brontë's novel.
ISBN 978-0-14-200180-6

Lost in a Good Book
Now a celebrated hero, Thursday Next finds herself enlisted as a Jurisfiction apprentice to none other than the man-hating Miss Havisham from Dickens's *Great Expectations*.
ISBN 978-0-14-200403-6

The Well of Lost Plots
Peace and quiet remain elusive for Thursday Next when she discovers the Well of Lost Plots.
ISBN 978-0-14-303435-3

Something Rotten
Thursday Next finally returns home, but Swindon is far more sinister than she remembers—for something is rotten in the state of England and only our heroine can hunt down the villains.
ISBN 978-0-14-303541-1

Thursday Next: First Among Sequels
There is a serial killer on the loose in the Bookworld, and Thursday Next will have to team up with her written self in order to discover just who is stalking literature's sleuths.
ISBN 978-0-14-311356-0

Shades of Grey: A Novel
Eddie Russet belongs to the low-level House of Red and can see 58 percent of his own color—but no other. He is content with his limitations—until he meets Jane.
ISBN 978-0-14-311858-9

The Nursery Crime series, featuring Detective Jack Spratt
The Big Over Easy   ISBN 978-0-14-303723-1
The Fourth Bear   ISBN 978-0-14-303892-4

PENGUIN
BOOKS

www.jasperfforde.com
www.thursdaynext.com • www.nurserycrime.co.uk